Giles Arthur (1849-1918) = Josephine Marie (1855-1890)
Railton   Simon

Andrew William (1875-1937) = Charlottte Hester (1875-)
Railton   Michael

Malcolm (1877-)=Bridget (1880-1917)
Railton   Kinread

Rupert William (1895-1921)   Caspar Arthur (1893-)=Hon. Phoebe(1894-)
Railton   Railton   Mercer

Marie Simone (1876-)=Marcel (1870-1917)
Railton   Grenot

Ramillies Giles (1895-?)
Railton

Alexander Percival (1917-)
Railton

Paul (1895-1914)
Grenot

Andrew William (1918-)
Railton

Denise (1898-)=Edward (1896-)
Grenot   Farthing

Hester Charlotte (1920-)
Railton

Clifton (1920-)
Farthing

(Colonel) Bradley Brinsley (1858-)=Penelope Diana (1864-)
Farthing   Newman

Edward (1896-)=Denise(1898-)
Farthing   Grenot

Clifton(1920-)
Farthing

Bradley Bartholemew (1895-)=Rachel Roman (1897-)   Maude Elizabeth (1896-)=Matthew John (1894)   Arnold Wilson (1898)=Mattilda Jane
Farthing   Preece   Farthing   Marlowe   Farthing   Henderson (1899-)

Bartholemew Brinsley(1917-)
Farthing

Luke Brinsley(1918-)
Marlowe

Wilson Brinsley(1919-)
Farthing

Rebecca Louise (1918-)
Farthing

Susanna Mattilda(1921-)
Farthing

THE
SECRET
FAMILIES

BOOKS BY JOHN GARDNER

JAMES BOND NOVELS

License Renewed
For Special Services
Icebreaker
Role of Honor
Nobody Lives Forever
No Deals, Mr. Bond
Scorpius

THE BOYSIE OAKES BOOKS

The Liquidator
Understrike
Amber Nine
Madrigal
Founder Member
Traitor's Exit
Air Apparent
A Killer for a Song

DEREK TORRY NOVELS

A Complete State of Death
The Corner Men

THE MORIARTY JOURNALS

The Return of Moriarty
The Revenge of Moriarty

THE KRUGER TRILOGY

The Nostradamus Traitor
The Garden of Weapons
The Quiet Dogs

NOVELS

The Censor
Every Night's a Festival
To Run a Little Faster
The Werewolf Trace
The Dancing Dodo
The Last Trump
Flamingo
The Secret Generations
The Secret Houses

AUTOBIOGRAPHY

Spin the Bottle

COLLECTIONS OF SHORT
STORIES

Hideaway
The Assassination File

THE
SECRET
FAMILIES

JOHN GARDNER

G. P. PUTNAM'S SONS
New York

G. P. Putnam's Sons
Publishers Since 1838
200 Madison Avenue
New York, NY 10016

Library of Congress Cataloging-in-Publication Data

Gardner, John E.
   The secret families.

   The final volume of a trilogy which began with The
secret generations and continued with The secret
houses.
   I. Title.
PR6057.A63S38   1989   823'.914   88-32503
ISBN 0-399-13397-6

Printed in the United States of America
1 2 3 4 5 6 7 8 9 10

The author gratefully acknowledges permission to reprint the
following material:

Lines from "Stopping by Woods on a Snowy Evening" copyright ©
1923 by Holt, Rinehart and Winston and renewed 1951 by Robert
Frost. Reprinted from *The Poetry of Robert Frost,* edited by Edward
Connery Lathem, by permission of Henry Holt and Company, Inc.

Lines from "The Waste Land" by T. S. Eliot from *The Waste Land and
Other Poems* by T. S. Eliot. Reprinted by permission of Harcourt Brace
Jovanovich.

Lines from "Heavy Date" by W. H. Auden from *W. H. Auden:
Collected Poems,* edited by Edward Mendelson. Copyright © 1945 by
W. H. Auden. Reprinted by permission of Random House.

Lines from "Missing" by John Pudney from *The Collected Poems of
John Pudney.* Reprinted by permission of David Higham Associates,
Ltd.

Lines from *Doctor Zhivago* by Boris Pasternak, translated by Max
Hayward and Manya Harari and Bernard Guilbert Guerney. Copyright
© 1958 by Pantheon Books, Inc. Reprinted by permission of Pantheon
Books, Inc.

For
Charles
and
Nancy

AUTHOR'S NOTE

This is the final volume of a trilogy which began with *The Secret Generations* and continued with *The Secret Houses*.

Each of the books can be read out of context. They are stand-alone works. The links which make up the trilogy are the series of characters which grow through the entire work—members of two families, the British Railtons and the American Farthings, together with several characters I have already used in the Kruger Trilogy.

Each novel is set in a particular period of recent history, and fact is surrounded by fiction so that there is a continuation of a sense of saga throughout the series. I should also add that these are not kiss-kiss bang-bang thrillers, but, I trust, true novels, dealing in turn with Enthusiasm which moves, in the second book, to Identity and, lastly to Disenchantment.

I have always believed that novels of espionage require three essentials. First, the protagonists must live on the page, with a past, present, and future; second, there has to be a puzzle which is successfully unraveled by the end of each book; lastly, they must lead the readers into believing they are getting a quick peep behind the scenes of a world mostly forbidden to them. I have tried to keep to these rules throughout these three works.

Thanks go to the large number of friends and colleagues who have given me their help and advice. Most will remain nameless for they know who they are. The others have well-known names which grace the spines of countless textbooks and works concerning the history of the great intelligence agencies of the secret world.

Finally, in the merging of fact and fiction I have taken liberties with certain aspects of secret history. Any theories advanced in this, and the other two books, are products of the "what if?" area of my imagination, and not necessarily the truth behind the known stories.

This is particularly important in the current book. The central core
is a true operation and, as far as I can discover, I have taken only one
major liberty, which concerns the first debriefing, in London, of the
man who in real life was known as *Alex.* This was not quite how it
was done. However, the rest of the tradecraft and handling of this
defector-in-place appears to have been followed almost exactly as described. My final theory has been voiced by others, though Nigel West
in his book *The Friends* claims that the Secret Intelligence Service
have information that *Alex* was, in fact, executed. There *is* other
evidence giving a different picture, and the odd handling and tradecraft surrounding *Alex,* together with the final use put to the information, known to the CIA as *Iron Bark,* and the SIS as *Arnika* and *Rupee,*
does make one wonder about the truth.

—J. G., 1988

There are secrets in all families.

George Farquhar:
The Beaux' Stratagem

THE
SECRET
FAMILIES

PROLOGUE

London: April 1961

On that particular night all ongoing operations appeared to have come to a sudden, unexplained halt, and the entire strength of the Watcher Service of Five—meaning the surveillance teams from the British Security Service, MI5—were gathered together in one place: at the Marble Arch end of Oxford Street, just across from the northeast corner of Hyde Park.

There are three well-defined groups within the Watchers—drivers, eyeballs, and footmen. Some of them were heard to complain that they were not in the job to work for the Secret Intelligence Service, MI6. What, they asked, had the SIS ever done for them? But the griping probably stemmed from the fact that, even for England, it was a chilly night. The whole of April had been bad, and now, during this last week, the men in the waiting cars had the engines running and the heaters turned on. Later, the SIS people would have to reassure the subject of all this activity that Five just did the job, and had no idea what it was really about.

On the pavements, and in doorways, the footmen still wore winter coats with collars turned up.

The target area was a dream to cover. Even now, at midnight, the traffic flowed freely, and there were plenty of people on the pavements. In spite of the Street Offences Act, the lanes and roads which web their way behind Oxford Street and the Edgware Road contained hotels galore which catered for customers by the hour—casual pickups, professionals, and dedicated amateurs still blatantly used the area. The footmen merged easily into the local color.

Cars were parked at both ends of Bryanston Street; another in Seymour Street, and two more in the Edgware Road. A pair of mobile units did a slow round-robin, taking in Oxford Street, Edgware Road, and passing the parked eyeballs at the ends of Bryanston Street. One of the

13

mobiles did not belong to the Watcher Service. Its call sign was Oscar Bravo One, and it was manned by members of the Secret Intelligence Service.

Less than a mile away, in Mayfair, in an apartment near the corner of South Audley and Mount streets, a dozen men and women waited in a large room which looked as though it was prepared for a surprise party.

Two long tables had been set up, decorated with champagne, caviar, and smoked salmon. The entryfone downstairs would buzz every few minutes, followed by a quick exchange with a short, tubby, and rather brusque girl who appeared to be the doorkeeper. A few minutes later another guest would arrive.

The similarity to a surprise party ended with the food- and drink-scaped tables. There was no lighthearted relaxed chatter, no laughs or loud conversation. It was as though something momentous was about to happen and the gathered spectators remained uncertain, anxious about the unknown. American accents were mixed with British and all were very low key. Tension could be felt, like static, in the whole building.

At five minutes to midnight the entryfone buzzed again. There was the familiar exchange, and a minute later, Sir Caspar Railton, now looking weighed down by all his years, was ushered into the room, his nephew, Donald, escorting him, one hand on the old man's arm.

Maitland-Wood bustled forward, making a fuss, full of so-glad-you-could-come, and it's-an-honor-to-see-you-here.

"It'd better be damned good, Willis. When I retired I left forever, this time. I'm no prima donna. Don't want to keep making comebacks, you know. Anyway, old Phoeb dislikes me goin' out of an evening anymore. Says it plays hell with me chest."

"You won't be disappointed, Sir Caspar. This is the one we've all been waiting for." There was something unpleasantly oily about Maitland-Wood.

Caspar grunted. "Make all the dreams come true, so young Naldo tells me. Going to make all your fortunes, I hear." The old man glanced up at his nephew, Donald, who since childhood had been known as Naldo. As a baby he had difficulty pronouncing his name.

The telephone rang, and the room became full of statues. A young man with longish fair hair picked up the instrument and quietly said, "White's Restaurant."

A slightly accented voice at the distant end asked if they were usually very busy on Friday nights, and the young man told him they had only one table left—"It's a table for five at ten o'clock," he said. The distant voice said thank you but that was too late.

As soon as the line was closed, the young man opened an adjacent door, revealing a battery of typewriters and teleprinters, all manned by young women. "It's 'go' in five minutes. Now!" he commanded crisply.

In the second room, a young woman manning a radio spoke into a microphone, "Oscar Bravo One. This is Cissy."

There was a crackle in her headphones. Then—

"Oscar Bravo One. We read you, Cissy."

"Your client's ready for you now."

"Roger. Wilco. Oscar Bravo One."

The girl raised her head and gave the thumbs-up.

"On the way," the young man told the assembled company. There was no reaction, except for the turning of a few heads, and a slight increase in the tension.

Over in the Marble Arch area, the dark Rover car that was Oscar Bravo One turned into Cumberland Place, pulling up at the staff entrance to the Mount Royal Hotel, Bryanston Street. As the car stopped, so three men hustled at speed, very close together, from the door. Within seconds, the Rover was negotiating the sweep around Marble Arch, picking up speed as it entered Park Lane. There was another car almost on its bumper, and a motorcyclist cut in between two buses to take station in front of the Rover. Five minutes later the small convoy pulled up outside the house near the junction of South Audley and Mount streets.

The men and women in the big room upstairs stood, silent, watching the door. Five men in topcoats ushered in a sixth—bareheaded, medium height, his dark hair combed straight back, his features undeniably Slavic and creased with good humor.

Willis Maitland-Wood stepped forward. "Ladies and gentlemen, he's here. I want you to meet a very brave gentleman. This is *Alex.*"

There was genuinely warm applause, and a sense of relief passed, like a long sigh, through the room.

"It's good to meet you all at last." *Alex* spoke very good English. "But we must get to work. There is much to be done." He smiled, embracing the room with sparkling eyes as Maitland-Wood handed him a glass of champagne.

PART ONE

THE FAMILIES ENCIRCLED

(1964)

ONE

1

Old spies do not fade away: they die. Caspar Railton would have freely admitted that he had been living on borrowed time for the past forty years.

At the age of twenty-one, Caspar had been terribly crippled by a shell during the bitter fighting around Le Cateau in the opening months of the First World War. At the time the doctors considered that, with care, he might last ten, maybe fifteen, years. Caspar's body inevitably suffered from circulatory problems, and few would have thought he would ever reach the age of seventy-one. But he did, dying the way he would have wanted: at The Travellers Club directly after lunching with three other old spies.

"Our family seems to make a habit of dying or being married just before Christmas, eh, Naldo?" Caspar's cousin, James Railton, leaned heavily on his son's arm, his face set in an expression that fell between grief and philosophical acceptance, shoulders braced against the biting wind which swept the graveyard. He was Caspar's age, give or take a month. "You'll think it's hardly worth my going home from this boneyard." He spoke to the earth that now covered the plain coffin with a simple brass plate: CASPAR ARTHUR RAILTON KCB DSC 1893–1964. The old jest was obviously addressed to his dead cousin. They had been as close as brothers down the years.

Naldo Railton was unusually emotional. He had been close to his Uncle Caspar. At times Caspar seemed more of a father to him than James, and during the service in the old Parish Church of SS Peter & Paul, Haversage, Berkshire, he had wept within himself—particularly when his cousin Andrew had read, not from Holy Writ, but, as Caspar had required, from Shakespeare's *Tempest*. Prospero's great speech, ending with the words:

> *"And, like the baseless fabric of this vision,*
> *The cloud-capped towers, the gorgeous palaces,*
> *The solemn temples, the great globe itself,*
> *Yea, all which it inherit, shall dissolve*
> *And, like this insubstantial pageant faded,*
> *Leave not a rack behind: we are such stuff*
> *As dreams are made on: and our little life*
> *Is rounded with a sleep."*

It was typical for any Railton to choose Shakespeare rather than the Bible, and even more typical of Caspar to instruct this passage to be read at his funeral. It did not please the vicar but he had little say in the matter. The Parish of Haversage was in the Railtons' gift—for they had owned much of the place, together with surrounding land, for generations.

Naldo glanced over his shoulder at the black huddle of departing mourners, whom he would see shortly at the main Railton property— Redhill Manor, perched under the shadow of the Downs, looking across the chessboard of fields and red rooftops of what had once been the small market town of Haversage, on the Berkshire/Oxfordshire border.

These mourners were nearly all family, a mixture of British Railtons and the American Farthings, relatives-by-marriage and a shared trade. Naturally enough, there were also a few of Caspar's close colleagues from the Secret Intelligence Service in which he had worked so hard, and for so many years. Above them all, Naldo spotted Herbie Kruger— for who could miss him? Big Herbie as everyone called him, head and shoulders above the rest in that unresolved posse of black-clad men and women being helped into the dark, shining limousines. Herbie seemed to be looking directly at him, as though trying to convey a message. In his head, Naldo heard a voice.

"Now it begins."

He was sure it was a Shakespearean line, and the voice that of some actor he had seen play one of the tragedies, yet it seemed to come from the earth that now covered his dead uncle.

"Now it begins."

To his surprise, Naldo realized it was his father speaking, still looking intently at the ground. At that moment it became suddenly clear to Naldo what his father meant.

At Redhill Manor, the mourners gathered, trying to make the wake for Caspar into a happier kind of family reunion. The Manor, which had been the Railtons' family seat for centuries, had changed little. As the beautiful building grew older, so its weathering gave it more charm and character: after all it had belonged to Railtons since Henry VIII had granted the land to the family in the sixteenth century. Only those who lived there, and made their mark on the house and estate, showed age and weariness.

Sara, who had been brought to Redhill by Naldo's grandfather as a very young second wife, still lived there with her husband, Richard. It was Sara and Richard who had forged the bond between the Railtons and Farthings, for Richard Farthing had married Sara after her first husband's death. As the years went by, so they adopted the name Railton-Farthing, not out of any pretension, but for purposes of making stronger ties between the two families.

Inevitably, things had changed. Richard—Dick to all the relatives—had become a sick and failing man in his eighties, while the once young and vibrant Sara was crippled with arthritis: though she was still capable of showing flashes of her old self. They were tended by their niece, Josephine, who had been through so much hardship during, and after, World War II. Jo-Jo, as everyone called her, looked much older than her forty-eight years, and at times needed the help of two permanent nurses who, together with a "daily" cleaning lady and a rotund and cheery housekeeper, always referred to as "Stalks," had long replaced the butler, housemaids, cook, and small regiment of servants.

Sara and Dick continued to pine for their daughter, Caroline, who had spent much of the Second World War with Josephine, and was still far away in America. She was due to return to England during the following year, like Jo-Jo shattered by her experiences since 1945, which were the true cause of her prolonged absence from Redhill.

Both Richard and Sara—who had not been at Caspar's interment—greeted family and friends as they arrived, while one of the nurses looked after Caspar's widow, Phoebe. She had always, since anyone could remember, been called "Old Phoeb," and now, at seventy years, had indeed become almost prematurely ancient with the onset of Parkinson's disease, which made her hands shake like some terrible, sick clockwork toy. Phoebe was truly prostrate with grief. She had loved Caspar deeply since they were both in their early twenties. Years had not wearied that love. They were like Naldo's father and mother, and the same as Dick and Sara. Some people said marriages were not made like that anymore.

Naldo's father, James, traveled to the Manor with his wife, Margaret Mary, in a hire car, while Naldo drove Barbara and their two children:

21

Arthur—a tall, astute sixteen-year-old, down from Winchester for Christmas—and Emma, who was at the exclusive St. Mary's School, in Haversage.

"I always thought Great-Uncle Caspar a cheery old buffer," Arthur said, in the patronizing manner of public school boys of his age. They were negotiating Red Hill in the blue 3.5 liter Rover. "Never talked much about himself though." The boy continued as though everyone hung on his words. "Always turned the conversation over to you. Used to ask him something, and then find myself going on about my own life and problems."

"You haven't got any problems, Art," from his sister, a shade cattily. "Except for your pimples, of course."

"Like the boys from the grammar school you ogle all the time," her brother snapped.

Barbara chuckled, and Naldo thought, if they only knew. Caspar had been ADC to the first "C"—the shortened title for CSS, Chief of the Secret Service—during the 1914–'18 war, and had gone on to greater things in the same Secret Intelligence Service, MI6. Naldo himself had seen his uncle at work as a skilled interrogator, and knew how this extraordinary, physically crippled man had set up networks, run agents, and knew the trade backwards. Naldo had even been on a postwar operation with his uncle, together with Dick's nephew, Arnold Farthing, and the then fledgling Kruger, the man he had glimpsed from Caspar's graveside. In fact he had first met and courted Barbara while that operation was running.

That morning at Redhill there was much talk of Caspar, and also a great deal of shop concerning world affairs. At the time there was grave concern throughout the Western world at what appeared to be the beginnings of a closer United States' involvement in the affairs of South Vietnam, which faced a full-blown Communist assault from the North. "Can't see how the Yanks can avoid being dragged in. Really they're in already, and their hardheaded foreign policy means they've got to show a heels-in stand against Communism," one senior intelligence officer was saying to Barbara, who nodded gravely. Naldo had talked about the problem at length, so the intelligence man was preaching to the converted.

For years the Americans had tried to stabilize that small and split Southeast Asian country. At the end of World War II they had backed the Viet Minh revolutionary leader Ho Chi Min. Later, they had put in military advisers, and "technicians"—another word for skilled intelligence and training officers.

22

For the past decade the United States had actively supported the politically ambitious Ngo family, conniving to maintain the South Vietnamese leader, Ngo Dinh Diem, who had dealt crushing blows to the Communists in their midst. But last year had brought great changes. Diem was known to be talking to the Northern Communists, playing them off against the Americans, who had become embarrassed by his ruthless and corrupt regime—run in conjunction with his brother, Ngo Dinh Nhu, together with the latter's powerful wife, Madame Nhu.

On November 1, 1963, Diem's generals and rebel soldiers completed a bloody coup in which Diem and Nhu died—shot and dumped into the back of an armored personnel carrier, part of the American aid. Madame Nhu and her entourage fled. Three weeks later, President Kennedy was himself killed, in Dallas, by an apparently lone assassin, Lee Harvey Oswald.

Now, in Southeast Asia, the signs of a forthcoming bloody war were there for all to see. There was little chance of the United States extricating itself from the potential bloodbath. As Naldo mingled with his kinfolk, and his uncle's old colleagues, that morning, he heard snippets of conversation which ranged from the American dilemma, to the recent fall of the British Conservative government which had led to Harold Wilson becoming Prime Minister. "Wouldn't have happened but for that damned girl," Sara said loudly.

Certainly, the change of government could in part be attributed to a great scandal during the previous summer, which contained all the ingredients so beloved of the gutter press: a Conservative Minister— the Secretary of State for War no less—caught with his hand in the sexual till, though forthright Sara had used a more apt anatomical simile. The Secretary of State for War had conducted an illicit love affair with a lady who was also engaged in similar assignations with the assistant Naval Attaché of the Russian Embassy: almost certainly a member of the GRU. These people were to become household names—Profumo, Ivanov, Keeler, and her so-called pimp, Stephen Ward. There were court cases, and one suicide: Ward, who claimed he was working under the instructions of MI5. Years later this was proved to be true, but the groundswell of this *cause célèbre* had certainly gone a long way towards toppling the government.

As he passed through the room, Naldo also heard the trivia of the times: last night's TV play, and the latest movie in glorious technicolor—"I say, have you seen the new James Bond film, *Goldfinger*. Really super," from some young braying relative. Or comments on

23

pop stars—"Damned cacophony these rolling people, what're they called? Stones, is it? Ought to get their bloody hair cut!" loudly from old Dick.

Politically, Harold Wilson was in Number 10, and saying little; Lyndon Johnson was in the White House, becoming dangerously bellicose; and Nikita Khrushchev, the outspoken and aggressive Russian leader for the best part of a decade, had been ousted from the Kremlin, his power taken by two men whose names as yet meant little to those at Caspar's funeral—Leonid Brezhnev and Aleksei Kosygin. As for himself, Naldo simply wanted to get away, to be alone for a while and think of his dear dead uncle. Politics, terrorism, wars, rumors of wars, shifts in power held no magic for him.

He threaded his way through the drawing room, hoping to seek peace in the rose garden, which had always provided a kind of sanctuary at Redhill.

Naldo reached the door before he sensed that Herbie Kruger, who stood huge and ungainly by one of the tall windows, was at the funeral for more reasons than his own need to pay respect.

Pausing, Naldo quickly took in the presence of his dead uncle's colleagues. He could not miss the pompous Maitland-Wood, C's current food taster; and the reedy, skeletal figure of "Tubby" Fincher. If Maitland-Wood sat on the right hand of God, then Tubby was firmly planted on the left. "Have care," a voice whispered in his head. Today, in this big and wonderful old house, nestling below the Berkshire Downs and the old Roman Way, there were pitfalls, swamps, and quicksands. "Have care, this day." Naldo turned from the door, shouldering his way towards the window and Kruger.

"What's up, Herb?" he said quietly on approaching the German, who was now a naturalized British citizen, still working for the SIS.

"Read me like a bloody book, Nald, eh?"

"Sometimes. I have the right, old son, I helped train you."

Kruger nodded his head, an exaggerated movement, like an ungainly Buddha. "True. You. Arnie. The boys at Warminster. Even the old bugger Maitland-Wood. He was first officer to interview me when you brought me back to England." He paused and visibly swallowed. "Then there was poor old Caspar, of course." There was a catch in his voice, but most people knew that Herbie wept easily, especially in drink or when listening to the works of Gustav Mahler. Only Naldo, and the few people who had run the agent, knew that his tears were part of a very elaborate cover built, brick upon brick, over the years. Herbie could turn on what he called "the blubbings" like a tap.

"Spit it out." Naldo looked across the room to see his fourteen-year-

24

old daughter deep in gloomy conversation with Alexander, one of Caspar's sons—still in the trade and working at the so-called Government Communications Headquarters (GCHQ), now firmly established in Cheltenham. Alexander's brother, Andrew—a solicitor who looked like one—spoke rapidly to Maitland-Wood, who paid no heed, only nodding occasionally as he square-searched the room with his eyes.

"Okay, I spit." Herbie gave a rueful smile. "Arnie wants to see you. He says very personal. Most covert. *Typische* CIA, hu?"

"Been a long while." Naldo had not seen Arnie Farthing for around six years, though there had been a time when they were never out of each other's pockets. The special relationship which existed between the American CIA and British SIS had become strained and full of mistrust when the Soviet penetration agents had been unearthed, too late, in the past decade or so. That had been the time of what the Press called the Cambridge Spy Ring. Guy Burgess, Donald Maclean, and, much later, Kim Philby—potentially the greatest defused threat of all, for there had been one very brief tarnished moment when the C of the time had put Philby's name forward as his successor.

What rankled, on both sides of the Atlantic, was the fact that a CIA officer—formerly of the FBI—had made the Philby connection, putting together the jigsaw of his treachery long before anyone else; and even then the Brits took little action. At the end, when Kim made a kind of confession before skipping to Moscow, he was still in the employ of the SIS.

It was only in recent years that the SIS and CIA had resumed a close, if uneasy, partnership, and only then because of a fluke, a defector in a million, a man with enchanted information, from whom the two intelligence communities shared the product and so, people believed, had brought the world back from the brink of another war.

Now Naldo wondered if Arnie had been pushed towards him because of new information. Only eight months previously, the so-called "fourth man" in the Cambridge conspiracy, Anthony Blunt, had made a reluctant confession to having been a spy for Russia—the confession carrying with it a promise of immunity. A very tight circle within the British intelligence and security organizations knew this truth. At the time, they said it would be a disaster if all the facts were leaked to the entire American Agency. Certain people had to know, but it was a careful knowledge. The Brits suspected the CIA of being leaky. After all, there were many senior members of that service who had told Philby more than they should, and ended up with red faces. In turn, the CIA feeling was that the British intelligence service was, as they would say, like a piece of Gruyère.

"Know what he wants, Herb?"

"No clue, Nald. Just that it's urgent."

"Where'd you see him, Bonn?"

Kruger's eyebrows twitched, and he shifted from foot to foot. He had run a superlative network in East Berlin, cryptoed *The Schnitzer Group*, until the building of the Wall had decisively split that unhappy city in two during the August of 1961, three years before. Herbie had got out in his socks, as the old argot had it. Since then, Naldo knew that he was working under a very tight trade cover, and without the knowledge, or sanction, of the BfV or BND—the West German Security and Intelligence Services—running his *Schnitzer Group* at long range. The Germans took a dim view of people operating on their patch without even a by-your-leave. Herbie was in and out all the time, doing the Bonn-London shuttle. They would not let him get within spitting distance of Berlin.

Now the big German gave Naldo a sly look and nodded. "He make a special trip to see me. Last week. From Berlin. I had just heard of Caspar's death." He paused, looked away, then back again. "So had Arnie. He's forbidden London at the moment. So he give me telephone number." Almost under his breath, Kruger rattled off the Berlin number and Naldo repeated it. "He says to ask for Mr. Dove. If okay he will say it is good to hear from you again. Those exact words, okay? You are Mr. Cline. Time will be plus three hours. Whatever place he gives you, on the telephone, the meet will be in lobby of Kempinski. You got it?"

Naldo nodded and started to turn away, but the big man rested a hand on his forearm. "Sorry about Cas, Naldo. Truly sorry. He was good. One of the best."

"Sure, Herb. Thanks."

Much later, Naldo thought the two first threads came together on that day at Caspar Railton's funeral. First with the words, "Now it begins," by the graveside; second with Herbie's "Arnie wants to see you."

That was when it all really started.

2

Arnold Farthing had risen in his chosen trade. Two weeks before Caspar Railton's death and funeral, he had received a Flash signal to return to Washington. He was, at this time, Head of Berlin Station—an appointment, in those years of the Cold War, of not only responsibility, but also danger.

He got into Dulles International around eleven on the morning after his recall, taking a cab into town and going straight to the small pretty house in Georgetown, owned by his family for many years and always used by Arnie when in Washington. His wife, Gloria, stayed on in Berlin, for he expected to be away for only three or four days at the most. By telephoning ahead, Gloria had made certain that the house was prepared for him: food in the refrigerator, clean towels in the bathroom, fresh sheets on the bed, and the heating turned on. Nights in the fall could be very chilly in Washington.

Arnold showered and shaved, changed his clothes, then called the Agency. A car would be sent for him at once. Tired and lagged, though he was, Arnold waited on the corner for the limo with smoked glass windows to arrive. They took the two usual sweeps across Washington Bridge, using the turning circles at each end to make sure nobody was dogging their tires, then drove north on the Washington Memorial Parkway, crossing under Key Bridge and on into the Virginian countryside. It was fall and the view—the trees brown, gold, and blazing with fire in weakening sunlight—never failed to excite him.

They passed the sign to Turkey Run Creek, then turned off after the indicator for the Federal Highway Commission, onto the exit marked unashamedly CENTRAL INTELLIGENCE AGENCY, LANGLEY. The sign had only recently been replaced. During Kennedy's Presidency it had disappeared. The President had been appalled that the United States Intelligence Service was so publicly marked—even though everyone knew exactly where the Headquarters complex stood, deep among the trees, guarded by dogs, wire, and sensors.

The driver took the car right into the basement, saying that Arnie should see the people at "reception." At the desk there was a message for him to report to the head of Counterintelligence—James Jesus Angleton, already a legend in the Agency. They jested of Angleton that he would be buried in an unmarked grave to preserve his anonymity.

Angleton had been known variously as "the Cadaver," because of his gaunt aesthetic appearance, and "the Poet" because of his love for poetry—there were always collections of Pound, Keats, or Eliot in his office, sometimes almost hidden by the mounds of paper which grew, like snowdrifts, around him. He was behind his paper-littered desk now, a cigarette between his fingers. There were three other senior field officers ranged about the room. "Heck," Arnie said, "the Sovs must be having a ball, looks like you have every European Station Head over here."

"You're not far wrong. Nice to see you, Arnie," Angleton's thin hand seemed to shoot out from the piles of paper to grasp at Arnold's huge paw. The office was cold, and Angleton apologized. "They still haven't got the heating and air conditioning right after three years," he said. "I hear we might sue the contractors. This campus is a mess."

The three other officers said their hellos. They were all known to each other.

"I'd only just started putting these guys in the picture." Angleton dragged on his cigarette. "There're ten other boys in town, and another seven expected any minute. As I was saying, you'll be in Washington for about three days. Nobody wants the whole European team here with Mother—let alone the other far-flung Heads—but there's no way to avoid it. We're getting a necessary briefing from our Cousins, the Brits, and this is the only totally secure way."

"More trouble?" The Head of Station from Sydney, Australia, raised his eyebrows.

"I don't think you'd call it trouble." Angleton's face seemed to alter, going into a reflective mode. "No, not trouble, but a slight embarrassment. That's why this is all silent as the grave. They've finally come up with the 'fourth man' as their tabloids would call him. Only, to lay the ghost, they've had to give him immunity from prosecution. The files won't be unlocked until around the time Gabriel blows Taps."

"The long march still goes on then?" Arnie said it almost to himself. The Russians, they all knew from defectors, had started what they called "the long march through the institutions" by recruiting likely penetration agents in the 1930s—men and women who stood a real chance of being placed in positions of responsibility within the government establishments and political power bases of every non-Communist country in the West.

"It would seem so." Angleton sounded briskly cheery about the whole thing. "Our Cousins took a fancy to him quite a while ago. A little hint here, an inconsistency there. Since the early fifties, I gather. But we had a small hand in the final unmasking—Uncle Sam, I mean, not *us* as in the Agency. FBI had a line on a U.S. citizen—Michael Straight, son of the famous Whitney Straight. Michael was up at Cambridge with all that gang, Burgess, Maclean, Philby, and the final mark. He spilled the whole can of worms. Juicy evidence, including a direct approach from the man concerned. Five could never prove anything in a court of law, mind you—and I shouldn't imagine they particularly wanted a court of law." He gave a dry little laugh. "But they needed cooperation. Don't we all? They certainly had to get a confession." Another laugh, short and unsweetened. "This fourth man, in the little nest of Communist spies, is none other than the famous art historian, former Surveyor of Her Majesty the Queen's pictures, and a 'Sir' to boot . . . "

"Or to cripple," said one of the others, his voice jaded.

"*Sir* Anthony Blunt. He sang, it appears, and there's some interesting product—so far, that is. They only began to work his jaw in the spring, but they feel there's urgency. They've brought an interim report. As I say, interesting."

"Interesting or *dis*interesting?" Arnie asked.

"Now, there you have it. Even the Director hasn't been put into the picture yet. A little bit of both, I suspect. Most of them have turned out to be hollow men, stuffed men, when taken apart." He lit another cigarette and inhaled. "Right, gentlemen. The Director and I are talking with our Brit Cousins tonight. We all meet here at ten in the morning. Room 56, nice and sterile."

They muttered their okays and thanks, then, just as they were about to leave, Angleton spoke again—"Oh, I'd appreciate it if you weren't seen together in town while you're here. In fact, we'd all appreciate it if none of you went out much. Don't want to draw attention to this little convention of spooks."

They smiled, nodded, or looked disappointed, depending on well-laid plans. Arnie asked when the Brits had taken this Sir Anthony Blunt apart, and Jim Angleton said, "April 23rd. That's when they nabbed him anyway. He's given them a lot of old stuff, but a few new leads. You must admit to the elegance of the Brits. April 23rd—St. George's Day, and William Shakespeare's Birthday."

Arnold Farthing went back to Georgetown, had a light meal, showered again, set his alarm and dropped into a sound sleep. The telephone rang at four-thirty in the morning. To begin with he thought he was back in Berlin, but, as he groped for the bedside lamp, Arnie immediately knew where he was. By the time he answered with a quiet "Yes?" he was wide awake.

The caller identified himself—all sensitive personnel were equipped with both cryptonyms and street names. The caller used James Jesus Angleton's street name and asked for Arnie by his crypto.

"I know it's early," Angleton said very quietly, "but I wonder if you could possibly come over to the office. It's rather urgent, I'm afraid."

"Of course." Arnie already had his feet on the floor.

"Just come straight up. I'll be alone and waiting." He hung up.

3

Angleton looked tired, and even more haggard than usual. "Arnold, I'm sorry," he said as a salutation, and for a moment Arnie thought it was some dreadful news—perhaps Gloria or one of the kids.

"This is difficult, and very embarrassing, considering our *particular* common interest," Jim Angleton began. He lit another cigarette from the one he had just finished smoking, then coughed. "Personally, I'm furious, but what can I do?" His body sagged, and, for a brief second, Arnold was reminded of the old photographs of revolutionary soldiers in the Spanish Civil War dancing with the disinterred corpses of nuns. Some had waltzed with ragged-robed skeletons.

Arnold now knew it was indeed dreadful news, though not to do with his family. Angleton's discomfort made it very personal. The gaunt man gestured towards a chair, the movement economic, like his spare frame.

"The Blunt debriefing, Arnie," he began, then took another long inhalation on his cigarette. "I'm sorry, but the Director's cut you out."

"Why?" This news was disturbing rather than downright bad. Steel seemed to line Arnold's voice and manner.

"Because the Brits have asked that you be removed. They don't want you privy to it. I fought for an hour or so, but they're adamant."

"Why?" Arnie repeated, pushing the word at Angleton like a battering ram.

"They claim it's because you're too close to an old British family which they have come to mistrust."

Arnold was quite still, not even blinking. "Railtons," he said looking hard at Angleton, who made no response. "Jim, who are these idiots?"

"Two from MI5 and three from the SIS. Five got Blunt and did the debrief, but the product has gone to the SIS." He mentioned five names. Arnold recognized four of them. The fifth was vaguely familiar, but Arnold only associated him with electronics. A man with wire coming out of his pockets.

Angleton lowered his voice. "My personal view on that is clear. I have to go along with them, but I'm doing the one possible thing which might put the business in perspective. They're not going to like it, but, then, I'm not going to tell them. They can be highly embarrassed—but so can we." He motioned towards a door which, Arnold knew, led to a small private office—sterile and sanitized—which Angleton kept for highly sensitive matters. "I've pulled two files from the archives. Signed for them myself." He did not look Arnie in the face, and his voice dropped almost to a whisper. "When you read them you'll know how I feel. They're *Eyes Only* for the Director and two other men—one is myself. I shall deny ever showing them to you. You've got a couple of hours. You're a quick study, as they say in the theater, and it would be a good thing if you read, brain-marked, looked, and learned from the files. After that, you must do as you think fit with the information." It was a quarter to six in the morning. "Two hours," Angleton repeated.

Arnold gave a wry smile and quoted from Robert Frost—

"But I have promises to keep,
And miles to go before I sleep."

Angleton gave him a bland look and repeated the last line, just as Frost had repeated it—"And miles to go before I sleep." Both men knew that "Stopping by Woods on a Snowy Evening" had been one of the Kennedy brothers' favorite poems.

Later, Arnie was to know that this was an extraordinary expression of trust on Angleton's part. One he would live to appreciate.

The two thick folders were flagged Cosmic, and had linking cryptonyms—*Elephant:Recent* and *Elephant:Six.* He opened the second one first and saw that, inside, under the crypto, were the words—*Analysis of last Iron Bark Material.* He began to read. Five pages in, Arnold Farthing sat up as though stung. Spread over four pages the name *Caspar Railton* appeared no less than twenty-five times. He spent an hour running through the whole document, then returned to the four pages which seemed to be central to his being cut out of the Blunt product. He memorized the pages, then turned to *Elephant:Recent.* This time he did not even sit up, for a genuine gasp of surprise escaped from his lips. He was looking at transcripts and photographs, recently taken, of a man he had thought was dead.

So, it was at that moment, Arnold realized the purpose of the complicated dangerous dance Jim Angleton had led him through during the past few years.

TWO

1

There had been some light snow around Berlin at the end of November that year, but now the streets were clear and days bright and crisp, with the kind of cold that bit into your lungs. As ever, the Kurfürstendamm was bustling in the pre-holiday rush. People were wearing a lot of fur, and the stores bulged with Christmas goodies. Everywhere there was opulence in the shop windows.

Naldo waited at a crossing, glancing to his right, hardly noticing the dark ruins of the Kaiser-Wilhelm Gedächtniskirche, its scarred and lopped-off stump of a spire a permanent reminder of World War II's devastation. Somewhere to the right, a huge metal circle, surrounding an inverted Y, rotated slowly, advertising Mercedes-Benz from the top of one of the relatively new tall buildings. Together with the obscene dividing Wall, these were images of Berlin already known all over the Western world. They were familiar from television newscasts, and the spy films which were such a booming offshoot of the Cold War.

To Naldo, the views were not even part of the scenery anymore. He watched other things—parked cars, and license plates, hands, faces, shoes, shopping bags, and the way people walked. Naldo abroad seldom traveled in a straight line, for being tall and distinctive he was an easy target for surveillance teams. He was also very good at avoiding them.

He had spent so much time here in Berlin since 1945 that there were moments when he almost forced himself to remember the city as it had been—broken, shattered, ruined, but with a sense of spirit and determination deep within the collective roots of its people. Compared with '45 it was now unrecognizable, and, in a way, even more distasteful, for the authorities were hell-bent on holding up West Berlin as a gleaming, glittering Christmas-tree carrot, tempting those locked behind the Wall in the East.

He crossed the broad street, almost marching with the regimented civilians, then began to walk west towards the Bristol-Kempinski Hotel. From behind the windows of a respectable looking café he heard the thump of the Beatles singing "It's Been a Hard Day's Night." He paused to read the menu in the window, though could not have told you what they served inside. Four Liverpool lads seemed to have taken over the world. He wondered if you could hear them singing "Hey! Hey! Wait a minute Mr. Postman!" in the Eastern Zone.

The foyer of the Kempinski was warm. Tropical fish swam in aquariums set into the walls. There was a feeling of almost intense orderliness. It was ever thus. Even in the dark, cold, and cruel days immediately after the war, there had been a sense of order in the chaos of the sacked and ruined city. The old image haunted him—the black-clad women sifting through the rubble; human chains passing brick and stone among a cloud of dust.

Arnie Farthing sat in a corner, stretching his long frame in an easy chair, coffee on a silver tray in front of him. He had chosen the one table from which every entrance and exit could be seen.

Naldo put his right hand in his coat pocket—it was a very old signal they had once used to mean that everything was clear.

Arnie rose, his battered pugilist's face splitting into a smile, though his eyes, as usual, said nothing. Nobody could read Arnie through his eyes.

Thrusting out his right arm, he took Naldo's hand in his. They were both large men, big-boned and broad-shouldered. At last, Naldo sat next to Arnold, ordering more coffee from the waiter, who appeared as though from the woodwork.

"Great to see you, Arnie. How's Gloria?"

Arnie Farthing had met his bride while on the same op during which Naldo had met Barbara. They—Arnold Farthing and Gloria Van Gent—had married a year later. Now there were two more fine Farthing sons whom, depending on his mood, Arnie referred to as Romulus and Remus, or Amos 'n' Andy. Their real names were Michael and Paul.

"You worry about the kids? Teenage adults now." The Englishman punched his friend lightly on the shoulder.

"Yeah. Yeah, I worry." The smile fell for a moment. "I see looks in their eyes. I don't think they like the way I earn my daily bread."

Naldo nodded. "The times they are a-changing—as the man sings. Recruit them, Arn. My family learned that trick a couple of hundred years ago."

There was a pause: around fifteen seconds. Then, "Sorry about Cas." Arnie looked at the floor.

"Yep. Rotten, but he had good innings. Thanks for the wreath."

Arnold had sent a wreath with a card that said, *The Symphony is ended. RIP A Minor.* Only a very few people would know the message came from Arnie. Only a minimal number had known about the operation called *Symphony,* for it was run by the, then, Chief of SIS, under the most covert circumstances, and connected with Caspar's reputation and loyalty.

"You okay? No lice?" Arnold raised his eyebrows, his mood changing, with eyes flicking towards the street door. On the telephone he had made a cryptic remark which bade Naldo watch his own back when coming to this meeting.

"I've been dry cleaning for the last hour. If anyone's on me it has to be the invisible man."

Arnie gave a wide smile. "There've been sightings of him in *this* city."

"I even stopped to buy a present for Gloria. Took me half an hour—just to show you I haven't lost the touch." Naldo placed a beautifully wrapped package on the table. It contained a small golden bear—Berlin's symbol. The wrapping showed it had been bought at Sedlatzek, distinctly up-market. It was the kind of thing you put on an expensive charm bracelet.

There was one primary rule, which rarely failed, when you were dry cleaning, which in the real world means shaking or detecting surveillance. Go into a very expensive shop and stay there for a long time: anyone on your back could usually be flushed or spotted.

Arnold tore at the paper and laughed when he saw the bear because it reminded them both of Eberhardt Lukas Kruger—Big Herbie, whom Arnold had passed on to Naldo in this very city some eighteen years ago.

In the DP camps, the young Kruger had ferreted for Arnie, rooting out Nazis. When Farthing was recalled to Washington he left the lad in Naldo's care. "How is he?" the American asked.

"You know how he is, Arn. You paid him a visit."

Arnold grunted and the coffee arrived. "He's done great things. Come a long way," he said when the waiter departed. "And you, cousin, what did you tell your office?"

"That I had to see a source. I gave them a name, and I'll have to meet him today. We've got an arrangement for this afternoon—fallbacks every two hours until midnight." In reality, the "him" was a "her."

Arnold nodded, and Naldo stopped speaking, waiting to see why the American had asked for this deliberately clandestine meeting. At last Farthing said, "This is a family matter."

"Which family, Arn?"

"Come on, we belong to the same family."

"By marriage, or trade?" Naldo gave a little questioning smile, with the hint of a raised eyebrow.

"There's ceased to be any difference. I have something you should know. Something we should all know."

"For free, Arnie? You're giving me something for free?"

Arnold smiled, a pleasant and open look, and Naldo wondered if he was about to lie. With Arnie you just could not tell, but they all lied to each other. It was their common parlance.

"Nothing's completely for free. You know that."

"And what you've got is family business?"

"Very much so. Warnings. The hoisting of distress signals. There are maroons being fired all over the place. We're in trouble. Both families."

"And the price?" Naldo sounded almost disinterested.

"Possibly your covert assistance. Maybe I'll ask you to lift the odd file, or something. Just remember it's family. I think you'll find plenty you *want* to give."

"I have very little to give." Naldo made a gesture, opening his arms like someone who had experience of haggling in bazaars, smiling as he did so to show he was joking. Then, as though suddenly thinking of another subject—"There is, however, a matter I'd like to resolve. There have been whispers. Rumors. Unconfirmed on the grapevine."

"Then ask away. If I know, I'll tell you, simply to convince you of trust and faith on my side." Both voice and face changed, as if the world had tipped. In the few seconds that had passed, Arnold appeared to become a man who had just had some terrible blow: his wife dead, or his own health damaged beyond repair. "Ask. You'll find we have to reestablish a lot of trust, because it's going to be difficult for *you* to believe what I have to say."

Naldo thought for a moment. Then—"Okay. Tell me about Dallas. A little over a year ago."

"Bad business." Arnie sounded like a poker player.

"Yes. Everyone in Britain was shocked." Naldo shook his head, a half-sad movement. "Though, if I hear it right, not all of your people were as heartbroken as the rest of the world."

"Could be. President Kennedy was out for blood. Wanted to scatter the Agency to the four winds." Arnold Farthing the open and honest broker.

"Because the Agency made him look foolish over the *Mongoose* fiasco?" *Mongoose* was the Bay of Pigs incident—a CIA-backed attempt to stir up revolt in Cuba and remove power from Fidel Castro. The Agency had told Kennedy it could not fail. The military had told him it could not fail. Nobody told him of the reservations felt in certain quarters within the Agency and the Pentagon.

The President ordered *Mongoose* to go ahead, and the operation was a disaster. Because of this, Kennedy was to suffer at the hands and tongue of the Russian leader, Nikita Khrushchev, who verbally beat him to a pulp at the Vienna summit some months later. "Castro wasn't a Communist, but you've made him one," the Russian leader was reported to have said. Kennedy was furious with the Agency and initiated a purge.

"So *were* your people involved?" Naldo asked. "*Are* we seeing a whitewash?"

Arnold sighed. "The answer's no—and yes. No, our people weren't involved. Yes, we're seeing a whitewash. That should be obvious."

"Well then, did the butler do it?" The line did not sound frivolous the way Naldo said it.

"No." Arnie let his hands rise a couple of inches, then fall back onto the arms of the chair. With the gesture came a small sigh. "No, Oswald might, or might not, have pulled the trigger. Who knows? But he who aims the rifle can be a different person to the one who pulls the trigger. In this case, it was, I believe, a Vietnamese family who aimed the rifle." He sighed again. "Though the others don't want to admit it, even to themselves."

"Go on." Naldo leaned forward.

But Arnie shook his head. "No. No, you really don't want to know the details of that one. I mean it, Nald. I have something far more serious for you."

"More serious than Kennedy's murder?"

"Much more serious for our respective families, yes."

"Just put me out of my misery on the Kennedy count first."

Arnold made a small facial movement of capitulation. "Okay. All I can tell you is that one very experienced field officer went private from the Agency because of it. He went off to bring back the proof; the whole proof; and nothing but the proof. And when he did, they just shredded it and dropped it into a burn bag. They've probably shredded him, and dropped him into a burn bag as well. It's easier for everybody to stick with the one determined, crazy assassin theory. Nobody wants to sully the President's memory. That would happen if you proved his death to be a simple revenge killing, carried out by a corrupt and ruthless family called Ngo, who imagined—rightly or wrongly—that JFK signed the warrants that brought about the coup in South Vietnam. A vengeance killing is squalid. A lone nut marksman you can live with." He leaned towards Naldo. "Now, let me tell you what I came to give."

Naldo smiled and cocked his head on one side.

"Blunt . . . ?" Arnie began.

"The bad Sir Anthony? What *of* him?"

"I should not even know Blunt exists, Naldo. They've cut me out of the action. No access to the confession. No briefing." He paused, gall and wormwood in his mouth. Every word he spoke was pained with bitterness. "They cut me out *because of family ties*—Railton ties and Farthing ties."

"Why?" Naldo could hear the strong note of alarm in his voice.

"That's what I asked, and now I think I know. Blunt is not important to the equation. But, sure as hell, my being barred from knowledge is a whirlpool of worry, and *very* important, because it raises questions. I'm going to tell you the story."

"Go on." Anthony Blunt's confession that he had spied for the Soviets when he was an MI5 officer, was a secret kept very close indeed, on both sides of the Atlantic.

There was a moment's silence while both men tried to look into one another's minds. Then Arnie continued. "Okay. I'll tell you what I've got. After that you might feel it wise to pool our resources. A couple of weeks ago, I was called to Washington. . . . " He told the bare facts of what had happened, using sparse language, wasting no words.

Naldo listened, his heart sinking. He knew that, as the Agency's Head of Berlin Station, Arnold Farthing worked directly to Counterintelligence—this being a euphemism for many things: mainly to monitor and capitalize on the activities of any foreign intelligence agency, and everyone knew that meant Allied as well as potential enemy agencies. They were also responsible for penetration agents, either way—into foreign agencies, out of agencies and, naturally, the penetration of their own service. CIA Counterintelligence would be high on the list of people to be briefed about Blunt.

Arnie now related the story of his early morning call, and the summons to Angleton's office. "He told me outright that it had to do with my family connections. In particular, connections with a British family. He didn't name your people. But I did, and he reacted. It would seem that our families are tied too close for some people's peace of mind.''

"Yea, even unto the third and fourth generation?" Naldo said it like a man making some automatic liturgical response.

"It isn't funny, Naldo." Arnie was quite sharp, making little biting movements with his mouth as he spoke. "No quips. No setting the table on a roar, as you bloody Railtons would say, quoting your beloved Shakespeare."

"Okay. Sorry. Go on," Naldo sounding more sober.

"Jim Angleton's a tight bastard, but he has great loyalties. He did us all one hell of a favor." Arnold went on to speak of the two files, though did not reveal their contents. "Before I left the building I saw Angleton again. He said there was a chance that I would be posted home and put behind a desk. He'll hold it at bay for as long as possible, but it was a plain warning. He also repeated that I should make use of what I'd read in his files. So, I went down and took a peek at another pair of files, off my own bat. It turned out to be more than interesting. I pulled the files for *Corby* and *AE-Ladel.* You recognize those names, Nald?"

Naldo nodded. *Corby* was the crypto for a KGB cipher clerk in the Soviet Embassy, Ottawa, Canada, who had defected back in 1945. *AE-Ladel* was a more recent, and equally alarming defector—a KGB major. Together, these men had provided not only a terrifying picture of Soviet penetration of the Western intelligence agencies, but also a whole new thesis on KGB operations against the West. The pair were harbingers of fear, suspicion, and an indication that the West was losing the Cold War. Above all, they had led to the fingering of Burgess, Maclean, and Philby, though these three had slipped the net. On both sides of the Atlantic, they had pointed to other agents. Some were quietly moved to places where they could cause no trouble; some had been arrested; at least three had disappeared. The Soviets had no compunction when it came to blown agents.

"Good. I'm glad your memory holds *Corby* and *Ladel.*" Arnold did not smile, nor did he sound happy. "Because the files Jim Angleton let me take a peek at contained the very *latest* material on *Alex.* Remember *Alex,* Nald?"

Naldo gave him a quick affirmative nod. Then Arnie let out a deep breath, as though he was exhaling smoke, and said there was a very important question he had to ask.

"Ask." Naldo was now concerned.

"Did you have anything to do with *Alex,* and the *Iron Bark* material? It's important."

For a second, Naldo thought Arnold was talking about Alex Railton, his cousin who worked at GCHQ. Then, with the mention of *Iron Bark,* he realized what was meant. "Yes. Yes, I did. Not the recruitment, but, yes, I was involved."

"And your late Uncle Caspar? Wasn't he pulled out of retirement for some of that?"

"I carried the messages to him. Carted him along to the sessions."

"Would you tell me exactly what happened? What you were told? What you heard? It's important for all of us."

2

They all lied, Naldo thought again, wondering if he should talk, and, if he talked, should he tell the truth?

His brain worked quickly, sifting what Arnie had laid out so far. Because of his connection with the Railtons, Farthing had been aced out of the enclosed circle of knowledge concerning Blunt's confession—the admission of an old spy that he had for some time in the past betrayed his country to the Soviets. Why should they bar that particular knowledge to Arnie? Naldo realized that he was also excluded from the Blunt material, or *Hypermarket* as they called it. He had not thought much about it before, as his exclusion was in the need-to-know category, so he had always assumed there was no need for him to be on the *Hypermarket* list. Then he thought of another strange thing concerning *Hypermarket.* It was Five's show, but the Secret Intelligence Service had been cut in and taken control. He recalled something else that was odd. The tapes and transcripts had been taken over from Five by the SIS. It was said they had them locked in a secure vault. You required the signatures of the Holy Trinity and St. Michael the Archangel to get near them.

"I just need to know what happened. What you saw and felt," Arnie prodded.

"Why?" Naldo was still uneasy, unconvinced.

"Why?" Arnold parroted him, remembering his own steely response to Jim Angleton. "Why? Because if you don't, I have to work blind, and there's going to be all hell let loose." Then, as an aside, "There's going to be hell anyway, but we might avoid some of the personal horrors." He paused again, then said, "If I told you there is twenty-four-carat, Grade A proof that *Alex* is alive and well, and living in style, would that help?"

"But they executed him . . . "

"That was the sentence of the court." Arnold paused for a deep breath. "In fact, they sprung him. Set him up for life. Good old *Alex* sits in the sun, with the best Stolichnaya, as many women as he wants, and every luxury the Kremlin can afford to give him. His wife, the General's daughter, lives with shame in her widow's weeds. It has to be like that, to keep the fiction alive. *Alex* is dead, but he has risen. *Alex surrexit. Alleluia!*"

"Come on, Arn. Didn't I hear they were about to publish his diaries. His testament that he risked smuggling into the West?"

"Balls. He risked nothing. There was never any question of risk for that man. Yes, they're working on the so-called diaries. I can even give you the names of the guys who're doing the job. It's being concocted, Naldo. Concocted from all those tapes and notes, taken while you, Uncle Sir Caspar, and two dozen others sat open-mouthed, hardly daring to believe the luck of what had fallen into your laps. Tell me what happened—what you were told; what you did—and I will unfold the truth and open your eyes."

Naldo frowned, not liking what he heard. *Alex* was the cryptonym for Colonel Oleg Vladimirovich Penkovsky of the GRU, a man who had provided the British and American intelligence services with information beyond price. The brilliant agent of conscience, heralded now in the West as one of the bravest defectors of all time; a man who had stayed in Russia, collecting information for the NATO powers, risking everything, passing his intelligence to the SIS and CIA at brief, dangerous meetings in the West, or through couriers and cutouts within Russia and Eastern Bloc countries.

What Penkovsky gave was pure gold. He had been a source without parallel in the history of the secret trade. A magic spy of the kind all intelligence officers dream. Through him, they said, President Kennedy had been able to outflank the Russian Khrushchev and brilliantly avert a nuclear war. It was only in the previous spring that Penkovsky had been tried, in Moscow, with his British courier. Penkovsky had been shot; the courier went directly to jail—via Lubyanka to Vladimir Prison. If Penkovsky was still alive, as Arnie claimed, something was very wrong.

"From the beginning, Nald. Please," Arnold was almost pleading.

Naldo nodded. "Okay." And he began to talk quietly. For him it had begun three and a half years ago, April 1961 in Berlin, with a ringing telephone in the middle of the night—"Isn't that always the way?" he said.

THREE

1

Naldo told it just as he remembered it from three and a half years ago. The telephone was ringing beside his bed in the safe house off the Knesebeckstrasse. He had only been asleep for an hour, and it was four in the morning. Big Herbie was in the spare room, in from the Russian zone for a forty-eight-hour debrief which had not gone well.

"It was the office. Our Berlin Station," Naldo now told Arnie. " 'Ginger's looking for you.' That's what they said. Funny how you remember the bloody crypts and passwords. *Ginger* was London that week. 'Looking for you' meant proceed London fastest. If the cable began with *Ginger* it was Flash." This last is the highest priority coding of any cable.

"So you went?" It was more a statement of fact than a question.

Naldo smiled and nodded. Do not tell him more than necessary. In reality he had not gone quickly. His subconscious dredged it back now. Herbie had a problem. That was why they had been up talking until three in the morning. Herbie was like a cat all night, pacing up and down, unnaturally nervous. Late on he came around to it. "Nald, switch off the bloody tapes. I need talk with you—man on man." He could see Herb, who had now settled, his bulk filling the chair, a glass in one hand and the remains of their meal still on the table behind him.

"I had to finish up what I was doing," Naldo told Arnie. "Servicing an agent." He did not mention Herbie, nor Herbie's problem. The big German was desperately in love with one of the girls he had recruited—Ursula something or other. They had talked it through, because Herbie wanted her out and there was no way Naldo could do it. The poor man was besotted and unhappy. Naldo remembered saying to him, "Herb, you know the rules, you know how to behave. You don't get emotionally involved with one of your agents. Okay, it might be good cover to live with her, but if you get your head down there below your heart it goes sour. Believe me." He almost said, "Believe me, I know." It was Railton history that one of the family had allowed it to happen, during the '14–'18 war, and had suffered for it.

He settled for "Enjoy, but unzip the hearts and flowers."

Predictably, Herbie had asked, "What's with hearts and flowers?" Then he had become angry—"You think I do it on purpose, Naldo? You think I want it happening? No man is in love for purpose. Hits you like bloody sleigh hammer . . ."

"Sledgehammer, Herb." After all this time, Naldo still automatically corrected Herbie Kruger's version of the English language, which always got jumbled when he was upset or tense.

"Hits you like bloody sledgehammer, love. I want marry this girl. She's first girl to make me happy in mind and bed both. *Verstehen?* I want her out for my pension. At least ask for me. Ask them."

There and then, in the spring, nobody had a clue about how the political situation would develop that summer. There was no hint that East-West relations would deteriorate quickly, with hordes of people coming over from the East, and the Berlin Wall going up overnight. Then the confrontation, the temperature rising, the threats and the concern that someone would get trigger-happy.

Later in the year was a time of anxiety and panic, with agents running in all directions and networks being left to the wolves. But in April, Naldo knew it was no good even mentioning Herbie's request to London. Maitland-Wood, pompous ass that he was, would have laughed in his face. But, to keep his agent happy, Naldo lied to him, telling him that he would give it a whirl back in London.

So, Naldo did not get into Heathrow until nine that night. It was raining and very cold: London had not yet fully acquired the delicious patina of the season. Spring was a little late that year, and at the office it was winter in the shape of Maitland-Wood.

"Where in God's name've you been, Railton? They were onto you at four this morning. It's logged at three forty-five. Then Berlin came back and said contact was made at four o'clock. Time, Railton, is—as the lawyers say—of the essence."

He was red in tooth and claw, but Naldo always found it easier to ignore the outbursts. "There was an agent. I was servicing him. Time was of the essence there as well. My agent had to get back into the East. Limited trip out." God, Naldo thought, how dated that kind of language sounded now, even at the distance of three and a half years. Their trade was like fashion, it changed constantly.

"Sod the agent!" Then a pause, and, "Who?" as if he did not know.

"Blunder. He won't get over again for a month. He has very good assets. A lot at stake."

Now, sitting in the Kempinski, he realized he had even dragged "Blunder" up from the past. Why had he used a street name to Maitland-Wood? Heaven knew, for C's deputy was familiar enough with Big Herbie.

"Well." Maitland-Wood gave him the grave and serious look. "This is the hottest thing to come our way in a lifetime." He went through the essentials—not just bare, but stark naked. They were about to open up a defector-in-place. Crypto, *Alex*. In the real world a GRU colonel, highly connected, experienced, decorated during the Great Patriotic War, and now not only with an extensive knowledge of missile technology, but also with access to it. *Alex* had already provided documents and film. "Everyone's crazy about him. Salivating," Maitland-Wood said.

Grosvenor Square, which really meant Langley, was being cut in, and the wonderful *Alex* was already in London with some visiting firemen: a trade delegation. On the following evening they were throwing a party for *Alex* and doing the first debriefing.

"All taken care of." Maitland-Wood puffed like a frog. "We've borrowed nearly all Five's Watchers, and the SB're going to help. We're springing *Alex* from the hotel where his entire delegation is staying. Open him up, then pop him back. Every night while he's in London. Cheeky, eh?"

Naldo personally thought it was not simply appalling tradecraft, but also damned dangerous. You did not tell Maitland-Wood things like that, so he sat, listening in silence to the means—how, once the other Sovs were snoring, *Alex* was going to be smuggled out to their largest safe house, where everything had been laid on. When he finally broke silence, Naldo asked what he was required to do—"Especially if everything has already been laid on, sir." The sarcasm was lost on BMW, as most people called him: Bloody Maitland-Wood.

"Touchy matter." C's deputy thrust his thumbs into his vest pockets, rising and falling on the balls of his feet. To Naldo he looked like the caricature of some pompous local small-town councilor.

"Yes?"

"Your uncle, actually. Sir Caspar." Caspar had been given a knighthood on retirement a couple of years before, in '59. He was already overage then. But for his years at Sandhurst, and the few months he had been on active service in France, in 1914, Caspar Railton had given

43

his entire life to the Secret Intelligence Service—he personally did not count the couple of years out in the '30s when he had resigned out of pique.

"But my uncle's out now, sir. Private. What do you want with him?"

"W–e–ll." Maitland-Wood gritted his teeth and drew out the word on one sustained note, neither rising nor falling. "Well, he's a very shrewd old hand." He was taking his time, and not looking Naldo in the eyes. "Shrewd. Knows what's what. Has a nose. As *Alex* is such a big fish we thought it might be an idea if he came and ran his eyes over the chap. Get his measurements so to speak. Look and listen, actually."

"But you said this man's bona fides were well established."

"Oh, they are . . . They are. But, well, he really *is* the biggest fish we've ever netted. We thought old Caspar would like to see and hear for the pleasure of it."

Now, in the Kempinski, Naldo told Arnold Farthing what he really thought. "They were showing off. In their own nasty little way they were humiliating Caspar. That's how I read it at the time, anyhow. Rubbing his nose in a super magic source the like of which Caspar had failed to haul in during his time. After all, he was Deputy to C for the last ten years of his working life. I think he only stayed on in the Service because of that appointment. Particularly as they'd already humiliated him once with that damned network investigation." He spoke of an SOE wartime cell in France which Caspar had run, long range, from London. Something had gone horribly wrong and, when the fighting was done, there had been a Board of Enquiry which tried to hang the blame on Caspar.

Arnold Farthing gave a curt nod and looked up, suspiciously, at Naldo, then away again. "But he went along with it, didn't he?"

"Of course he did. Why shouldn't he? Everyone was starry-eyed, including myself come to that. It was Caspar who actually originated the phrase that *Alex* was 'the great agent of conscience.' Christ, Arnie, it *was* impressive. I couldn't follow all the technical stuff, but it was obviously very good indeed: really up-market, the missile intelligence, I mean. The boffins went crazy about it. You must've seen most of the product."

Arnold Farthing made no comment about seeing the product. "And you babysat Sir Caspar on *all* the debriefings?" he asked.

"There were only three sets. Two in London. One in Paris. About five nights each. All the other stuff—the pix of documents and all that—were brush-dropped or dead-dropped in Moscow and run through the Embassy."

Arnold nodded, indicating he knew all that. "You did *all* of them with Cas, though?"

"Yes."

"Paris, and the girls? What the Ks would call 'swallows'?" K was the diminutive they all used for KGB.

"Yes, we took girls over to keep *Alex* happy. There was an unfortunate incident in London when he tried to use some tart. We couldn't take the risk again, so we supplied him."

"They were girls you could *trust?* Trained and everything?"

"I gathered we'd used them before. Baiting honey traps. Safe as houses." He smiled.

"Caspar condone it?"

"He didn't know. I knew because we all had to keep *Alex* sweet."

"Why did they ask you to mind Caspar? Why not Alexander, his son? He's in the trade, after all."

"Cryptoanalysis, ciphers, Comint. They're Alexander's speciality acts. Different end of the business, isn't it? Alex Railton's not a field man—the little shit. Anyway, they worked out that I was closer to the old boy."

"Don't like Alexander much, do you?"

"Nor my cousin Andrew. Alexander's a stinking shit, for Christ's sake. Arn, *you* know what that runt did to Caspar."

"Tried to drop his father in the mire when they investigated the network business right after the war. You think I'd forget that?" This was Caspar's first humiliation that Naldo had already mentioned earlier.

Arnie continued. "Of course I bloody remember, and it worries *me*, Nald. You needn't keep bringing it up. It bothers the hell out of me."

"Oh?"

"Later," sharp, as though pushing Naldo, hurrying him through his memories, his version, in order to get to the heart of the matter, which was the reason he had arranged this meeting in the first place. "You heard all the face-to-face debriefings, though. You heard them with Caspar. What did *you* make of the wonder spy? What did you really make of Penkovsky?"

"Bit full of himself. You know what defectors're like, Arn, unpredictable, nervous as a rule."

"Was *Alex* nervous?"

Naldo thought for a good thirty seconds. "No, come to think of it he never showed nerves—except about Five, about the security service. He wanted nothing to do with Five. Paranoid about it. Apart from that he was very relaxed. Liked the trappings as well. He was dead pro during interrogations. Gave chapter and verse on everything; and he was like a kid on Christmas morning when they gave him the gee-whiz stuff—the camera, film, pen, all the bloody James Bond stuff. He liked that a lot. Otherwise, he always seemed to know what he was talking about. Never stuck for an answer. Convincing. I was convinced—still am."

"You were there when he asked for the money?" Arnold's battered, craggy face was set in a frozen mold.

Naldo hesitated. "Yes. Yes, I was. Right at the end of the first, or maybe the second session during the first London trip. One grand for expenses. Bit embarrassing at the time. Reasonable enough, though."

"Wasn't really in line with the 'great agent of conscience,' was it?" Arnie did not even pause for a reply. "Did anyone—like Willis BMW, for instance—talk to you about the recruitment? *Alex*'s recruitment?"

"Only the bare essentials. The stuff on record. The stuff we all know."

"Oh, yes?" If Naldo had not known the American as well as he did, he would have thought Arnold was sneering. "So tell me. Tell me what they told you," Arnie prodded.

"You know it, Arn."

"Never mind what I know. Pretend you're briefing me. Tell it just as you heard it. No frills, just the straight feed."

Naldo shrugged. "Okay, he made contact with this bloke we had coat-trailing in Moscow. Gave our fellow a bloody great envelope full of shit-hot, gee-whiz intelligence. That was the first of many contributions *Alex* handed over. It wasn't surprising they snapped him up."

"And when it went sour? What'd they tell you about that?"

Naldo made a little sigh of exasperation, as though this was all a waste of time. Arnold nodded him on and Naldo shrugged again. "*Alex* got nervous. There was a plan activated to get him out—him and his family. Then our bloke had a dinner date with him, in Moscow, but *Alex* signaled it was no go. Fallback at the airport at six the next day. Should've been noon, but *Alex* pulled rank and got his contact out."

"And that was when exactly, Nald?"

"July '62, I think. Yes, I'm sure."

"*Alex* was giving off warnings like a goddamned alarm system, right?"

"Yes, but . . ."

"But it went on, didn't it? He was still passing information, and the courier was popping back behind the curtain—right?"

46

"That was how they told it afterwards, yes."

"And nobody thought it odd? Nobody said, 'What a bloody silly way to run a railway.' Even though the Ks were on his back, *Alex* went on pushing the stuff over, and the courier returned with an escape plan—returned behind the curtain, to Budapest?"

Naldo saw the inconsistency and folly of that kind of behavior. He frowned.

"So," said Arnie, "it shouldn't have come as a surprise when *Alex* got himself pulled. In Moscow. October 22, 1962?"

"No, it shouldn't have. But where's this leading? Arn, you know it all, so why . . . ?"

"And they pulled the courier in Budapest. November 2, 1962. Surprise, surprise."

"I said if . . ."

"And you believed all of it? Big trial. Western Press have field day. Extra! Extra! Read all about it! Briton and Ruskie held on spy charges. 'We do not know these men,' says Foreign Office. Tcht!" Arnold made a noise of contempt. "So, your guy goes off to the slammer. Colonel Penkovsky—*Alex*—gets a bullet through the back of his head, in the Lubianka cellars. You believe that? Taken in like all the others, Naldo?"

"*Was* I taken in?" Naldo felt icy cold.

"Like a stray dog. Taken in, fed, watered, kept warm."

"How, Arnie?" He sounded calm, but his old friend had him needled, jumpy under the skin, like a junkie going cold turkey. "How and *why*? Didn't *Alex* provide the Cuban missile intelligence? And didn't he pass enough technical stuff to let Kennedy go right to the brink with the Russians? Or did we all just imagine that?"

The American shook his head. Slow, tiny movements. "No. No, that was real enough. *Alex*—Colonel Penkovsky—provided unbelievably good intelligence. Russian missile and rocket capability, order of battle, just the kind of thing we all needed. And, yes, that information allowed everything to be taken to the brink, then drawn back."

He paused, but there was no comment from Naldo.

Arnie continued, "It was serious business. The fall of '62. A couple of years ago, Nald, but it seems a lifetime. In October 1962 Oleg Penkovsky got himself lifted, and Jack Kennedy faced Nikita Khrushchev across the baize boards, playing a game called brinkmanship. The Cuban Crisis. The missiles of October, right, Nald? Twelve days that shook the world, okay?"

"That's how I remember it."

"Sure, that's how you're meant to remember it—and most of the world with you. Sure, the Sovs had missiles and technicians on Cuba, a stone's throw from the U.S. of A. Jack Kennedy says, that's too close, get your missiles off the island or we'll turn your country into glass. Belligerent old Khrushchev has a convoy chock full o'missiles heading straight for Havana. Confrontation. The whole world goes to the brink. Khrushchev threatens a preemptive strike. Lights burn through the night in the White House, and Kennedy calls his bluff. Comrade Nikita backs down. Why? Because President John Fitzgerald Kennedy has all the facts, ma'am. Yes, sirreebub. JFK has the Russian order of battle, the missile and rocket capability, the works, right there on his desk. So he knows they haven't got the hardware for the real business."

Arnold paused for effect before he went on—

"And how does Jolly Jack Kennedy know? He knows from *Alex* aka Oleg Vladimirovich Penkovsky, who has shown that greater love hath no man than to lay down his life for the free world. He knows from Penkovsky, the enchanted agent who is disillusioned with the Communist ideology in general, and Khrushchev's Russia in particular . . . "

"It's not . . . " Naldo began, but Arnie held up a hand as though to say, "Let me finish."

"We get all this vital information from Oleg, or *Alex* as he likes to be called. We get it from a man who is so disillusioned that he trots off to the nearest Englishman he can find who's doing auditions for the defectors' opera in Moscow that week. He finds him and thrusts a velvet sack of true gems into his hands, saying that he's fed up with his lot. Bored with the dacha; the swimming pool; being married to the daughter of an honored general; holding high rank and a few honors himself; special privileges; doing the weekly shop at the Beryozka stores: Christ, he could probably get Beatles and Stones tapes for the kids." Arnold stopped again while a bellboy held up a board, progressing through the lobby, trying to find Herr Felton. "But not Dylan. I'd say not Dylan, or Baez," he said quietly. Then—

"He's so disillusioned, Nald, that he gives us everything our hearts desire. Then he goes back to work in Moscow, and even volunteers to do other officers' night duty for them. Volunteers, so that he can have more time to snap the documents we're all crazy to get our hands on. Didn't anybody learn anything about method from Philby? 'Kim's so conscientious,' they used to say. 'He stays on late at the office every night.' They didn't ask why, until later, when they woke up and realized he was taking pix of classified material. And Penkovsky's supposed to be using the same, tried and true, Soviet tradecraft in *his* Moscow office. You believe *that?*"

Underneath, Naldo was becoming more and more angry. "Okay. Yes. Yes, I went along with what Penkovsky did."

"Naldo, my dear old buddy, and relation twice removed, of course you went along with it; your Service went along with it; unhappily, even Caspar went along with it. The boys from *my* Company went along with it—in spite of what they already knew. I repeat that, they all went along with it *in-spite-of-what-they-knew.*" He clipped off the words like scissors cutting a tape. "C knew it as well as our own Director. Naldo, Willis BMW *must* have known as well, and so must the boys from Langley who sat listening to Penkovsky. They must've looked at the product and said, 'Jeez, the secrets of a lifetime. This guy really has got balls.' Even though they knew damned well that he was throwing a lot of what the Ks call barium mixed up with what they wanted to believe."

"In *spite* of what they knew, Arnie? What *did* they know?"

Arnold leaned closer to Naldo Railton, "Our people should really have known better. Did anyone ever tell you, or Caspar, or anyone else, the true facts about *Alex?*"

"What facts?"

"They're all there, plus a great deal more, in those dossiers Jim Angleton pointed me at in Washington. They're ciphered *Elephant* by the way, in case you run into them on your side of the water. It appears that, for years, Penkovsky was hurling himself at us. He'd been soliciting the Agency and your Firm for a long time before he grabbed the coattails of that luckless courier in Moscow. Nald, he was whoring. Offering himself to you Brits, and our guys, a good five years before Nikita Khrushchev came to power.

"Everyone had him tagged. He was a fucking dangle, Nald. Again and again memos went out saying don't touch this guy. My own boss, Jim Angleton himself, warned everyone, time and again, even *after* he became *Alex* the magic agent. When the chips were down, Naldo, everyone conveniently forgot.

"Eventually, because you Brits picked him up, they took a look at the jewels he was peddling and said, 'Shit, this is a crock of gold.' What they should have been saying was, 'Gold? This is a crock of shit.' Naldo, you're going to hate this, but most of what Penkovsky gave us was manure of the finest quality."

"You can prove this?" Naldo felt the familiar invisible cold hand

49

lying on his stomach. "Prove it from the files in those sterile vaults at Langley?" he asked again, but now it sounded flat.

"If I'm ever allowed into those vaults again, I can prove it. Those files Jim Angleton pulled for me give you chapter, verse, page number, the full works, together with a little logic. And the files give more than proof. They add a new dimension. The afterburn of the Penkovsky business is something that could be a real threat to your family, and to mine. It could just about put your Railtons and my Farthings out of circulation, and turn us all into lepers."

2

Arnold called for more coffee, and when the new pot was set in front of him, he poured for them both, leaned back and took a sip.

"Okay, let's see what you think, when I tell you about the way it really was according to the *Elephant* files. The way nobody bothered to tell you—or, worse still, tell Caspar. Could be everyone was honestly mesmerized with all those doubloons and pieces of silver *Alex* handed out. Maybe it all looked so good they genuinely wanted to forget the truth: really allowed their memories to become selective. It's possible. But that was then. Now, unhappily, is now, and it's almost time to pay the piper."

Arnold gave Naldo a sad smile of true affection, then started again. "Back at the end of the war, when I was spending a lot of time in Cockroach Alley, those stinking old huts along the Reflecting Pool and the Mall: the Agency's first resting place. Back then, we thought our families were in a mess, and we sorted it out, with Caspar's help. This time it's much much worse. How many family—both sides, yours and mine—are still in this business?"

"We make two." Naldo's laugh was flawed. "Three if you count Alex of GCHQ. You want to add in those who're retired or dead?"

"Well, the retired, and the recently dead, yes."

"Caspar. Dear old Dick. My Aunt Marie, and Denise. My own father." His father's voice, standing by Caspar's grave, came loudly into his head. "Now it begins."

"Don't forget another Farthing with heavy Railton ties. Clifton."

"I didn't know."

Clifton was the son of Denise Grenot and her Farthing husband, Edward. During the 1914–1918 war Denise had worked behind the

German lines, in Belgium. A Farthing had saved her life, and she was very much a Railton. Her mother, Marie, Naldo's aunt, had married, and deserted, a Frenchman during that same first war. For a long time, Marie had been seriously suspected of duplicity.

"Clifton's on the Soviet and Eastern European desk at Langley. Speaks Russian like a Muscovite. Walks like a Russian as well, you know, from the upper part of his body, not from his legs." Arnold sounded a shade smug. "He did the training at the Farm, but that was years ago. It wouldn't surprise me if he turned up in this city one of these bright days, en route for all stations to Moscow—for us, of course. Very gung-ho, Clifton." The Farm was the name they all used for a secret CIA training facility at Camp Peary, near Williamsburg, Virginia. "He's spent time in the field. Clifton's very experienced. Europe at the end of the war, then Eastern Bloc *and* Southeast Asia," he added, almost as an afterthought.

"We're old in the trade," Arnold continued quietly. "Not only the times, but the people are a-changing, Nald. How many in our families can be marked down as traitors?"

Naldo winced within himself. He knew now where Arnold was leading him, and it was a place he did not wish to visit—the territory of treachery near at hand. "You want to count the two girls?" he asked, and Arnie nodded.

"Two really big ones that we don't talk of anymore, and four who were just plain foolish."

"Puts you ahead, though. Makes you vulnerable, and don't forget, Nald, there was one investigation. One more suspect."

"You mean Cas? How many more times? He was cleared, for God's sake."

"He *was* investigated. You can't hide it, Naldo. Once a suspect, always considered a risk."

"Caspar was cleared. He worked as C's Deputy for ten years after that."

"When did that make any difference? Sometimes it's best to keep suspects close, where you can control them."

Naldo did not look at the American. At last he said, "Well, maybe. But what's this got to do with the *Elephant* files, and you being cut out of the *Hypermarket* material?"

"That what they call the Blunt product? Well-well. Naldo, it's got everything to do with it. That's why we should both watch our backs. You hungry, Nald? I can't tell you everything here."

"I'm hungry, but not for food. I want to hear about *Alex*. All of it."

51

"Maybe we should get some lunch," Arnold said. "It's a strain on the throat, sitting and muttering like penitents in the confessional. So, possibly we should have lunch, and then go somewhere quiet. I was going to give you the whole wretched story here, but, perhaps we should be kinda careful."

"It's your game, and your neck." Naldo did not like the way things were shaping up. There was a tension, an anxiety, an uncertainty about Arnold. He had known Arnie for a long time, and the man was as cautious as a deer going to a water hole. Now he was suggesting further caution, which did not predict any peace of mind.

Arnie gave him what used to be called an "old-fashioned look." One eyebrow raised, and an expression of disapproval. "In fact, it's your neck as well; and a lot of other necks. Best take care."

Naldo experienced the same unpleasant sinking feeling in the pit of his stomach, a well-known occupational sixth sense. Arnold had something *really* unpalatable lying festering in his mind.

"Whatever you say." Naldo spoke quietly. So they got a table, then and there at the Kempinski, and lunched with care also. Some soup, smoked salmon, and salad. No pudding. No alcohol. Afterwards, Arnold went to one of the telephone booths in the lobby.

He returned, frowning. "Not the kind of day to go for a stroll in the Zoo, and I can't use one of our normal safe houses," he said. "You mind a green house? It's okay, and we have full access to the mirrors and tapes, which means we can switch them off."

Naldo nodded. "As long as nobody starts any rumors about us."

Arnie gave a short, uneasy laugh. Green houses were places the trade used for entrapments, honeytraps. As such, the houses were always fitted with the best in hidden cameras and bugs.

3

The doorman summoned a cab which dropped them off near the Charlottenburg S-Bahn. The house—a second-floor three-room apartment—was five minutes' walk. They made it fifteen, sweeping the street twice. Arnold was on edge and made certain they had no watchers on them.

It was a pleasant apartment, well-furnished, and without gimmicks likely to put clients off. The rooms smelled fresh and clean, as though someone knew it was to be used. Arnold showed Naldo the two-way mirrors and the observation room, also the main controls hidden away in a broom cupboard. Naldo, for his part, took another look around, just to be on the safe side. Then, together they checked that everything was deactivated before sitting facing each other in the small living room, which had no mirrors anyway. They were reserved for the bedroom, which was decorated, as Arnie remarked, in *poule de luxe.*

"Okay, so you say *Alex* was a plant, and you can prove it?" Naldo was like an accused man awaiting a verdict. He wanted to get the bad news over and done with.

"I can prove he's still alive and well and living it up in a dacha near Sochi."

Naldo nodded. He knew that Sochi was a Black Sea resort favored by the Soviet privileged because of its mild climate. Nobody spoke of the prison camps and the special psychiatric hospital nearby.

"What kind of proof, Arnie?"

"Photographs. Statements. Transcripts, with cross-refs to tapes. The tapes certainly exist, and there's mention of film. But the statements and pix are enough. He's there. No doubt about it." Arnold gave a pleased grin. "It seems *Alex* was first spotted last year by one of our floaters. Unconfirmed, but worrying. A lot of Agency people were always worried about *Alex.*"

"So?"

"So they put in some plumbing—one-time tourists, a couple of journalists, all working through Tchaikovsky Street. They came up with the goods." By Tchaikovsky Street he meant the U.S. Embassy in Moscow.

"Put it in perspective for me, Arn, because I don't quite see where it's all leading and what it has to do with our families."

"Okay, I said *Alex* had tried it on long before you Brits netted him. Well, I *do* mean tried it on. You couldn't stop him. Anywhere our people went in Russia—embassy parties, diplomatic functions, even little soirées for visiting firemen—Penkovsky would be around, lurking behind pillars or doorways, shoving envelopes into people's hands, talking about coming over. He was such an obvious dangle that Langley eventually warned everybody off; and your people knew about it. The memos went through both SIS and Five. They'd already made up their own minds, because the Comrade Colonel had also embarrassed them."

"But we finally picked him up."

"I guess that was a field error. The guy your people used was only a floater. Not a pro. I guess someone didn't warn him. He saw it as a chance and took the bait."

"And *Alex*'s bait was a sackful of jewels, Arn. Explain. Why?"

"How does anyone explain, except to say that most of the jewels were paste repros. His profile still doesn't fit. It never did. *Alex* did it under discipline. When he was finally taken as a live one, nobody could see the wood for the trees. Just on track record, to say that he was an agent of conscience isn't enough. No offense to Caspar, because he probably didn't know the record. Neither did a lot of the others."

"But the intelligence . . . "

"Break it down, Nald. Go root in the files and see what he gave us."

"But he gave us a great deal."

"Wrong. You examine all the stuff, piece by piece. Everything. Some of it sounded terrific at the time, but in the terrible clarity of now, the majority was already known, or intelligently guessed at. Oh, sure, he gave us little bits of tittle-tattle, scraps picked up from his father-in-law's table, and the sum total of that was the strength of the military power, compared with the weakness of Beria's Secret Police. Remember Lavrenti Beria, Stalin's thug? You recall what *Alex* told us about his death after Stalin died? How the military lured him to the Moscow General HQ, shot him and burned his body. And *that* gets important if you want to follow this whole thing through. Remember *Alex* was GRU, which means military not NKVD, as the Ks were then. He was, to use their language, a 'Neighbor.' But, from the files I've seen, it would appear that they were all in on this. The Ks and the GRU. It became necessary for some kind of alliance between them."

"He gave the missile details. Technical and tactical." Naldo sounded lame, halfhearted, and he knew it.

"Uh-huh. So he did. But only just. Remember, all that was *military* stuff." There was something machiavellian in the way Arnold spoke. "Never once did *Alex* give us a clue as to *intention.* All he did was give us missile capability. He showed how the *military* handled the missile sites; how they went about the work; he also showed that the missile gap between the Soviet Union and the United States was much smaller than our analysts had originally computed."

"Yes. But the missile information *was* central to the power play at the time of the Cuban Crisis. Surely . . . "

"Nald," Arnold interrupted quickly, "that was the whole point. Well, almost the whole point. You have to ask yourself about the timing. When did *Alex* give us this wonderful knowledge? The answer is that he gave it *just* when we really wanted it. Kennedy needed it desperately; the Agency needed it three years before; the Pentagon was asking for it almost from the moment we knew the Sovs had an atomic capability. *Alex* gave it *just* in time for the supposed Cuban Crisis, and—this is damned important—he got himself pulled by the KGB at *just* the right moment. *Just* as the Cuban business was heading into its final phase, they removed him; and, for safety, his courier as well."

"I don't get it. Why, Arn? Why should the Sovs mount an operation which turned out to be an information op, *not* a disinformation op?"

"The end product." Arnold held up a hand. "The end product, plus a neat piece of disinformation, which is revealed only now that we know *Alex* still lives."

Naldo looked at him, saying nothing. Waiting, his face a blank, reflecting his mind.

"Go check it yourself. Every scrap of *Alex*'s product, with the exception of the important, though limited, missile intelligence, was worthless. Your people, and mine, fell on the stuff and were blinded by its brilliance, mainly because we required the core, the heart of the product." Arnold leaned back, spreading his hands wide. "It was the Emperor's Clothes time. There *is* nothing there of any value, except for the missiles."

Somewhere in the street below there was a crunch, as though a couple of cars had been in a fender-bender. Angry voices floated up to the window.

"And the object? The bottom line of a Russian op like this?" Naldo's brow was creased.

"Cuba."

"Kennedy stopped more missiles going to Cuba, with the dirt we gave him from *Alex*. That's plain enough. It saved the world from nuclear disaster."

"Sure it did." Arnold allowed a short pause. "Kennedy also gave guarantees to the Russians. Never again would America allow its bases, or agencies, to assist in an attempt to dislocate the new Cuban regime. No invasion of Cuba from U.S. soil. Not ever. Quoth the Raven, never more. *They got what they wanted.*"

Naldo raised his eyebrows. "But, if I follow you, *Alex* was trying to sick intelligence onto us, and your people, long before Khrushchev came into power."

"True. Who knows why? Testing the water perhaps. Getting a man in. A penetration operation that went wrong. Probably the object changed with the circumstances, the prevailing political and military policy. Like I said before, we alter the object of operations like designers change fashion. We dance to the tempo of the time. If the beat changes, so do we. But, in the end Penkovsky's op went right. We know that, because, instead of lying cold, in an unmarked grave, Oleg Penkovsky is living it up on the Black Sea. Isn't that the clearest proof we have? That, and the fact of him being GRU. Military?"

Naldo thought for a few moments. "That's it? That's the lot? The GRU push him at us for years, then finally get us to bite just when they want, in order to stage a confrontation in which they appear to be the losers? Why should Khrushchev allow an operation like that to be run? He called the shots. He wanted the missiles on Cuba."

"Who said *he* did call the shots on this one?"

"He was the *capo di tutti capi,* as they say in certain circles."

"He also liked the brinkmanship. He wanted a big bang. The military did *not.* Because they knew they couldn't get away with it. Looking at it now, the whole thing was a GRU and KGB double play to draw Khrushchev's teeth; to defuse an untenable situation; and to provide big breadwinner Khrushchev with a nice bonus. They gave him Cuba: safe, clean, once and for all. In the long run that would keep the Comrade Chairman happy."

Outside the shouting had died away. Arnold glanced up as though the new silence had become a sinister sound. Across the rooftops snowclouds had started to gather, and darkness was closing in.

Then Farthing spoke again. "Who, in Russia, bore the brunt of the blame after it was over? Certainly not the GRU. KGB were the patsys, weren't they? Khrushchev did an awful lot of hirings and firings. And Oleg Penkovsky reaped a golden handshake instead of a bullet. How would it be if the Ks had agreed to be the fall guys? Agreed so they could protect very important assets?" He stopped talking and lit a cigarette. Naldo did not recall ever seeing Arnie smoke before. Now he drew on the Marlboro in long, quick drags, as though someone might stop him before he finished it.

They sat together in silence for a long time—ten, fifteen, twenty minutes, each thinking of the ultimate conclusion. Naldo rose and walked to the window. Looking out at the first snowflakes, corkscrewing in the streetlights, he asked, "If all this is solid, where do we come in? Why should it hurt *our* families, Arnie?"

Arnold bit his lower lip. "It's there, in the *Elephant* files. I memorized the important bits, and I'll give you the full text. But, first, look at the small print. The detail. The handling. You were there, Nald. You were there in London—twice—and in Paris. Think back. What did you really feel about the handling? At the time what did you think about the tradecraft? Didn't you say it stank?"

"It was Godawful. Insecure. Dangerous . . . ."

"And Penkovsky himself?"

Naldo nodded. "Worrying. Bad discipline. Leaky as a sieve. They had to keep plugging him, hence the hired whores in Paris."

"And the one grand in sterling your boys gave him. Know how he spent that?" Once more he answered the question himself. "He blew the lot on expensive presents for his wife and brother officers in Moscow. Don't you think *they'd* be a little surprised at the amount of money he had to throw around if they weren't in on it? They must've laughed like gurgling drains."

"You put money into the pot as well." Naldo tried to sound accusing.

"Oh, yes. A lousy three hundred bucks a month, and I'm not going to defend *our* handling and tradecraft either. I wonder who had the bright idea of taking him out of London for over eighteen hours so that President Kennedy could shake his hand? *That* happened. Clever, huh? He could have been spotted, missed by the delegation. Anything."

"At least we didn't let him meet the Queen, and that's what he wanted. The man was a prima donna. His contact took him to Badminton, the Horse Trials, just to look at her Majesty from a distance. Had the hell of a job restraining him. He wanted to go over and introduce himself."

"The whole thing was fiction, Nald."

"The *whole* thing? I don't know how anyone got away with the tradecraft and handling. There was that lunatic business of making him a colonel in the British and U.S. armies. Taking his picture in both uniforms. They had a field day with those at the trial, remember?"

"Right, and a good laugh as well, no doubt. You do know that *Alex* was the name he preferred to be called by friends out in the real world? Who the hell ever uses nicknames for cryptos like your people did?"

Naldo Railton's face was that of a deeply worried man. He shied away from where the whole story was taking them.

"And didn't you say he got edgy in London when he knew Five were involved and keeping an eye on him?"

"He panicked and blustered. We had to reassure him again and again that nobody in Five knew who he was; or what the operation entailed."

"Right. Because, like other defectors before him, *Alex* gave the impression that Five was shot, deeply penetrated."

Naldo gave a curt nod. At least two defectors had fingered Burgess, Maclean, and Philby, who was part of the Secret Intelligence Service. Together they had stuck to what they knew—that there was a ring of five highly placed penetration agents within the SIS and MI5. The two Foreign Office men and Philby made three. Blunt's confession, earlier in this year, brought the total to four. So there was probably still one on the loose. Everything pointed to MI5 still being penetrated.

"Blunt was long out of Five when he confessed, right?"

Naldo gave a very short nod.

"So we can count him out?"

Another no-comment nod.

"Oleg/*Alex* was still fingering Five as being leaky."

"Yes."

Arnie sighed. "Remember, Naldo, that someone once said the price of freedom is constant paranoia. Let me give you a 'what if' situation. *Alex* was a plant. We know that now, so what if he wanted to misdirect everybody in your Service? What if his other job, apart from the missiles, was to take the heat off any suspicion that your Firm, the Secret Intelligence Service, was penetrated, and continue to point a finger at Five?

"By showing fear of Five, *Alex* was performing a song without words. He was saying, watch out for Five, they're still bugged; they're penetrated to hell. You boys are okay. Since Kim, nobody's got into your pants. Yet the truth, Nald, is that your SIS is the penetrated service, and Five is as clean as a whistle."

"So where do you take it from there?" Naldo still sounded unconvinced.

"Nobody's going to admit out loud that *Alex* was a double, are they? To admit that is to explode one of the great successes of all time. So the history books have got to say, look at this, Oleg Penkovsky was the wonderful agent of conscience. Without him, the world would be a desert. But, in secret, a small faction knows that the truth is the opposite. I have heard voices on the wind, Nald. In your untight little island they're still saying there's someone operating in Five. Those of us who know that *Alex* is alive, and well and living in Sochi, have our doubts. Isn't it more possible that the Sovs had, and might still have, an agent in place, high in the pecking order of your own Service?" He spread his hands again, in the gesture he had used on and off all day. Frank and open Arnold. "It's no secret that Five are still hooked on the original bait."

Naldo turned, stared at the ceiling and whispered, "From where we sit it seems like a witch-hunt."

"Uh-huh, now we're getting to the nub of why I brought you here. I've said it all, except the stuff memorized from the *Elephant* files.

What if Five's as clean as a whistle? What if they're jumping at shadows, investigating ghosts? They're so lost in the maze, Nald, that it wouldn't surprise me if they eventually fingered some poor senior bugger, just to satisfy themselves that they'd done the job. But, what if *Alex* did two things? What if he told us about the missiles in plain language, so they could get guarantees from Jack Kennedy; and, more subtly, by inference, he underlined what everyone believed: that your Five was a major target? What worries me, Nald, is that any minute they're going to open a new inquest. This time within your SIS, using evidence from what I've seen in the *Elephant* files. Your Service wouldn't be alone. There's one going on inside Langley at this moment. Already heads have rolled."

"I'm to believe this?"

Arnold's face and voice took on a pleading note. "You'd better believe it, Nald. Like you'd better believe we've got to get ourselves some protection. We have to take a look at the Blunt confession. We have to, because I think Blunt's put in some heavy disinformation as icing on the cake. I'm pretty certain you've had some access to Five's tapes. Now we need further access. We need to know what's really been said. All of it."

"I've got news for you. I'm excluded from *Hypermarket* as well, though nobody's made a big thing out of it. Just need-to-know and all that." Naldo smiled at the irony. "You think Blunt's fingered people? Like Penkovsky, he's drawn fire from the SIS and put Five up as the real target?"

"I think he's probably done more than that. I think he's named names, just in case something has gone wrong. I think he's pointed the finger. Poured new poison into people's ears; and remember, Nald, this is just the start. They've only been at Blunt since the spring. He can go on talking for the next six years or more. The guy can make it up as he goes along, can't he? That's what these people do to muddy the pools. This is a terrifyingly clever piece of work, Nald. It's Chinese boxes, *matryoshkas*, nesting dolls; infinities of distorting mirrors. When I discovered that friend *Alex* was alive, I came across some even more alarming matters." He took a short breath, as though steeling himself. "Nald, I know who the prime suspects are in your Firm, and mine. Apart from small-fry that is."

"So *you* can name names?"

"I can name ones I believe have been planted, yes."

The silence seemed to go on for a long time. Then Arnold spoke again—

"As far as any internal investigations go—within my Agency, or your Firm, or Five—I believe the object will be merely a question of balancing the books. Setting the record straight. If they can say, 'He was one, he *is* one, and so is he.' That will satisfy them. It really doesn't seem to matter how the Inquisition fiddles the figures, just so long as everything tallies at the end of the day." He took a deep breath, inhaling through his nose like a diver about to go off the top board. "Any day now, Naldo, they're going to finger your late, beloved Uncle Caspar as the KGB's second-biggest mole in the SIS. And he isn't around to defend himself. There's chapter and verse on Caspar in the *Elephant* files. More, those files make further suppositions."

"What kind of suppositions?" Naldo's face flushed red with anger.

Arnie made a strange gesture, a moving of the head. "From Caspar Railton, they seem to think that it's not a huge leap to encircle *our* mutual uncle, Dick Railton-Farthing. He would be classed as both SIS and CIA. It doesn't take a massive intellect to see who gets the treatment next."

"You, Arn?"

"Of course. And you also, Naldo."

"Fuck off," said Naldo with some feeling.

They sat in seething silence for a while. Then Naldo looked at his watch. "Christ, it's almost six o'clock."

"Time flies when you're having fun." Arnold was not being funny, or pleasant.

"Fuck off," Naldo said again, reaching for his coat. "I'm going to call Barbara, but not from this place." Six o'clock in Berlin was five in the afternoon in London. At the time of leaving, and walking out into the snow, Naldo did not intend to return. Arnold's conclusions were bizarre and obscene. He wanted nothing to do with them.

FOUR

1

Just as Arnold and Naldo were settling down to talk, in the so-called green house near the Charlottenburg S-Bahn, Berlin, so Naldo's wife, Barbara, was, for the first time in her life, experiencing the onset of jealousy. She was not jealous of her husband, in spite of his long absences and the natural disinclination to talk about his work in any detail. She was no stranger to this kind of life, for her maiden name was Burville, and the Burvilles had, for centuries, been a military family. In any case, her marriage to Naldo had lasted for seventeen years with only the usual *sturm und drang,* plus a liberal share of *angst.* But who was counting?

Barbara was used to her parents, brother, uncles, and cousins disappearing abroad for long periods. Sometimes disappearing forever, for as a child she had been an Army brat.

Later, in World War II, she had done her own stint, in the Women's Auxiliary Air Force, preferring this to its Army equivalent, the Auxiliary Territorial Service (ATS). Now, on a winter afternoon, at the age of forty-five, she felt dissatisfaction: a sense of having missed out somewhere along the line. She knew, like Muriel Spark's Miss Jean Brodie, that she was in her prime.

She had a loving husband—when he was there—and a couple of children of whom she was justly proud, but somehow certain variations on the theme of life appeared to have passed her by.

It was something that happened to many women of her age during the 1960s, when life and its mores suddenly burst wide open, warped, doubled back, changed everybody's perspective, and altered lives out of recognition. Youth was on the move, there was a new freedom in the air, and Barbara wanted to grasp at it before she went really over the hill. At her age she knew her body was certainly not yet even at the brow of the hill.

The first cause of disillusionment was a childhood friend with whom she had lunched at the Connaught Hotel. Barbara had been at school with Vivienne Long, and later was her bridesmaid when she married Lord Anthony Short. After twenty years, the obvious quip was getting somewhat tired, but Vi Short *never* appeared to tire, just as she refused to age. She had married well—some said she took Tony simply for his estate in Scotland, and the magnificent Regency house in Chelsea, plus a generous allowance. She was a year or so older than Barbara, but had shared secrets with her since adolescence. So, Barbara knew, with delicious detail, that Lady Vi had taken lovers, when and where she felt like it, down the years of her marriage.

After lunch, during which Vi Short had spoken at length, with all the disturbing minutiae, of her latest conquest—a stockbroker not quite young enough to have been her son—Barbara set out to do what remained of her Christmas shopping. As she waited for the doorman to get her a taxi, she was aware of someone else coming out behind her, down the steps of the Connaught. She turned, to see a man of, she guessed, around her own age. He was not particularly striking, medium height, smartly dressed, with a dark single-breasted Aquascutum topcoat over what seemed to be a suit. The coat had a fashionable narrow velvet trim around the lapels and neck, and nobody could miss the single red rose pinned, rather rakishly, to the right lapel.

The man smiled and bowed his head in Barbara's direction, and at that moment the taxi arrived. Barbara asked the driver to take her to Harrods, and noted the cabby's sigh, for the pre-Christmas traffic through Knightsbridge was murder. It was only when she was seated in the cab that Barbara realized she had felt rather flattered by the stranger's obvious glance. The look, smile, and bow bore all the hallmarks of someone who had been attracted to her. Ten years on, someone like Barbara might well have put him down as a sexist male chauvinist pig. At the time no such thoughts entered Barbara Railton's head.

The cabbie was disinclined to talk, so the journey was passed slowly, backed by the radio, with Petula Clark belting out "Downtown," and the up-and-very-much-coming Cilla Black tearing at adolescent heartstrings sobbing "Anyone who has a heart." Barbara wondered what Naldo was doing—he expected to be back either late that night, or by tomorrow evening, though she had no idea where he was. They had only recently come back to London from the Berlin posting, and this was to be their first Christmas in England for five years: a true Railton Christmas, to be spent with the entire family at Redhill.

She watched the pavements as they negotiated the traffic, and seemed to see nothing but miniskirts, short fur coats, young men with shoulder-length hair, who wore flared trousers or jeans under knee-length coats.

The shop windows were full of good cheer, and the crowded pavements reeked of youthful arrogance. So, it was at that moment, as they approached Harrods, that Barbara had this sudden shaft of jealousy and realized with some humor that she felt exceptionally randy. In plain terms, she was a woman in her mid-forties who fancied a temporary change in partners.

Vaguely, the danger of such an adventure—unlikely in any case—crossed Barbara's mind. Many serving intelligence officers claimed their work restricted and frustrated their private lives, because they could share nothing with their nearest or dearest. Of course this was not the whole truth, certainly not as the Railtons and their American cousins, the Farthings, believed. Families did know about the job. They *had* to know, just as they had to accept the sudden guarded telephone call, and the unexplained absence. The family of any career intelligence officer knew well enough what sort of job he did, and for the most part they remained silent. That was that. A fact of life.

As she paid off the cab, she vaguely noticed a familiar figure alighting from another taxi behind her. It was the man with the red rose, and, even then, it did not concern her. She wandered through the food hall, made a mental note to order the veal and ham pie that Naldo liked so much. Then she took the elevator up to the toy department. There was a particular model kit that young Arthur wanted, and she had thought of getting Naldo something absolutely outrageous, like one of the new Scalectrix sets. She could just see Naldo, with cousins, uncles, and children spread out across the floor at Redhill, controlling electrically powered model racing cars around a track. The more she thought of it, the more it appealed to her. Anyway, she was feeling profligate that afternoon. It might be a good idea for her to spend some money on a completely frivolous gift.

She found the model kit easily, then headed to the area where assistants were busy showing off the Scalectrix tracks, and tried to make up her mind whether to be relatively economic with the purchase, or go the whole hog and buy the most expensive one she could see.

"Kids are hell to buy for, aren't they?" The voice was pleasant and unaffected. She looked up and found herself thrown into a schoolgirlish flustered state as she recognized the man from outside the Connaught, the one with the red rose. In the far corner of her mind she knew it should not have surprised her, as she had been conscious of him outside the store.

"They're hell to buy for—kids," he rephrased it and she caught the scent of an expensive after-shave—Aramis she thought—and found the man's amused gray eyes quite disconcerting.

"Yes," said Barbara lamely. Then, pulling herself together, "Yes, they are, but actually I'm shopping for my husband."

He laughed, and she liked the way his eyes laughed with his voice and mouth. She also liked his thick graying hair, and the lips which were a shade too thick, and then felt foolish for thinking like a character from one of the women's magazine stories she sometimes read at the hairdresser. "Your husband's a lucky man." He smiled. "I wish my wife would buy me one of these. All men are kids at heart."

She summoned up the courage and asked, "Are you following me? You were outside the Connaught as I left."

He smiled again. "Of course I'm following you—though, by chance, you *were* going my way."

"You often follow strange women?"

"Never, until today. Sorry, I didn't mean to offend you, but, well, you looked so bloody attractive and I just wanted to talk to you."

"Oh!" She felt a little flush of blood, not to her face, but in the depths of her body as she realized what was happening. He was trying to pick her up, and she found it a very pleasant experience. Nobody had tried to pick her up for years. In any case, Service wives were warned about this kind of thing, but only on foreign postings. Before she realized it she was telling this highly desirable man that she was flattered.

"Philip," he said, slipping the glove off his right hand and extending his arm. "Philip Hornby."

His palm was very dry.

"Oh, my children have got some of your trains," she said without thinking.

"Alas, a different family," he said, laughing again.

She introduced herself and he said that now they had the formalities out of the way, couldn't they have tea together?

"I have to get my husband's toy first." There was no question in her mind about having tea with him. In fact, far away, hardly even noticed, she knew that she would have more than tea. The lunchtime conversation with Vi had worked its tiny wickedness. "Maybe you can help. I don't know which one to get for him." She waved a hand towards the boxes of Scalectrix.

"Has he asked? Put it on his list?"

"No, it's a surprise. He'll be angry and then adore it. Him and half the family."

"Then get him the biggest and best you can find."

She did just that and had it charged, asking them to deliver. "It must be this week," she told the assistant. "We're going away for Christmas."

"Certainly, madam." The assistant rechecked the address—just off Kensington Gore, the house to which Naldo had first taken her. His father and mother had bought it during the First World War. It slid through her mind that a new decision would have to be made at Christmas. Caspar had asked that the famous Railton property in Eccleston Square should go, not to his children, but to Naldo, should Phoebe wish to move. "That area is easy for us, madam, probably on Thursday if it's convenient."

She hardly heard what the woman was saying, so it had to be repeated. "Oh, yes, that'll be fine." Then, turning to Philip, she put on her wide smile and, surprising herself, said, "Shall we have tea now? I'd like that very much," and, taking his arm, she almost led the way to The Silver Spoon which was Harrods' tea room.

They drank Darjeeling, ate little triangular sandwiches and cream cakes, talking for over an hour. He was in advertising—"The managing director, in fact"—and lived with his wife and three young children in Suffolk, near Lavenham, but kept a pied-à-terre in London. "Just around the corner, actually. Hans Crescent."

She was thrown for a second. Hans Crescent had a reputation within the Railton family. Years ago, one of Naldo's relatives had kept a German agent in Hans Crescent. She had been murdered there. "Nice," was all Barbara said now, and thought Naldo would have been proud of her as she gave nothing of the real life away. Naldo, she said, was a civil servant—"Very dull, really. Ministry of Transport. Dashes around the country telling people about their roads."

They discovered, just as, years before, she had found with Naldo, that they had similar tastes in books, music, cinema, and theater. He suggested they might go to see the new film version of *Tom Jones*—"I hear Finney's terrific in it."

"When?"

"Can you make it tonight?"

She thought for twenty seconds, she could always say she had been with Vi if Naldo *did* come back late. "Why not? I'll have to nip home and change, though. My son and daughter are around. I like to make sure they're okay." If anything went wrong she could telephone him. "If you let me have your number."

"Sure." They exchanged numbers and Hornby said he could pick her up.

"No. No, I don't think that would go down at all well. Let me phone you, and *I'll* pick *you* up. How about that for a deal?"

"Right," he said, giving her the address, then slowly standing up. "I'll see you into a cab."

She thanked him for the tea, and the nice afternoon. Almost as an afterthought, as she was getting into the cab, she gave him a quick kiss on the cheek, then wondered why. It was something that, until this moment, she would never normally have done to such a relative stranger. Riding back to Kensington Gore, Barbara felt a twinge of guilt, there one minute, then gone the next, overcome, suffocated by the feeling that it, whatever "it" was would not hurt anyone. They had talked of poetry over tea, and discovered a mutual passion for the modern giants. It should not have surprised her, that, as the cab bore her away, T. S. Eliot sauntered through her head: *The Waste Land*—

> *When lovely woman stoops to folly and*
> *Paces the room again, alone,*
> *She smooths her hair with automatic hand,*
> *And puts a record on the gramophone.*

Damn, she thought. She did not really like Eliot. Auden was her poet, and she knew all too well, that, lovely woman or not, she would stoop to folly.

Behind her, Philip Hornby walked down into Hans Crescent, went into his building, and rode the lift to the fourth floor. He did not even take his coat off before dialing the number. They answered at the third ring.

"Flashman, here, for Brown," he said.

"Brown speaking."

"Flashman. She went for it. She's careful, but I think, sadly, she's a definite security risk. Give me a day or two."

"All the time you want. Call me tomorrow." Brown hung up.

Her key was in the lock as the telephone began to ring. Arthur had already answered it and now held the instrument out towards her.

"Dad, for you," he said, and disappeared quietly up the stairs. She could hear Emma thumping out Chopin, very badly, in the music room, as they called one of the spare bedrooms above.

"Sorry, love, won't be back until tomorrow. Afternoon probably." He sounded flat, matter-of-fact, and she knew he was somewhere on the Continent because of the tiny delay and particular sound on the line.

"Can we plan for tomorrow?" she asked.

"Why not? Get tickets for a show. I should be free, okay?"

"I'll try, darling. Take care—Oh, I'll be out tonight. Cinema with Vi."

"Have a nice time. Love you."

"Love you," in an automatic voice as he hung up. Naldo was rarely demonstrative on the telephone. Any exchanged endearments had become almost liturgical.

Words without thoughts never to heaven go, ran through her mind. Shakespeare was catching.

Barbara went into the drawing room and put on a record. Mahler, which Herbie had given them for Christmas last year. The Second: Bruno Walter and the New York Philharmonic.

2

Naldo cradled the telephone and stood, looking at the instrument. The snow had become heavy, and he had trudged two blocks before finding a small hotel where they had a coin telephone unlinked to the switchboard. All the way he fought an icy wind, which carried the stinging flakes into his face. Direct dialing had not long been in use, and was still not available in some parts of Europe, so he put his call to Barbara through the operator, reversing the charges.

"Cold out?" Arnold looked up from the book he was reading as Naldo stomped his feet on the small mat inside the door. He looked fifteen years older: grizzled, with hair and eyebrows crusted with snow, his face florid from the freezing wind. He had taken his time about getting back. The obscene things Arnold had suggested made him more cautious. In this kind of weather any watcher could have been forgiven for getting spotted. Naldo was ninety-nine percent certain that nobody was on his back.

"Get me a drink, Arn. I bloody need it."

"Alas"—Arnold did not really look pained—"the beloved Den Mother, who cares for all our safe and green houses, makes it a rule. Like ships of the U.S. Navy, we do not carry alcohol except for special, authorized occasions. Barb well?"

"Going out to the movies." Naldo still felt angry, but knew nothing would be gained by a falling out with his old friend. He rubbed his face, driving circulation back into his body, stamping his feet. "Going out with Vi Short."

"Ah, the delectable Lady Short."

"You've met Vi?"

"Once, at some function. Grosvenor Square. An unhappy, unful-filled lady, I thought."

"Vi? She's had enough filling for any redblooded girl." He stopped to see that Arnie's face was set in a smirk.

"Arn, you didn't?"

"I'm saying nothing that incriminates me."

"You sly old devil. The gorgeous Gloria was left in Berlin, I presume?"

"You presume right. From there on in I plead the Fifth."

"No booze, huh?"

"Not a drop in the house. Only two books as well—apart from a load of porno stuff that our dear girls, or boys, use on clients, I suppose. The Bible and Shakespeare. It's a Gideon Bible, which must tell you something about how the accounts are run around here."

Naldo nodded unhappily. The drapes were drawn to shut out the night. He went over and lifted one corner, peering down into the street below where the wind was blowing little drifts of fine snow along road and pavements. Below him not even a shadow stirred in the streets. The one percent still bothered him. Naldo only bet on certainties.

Arnie Farthing started muttering to himself, just loud enough for Naldo to hear—"Oh really, Arnold. How nice, Arnold. And which one are you reading, Arnold? As you ask, Nald, I am reading the complete works of William H. Shakespeare—the Cambridge Text with notes by John Dover Wilson, no less. First published in 1921. How strange, Arnold, we have an edition just like that at home. We don't have a Bible though. For us Railtons, William of Stratford is our Bible."

"Stow it, Arn. You're getting boring."

Arnold gave a short laugh, one note pitched high. "I can see why you bloody Railtons are so attached to this guy. I found a piece here, in *Richard II,* which could have been written of Railtons, only it's about kings."

"No!"

But Arnold continued, "Substitute Railtons for kings and you're away—

> For God's sake let us sit upon the ground,
> And tell sad stories of the death of Railtons—
> How some have been deposed, some slain in war,
> Some haunted by the ghosts they have deposed . . . "

"Stow it, Arn."

"Strikes home though, doesn't it?"

Naldo saw there was no beating him—"Okay! Enough!" he held up his hands in surrender.

"Strikes home, yes?"

"Arn." There was serious warning in Naldo's tone. "You've hauled me over to this blighted city; fed me full of filched information which boils down to the supposed fact that Oleg Penkovsky, wonder-spy, has not been executed, but lives in luxury on the Black Sea, which indicates he wasn't the man we thought. Right?"

"Right, except there's no supposed about it."

"We'll see."

Arnold opened his mouth, but Naldo held up a hand. "Wait! Let me finish, just to make sure I've got it right. You also tell me that the Firm for which I work is about to nobble my late Uncle Caspar and name him as a Russian penetration agent. Right?"

"Oh, I don't think they'll name him out loud, unless some idiot begins to ask questions in your House of Commons. That *is* the way these things are usually leaked, isn't it?"

"As a rule, yes. But you continue by suggesting that those of us with kinship to Caspar might also be put through the mill."

"True."

"And, by association, members of your own family?"

"Yes."

"I don't follow any of the logic. I can't see why Penkovsky being a disinformation agent makes Caspar, or Dick, or you . . . "

"Or Naldo Railton?"

"Okay, or me. I don't see the connection. Why should we be sought out as possible suspects?"

"Because we're here." Arnold looked up blankly at Naldo's frown. "Because we've had the opportunity, and because we're interconnected. Also, because that's what the files say at Langley."

"So you said," angry again, his face flushed, body tensing like a man about to make a physical attack.

Arnie pushed at air with his hands, in a fending-off motion. "Sit down, Nald. Sit and hear me out." He stopped, waiting for Naldo to back off. "You got incensed before, when I first brought it up. Rightly so. I'm not cool about this. But hear me out."

A long silence stretched between the two secret men. Then Naldo gave a shrug and sat down, close to the small electric heater that warmed anyone who could get within six inches of it. Arnold saw the movement and said his outfit did not bother about keeping places like this warm. "It encourages the clients to get cozy more quickly." He gave what in any other man would have been called a shy smile.

"Right. I'm waiting. You said you'd committed the thing to memory."

Arnold tried another smile. "Conned it by rote, as Shakespeare would say."

"Go on." It was the kind of tone nobody argued with.

Arnold reached out, touched Naldo's sleeve like a conspirator. "It was in the final batch of stuff *Alex* sent over. Just before they lifted him. The produce included two military pamphlets which, it appeared, we already had. Also a correction to an earlier pamphlet he had provided. That was useful. Then there was a coded signal. The whole lot came on two microdots. The bit I learned by heart was the decrypt of the signal."

He breathed in, closed his eyes, as though settling to bring the words to the front of his memory. " 'I fear we have not long.' That's how it began. Then—'Unless I am wrong the State Organs have caught up with us. This is why I am sending these out now and not waiting in the hope of meeting up with my friend. I suspect we have been blown and this is an urgent warning. There is penetration of the British Secret Department, though I suspect he is retired. I have met him in London. By chance I had sight of a highly sensitive document in our files. The State Organs had given us information so that wires would not be crossed. When I saw this document I became terrified. They have insinuated an agent at top level into the SIS. Before, I thought the only danger was from your Counterintelligence Security. I was wrong. Since the late 1930s there has been an agent of influence working within the Secret Department. This man is now retired, but I believe I have met him. I do not know his real name, but he belongs to an aristocratic family which has links with the world of secrets going back for centuries. This man's cryptonym is *Dionysus.* His dossier was Sovbloc Red, and suggests that he still provides high-octane material via a relative

who is known as *Croesus*. This man might be a son. Further details
are that *Dionysus* was seriously wounded in the First Great War.
Croesus is a Sovbloc Green. Also a member of the same family is what
we call a *shifr odtel*. There are also links with an American family who
have people in the trade. Former members of the British family have
worked for us in the past. He has blown us all.' It was signed, *Alex*."

"The Railton track record," Naldo muttered.

"Not altogether. I believe that side of things was added as a sweet-
ener to see if we would bite."

"You said there was mention by name."

"The analysts locked on very fast. Caspar is put up as obvious, and
yourself, of course. The *shifr odtel* is off the hook—your beloved
Alexander." In Russian secret terminology a *shifr odtel* is a codebreaker. "The analysts do a very good job. We all get a mention—
Caspar, you, myself, Alexander, your Dad, Dick. Everyone. That's
the good news—there was a series of memos running between Langley and London. London dismisses the possibilities. In a word they
say preposterous."

"So, what's the bad news?"

"There is a Flash Cosmic file attached. It emanates from London just
four days before the Blunt product team came over to brief Langley.
The briefing from which I was barred."

"And it says?"

"New evidence demands a reappraisal of the loyalty of certain members of the Railton family. It gives a reference back to the last Penkovsky signal, and the memos that followed poo-pooing the whole
thing. The signal says that, while Caspar is dead, his file has been
reopened. It also says that there will be a fresh look at the working
lives, and operational defects, of all who come under the blanket of
Penkovsky's accusation."

"Shit."

"That's what we're in, old friend. I should imagine Jim Angleton has
argued using the most recent information, that *Alex* lives and
breathes. But, if he did argue that way, it made no difference to the
Brits. They still kept me out of the Blunt product briefing. Hence my
reason for needing to see that file."

"Yep." Naldo gave a long sigh, and Arnold left him with his
thoughts for a few moments before asking—

"You were at the *Alex* briefings, Nald. *Did* Cas actually meet the
bastard face to face? I mean was there a full-blown introduction?"

Something stirred, just under the surface of Naldo's consciousness.
An itch. An itch he could not scratch. He thought back to the meet-

ings in London and Paris and, as he did so, even the smells returned—smoke, fish, alcohol, the particular cologne Caspar always used. He stood up, with the pleasant, mannish smell almost there in his nostrils, and at that moment a whole scene flashed into his mind, and out again. Mentally he grabbed at it, pulling it back to the present. Caspar standing by a door, a glass in his hand. Willis Maitland-Wood, one hand on Penkovsky's shoulder, and the Russian's hand reaching forward to grasp Caspar's. As the picture came, so the words followed. "Sir Caspar, it's a pleasure to meet you. Have heard a lot about you, and here you are, in the flesh."

That was over three years ago. Now he had the look in Penkovsky's eyes; how they glittered and how the Russian gave a little nod to Caspar, then turned and smiled broadly at BMW, who gave a tight smile.

"Fucking Judas," he said. "Yes. Yes, Arn, I think *Alex* fingered Cas. I was there. I can see it all now. Even the reason Bloody-Maitland-Wood required Caspar's presence." Briefly he described the scene.

"Careful, Nald. Don't jump at shadows." Arnie shook his head. "Penkovsky wouldn't have shown himself to risk something like that. Certainly not in front of BMW."

"I'll kill him!" Naldo felt that he had been physically penetrated. He thought he knew what a victim of rape must feel. Revenge flowed through his head, as though his blood was made of some new potent liquid. "I'll go to bloody Sochi and kill him with my bare hands."

"Naldo." Arnie had come over to stand beside him. "I think that would be a good idea, I'd kill the bugger as well. But we must know what Blunt has said to reactivate something that was dismissed as a fairy tale at the time. After that, well, we might just find some way. Can you get the Blunt material? *Hypermarket?*"

"Depends what word is out about me. Depends if they've already put me in the leper colony or are just doing a light watch, with the brains working on old files. If they haven't got at Herbie, then there's a chance."

"How?"

"Herb has access. Don't ask me why, because I can't tell even you. But he has access. I'll try him." He locked eyes with Arnie. "You do realize this is ongoing, don't you? I mean, they're still working on Blunt."

"Sure, I know that. But, whatever he's said, he's said already. If we can take a look now, Nald, I think we just might be able to do something positive. Can you go invisible?"

Naldo turned towards him. "That's one thing that both Cas and my father taught me. Always keep a hole you can drop into. That's what they both said. Preferably a hole about which nobody else knows. Yes, Arn, and we've got a bloody good hole to drop into, haven't we?"

"Naturally. Let's make use of it. That's what Cas would've wanted."

They sat down and began to talk. Setting up telephone code words; meeting places; Flash signals; all the things they would have to do in order to mount their own kind of operation. It had to be secure. Even more so than usual, for what they planned had to be kept from their own most trusted people. They both knew that they were quite alone in this. Alone and outside the law. It was possible the pair of them might even have to cheat their own agencies. The two men were still there at eleven o'clock, but by then they had the makings of a plan. It was far from foolproof, but they calculated—providing the requisite parts of *Hypermarket* were forthcoming, and showed what they suspected—it stood around a sixty percent chance of working.

Naldo's mind ran in angry circles. He was aware that chivalry, honor, love of country and family were considered unfashionable, but he had more than loved his uncle. To Naldo, Caspar had been a giant within the world of secrets; totally reliable; undoubtedly trustworthy. For anyone in the Secret Intelligence Service to even suggest Caspar Railton had betrayed his country was anathema to him. In Naldo Railton they had perhaps chosen the one person who would go to the ends of the earth, die even, to save family honor, and, particularly, the reputation of his uncle.

At eleven-thirty, Naldo, keeping to his original cover, left to make his meeting with the source he had used as an excuse to come to Berlin at all. She was a young girl from behind the Wall who had cast-iron reasons for coming over once a month. She worked for an East German textile company that was putting out feelers for work in the West—all above board, with documentation and special permission from the DDR Department of Trade. So far everything the girl had given to him was good and checkable. There was no reason to think she was entrapment material or a double. Quite the opposite.

Naldo knew her only as Helga, and she brought small pieces of gossip, and, sometimes, a few troop movements. She provided nothing shopworn. From the first she had made it very obvious that she fancied Naldo—whom she knew as Mr. Gray—and certainly wanted to bed him. She had tried, but he had always kept her at arm's length, sticking to the first rule of running agents or sources.

It had stopped snowing and the temperature was rising, sending a light mist from the pavements. As he pushed through the slush, he decided that tonight would be different. He either had to get drunk or have a sexual encounter. It was not difficult for Naldo to decide which would be better for his soul. Have Helga tonight, he thought. Then, tomorrow recruit old Herbie.

3

After it was over, she lay in his arms, and wondered, why? Aloud she asked—

"Why? Why tonight? And why me?"

"Because we were there." He gave a kind of laugh, that sounded hollow. "Because we met and talked and wanted each other, I suppose. You did want me, surely?"

"Oh, yes. I wanted you," Barbara said. "This is the first time I've been unfaithful in all the years of my marriage, and here I am, mother of two as they say in the popular press, in bed rutting like a bitch in heat."

"It's sometimes necessary." Philip Hornby leaned over and kissed her.

"I think it was that scene where Finney and the girl virtually did it over the meal. God, that was sexy." As planned, they had seen *Tom Jones,* and Barbara had felt her body go hot then moist during the famous scene where Tom and the girl manage to convey a bedful of sensual lascivious nuances into the act of eating a meal. If she had not known it before, it was then that Barbara really knew she would give herself to this stranger.

On the wall facing the bed in Philip Horby's flat, there was a large copy of some painting by, she thought, Bruegel. She knew little about the artist, and could not have told him Bruegel's dates, let alone the painting's name. But it was all snow and people: a village in winter and in trouble, for mounted soldiers rode, with menace and plumed lances, down the main street. It looked as though they would crush anything that got in their way.

"So, where do we stand?" she asked now.

"We're lying," he chuckled, kissing her ear.

"I mean, do I see you again?"

"I should damned well hope so. Cigarette?"

"Just one. Then I must go."

"Why not stay the night?"

"I can't do that. I have children home from school. Christmas is nearly on us." She blew a long stream of smoke through pursed lips.

"And you're going away for Christmas?"

"Family tradition—my husband's family. They have a place in the country and all family members who're in England gather there. We even spent our honeymoon there, over Christmas. It wasn't in the least bit embarrassing either. I thought it would be, but Christmas at Redhill is really something quite special."

"Redhill?"

She told him about the manor, and the Railton family: how they were descended from Pierre de Royalton, one of Duke William's knights who had distinguished himself at Hastings in 1066; how Henry VIII had given the family lands around Haversage at the time of the Reformation. She mentioned that her husband's great-uncle had been a Foreign Office mandarin who had died, taking many secrets to his grave, and how Naldo's great-grandfather was General Sir William Railton VC, who had taken part in the blundered charge at Balaclava.

"Real roots," Hornby said. "Not like my lot. My father was a cockney from Hackney, and my mother worked in a drawing office. Mind you, the old boy pulled himself up by his bootstraps. Sort of laid down a trail that I could follow. Self-made. Looks like you've got the real thing."

"What's the real thing?" She laughed, turning her head towards him, a puzzled expression in her eyes. "You care about things like that? God, there's nothing upper-crust about either of our families— my husband's or mine. We're all Army and civil service. Sure there's a bit of history, but nothing special."

They lay, side by side, on their backs, smoking quietly, their free hands resting on each other, and Barbara felt like a young girl again. She stubbed out her cigarette, rolled on top of Philip and mounted him, riding towards a winning post of pleasure. He had a surprisingly hard and firm body, with good muscle tone. He probably worked on it, she decided. Their lovemaking had been more intense than sex with Naldo. With Naldo it was always a great, funny game. They laughed a lot and did stupid things. It was true sport with Naldo. This was more like a tender poem, and she could not decide which was best. Later she realized that each was as good as the other. They were just different. Like the techniques of Naldo's job, she thought.

"I haven't felt like this in years," she said after the second time. "Damn it, I don't even feel guilty."

75

"You probably will." His face was turned from her, and she wondered if he did this often. "You know about all that kind of thing, of course?" She was not really questioning.

"Just one or two illicit incidents. It happens when you're away from your partner a lot. Happens to men anyway."

Barbara wondered if it happened to Naldo, and decided it probably did.

She liked the way Philip watched her dress, his eyes showing pleasure in the sight of her body naked, and then half-clad.

"So, what do we do?" she asked. He was getting out of bed and she told him to stay where he was. "I can see myself out. Big girl now, you know."

"If you say so. Look, Barbara, why don't you give me a call after Christmas. We can decide then."

"You're putting me off," she said, unworried that it might even be true.

"No. I could even fall in love with you, given half a chance."

"Don't," she replied seriously. "Please don't. I'm not going to hurt anyone."

He nodded and said he was going away for Christmas also. "I have to be back in Sussex tomorrow. I'll be there until we go. Get in touch after Christmas. If you don't, then I'll pester you with phone calls."

She got a cab easily, and felt happy all the way home. There was something very satisfying about illicit sex. Vi had certainly been right about that. Then another snatch of poetry came into her head, and she smiled to herself. Eliot had not been a bad omen, because Auden had followed on his heels. She muttered the lines to herself, like someone in prayer—

> "Love has no position,
> Love's a way of living,
> One kind of relation
> Possible between
> Any things or persons
> Given one condition,
> The one sine qua non
> Being mutual need."

Thank God for you, Wystan Hugh Auden, she thought. You're my little crystal ball, and you always provide the right words. Not like Thomas Stearns Eliot, who I can never quite understand.

Back in the Hans Crescent apartment, Philip Hornby was running the tapes back, and checking that the cameras behind the copy of Bruegel's *Massacre of the Innocents* had taken their standard four frames a minute. The things I do for my country, he thought. When everything checked, he called Brown and a tape responded. After identifying himself, Hornby said just four words. "She's in the cage." Then, after a moment's pause, he added, "I'm going home. You can send in the technical boys to clear up."

4

When he was in London, Herbie Kruger used a small office, tucked away in a side street across from the Cenotaph in Whitehall. The building had four such sets of offices and was generally known as the Annexe. More often than not Herbie worked there alone—with three telephone lines, one a direct patch through to Maitland-Wood's office. Occasionally they gave him a schpick—a word they all borrowed from KGB, meaning a novice. Herbie's schpicks were usually just out of training from Warminster.

Naldo got into Heathrow at midday, checked his small overnight bag into the luggage facility run by Five's B Division and the Special Branch's airport security, then called Herbie at the Annexe from a pay phone, just to reassure himself that the big German was in town. Herbie answered the phone himself, which meant no schpicks were assigned to him. When they were, Herb always made them answer the telephone.

Naldo said nothing. He just heard Kruger's voice and put the telephone down. He then took a cab to Trafalgar Square and called Barbara from a pay phone. She sounded very perky and told him she had got a couple of tickets for *Maggie May*, at the Adelphi. "It got great reviews, and you like Rachel Roberts, Nald. When we saw her in that film you said she had 'earthy' qualities, which probably meant something highly sexual."

"Ah, Rachel Roberts, yes. Good. Be home this afternoon sometime, Barb. Love you."

"Love you." She did not hesitate. No guilt had haunted her dreams, or the waking morning. Barbara simply felt refreshed and rejuvenated. She wanted Naldo sexually, not to compare, but for reassurance. Yet she had telephoned Philip Hornby that morning. The phone just kept ringing out. Up and away to Sussex, she thought, and realized that

while he had her London number she did not have his near Lavenham.
Crafty sod, she smiled.

It was a little after one o'clock when Naldo arrived at the Annexe.

"Nald, what you doing in this throat of the woods?"

"Neck, Herb. Neck of the woods," Naldo prompted.

"Throat. Neck. What's the difference?" Herbie gave a wide grin and
a wink, suggesting that he had been pulling Naldo's leg. He opened
his arms and gave his old friend and one-time controller a huge bear-
hug.

"Came to see you, Herb."

"Talk over old times?" Kruger tilted an eyebrow.

"Thought we might go out to lunch. You still eat lunch?"

"Do I eat lunch? You take me to Travellers Club, Nald? I like
Travellers."

"Maybe."

It was cold outside, and London was bursting at the seams with the
pre-Christmas rush. On the street, Naldo hailed a cab and told Herb
he knew a good place in Soho. After lunch, during which Herbie
talked food from his half-remembered childhood, Naldo asked if he
minded walking back through the Park. He did not broach the subject
of the Blunt interrogation until they were well out in the open in St.
James's Park. The scenic route.

"Need a favor, Herb." He was so casual that Kruger only gave a
grunt, and Naldo had to repeat the line.

"*You? You* need favor from me? You're big league, Nald. I'm only
errand boy now."

"Come off it, Herb. I know what you're doing in that little broom
cupboard they call the Annexe. I'm asking a dangerous favor."

"Such as?" They continued to walk, Naldo with his erect, near
military bearing, Herbie lumbering along with uncoordinated gait.

"Such as a look at some files."

"You got files of your own, Nald. What you want with mine?"

"They're not yours, but they're highly restricted. I can't get access.
I know you can. I want a peek. You can provide."

"You asking as a friend? Or is this tricky?"

"Maitland-Wood's a little tricky."

"Oh, that all? Old BMW. Ja. Okay. Anything, Nald, if it will put
back up Maitland-Wood."

"I want to see the Artist's inquisition files. *Hypermarket.*"

"Oh, *Mensch!*"

"And listen to the tapes if you can get them."

"Oh, shit!"

"Difficult?"

"Bloody Ambrose Hill have diarrhea." Ambrose Hill was Head of Registry and guardian of many secrets. "He's like he was married to those bloody files. They keep them, and the tapes, in a nuclear shelter, Nald."

"But you have access."

"Sure. Yes, sure I have access. But you know they get updated every couple of weeks. They took off one inquisitor and just put a new man in. Can go on into twenty-first century." He gave a big sigh. "Yes, okay, I have access."

"Well?"

"Only in Registry. You want to see and hear those things you do it in safe room—you know, the one right down below Registry, with the baffles so there's no sound stealing. Nothing. You listen on headphones and you read for limited time only. Hill puts one of the knuckle-draggers outside door, and he spot-checks. I know. Been through it all."

"For me, Herb—because I'm having problems with BMW—would you take in a camera and a little machine, a tiny recorder? In secret, of course. I need to see, and, if possible, hear a lot of that stuff."

"There *is* much, Nald. A great deal. Would I do it?" Herbie moved his body to and fro, as if to suggest, maybe. "I got to have good excuse, Nald. Got to have reason."

"If a very good reason suddenly came up, would you do it? For me? You know, us against the world. It's really for poor old Caspar."

"Haaa." Herbie gave him a sidelong, knowing look. "You don't believe all that rubbish about Cas, do you, Nald?"

"What rubbish?"

"Ja, I thought you disbelieved it. Now, you give me a very, but very, good reason and I go play spies for you, okay."

"You know something about accusations against Caspar?"

Herbie lifted his bananalike hand, tipping it from side to side. "Maybe a little. Anyone tries putting shit on Caspar's memory'll have to deal with Kruger, ja?"

"Arnie's in as well."

"Like they say, the three muscatels." Kruger smiled wickedly.

"Musketeers, Herb." Naldo was certain the big man played with the language on purpose. "You'd do it?" He turned his head, making eye contact.

"You think I'd pull your pisser, Nald?"

"I think that would depend on who was holding your wrist."

Herbie guffawed. "No. Serious. If it's to shut this Caspar rubbish once for all, I do it with pleasure. I also show you what good spy can do. Just give me reason."

"How about this, then . . . " Naldo began to talk. Slowly a huge smile engulfed Big Herbie's large face. "You got a deal," he said. "You do it and we put one over on Bugger Maitland-Wood, okay? How soon?"

"Tomorrow?"

"Pity you can't do it this afternoon."

"No, it'll take a bit of time, okay? Eight, or half-past, in morning. Be at your office. You'll hear from someone. Maybe old Bloody Maitland-Wood himself. Better *they* should ask you. Safer than you going to them with a story. In any case, I'll have someone drop you a package with the hardware in the morning."

"What hardware?"

"Camera, and the little tape machine."

"Don't worry, I got my own. Friend in Japan gives me all the stuff I need."

"Really?"

"Yea, out of the good of heart. I got pictures of him fucking a young girl. I told him I might show them to his girlfriend in Tokyo who runs very efficient whorehouse. Jealous. Most jealous lady who runs House of the Paradise Gardens. You want introduction to her sometime?"

"Didn't know you'd been to Tokyo, Herb."

"You don't know a lot of things, Nald. I been most places since they pulled me out of Berlin. House of Paradise Gardens gives excellent value. You get nice hot bath and massage thrown in. Even get the wax treatment."

"What wax treatment?"

"Ahh!" Herbie put his finger alongside his nose. "They have this warm pool. Very warm. Three girls take you in warm pool. Massage you with oils—the girls have no clothes, eh? Then they take you out, put your do-dah on a marble slab, One girl, she go, 'Hyee-Yah!' Give it karate chop and the wax pops out of your ears. Good, yes?" Herbie exploded with mirth. Naldo was still chuckling as he left the Annexe.

It was not until he got to the top of Whitehall, where it enters Trafalgar Square, that Naldo realized he was the focal point of a whole watcher team. He spotted the two cars and the little white van on his way towards the Square. They made two sweeps, as though they wanted him to know they were there. In the Square he spotted the cars and four men, in pairs—two of them by one of the lions at the foot of Nelson's column, two across from him, in Whitehall itself. He went right, dodging the traffic in Northumberland Avenue, and glanced back, over his shoulder. The pair by the lion began to stroll in his direction. Nelson moved, the column falling against scudding clouds. He remembered being frightened of this odd optical illusion as a child. Now, as Naldo slewed right again, making for the Strand and Charing Cross Station, he felt a different kind of fear.

The thing that really bothered him was that they all worked like Eastern Bloc teams, not your standard everyday, run-of-the-mill Five, or SIS watchers. Also the men did not even disguise their intentions. They were all big, burly heavyweights. They looked like the men he thought they were—*Boyevaya Gruppa,* as the Ks called them. A combat gang. Trained killers, expert in the art of abduction and death.

Jesus, he thought, a Sov goon squad in the heart of London? This was crazy. They had an unwritten agreement with the Ks. You didn't wipe out each other's officers. Defectors, doubles, they were different. They would not kill him, here in the heart of the capital. If this had been Berlin things might be different—but why a hit? Unless someone had sold him to the Sovs. No, it had to be a lift, but why were they making themselves so bloody conspicuous?

He remembered something he had heard in Berlin. The footmen work in pairs. Usually four pairs to a *Gruppa.* Which meant there were another two pairs unaccounted for. Then he saw one of them—a man to the left and another to the right, at the bottom of the street as it emptied into the Strand. One of them glanced back, saw him, and crossed to join his companion. He lifted a rolled newspaper, tapping his shoulder twice, as he ducked the traffic, and Naldo was immediately alert for the sudden squeal of an oncoming car. In Berlin they had called that trick "fly squashing." A footman would signal with a raised newspaper and a Merc's fender would suddenly break your back.

But he reached the Strand safely. The couple had moved along to the left, lingering as though trying to make up their minds whether to traverse the road, towards the railway station, with its old cobbled forecourt, and the cross, ravaged by weather and time—the last of twelve crosses erected by Edward I at the stopping places of Queen Eleanor's funeral cortège as it made its way from Nottinghamshire to Westminster Abbey. Naldo wondered if this would be *his* last cross, as he began to follow the crowd of pedestrians released by the traffic lights.

Again, he glanced back. One of the pairs from Trafalgar Square had come into the Strand, hurrying. The other two men remained in place, but the one with the newspaper was holding it high, straight up like a torchbearer. You did not need to know about surveillance techniques to work out that the signal was for the final two-man team, and that they were somewhere ahead, near the station itself.

Naldo reached the forecourt, heading for the main concourse, then ducking into the Underground entrance. Once beneath the main station he stood a good chance of losing the team. The Underground complex at Charing Cross was difficult—several white-tiled tunnels leading from the main booking hall, plus a set of escalators. You needed a whole army of watchers ahead to cover all the permutations, and these men appeared to be set on wanting him to see them.

He thought he detected another couple within the booking hall, but lost them a second later as he banged coins into one of the ticket machines and set off, heading towards the tunnel to the right of the escalators. It would be difficult for them to outguess him. At the very last moment he made up his mind and lunged towards the escalator and began the downward ride.

He was halfway when he saw them, waiting at the bottom. Another pair, loitering between advertisements for Kayser Bondor stockings and the show he was supposed to see that night, *Maggie May.* He glanced back, wondering if he could jump from the down to the up-moving stairways. But there were two more of the same muscular kind on the escalator behind him, and yet another duo still waiting at the top. Boxed and buggered, he thought.

Naldo shoved his hands into his topcoat pockets. You always had some kind of weapon on you, they taught—a pen, a box of matches. He did not have a damned thing. He could not get at his pen inside his jacket pocket, two layers down. Feet and hands only. He stepped off the escalator and the two hoods at the bottom took a pace towards him.

FIVE

1

Naldo braced himself, stepping back with one foot and positioning his body close to the dividing line between the up and down escalators. The midafternoon rush was just starting to build, and people jostled, pushed, even shouldered their way around him. The larger of the two men had a florid complexion, there were blue veins showing on his nose, and his eyes glittered, alert, feigning friendliness. He smelt of garlic, strong tobacco, both almost overpowered by some sickly deodorant. He smiled, as did his friend, then gave a tiny bow, a kind of mock obeisance.

"Please excuse," he said, showing a top row of bad teeth. *"Spasibo—* Thank you, please excuse, you are right for National Gallery here, yes?"

"Yes," Naldo heard himself say. "Yes, National Gallery. Up there," pointing. "Cross the Strand, and straight up into Trafalgar Square. National Gallery. Can't miss it." His body was tense, as though waiting for the bullets.

"Can't miss it. Ah, thank you. Good." The hood looked up and shouted in Russian to his colleagues on the down escalator. He used the English for National Gallery and all four of them nodded, smiled, and thanked Naldo. The smiles were like those you read about in childhood fairy tales. The smile on the face of the tiger-wolf-crocodile.

The hoods from the down escalator had now joined them. The other pair stood at the top of the escalator, looking down with eyes like glass. The quartet nodded and started to move towards the up escalator.

"Again, thank you." The florid man gave another little bow. Then, in almost a whisper, "You see how easy it is, Mr. Railton? *Da svedah-nya.*" He was gone, not even looking back.

"Yeb vas!—fuck you!" Naldo had learned to swear in Russian from a well-informed espionage novel.

On the train to Knightsbridge, he noticed that his hands were shaking.

Barbara was out when he got home. There was a note propped up against the hall telephone, *Gone to buy enticing clothes. Love B,* it said, and Naldo smiled, feeling relief, just as he had felt postcoital guilt all the way back to London. Barbara had not used that little code for a long time. When they were first married she left notes for him all over the house. Soon they had, without talking of it, invented their own codes and signals. "Enticing clothes" meant that she had missed him, and wanted him sexually.

Naldo went into his study and telephoned the shop. He spoke the words that meant the conversation should be scrambled, and the duty officer made the correct response. Naldo counted slowly to ten, then pressed the tiny button built into the rear of the instrument, which was the primary phone on the line in. At each end they had pressed the scrambler buttons at the same moment and he asked for "Tubby" Fincher. By the time the connection was made, Tubby would know that all was secure.

"Yes, Naldo. What can I do for you?" Tubby always sounded tense, as though his position in the Firm had to be buffered by illusory smoke clouds. He made telephone callers think they were the last people in the world to whom he wished to speak.

"Did you know there was a Sov hit team in town, Tub?"

"No, what makes you think there is?"

"They just gave me the runaround. Showed themselves. Approached me, then buggered off with a cryptic word which told me I was an easy target. What's going on?"

There was a long silence. "How many?" Fincher asked.

"A regiment." Naldo had begun to doodle on the pad by his desk. "Two cars, a van, and four pairs of footmen. They looked like a *Boyevaya* gang to me."

"They all look like *Boyevayas* after you've served a month or two in Berlin." Fincher was not even trying to be funny.

"What's going on?" Naldo asked again. Looking down he saw that he had doodled several female thighs and torsos, clad in bikini briefs.

"Think you'd better come in and have a chat, Nald. Tomorrow do you? About eleven?"

"I'll be in anyway. I'm stationed here now, remember?"

"Not likely to forget. Tomorrow then. Oh, and keep off the streets, Naldo. A word to the wise."

"Going to the theater tonight. With Barbara."

"Be cautious," Fincher said, then sent their voices into oblivion by hanging up.

Naldo disengaged the scrambler, tore the page covered with doodles from his note pad, and wrote on the clean sheet, *Can't wait. Back soon. Love, N.* He carried it through to the hall and placed it beside Barbara's note. Then he again put on his overcoat and went out into the cold December afternoon. He hailed the first cab showing a light and got the driver to take him down to Leicester Square. Half an hour later he was walking into the Lyons Corner House. In the basement there was a row of public pay phones. He could have used the ones by the railings of Kensington Gardens, five minutes from the house, but nowadays they were even operating sound stealing on pay phones. He never used one within a mile of his home or office.

He asked for the Berlin number, deposited the money demanded by the operator, and waited for three minutes before he heard the distant *Nurrrrp . . . Nurrrrp.* Arnie picked up on the fourth double.

"Ja?"

"Oh, I think I must have a wrong number," Naldo said in German.

"Who did you want?"

"Fräulein Sender."

"I can get a message to her."

"Oh, thank you. Tell her Walter called. Could she call me tonight?"

"Certainly. Tonight you say?"

"Yes. She has the number." Naldo put down the telephone and walked back upstairs. On his way out he bought some violet creams for Barbara. She said they were "her favorite fruit," and always called them "violent creams." The telephone double-talk would already have set Arnie in motion. Within hours, the shop would be put into a situation demanding them to instruct Herbie to have another look at the *Hypermarket* /Blunt material.

Barbara was back, getting dressed, when he got home. He telephoned the theater and found out what time the show ended, then ordered a cab to take them right to the doors of the Adelphi, and another to get them into the Trattoo in Abingdon Road, where he now booked a table. Pasquale would see to it that a cab picked them up. Pasquale, like any good restaurateur, knew Naldo's ways: how he liked to sit at the back of the room so that he could see the entrance; how he should never be addressed by name, though Pasquale thought his name to be Mr. Douglas, and how he always had to call a cab from a firm known to him and with a driver known to him. He would check it was the right driver before letting Mr. and Mrs. Douglas leave the building. In truth, Pasquale did all these things, and, in private, thought Mr. Douglas was a fussy, stupid Englishman who liked to be seen as a big, powerful man. But, like all good restaurateurs he never confided these reservations to anybody else. In his own country you could always be wrong about this kind of thing, and he did not want to be caught out. Pasquale was a prudent man.

They enjoyed *Maggie May,* an amusing, dramatic, and sad musical about Liverpool dockers, strikes, and whores. Liverpool was the "in" city since the Beatles had made the breakthrough.

On their way out, Naldo felt eyes on him and turned his head. The big Russian with the bad teeth was patiently waiting to get from his seat to the aisle. He smiled at Naldo, who mouthed *Yeb vas* at him, though his guts did a slow roll of panic. The Russian raised one finger and gently prodded the air with it, smiling all the time. Naldo was pleased that there was a cab waiting for them, and even more happy when he watched for vehicle surveillance and found none.

They ate seafood, *Fegato alla Veneziana,* and, switching to French, *Crêpes au citron.* Barbara sat next to him facing down the long narrow room with the mirrors and greenery giving it an illusion of greater width, and Naldo stroked her thigh under the table.

When they got back to the house near Kensington Gore there was no waiting. They stripped each other in the darkness of the bedroom and fell backwards together onto the bed.

"And how's my little laughing cavalier tonight, then?" Barbara whispered, giggling and reaching for him. "My, he's got his rapier out. Kiss me, and talk very dirty, Naldo Railton. I feel really filthy." And she did. A tiny bit on the side helps the marriage along, she thought, then cried out with pleasure as he entered her.

The next morning, after Naldo had left, she called the Hans Crescent number just to hear the bell ringing in the distance and knowing it was doing so in the one room in which she had committed her only act of adultery. To her surprise a man answered.

"Philip?" she said, in a small voice.

"Who do you want?" It certainly was not Philip Hornby speaking, so she asked for him.

"Nobody of that name here," he said. "You sure you've got the right number?"

She repeated it, and he said, yes, that was the number. But there was no Philip Hornby at this address. "I'm doing some redecorating," the man said. "Redecorating for Mr. and Mrs. Barnes. Lived here for years."

She was mildly disturbed, then decided she had been taken for a ride—literally, she felt. "Rotten bugger," she said aloud. "Bet you borrow the place from the Barnes people." At that moment her own telephone rang. When she answered, the caller hung up without speaking.

2

Big Herbie Kruger's red telephone rang at just after ten. He had been in his office for over an hour, and the red telephone rarely rang. It was the one connected directly to the shop.

Maitland-Wood himself was on the line. "Can you get over here, chop-chop?" BMW asked. He always used obscure pidgin-English type phrases when speaking to staff who were not actually born in the UK. It was the wrong thing to do with a man like Big Herbie. "What's with the chop-chop?" Herbie asked, sounding his most puzzled.

"Fast—schnell-schnell! to you, Kruger." BMW thought at least he knew where he stood with Kruger. He had not served with the XX Section for nothing. XX stood for Twenty, or double-cross. Maitland-Wood had spent some of the war with Five and their unit at Ham Common, Camp 020, neatly doubling German agents or luring them into false flag operations. He found Kruger easier to deal with than some of the young university entrants they were getting into the Service these days.

At his end, Herbie banged the telephone onto its rests—"Schnell-schnell! Raus! Raus! Bloody Pinewood German," he exploded. Then he went silent and very still, a smile slowly spreading across his face. "Clever boy that Naldo," he whispered to himself.

"Uncomfortable, Kruger?" Willis Maitland-Wood scowled across his desk.

"No, fine. Quite comforting here." Herbie gave them his big grin.

"I mean," said BMW, taking a long pause between the definite article and the word "mean," "that *we,* here in this department, are uncomfortable."

Herbie knew well enough what he meant. Still grinning he looked around him. "Better than my office. You got all mod cons here, Mr. Maitland-Wood."

"Just shut up and listen, Herb," Fincher, seated nearby, snapped like a mousetrap.

"We've had access to a ciphered cable," Maitland-Wood continued. "Flash from Berlin via Langley. Need-to-know Flash. Last night. Early hours in fact. They followed it up with a very long dossier which went through the Grosvenor Square telexes this morning.''

Herbie, who already had an idea of what was to come, thought that BMW had a tendency to talk in a series of crossword puzzle clues.

"We've examined the cable, and the dossier. So has CSS. It was the CSS who instructed us to call you in.''

"Do I have to make educated guess, or you going to tell me things straight?'' Herbie asked. He had stopped smiling and sat very still, as though made of granite. Inside his head he thought, *'Was mir die Nacht erzählt*—What the night tells me. It was the title of the fourth movement of Gustav Mahler's Third Symphony. Somehow it seemed apt for Herbie to think of the titles of the third's movements now.

"Just listen, Herb. Mr. Maitland-Wood will tell you everything.''

"Cockroach,'' BMW said as if it had a wealth of meaning.

What the animals in the forest tell me—second movement, Big Herbie thought. Aloud, he said, "Insect,'' but not loud enough to be heard.

"Our American Cousins had a walk-in defector about four weeks ago. Berlin.''

"Didn't hear about it.'' Herbie's lips hardly moved.

"You weren't meant to hear about it.'' Willis Maitland-Wood felt this was not really his job. C should have done it himself. "They've given him the crypto *Cockroach.* For the CIA it's apparently insect time.''

"Ah.''

"Yes, just *over* four weeks ago to be exact,'' Fincher butted in.

"Four *weeks?*'' Herbie raised the pitch at the end of "weeks.'' It seemed the right thing to do. "Why they not flown the bugger back to Washington D.C. and put him through the grinder?''

"That's none of our business, Kruger.'' BMW on his dignity, even though *he* would never keep a walk-in hanging around on the operational turf for that long. "They must have their reasons.''

"Maybe he's no good. Maybe he's bloody double. Maybe bait; dangle, hu?'' Herbie knew well enough that *Cockroach* was just that. They had him well and truly sorted out in one of the well-equipped safe houses run by the Americans. They were doing their best to turn him, or feed him some carrots, pop him on a stick and dangle him back. *Was mir die Morgenglocken erzählen*—What the morning bells tell me. Fifth movement. *Cockroach* was a very low-grade radio mechanic, straight out of the KGB facility at Karlshorst. Knew nothing; no ambition; no interest except to go to America and become rich by being a well-paid radio mechanic. Naldo had told him all this yesterday. Arnie was keeping him for stock. He could put words in the man's mouth and *Cockroach* would not even know it, Naldo had said. Also, Arnie could do it at arm's length, without becoming involved on paper. Langley would gobble it up and give it to London, quick as a whore can pass on the clap. That is what Naldo had said, and Herbie believed Naldo in almost all things.

Cockroach, BMW now told him, was a specialized technical expert. "Radio, I understand. German, but a Party member and happy as can be to work for KGB."

Ponderously BMW came to the point, with a few prods from Tubby Fincher, who kept shifting his skeletal frame in a chair that seemed to engulf him.

Cockroach, it seemed, had positive evidence that *Daulis* had still been working for the Russian Service up to two years ago. Also he had positive intelligence that *Daulis* had twice made connections with one of Herbie's own network. *Daulis* was their name, that month, for Blunt. They all thought it was a terribly droll crypto, for in classical mythology Daulis was a nymph.

"This being the case," BMW droned on, "you are significantly involved. Maybe even compromised. We have the dossier and the dates. It is possible we shall have to ask our brethren from Five to have some strong words with *Daulis*. It's just, well, we should be sure of our facts. We thought you might like to check your own files. Just to see if they were possible: the two meetings with your fellow, I mean."

"Which fellow?" Herbie had assumed a hard, angry expression. The kind of reaction they would all expect from him, for he agonized greatly about his network, known as *The Schnitzer Group*. He was constantly complaining to Fincher and BMW of the difficulties of servicing them long-range.

"Your man? Yes. Real name, Willy Blenden."

"Shit!" said Herbie. Then, once more, with feeling, "Shit!" And again, for the insurance, "Shit!"

"May not be true, Herb," Fincher tried to soothe him.

"And then again it could be truth. I need time. Go through my stuff." He paused, then put the boot in. "Shall need access to *Daulis'* files also. Today. Straight off. There was some stuff didn't quite add up, last time I checked. I need the Watchers files as well. Watchers on *Daulis*, I mean."

"Sure, anything, Herb," Fincher said. "They've been updated since you last poked around in them anyway. It's going to be another year, at the least, before they've finished with our artistic gentleman. But, anything you want."

Yes, anything, they both said. Anything you like, keys to the king-
dom. Complete freedom in the Registry. Oh, my, Herb thought. My
God. What I learn from love. Love of job; love of pension. Nald, you
and Arn have just scared Mr. Maitland-Wood and Mr. Fincher shitless.
Probably CSS as well. Because we all know everyone's agreed that
Daulis, aka Sir Anthony Frederick Blunt, has been out of the trade for
a long time now. Also he's been more than cooperative. Named names.
Whispered poison. Even though he has shown no hint of remorse.
Naldo, you bloody genius.

They gave him all necessary forms and clearances there and then.
In triplicate if he wanted them, praying that he could check and come
back to tell them this bloody *Cockroach* was out of his tree, and they
were off the hook.

They even telephoned Ambrose Hill, while Herbie stood there, and
told him that he was to give full and complete cooperation to Mr.
Kruger.

"Almost give me a medal, Nald," Herbie said later when the two of
them sat down in a very secure room and talked, with Herb handing
over several rolls of exposed film.

"They'll give you a jockstrap medal when you tell them they're off
the hook, Herb. When you say he's been a good boy since way back.
But they won't be thinking of medals when we finally show that he's
been leading them a dance around the houses: naming wrong names
and spreading gloom and suspicion." Naldo smiled, "But not yet,
Herb. Keep the options open. Keep digging, would you. Keep beavering
away until I surface again."

"You going invisible, Nald?"

"Yes. And it's three-wise-monkey time for you, Herb."

"For you, Nald, I make it four, okay?"

But that was a couple of days later, seated among spices and canned
goods.

In the present, as Herbie was taking the elevator down to Registry,
so Naldo Railton was making his way from the eighth floor to the fifth
and his meeting with Tubby Fincher. They probably passed in the lifts.

3

The suite of offices on the fifth floor, which housed the CSS and his
immediate aides, was nested within the building. The rooms had no

windows; the walls contained noise-absorbant tiles, and electronic bafflers protected the area from external sound-stealing devices. Technicians swept the offices morning and evening, while one of the duty officer's standard jobs was to check the wastebaskets.

Naldo had the feeling that they had laid on the full works for him. One of the jumpers, pearls, and sensible-shoes secretaries showed him into Willis Maitland-Wood's office, where Willis sat behind his desk, wearing the look of a headmaster about to deal with some errant schoolboy. In a chair to his right, Tubby Fincher squirmed visibly. Standing just inside the door was one of the minders from Warminster. Naldo recognized him immediately. "Hello, Mr. Railton, sir," said the minder, like a gamekeeper tugging at his forelock.

BMW gestured to a stand chair set carefully before his desk. The minder's name, Naldo suddenly recalled, was Max. The runes did not read well, so he did not sit, but leaned, one hand braced on the chair back.

"All right, Max. Outside. See we're not disturbed." BMW nodded to the minder. Behind him, Naldo heard the door close. Then—

"Just tell us what happened." Maitland-Wood's attitude was officious and unfriendly.

"Please sit down, Naldo." Fincher looked acutely embarrassed.

"No, I won't bloody just sit down, Tub. I reported something really dangerous to you. In turn, you asked me in to talk about it in a secure place, and I find the heavy mob on guard. I presume your office *is* secure, Willis?"

"Oh, it's secure." BMW put aside any pretense of the meeting being merely a friendly get-together. "So, just sit down. There are other things we must talk about, and probably put to you. All right?"

Naldo nodded.

"First," Maitland-Wood began, "you went to Berlin two days ago to service a source. You were supposed to be in and out in a day. We put a safe house at your disposal, and we made certain you had no surveillance—from anyone."

"Right." Naldo took the same crisp, somewhat brusque, tone.

"You stayed the night, which was not in the schedule. Why?"

Naldo smiled straight into his face. "You read my request, Willis? If you did, you'll see that it says 'business scheduled within a twenty-four-hour period, *with some leeway either side.* Which, as you damned well know, means it could take longer. In fact, from Heathrow to Heathrow it took twenty-eight hours. Four over the hoped-for schedule. The reason? My source came in from behind the Wall. There

91

were three-hour fallbacks. We couldn't get it together until around midnight. That's a normal, secure operational necessity. Right?"

BMW nodded and made a note. He had a blank piece of paper in front of him, and his custom-made desk sported an inlaid marble panel. No bits of glass for BMW. His tradecraft was full of silly little luxuries, as though he used them to support his position.

"You came into Heathrow around noon, yesterday, Naldo. What did you do first?"

"Rang my wife."

"Mm-hu. Then what?"

"Took a cab to Whitehall. Dropped off at the Trafalgar Square end and walked up to the Annexe."

"Naldo, *please* sit down." Maitland-Wood did not look up, but Naldo sat at last, turning the chair sideways on.

"Why did you go to the Annexe?"

"To see Herbie."

"Why?"

"Because I'd promised him lunch."

"How and when did you arrange this with Mr. Kruger?"

"I didn't arrange it."

"You said you'd promised him lunch."

"When I last saw him, at my uncle's funeral, I said let's have lunch sometime? Herbie and I are old friends. In the past we've worked together. Very closely, as you know, Willis. He said he would love lunch. He likes to go to The Travellers, but I took him to Gennaro's instead. Old Herb can be noisy over lunch and one doesn't like to disturb the calm of The Travellers, does one?"

"You're saying you dropped in unannounced?"

"Got it." Naldo leaned back. "I thought it would be a little treat for him. He likes treats."

"You didn't want to discuss anything operational with him, then?"

"Our paths do not cross, operationally. You know that also, Willis. It was a friendly luncheon. Two old colleagues."

BMW made another note. "And you walked home with him?"

"If by 'home' you mean back to the Annexe, yes."

"During lunch, or the walk back, did you mention your uncle? Did the conversation veer in the direction of the late Sir Caspar Railton?"

"You what?" Naldo feigned puzzlement. "Veer in the direction? What kind of language is that, Willis?"

"It's a simple question. Did you talk about Caspar?"

"I don't understand you, but, yes, he was mentioned. We talked about old times. People like Herbie and myself miss Sir Caspar. I do, in particular.''

"Really?"

"Yes, *really*, Willis. He was a good intelligence officer, and an even better uncle.''

"You talked about the past, then?"

"We couldn't very well discuss the future, could we? Herbie and myself are not intercognisant now, as you already know.''

"Don't be flippant, Naldo. You'll see the reason for this line of questioning shortly, and I fear you're not going to like it.''

Naldo felt himself go very still, as though he could, like some reptiles, control his pulse rate, slow down and lock his muscles. God, he thought, it's coming. Now. Straightaway. In the back of his head he heard the old words, this time spoken in Caspar's bluff manner. "Now it begins." Aloud, he said, "We discussed a defunct operation which is still classified.''

"I see. The operation is dead?"

"And finished with. It was a long time ago. Herbie, Caspar, and myself were involved. I'm saying no more than that.''

"Why not?" Maitland-Wood had changed tack. He was polite, but pressing. He sounded like a doctor going through routine questions. If all the answers added up at the end of the interview, Naldo thought, he was going to tell the patient he had leprosy. Possibly, BMW considered, a lot of Railtons were already infected; and he might be right.

"Because, in spite of you being Deputy to C, I really don't know who has what clearance, Willis. We can troop in and have a word with C if you like.''

"That won't be necessary," BMW said, a shade too quickly. "You left Kruger at the Annexe. It was after that the trouble began?''

"Yes. Straightaway." Naldo went through his sighting of the Russian team and the events that followed. Finally he told them about seeing one of them at the Adelphi that night. When Naldo had finished talking, Maitland-Wood carried on writing. Then he sat back—

"Yes, there is a team in town, and that's odd, because they don't usually show themselves here in London.''

"That's why I reported it. In Berlin I would have understood . . . ''

"Don't you understand now?"

"I understand they're trying to make a point. I don't know why.''

"I see. Well, let me tell you some of it. Half of the team are newly appointed Embassy heavies. They came in with a new batch last week. Nobody likes it, and we're doing what we can. At least our

93

sister Service is doing what *it* can. The other part, the really nasty knuckle-draggers, are what the Ks call *Shavki*—trash-eating dogs. Like you gave Kruger a little treat, the Ks sometimes give their outside help little treats. These people came in to nursemaid a small delegation here for the talks going on at the Ministry of Trade. But they're not really doing their duties. The *Shavki* haven't accompanied their charges, nor have they spent any leisure time with their charges. They've been whistling around town, mainly with the pros from the Embassy. The Foreign Office has given them their cards. The *Shavki*, I mean. They've been PNGd and they go on this afternoon's Aeroflot back to Moscow." PNG was the smart acronym for *persona non grata*. BMW expelled air through his nose. "However, the teeth of the team are a different matter. Now, Naldo, you've agreed they were trying to make a point with you. What kind of point do you think they were making?"

"I said, if it had been Berlin, I would have looked at how I'd managed to get up their noses. Those people can be damned frightening, but we're not in the business of killing each other. If I *had* done something to really upset them, I suppose I'd have locked myself away for a couple of weeks, or taken them on and risked getting roughed up."

Maitland-Wood stared at the ceiling. "We're not in the business of killing one another." He repeated Naldo's words as though they were some kind of magic charm. "But, Naldo Railton, those kind of teams, the *Boyevaya*, the Combat Groups, *are* in the business of killing people. That's their trade. That's why we've PNGd half of them. That's why we're working on the other half. We don't like the Ks' Combat Groups on our ground. They're bloody dangerous."

"This is true." Naldo had no option but to sit there and roll with the punches. He knew BMW was about to bring a crushing left hook from nowhere.

"Yes, of course it's true. Just as what you've said is true. We don't go around taking each other out. It has never been written into any charter, but we all know it's counterproductive. Yet, there are times when people do get killed in this job. Tell me, in your wide experience who they *do* kill. Come to that, who we also sometimes expend. What kind of person gets the chop, Naldo?"

Naldo shrugged. "Defectors, before they've had a chance to talk; would-be defectors; proven doubles that we, or they, can't double back."

"In a word, traitors."

94

"*Some* traitors," Naldo said firmly. "Those traitors who are too far into the quicksands." He shifted his body in the chair. "When you work in the field, Willis, you haven't got time to make choices—religious, moral, or questions of honor. The whole of our job concerns traitors. The evaluation of intelligence is left to the clever people in this building, or buildings like it, who sift the stuff we get. They don't care how we get it, and I feel they often lose sight of the fact that we feed these clever brains with the offal of traitors.

"Every bloody asset I've had to deal with throughout my career has been a traitor. We're all traitors to somebody."

There was a long silence, broken at last by Maitland-Wood, who spoke as though he had not heard any of Naldo's short speech. "Defectors; would-be defectors; doubles. Sometimes couriers? Right? And in your vast experience, Naldo, what type of person is given a warning before he gets chopped?" BMW was not good on the heavy sarcasm.

"Oh, I suppose people who are thinking about defecting; or people who own information that they're likely to spill to the wrong agency."

"Quite. I must put it to you, very seriously, Naldo. Do you fall into any of those categories?"

"Me?"

"Well, my dear Naldo, it was *you* who received the gypsy's warning. You were the target of these thugs."

"That's exactly why I reported in. Immediately. I told Tubby here as soon as I could get to my phone."

"Being conscientious, you would do that anyway. You're sensible enough to realize that we, or our brothers in Christ who are Five, could have been shepherding this band of Russian acrobats."

"But you weren't, Willis. If you had the dogs on them, I would have known."

"Railton the omnipotent, eh?"

"No, Railton the professional. I've already seen most of it. If you'd had people piggybacking those hoods, I really would have known, Willis."

"They were warning you, though. You admit that."

"I admit that. I don't know why they were warning me. Perhaps I have, inadvertently, trodden hard on someone's toes. I might even have accidentally lanced one of the big boils at Moscow Center. Who knows? It could even be an error. Mistaken identity. I don't know, Willis. I don't know why. I do know they were putting the frighteners in."

Again a longish pause while Maitland-Wood made a note with his slim silver ball-point pen. Then, for the first time, he looked up, straight into Naldo's face. "You would, then, deny that at any time you have provided the Russian Service with intelligence?"

"Come off it, Willis."

"No," he said, his voice seeming to be filtered through several layers of granite chippings. "I am asking you officially. You deny having worked as a double agent, for us and the Russian Service? You deny any complicity in running, or servicing any Russian agent in place for the Russian Service? You deny having any preliminary meetings with Russian officers to discuss your own defection?"

"You're joking!" *Now it begins.*

"Just answer the questions."

"I deny them. I deny all counts. No! No! And no!"

Maitland-Wood nodded, then gave a friendly shrug. "Well, you'd deny it anyway. Three times, like Peter with Christ. On our part, I should tell you there's not one iota of evidence that you have, in any way or manner, conducted yourself as a potential traitor."

"I should bloody well think not."

"It was necessary to put the questions formally."

"Willis, what's all this about?"

"You were warned that something unpleasant would happen to you if you followed a certain course of action, Naldo. We think we know exactly why a little cautious, if heavy, advice came your way."

Naldo waited.

"I'm sorry to be the one to tell you this." BMW did not smile. "Several officers of this Service, and from Five, are involved in an investigation concerning a member of your family. And, unfortunately, he's not available to defend himself. You see it's quite possible that your uncle, the late Sir Caspar Railton, was a long-term Soviet penetration agent."

Though he was half-suspecting it, the confirmation went through Naldo like a sword. He felt betrayed and violated, just as he had when Arnie suggested it. He hoped his face showed none of this.

The two men sat looking at one another. Then Naldo said, "Could Cas ever have had the time?"

"Meaning?" Maitland-Wood asked.

"Meaning that I once heard a very great spycatcher say that if you wanted to wear a moleskin jacket, you should look for a time when your target could have been nobbled. In plain language, there never was a time when my Uncle Caspar could have been turned, burned, buggered, or branded. He went from school to Sandhurst; from Sandhurst to France; from France to a long spell in hospital, and from thence to this Service, which was only just taking flight."

"Four things, Naldo." Maitland-Wood's voice had become almost kindly. So much so that Naldo's antennae bristled at the uncharacteristic trait. "One, your Uncle Caspar was, in fact, recruited to this Service by a former relative who later became completely discredited. I don't have to give you the details."

No, you do not, Naldo thought. Everyone in the family knew that story, and his treacherous ancestor's private papers stayed under lock and key at Redhill. BMW went on—

"Two, with respect, while your family has undoubtedly served country, king, queen, and honor with great gallantry, it has also had its fair share of, shall we say, rotten apples. From a Service viewpoint, the Railtons are tainted goods. Three, Sir Caspar himself came under suspicion towards the end of, and just after, World War II . . . "

"He was completely exonerated, Willis. We all know that. There was no hint of Caspar having been even indiscreet . . . "

"And, four!" Maitland-Wood overrode Naldo, raising his voice. "Four, there *was* a period when he was away from the Service. Out completely. There is very little of his history left available to us from *that* period. What is clear shows that he was, at the very least, stupid enough to make long-term friendships with some highly dubious characters. The opportunity for Caspar to be turned *is there* . . . "

"When? What're you talking about, Willis?"

"From August 1935 until September 1938, Caspar Arthur Railton was out of the Service at his own request. During that time he traveled a great deal. He met a lot of people. We know who some of them were."

"So, we all meet people who turn out to be undesirable. I'd bet he provided an accurate picture of his contacts and movements when he came back in again."

BMW gave a rather Gallic gesture, using hands, shoulders, and face. "Unhappily, no."

"What's your supporting evidence?" Naldo kept his anger at bay. After all, he knew there was a fair chance of some of the supporting evidence—from *Alex*, Penkovsky—being blown to blazes. If Blunt had also added poison, he would soon be in a position of knowledge and, therefore, ability to neutralize whatever had been said.

"Naldo." It was Tubby Fincher who spoke. "Naldo, unhappily there is some very damning evidence."

"Where? How?"

97

"At the moment it's restricted. There's also some rather unpleasant verbal evidence."

"Substantiated evidence?" Naldo feigned slight mollification.

Tubby tipped his head from side to side, as some people might do with a hand. "More or less," he said.

"And you all think, because I'm a Railton, I'm well tied-up with my late uncle, and treachery, which I cannot, incidentally, believe."

"No." Willis Maitland-Wood was now firm but friendly. "No. But we think the Soviet Combat Gang were warning you to stay out of any investigation."

"They could have been laying false trails, Willis. Thought of that?"

"It's a possibility."

"So what do you want of me, then?"

"A little family assistance. The kind of thing best left to experts."

"Which means it could be something illegal." Naldo smiled, the way a murderer must smile when putting a victim at ease.

Maitland-Wood ignored the comment. "Your family," he said, "have a famous property. The house in Eccleston Square. It was owned by your great-uncle, the famous Giles Railton, and eventually passed to Caspar. Right?"

"Yes."

"Have you been there since the funeral, Naldo?"

"No."

"Is anyone living there?"

"No."

"We want to have a look-see."

"You mean you want to turn it over."

"As you wish. We can get a warrant, but it'd be easier all round if we had cooperation. We'd like you to get permission from Lady Phoebe."

"Permission for your so-called technical boys to take it apart and put it back together again?"

"Permission for us to go in. Look. Examine Caspar's papers, maybe remove some of them. Yes, that's about the size of it."

Naldo scowled, a shaft of concern went through his mind. "You really believe all this, don't you, Willis?"

"All of it, I fear. Yes. I have no doubt whatsoever that your Uncle Caspar was a Soviet penetration agent. Sorry, but the circumstantial stuff is *very* strong."

"I'll talk to Phoebe. And I insist on the right to come with you during the search." Naldo smiled inwardly, knowing that it was himself, not his Aunt Phoebe, from whom BMW should seek permission. "Agreed?" he asked.

Slowly BMW nodded. "Thank you, Naldo."

"When?" Naldo asked from the door.

"Yesterday. But we'll settle for tomorrow."

Naldo wondered if there was already surveillance on the Eccleston Square house.

Max was still outside.

"The old man getting tough, Mr. Railton?" Max spoke like an old con, without moving his lips, but with his mouth slewed sideways as though he had suffered a stroke.

Naldo did not even nod as he walked quickly towards the elevators.

SIX

1

During his last five-year stint in Berlin, Naldo Railton had worked out of an anonymous gray building, close to Gatow airfield. There, as assistant to the SIS Resident, his cover was diplomatic. Most of his time was spent in the field, though he remained directly responsible for ten operational case officers, around a hundred technicians, drivers, and desk jockeys, analysts, cipher clerks, and the like, who made up the bulk of the Secret Intelligence Service's presence in Berlin.

Throughout his tour, Naldo became almost paranoid over the use of tradecraft. He practiced it day and night, asleep or awake, twenty-four hours a day, every day. This was no game, from which some field agents got a buzz. Naldo, like his father and uncle before him, saw tradecraft as a way of life. A highly skilled agent had once told him that tradecraft should be second nature—"You don't go into a country where cholera or typhoid are rife without taking the normal medical precautions," this man had said. "You make sure you get your shots. Sure, you might still get the damned disease, but you stand more chance of remaining immune and alive if you've done something about it." Some people in the trade thought the rituals were a joke. Anyone, serving under Naldo, who showed a casual or flippant nature towards the everyday practice of their craft was in for a pasting.

The return to England, while not unexpected, had made him edgy and frustrated, but he still behaved exactly as he had done in the field. Those who could see it whispered that he was "Wall-happy." Naldo Railton was subject to the twitch, ready for retirement into some backwater of the Service. So murmured the Mighty Wurlitzer, as they called HQ rumors: a double-edged nickname, for it mirrored a long-running American intelligence media story-planting operation.

Indeed, after the normal month-long debrief at Warminster, while Barbara worked on refurbishing the house near Kensington Gardens, nobody appeared to have any serious occupation for Naldo at the shop. The shop was a high-rise building overlooking the Thames, housing the headquarters of the SIS, perched above the ground-floor offices of a great oil company.

When the debrief was over, Naldo had found himself working from a small, cluttered office on the eighth floor, above the canteen. It was here that London watched over its operations within the Soviet Bloc countries, and Naldo was given a special responsibility for East Germany, the DDR, about which he knew a great deal.

Below, on the fifth floor, there was no worry about the Mighty Wurlitzer. In fact, the rumors could have been traced straight back to the CSS's staff, who wanted people to believe Naldo was ready for retirement, possibly with a cut in pension. They had successfully propagated a similar whisper about Big Herbie Kruger, when, in fact, Herb worked from the Annexe with a special, and highly secret, title of Director Special Sources, East Germany. The powers on the fifth floor had initially planned that Naldo and Herbie would eventually work in double harness.

As far as Naldo was concerned, this small act of in-house disinformation had been abruptly aborted in late November. The reasons were dark, dubious, and not absolutely confirmed. But on the fifth floor nobody took chances anymore. All they could do was slowly decrease the amount of classified material which passed across Naldo's desk.

It was a situation which ran parallel to the events concerning Arnie Farthing in Washington, and had led, inevitably, to the painful interview in which Maitland-Wood laid the news on Naldo that his late uncle's career was under investigation. He did not have to say that Naldo was also under the microscope, nor that there was alarm because the surveillance team assigned to cover his recent trip to Berlin had lost him, somewhere along the Ku-damm, not picking him up again until he reached the safe house where he had spent the night with his source. The CSS's special aides would have been even more worried had they known of certain events which had taken place, first, in mid-November, and again, just after Sir Caspar Railton's death.

On their return from Berlin, Naldo's parents had thrown a small party for them in London. A few weeks later, Sara and Dick did the same thing over a weekend at Redhill Manor. It was at this second party that Naldo's father, James, arranged to dine with him a few weeks hence.

They met and ate at The Reform Club. "I prefer it here to The

Travellers," James told his son. "Not so many connections with past and present."

"Not to mention future," Naldo had said seriously. The Travellers was still known as The Foreign Office Canteen and you could bet on at least four or five members of the Secret Intelligence Service being there at any given time.

After dinner they took coffee on the balcony that runs around the first floor of The Reform, and it was at a secluded table that James told his son what was on his mind.

"It's your Uncle Caspar, Donald," he began. Only rarely did anyone call him Donald. Occasionally his father or mother would use "Donald," but he noticed it was usually when they were under stress.

"Old Cas and me, we're getting on," James said. "He'll go first, no doubt about that. His doctors have been very open with him. He hasn't got long. As for me, the first show took a lot out of me, and since the second unpleasantness I've begun to feel my age."

"Come on, Father, you've still got a lot of years left in you."

"Maybe. Yes, maybe, but I'm not as spry as I was and that worries me." He went on to tell Naldo, in confidence, what Caspar had prepared in his will. "Doesn't want either of his sons to have the Eccleston Square property, that's the top and bottom of it. He's afraid Andrew, being the shrewd lawyer he is, would sell out; and he knows damned well that Alexander would do it without a second thought. He also knows old Phoebe wouldn't want to stay on there without him, so he's leaving the place to you, and your children, with the usual proviso that it doesn't pass out of the family."

Naldo lit a cigarette and blew smoke down his nostrils. "I thought Great-Uncle Giles made that proviso years ago."

James nodded. "Well, he did. But Cas is concerned. Andrew's such a clever bugger with the law that he reckons they'd be able to break the clause in no time."

"That all?" Naldo asked gently.

"No. No, there's something connected with it, and it's a matter for someone like you or me. Got to be in the trade, you see."

"Yes?"

"Well, Cas put me under discipline on this one, but I think I'll have to let that go. Should tell him, but I think it's best I don't."

"You want to share it with me?"

"More than share it." He fumbled in the inside pocket of his jacket and withdrew a bulky, thick manila envelope, which he passed across the table. It was heavy, and Naldo heard a jingle, and felt metal inside.

"One full set of keys to Eccleston Square." His father's voice dropped to a whisper. "If your Uncle Cas dies suddenly he wants me to take certain actions. As I said, I'm not as spry as I was. Could be that the opportunities for me to do as he asks will be limited. You're a different matter. I'm passing his instructions to you. There's a note of the safe combination in there as well. I'd memorize it then destroy, if I were you."

"Right." Naldo knew there was no arguing with his father. "Tell me what's to be done, and I'll do it."

It took twenty minutes for James to go through all the points. When he was finished he made Naldo repeat everything.

When Caspar died, only a few weeks later, Naldo carried out the orders to the letter, and knew his father had done the right thing. There was no way in which James could have followed Caspar Railton's instructions.

As it turned out, the news of Caspar's death, in The Travellers Club after lunch in the first week of December, reached the shop long before anyone else. Sir Caspar had been with other old friends and one of them had the presence of mind to telephone the duty officer even before the ambulance arrived. It took less than ten minutes, from the DO receiving the call, to Naldo getting the news from C himself.

He tried to call his cousin Andrew, but he was in court. A message would have to be taken to him by hand. "And I can't be certain he'll leave straightaway," the clerk said. "It's a *very* important case."

So much for filial love and responsibility, Naldo thought, and telephoned Alexander in Cheltenham. He would leave as soon as possible, but could not expect to be in London for three hours at the soonest. "Has Mother been told?" At least he asked *that.* Naldo told him, no, and he was to leave that to his father's old Firm.

C came with Naldo, who had taken the precaution of telephoning Dick and Sara first. Together, they broke the news. Phoebe was herself a sick woman, and Naldo could not recall seeing anyone else take news of a death so badly. Now he knew what "prostrate with grief" really meant. She made wild statements; asked foolish questions. "Is Alex coming back? Has James been told? I think Alex phoned James."

C quickly melted away when Andrew arrived, with his wife, and together they made the arrangements. Alexander eventually got in from Cheltenham, and the two sons and one daughter-in-law set off in convoy to take their mother to Haversage, and from there to Redhill. Everyone knew that Caspar would be buried with the rest of the family at Haversage.

103

"I'll have to come back to London tonight," Andrew had said petulantly before they left. "It's just like Father to die when I'm in the middle of an important case. Difficult judge as well."

"Your father *has* died, Andrew. For God's sake . . . "

"It isn't as though we weren't expecting it." Andrew was putting on weight. When he stood upright the potbelly showed, even through his dark overcoat. "He's been living on borrowed time for years. I don't know if I can cope with Mother doing her deathbed scene either."

Naldo kept his temper in check. "I don't suppose your mother'll want to return here for some time," he said, grit in his throat. "I should lock the place and activate the alarms if I were you."

"No, you're not me, Naldo. Thank God. And thank God I'm not you. You *would* think of that, making sure the alarms're on. It's the bloody filthy trade you and my father shared."

"Actually, I was thinking about criminal activity," Naldo said rather primly, and Andrew moved away to the car in which his mother sat, shocked, cradled in her daughter-in-law's arms. When he returned, Andrew curtly said Naldo had better come with him, they would do the whole thing together. "And you can hold on to the bloody keys. The old man's left the place to you, I gather," Andrew snapped.

"I'd rather you kept the keys. At least until everything's been settled."

"Mother can have them, then. Place'll cost you a bloody fortune to run."

They went through the business and drove away, the two cars moving off into the traffic with none of the occupants giving Naldo a wave or look.

Later that same night, Naldo returned to Eccleston Square with his own set of keys and several items he had collected on the way. He switched off the alarm system and went straight to The Hide, the study on the first floor. It had been called The Hide, so family legend went, by his great-uncle, Giles Railton. It was a large room with an unusually big desk and a strange built-in filing cabinet. The cabinet contained drawers full of miniature soldiers—armies which went back to Roman and ancient Greek times, with all the accoutrements of war through the ages, from siege towers and ballistae to the howitzers and field guns just coming into service before the first war of 1914–'18. There were also large, rolled, handmade maps showing the terrain of hundreds of great campaigns. Giles Railton had claimed that reenacting the battles from the past helped him plan a secret strategy in his present. Naldo knew these things were, now, most precious, worth thousands of pounds in the specialist field of war gaming. Uncle Caspar had toyed with them, and he could recall being in The Hide as a child, with his father and Caspar as they tried to relive battles.

For the moment, though, he did not open the tall cabinet. Instead he pulled on a pair of woolen gloves, knelt on the floor, close to the window, and manipulated the tumblers and lock on an elderly, heavy Chubb safe. The mechanism was well-oiled and the door swung back without a sound. Ten minutes later he had been through everything, removing the long metal strongbox, opening it with a key from the house set provided by his father, and adding to its contents from the many bundles of papers neatly stacked on the metal shelves of the safe.

He closed the safe, turned the key, and spun the dial. Then Naldo went through the house, unlocking doors, then closing and locking them again, As he went, he left a small but unobtrusive trail: on the hinge side of The Hide's door, a splinter of matchstick, tiny and crushed into the jamb; over the lock of the master bedroom, a hair from his own head, pressed into place with two pinheads of wax. On the carpet, across the locked doorway of his uncle's old smoking room, he laid a tiny piece of cotton, matching the carpet itself, but left in such a way that it would be moved should the door be unlocked and opened. There was a sliver of paper tucked into another lock; another shaving of matchstick jammed into one of the doors downstairs, and telltale sprinkles of breadcrumbs, fresh on the stairs, invisible unless you went down on your hands and knees to look.

He set further traps, on the rear door and the windows, sprinkling an almost invisible powder, a fine aerosol foot spray he had discovered in Germany, inside the door and along the sills. He also did this to the front door interior, and, in the sixty seconds between setting the alarms and leaving, he arranged more small pieces of cotton.

As he drove away, on that night, he patted the strongbox on the passenger seat beside him. He had undertaken not to examine the files, and other items locked away in the box except in specific circumstances.

Now, as he stood waiting for the elevator, Naldo decided the time was almost with them for the opening of the box.

2

The telephone rang three times during the morning. Emma answered the first call and shouted to Barbara, "Daddy's not in, is he?"

" 'Fraid not. For him? Let me have it." She took the instrument. The voice at the distant end was cockney. "Just wanted a word with Mr. Railton, like."

"Sorry, he's out all day. Can I get him to ring you?"

"Nah, I'll ring back. Maybe tonight. Cheers," and the line went dead.

Barbara answered the second call, just after eleven. She knew immediately that it was long distance, from Europe, the line had that odd echo. She said "Hello" three times. Then, "Who is it?" before she heard a receiver go down. But she instinctively felt the line was still open. It was as though her senses could detect another ear listening.

The third call came just after midday.

"Barbara?" he said, as though uncertain of her voice.

"Yes, who . . . ?"

"Philip. Look, I'm calling from home. From Sussex. I can only stay on a minute. Just wanted to hear your voice."

"Philip! What the hell're you playing at?" She was angry, and had felt used after the odd call to his Hans Crescent number. Yet, now, as she heard his voice, she felt a twinge low down within her. Almost a pain. A desire. For a second, in her confusion, she did not even hear what he was saying. She had a need and desire for Naldo, yet this was different, as though the very fact of it being illicit made it more urgent.

"What d'you mean, what am I playing at?"

"Your Hans Crescent number."

"What about it?"

"I rang there. Stupid, silly thing to do. Just wanted to hear the telephone ringing. They'd never heard of you at that number."

"That's crazy, Barbara! Impossible! There hasn't been anyone there since the crack of dawn yesterday. You must've been misrouted."

"They gave your number, Philip. I felt a fool. Some people called Barnes."

"And what was the number you rang?"

"The same as I rang the night we went out."

"The number. Repeat it."

"One minute." She rummaged in her handbag for the little black address book. She had copied the number across one of the blank back pages, disguising it with doodles and other numbers. She had not lived with Naldo without learning some tricks. (Whose number's this? Let me see. Haven't got a clue. Some party guest, I suppose. Couldn't have been important. There's no name next to it.) She read the number into the phone.

"Barbara! You've got it wrong. Last two digits. They're four-three, not three-four."

"But it's the number I called you on the other night."

"Couldn't have been. You must have reversed that last pair of digits when you dialed. You sure you've got them written down like that?"

She repeated them.

"Well, you got them right the other night. Look, change them around now so we get no more mistakes."

She obeyed him automatically, then wondered why the hell she was doing this. "Philip," she said, "I really don't think this is a very good idea."

"What?"

"You ringing me like this."

"Why the hell not? I'm going to see you after Christmas, aren't I?"

"I don't know. Really, I don't know. It's . . . "

"It *was* very good. It can be good again. Not as if we're hurting anyone. I just called you to say I was thinking about you."

"Perhaps you shouldn't."

"Well, I was, and I've rung you. I'll ring again when I'm back in town. Okay?"

She was silent, and he repeated the "Okay?"

"I suppose so," she said. "But I can't promise to see you, Philip. I must go."

"See you soon. All my love."

She dialed the Hans Crescent number again, this time reversing the last two digits. It rang and rang.

"Nurrrp-Nurrrp," she said, half aloud, seeing the bedroom of his flat as clearly as she saw the embossed Sanderson's wallpaper of her own hall. "What the hell!" She slammed down the receiver. Naldo's my husband. I love him like nobody else. I have nice kids. All this for a few minutes' pleasure. It's just the same thing with a different body. It's nothing. Forget it. Eat. Lunchtime.

3

"Anyone come looking for me?"

Barbara thought he sounded tense, strung out, unlike the Naldo she knew in London. In London there was not the stress of Berlin or other foreign postings.

"A couple of telephone calls. One from somewhere on the Continent, I think. Rang off."

He thought that *she* had an edge of worry, a subtext in the way she replied. "And the other?" Naldo asked.

"Cockney accent. Sounded like the real thing. Said he'd phone back, later."

"Nobody at the door? No telephone repair men? Meter readers? Nobody left alone?" These were standard questions he asked Barbara regularly. She was also suspicious of any callers, official or not. Like all SIS officers, Naldo was a target, abroad or at home. He knew his own Service would periodically tap into his line, and it was more likely under the present circumstances. That was easy enough from the exchange, or junction boxes. What he always feared were the new, soulless, "infinity" bugs which, when inserted into a telephone physically would make the instrument into a live microphone. Every word spoken near the system could be heard by unseen listeners.

"I might have to go out tonight," he told her. "Let you know in a minute. Have to use the magic phone." He laughed, and knew it sounded false.

"Tea?" She felt Philip Hornby moving within her, but knew she really wanted Naldo to take her now, lead her upstairs, strip her and take her hard, even hurt her for being such a silly bitch and letting it happen.

"Yes, tea. Super. I won't be long."

God, she had almost confessed to him. She went through to the kitchen, filled the kettle and switched it on. As she waited, Barbara unconsciously smoothed her hair with the palm of her right hand.

From the study telephone, Naldo dialed his cousin Andrew's office. Yes, Mr. Railton was in, but with a client.

"Then you'll have to disturb him, I'm afraid. This is his cousin, Donald. Tell him it's urgent family business."

He was kept waiting, hanging on for a good five minutes. Then—

"Naldo? What's all this? I'm in conference."

"I have to ask you something, Andrew. It's very official, and we need to know now."

"What?"

"Does Aunt Phoebe still have the keys to Eccleston Square?"

"Yes. Why?" Andrew would make a good team with Willis Maitland-Wood. Willis playing soft to his curt, hard, and brutal.

"My immediate superiors want to go through your father's papers. Official. They can get a search warrant if you insist."

108

"They can do what they like, as long as they leave the silver alone. You be with them?"

"Probably."

"Hold you responsible, then, if anything that comes to me grows legs. As for Pa's papers, they can have the bloody lot, and those damned-fool toy soldiers. You'll have to get the keys off Mother. But the bloody house is yours now, anyway. Well, it will be, once we've gone to probate, and that's only weeks away. So it's up to you, Donald. Do what you bloody like."

He dialed Redhill Manor and spoke to Sara, who sounded depressed, as though Phoebe's grief had got to her. "Just tell her there are confidential documents that Caspar's office wants. I've informed Andrew." A courier would be at Redhill in the next couple of hours to pick up the keys. "Sara, love, could you make sure the keys are all there, and fastened in a thick envelope, addressed to Willis. Yes, *that* Willis. Willis Maitland-Wood."

On the scrambler he told Maitland-Wood that the keys would be ready if he sent someone to Redhill for them, and yes, he was quite prepared to be there himself. It was arranged for eight o'clock the following morning.

So, tonight, old son, he thought, we have to take a look-see. Find out if they have a team already on the place. Or if they've been taking a sneak preview.

He put on his heavy coat, stuffed the Eccleston Square keys in one pocket and a powerful flashlight in the other, rammed a hat on his head, and kissed Barbara.

"Naldo, a hat. You never wear a hat, except . . ."

"I won't be late." He saw the anxiety come welling into her eyes.

"Please be careful, Naldo. Please. I thought, now that we were home . . ."

"It's something and nothing. Don't worry your pretty head." Another squeeze. From upstairs he heard the Beatles drifting down, twisting and shouting.

His hand was on the doorknob when the telephone rang. Naldo picked it up and heard the overseas static, together with the faint whir of power being pulled from the line as Maitland-Wood's listeners strained to capture any illicit conversation.

"I have a call from Rome. A personal call," said an impersonal operator. "It's for a Mr. Diamond. Mr. Sam Diamond."

Naldo felt his heart leap into his mouth, he knew the sensation well, and could even recall the time when he thought the phrase melodramatic. "I think you must have a wrong number. No Mr. Diamond here."

"That is London, Kensington 0097?"

"It is, but there's no Mr. Diamond."

"Hold on a moment, please." There were faint stirrings on the line. Then, "Sorry you've been troubled. Italian gentleman. Seems to have given me the wrong number."

Naldo grunted and slowly put down the receiver. Bees buzzed in his head. When they checked, he was sure they would find the call genuine enough, a digit or two off, with a Mr. Sam Diamond at the other end. Arnie had made the rules about any of his telephone calls. An Italian gentleman wanting a Mr. Diamond meant that Arnold Farthing had been recalled to Washington. If it was a Mr. Sam Diamond, it meant that he was going invisible. Within the next hour Arnold Farthing would cease to exist. He would be a man who had dropped into a hole. The warning would mean that Naldo should follow him as quickly as possible.

He kissed Barbara, and then gave her a hug, holding her to him as though he did not want to leave.

At the door, he said, "Don't talk to any strange men."

Outside, as he turned towards Kensington Gardens, Naldo glanced back. A small black van was trying to get into a parking space almost opposite his house. Why were they always so bloody obvious in their own country? he wondered.

SEVEN

1

The Christmas lights straddled Regent Street. Angels raised long golden trumpets between Austin Reed and Aquascutum. Kaleidoscopic multicolored snowflakes shifted almost wearily in the cold December breeze that would bring rain before the night was over.

The traffic was clogged both ways, and Naldo had the taxi set him down at the corner of Denman Street and Shaftesbury Avenue. He walked through the short narrow thoroughfare, passing the Piccadilly Theatre, and crossing to the Regent Palace Hotel.

It was many years since he had taken this route. He remembered it last in 1944, replete with whores and soldiers on leave. The whores had beats all around this web of streets in Soho then. They used to call them the Piccadilly Commandos. Now, with the Street Offences Act, they were all but gone, leaving their traces only in the doorway of a clip joint. Unsummoned music crossed his mind. "String of Pearls," "American Patrol," and "Pennsylvania 65000." He thought of Arnie, and hoped he had made it to their agreed hole. As he approached the Regent Palace he saw, in a flash across the screen of his mind, the pink villa, the lake and ferries churning white under the mountains.

He walked through the crowded lobby of the hotel like someone who had every right to be there, stopping at the double bank of elevators where he loitered, looking for any familiar face before he took the side entrance that led into Glasshouse Street, around the side of the hotel. He crossed the street, heading towards the line of arches around the Piccadilly Underground station, dodging taxis and private cars. A cabdriver yelled an obscenity as he had to brake. "You too!" Naldo snarled under his breath.

Now, he wondered how much surveillance they had on him because of his dead uncle, so he began to go through a whole series of dry-cleaning moves which took the best part of an hour, by foot, Underground, and taxi. He ended up, deep in the heart of Belgravia, by a row of telephone kiosks half a mile from Eccleston Square, one hundred percent certain that no watchers were onto him. They would be there, though, near the Eccleston Square house. He would be exposed to them, and they could not be avoided.

Inside the first kiosk, he took out loose change and dialed Herbie Kruger's number in St. John's Wood. Herbie grunted his answer after four rings.

"Herb?"

"Yeah." At his home, on his private line, Herbie liked to let people think he had never learned to speak on the telephone. He shouted always, as though contact could only be made in that manner. Naldo had seen and heard him in offices, and on operations. His telephone manner at all other times was perfect.

"We meet for a drink tomorrow, Herb?" Naldo did not introduce himself, or say why he was calling from a public booth.

"Sure. When? Lunchtime or evening?"

"Make it lunch, okay?"

"Sure. Where you want to go?"

"Blue Posts, Berwick Street. How does that sound?"

"No problem. I got a wonderful story to tell you. You know, a joke." He pronounced it "yoke."

"Look forward to it. Say, quarter-to-one?"

"Anything you want. See you then. I'm not at work for two days' minimum." It was Herbie who hung up.

On returning from his posting in Berlin, one of the first things Naldo had done was to take a long country walk with Big Herbie. They had gone to Redhill for a weekend, and during the outing, on open downland, below the skyline and where nobody could possibly have a directional mike on them, the former controller with his former agent had worked out a series of drops, meeting places, and telephone codes. It was a simple intuitive action. Naldo had described it to Herbie as "A little secret money in the bank. We'll keep it between ourselves for a rainy day." Even then, he realized, the first signs of disillusionment were showing themselves. He had begun to mistrust his masters.

He recalled the conversation now as he walked away from the three crimson kiosks, and into his head came some lines from a sentimental Sinatra ballad, something about leftover dreams, and the rainy day they all told him about.

"Funny, that rainy day is here," the recognizable voice sang in his ear.

Neither Herbie nor Naldo would be at the Blue Posts public house in Berwick Street at twelve forty-five the next day. But, by midnight tonight, Herbie would be waiting for him, together with the required material. Herbie's "Anything you want," and "yoke," had signaled that he had managed to get the necessary material from the Blunt interrogation tapes and their transcripts.

Naldo trawled the Eccleston Square area for another half-hour, trying to spot watchers, and knowing in his heart that by now they would certainly have the house covered. He had to go in, check the snares, then get out fast. Doing it would undoubtedly alert the hounds. He could take every precaution, but BMW would know, in minutes, once he was inside the place.

Here's that rainy day they all told me about. Arnie gone to ground. Uncle Caspar's body lies a-moldering in his grave, but his life goes marching on under a microscope. The long and winding road that leads to Oleg's door. The Railtons and the Farthings sapped with a blunt instrument. Suspicion sat, like Long John Silver's parrot, on every shoulder—

> Suspicion always haunts the guilty mind;
> The thief doth fear each bush an officer.

There were no odd signs in Eccleston Square. A few parked cars. Nobody in them as far as he could see. Two houses had their ground-floor curtains drawn back, and you could glimpse the signs of imminent Christmas bright within; trees and flashing fairy-lights, cards on red ribbon. Other houses had their drapes drawn tight against the night and all its evils. The famous Railton place, which had seen many secrets walking to and fro, talking of Lord knows what mischief, stood in darkness, the front door bright and clear in the light from the nearby streetlamp.

In his pocket, Naldo's hand closed over the keys and flashlight. He sucked in breath, took a step into the light from the darkness of the wall where he had been sheltering. He hesitated for two seconds, no more, then walked quickly, with purpose, towards the building he had known since childhood as Uncle Caspar's house. Behind him he was certain he heard a scrape—a movement, as though another night animal of the city had taken a pace forward. Even the chill damp air was impregnated with heresy.

He turned the Banham key twice, hearing the dead lock click back, followed by the feel of tension on the spring. His hands touched only

113

the doorknob and he used his foot to kick the door closed behind him. Flashlight on. Sixty seconds to get across the eight paces, using the stepping-stones of memory to avoid the scattered lengths of cotton, to the small closet which housed the master control for the sensors. He did not even use the flashlight, for he knew the layout backwards. The little red light was beginning to blink off the seconds as he found the hole and inserted the second key he had sorted out by feel in his hand. The light blinked off. He was in, and the alarms were deactivated.

Naldo switched on the flashlight, running it around the hallway, focusing on the door. Really he did not need to go further, the transparent spray of powder on the inside of the front door had turned white and was smudged; while the tiny pieces of cotton he had arranged in a prescribed order were scattered, or had disappeared, proof positive that someone had been here since he had set the snares.

Slowly, he made his way through the house, and everything bore the indicators of penetration: from the crushed breadcrumbs on the stairs, to the missing slivers of matchstick and moved pieces of cotton. Inside, all the rooms were in order, nothing seemed to have been touched, but all the snares had sprung. A very professional job but for the alarms he had set, the miniature gins and mantraps. Spoor had been left screaming in the house, probably by several people, for, in particular, the breadcrumbs had been crumbled deep into the fibers of the carpet, the tiny pieces of paper, and slivers of matchstick were gone or had fallen from place, while the powder, sprayed at vantage points, was smudged and scattered heavily.

In The Hide, the safe had been tampered with. They had taken care to reset the numbers as he had left them—4-2-9—but the careful trap he had laid within was gone.

Naldo came sadly down the stairs, keeping close to the banister. Just as he had felt violated when they told him of the investigation into Caspar's working life, Naldo now sensed some filth rubbing off on his own skin. They had already tried to rape this house in Eccleston Square, and he was disgusted, feeling, as his American Cousins would say, sick to his stomach.

Quietly he opened the front door, meaning to go back and deal with the alarms. They stepped in front of him, one from each side, blocking his exit.

"Sorry, Mr. Railton, sir," said Max. "It's the Deputy CSS. Mr. Maitland-Wood wants you back at the shop."

Max's partner came in close and frisked Naldo expertly, and very fast. They took the keys and the flashlight, one of them going in to switch the alarm system. Max said again that he was sorry. "You're like those fucking SS Kat-Zed commandants, Max," Naldo barked.

"I'm only doing my duty. Only obeying orders." Max shrugged, looked away, and shrugged again as they led Naldo off to the waiting car.

2

Much as Naldo had expected, the vultures were gathered in Maitland-Wood's office. Tubby Fincher was there, and a sleek, trendy young man he recognized from the department they jokingly called Legal and General. The lawyer had the nerve to give Naldo a winning smile, which was more than anyone else was inclined to do. The young man was called Lofthouse, Naldo remembered.

Maitland-Wood wore his hanging judge look, and Tubby merely appeared to be embarrassed, like a young relative suddenly involved in an unnecessary and violent squabble between an uncle and aunt.

"Well, well, well. So the ingrate wanderer returns." BMW threw his hand dramatically towards the same chair that Naldo had occupied earlier in the day. "I trust, young Railton, that you have an explanation that will hold water."

Naldo was not going to play those kind of games. "And I trust *you* have a similar explanation, Mr. Maitland-Wood, sir."

"Don't be flippant. I want to know why you were in that house, how you obtained a second set of keys, and what you tampered with?"

Max whispered something to Fincher, then disappeared.

"He carried nothing from the house," Fincher said for BMW's benefit.

"Where did you get the keys? Why did you enter that house?" Maitland-Wood repeated.

Naldo smiled at him, knowing the smile was a smirk and would infuriate BMW even more. "You know any reason why I should answer that?" He continued to smirk.

"By God, I'll see you out of the Service, Railton. Just as we *will* get to the bottom of this, and probably hang out your Uncle Caspar's ghost where the Press and scum can destroy and exorcise it once and for all."

The smirk left Naldo's lips. "If you'd care to come into some public place and say that to me in front of disinterested witnesses, I'll sue you blind, Maitland-Wood. I don't care a tinker's fuck . . . "

115

"Watch your language," BMW snapped, starting to go crimson.

Naldo gave a short, derisory snort. "Then watch your words, *sir*, or I'll have *you* for breakfast."

A vein stood out, throbbing on Maitland-Wood's temple, and his cheeks blushed scarlet. At last he took two deep breaths. When he spoke it was with an unfamiliar, soft and calm voice, which made him sound even more sinister.

"Donald Railton," he almost whispered. "You kindly got Lady Phoebe to let me have the keys for the Eccleston Square house, your late Uncle Caspar's property. I understood that you had also approached your cousins, Alexander and Andrew, who were willing to extend permission for us to perform a search on the Eccleston Square property. It was arranged that we would do that, accompanied by yourself, in a family watchdog capacity, at eight o'clock tomorrow morning. I was concerned about you. Truly *concerned.* Naldo, I understand how even the thought of Caspar's life being investigated must alarm and hurt you." He could not know, only guess, how more alarmed Naldo had become since BMW had adopted the soft, sympathetic, approach.

"I instructed Tubby, here, to get some of our own watchers in. Naturally we want to keep this within the family, so to speak. The family as a whole, not merely *your* family. You must see that I was anxious when they told me you were in the house."

Naldo allowed his smirk to die. Fight fire with fire. He answered in a reassuring tone. "You were only concerned for two reasons, Mr. Maitland-Wood. First, because you do not have the correct facts. That's my fault. I should have told you the house is, to all intents and purposes, now mine. Caspar left it to me: in his will."

The mask slipped. "What?"

"You had no idea? I'm sorry, but, yes, for some time I've known it's mine. Caspar knew Phoebe didn't want to live there without him, and, for his own reasons, he was against the property leaving the family. He wouldn't pass it on to either of his sons. That his daughter, Hester, might want it, never crossed his mind. That's not surprising, since she couldn't even be bothered to come over from the States for her father's funeral."

Hester, at the age of forty-four, was living in Virginia with Luke Marlowe, son of one of the Farthing aunts and a distant cousin to Arnold. The pair spent most of their time just outside Williamsburg, where they sometimes "donned the dress" and worked as potters in the showplace of Historic Williamsburg. Hester had made it plain that she wanted nothing to do with the family trade. They would protest against anything, and the FBI had their photographs on file, taken at marches for black emancipation and the banning of nuclear weapons. During the war, Hester had served with the WRNS, but had turned into such a bubbling chatterbox that nobody dared to repeat a secret in front of her. Now, all that liveliness had gone, her heart and intelligence poured into good works and political causes about which she felt strongly. "Hester's like a Catholic convert," old Dick would say at Redhill, laughing. "Her conscience doth make cowboys of us all."

"So the keys you used . . . ?" Maitland-Wood's quiet voice had turned throaty.

Naldo nodded. "Were mine, yes."

After a long silence, Maitland-Wood asked what the other reason was. He looked troubled, as some high-powered executive will look when the signs of a wrong decision show on the balance sheet.

"Because you've already had the house turned over. As it was recent, I can only presume you sent a team in very fast, as soon as you received the keys. In and out like the ferrets your people are."

"Someone has been in the house?" Maitland-Wood sounded genuinely shocked.

"You know they have, Willis. Come on. How were they to know I'd salted the place? I did it some time ago, and they've left trademarks all over the house. They find anything interesting?"

"It's preposterous." Still maintaining dignity.

"If so, then you'll have to get the SB to turn it over. You're going to need a search warrant now. I imagine Caspar's lawyers'll hold you off in my name. I was trying to do the right thing. I wanted to check, to see if you'd jumped the gun."

"I see." He looked down at the marble inlay on his desk. "So we have to get your permission now?"

"Yes."

"Did you find anything interesting in the house, Naldo?"

"Not a thing . . . " He was about to continue when the telephone gave a discreet buzz. Tubby Fincher reached for it, said "yes" a couple of times, then, "I'll ask him." He covered the mouthpiece with one hand, speaking low to Maitland-Wood. "Paul Schillig," he mouthed. "Wants a meeting urgently."

Maitland-Wood took the phone from Fincher. "Yes, Paul?" They could all hear the electronic murmur from the earpiece. "Well, if it's *that* urgent, you'd better come straight over. No. No, I can't oblige you. We're in the middle of a small problem here." The voice at the distant end cracked again. "Really?" Maitland-Wood sounded intrigued and surprised at the same time. "Right. Fifteen minutes." He put the telephone down. "Schillig," he said looking around the room. "He has some disturbing news of an old friend of yours, Railton. Arnold Farthing seems to have gone invisible, as they say."

Naldo tried to look suitably alarmed. Paul Schillig was the Agency's Station Chief in Grosvenor Square, with cover as political affairs officer. The Agency, like the British SIS, had once given local Embassy-based chiefs of station and their staffs cover as visa- and passport-control officers. Now, most diplomats, and other members of intelligence organizations, knew that an American Embassy Political Affairs Officer was more often than not the local CIA Resident. If hostile embassies wanted to find out who was Agency material, they looked at the political affairs officers, and the list of FSR officers, Foreign Service Officers (Reserve), and they could take their pick. CIA people never had full Foreign Service cover.

Paul Schillig was very tall. He had unfashionably short light hair, a charming deceptive smile and a manner calculated to put even the most suspicious at ease. One wag in the SIS had referred to him as "Paul Schillig, he who makes Steve McQueen look deformed." It was an accurate observation.

Naldo, together with Lawyer Lofthouse, was banished to the anteroom when Schillig arrived. He came casting smiles and goodwill around him like some foreign prince. His height, just under seven feet, made everyone feel like a child in his presence.

In the anteroom, Naldo picked up the latest copy of *Intelligence & National Security* and half read an article on the part played by the old Hungarian branch of the KGB, the AVH, in the 1956 uprising. He read the words but took in little of the meaning.

After twenty minutes or so, the door opened and Tubby Fincher beckoned Naldo into the office. Maitland-Wood was still at his desk, looking distracted, while Paul Schillig, stretched out in one of the easy chairs, had allowed the perpetual mask of one who lived without friction to slip. A sense of worry filled the air.

"Sit down, Naldo." There was neither suspicion, anger, pleasure nor pain in the way he spoke. BMW, when pressed, could be a first-rate counterintelligence officer. The pompous bombast was simply another facet of character, used, Naldo often thought, as carefully as an actor might use false hair.

"You've worked with Arnie Farthing in the past, Naldo?" Schillig's accent was neither mid-Atlantic nor English. It leaned towards the kind of English you heard spoken among dons and fellows in university cities, with an occasional lapse of "Kan't" instead of "Carn't."

Naldo nodded. "It must be on record," was all he said. He did not ask why the question had been put.

Silence again, then Maitland-Wood turned to Schillig. "I think you should put Naldo in the picture. It seems we have to be nice to him if we're going to get to the heart of another matter. Though he has to answer an avalanche of queries." A trace of bitterness sounded below the words, as though the subtext of his sentence was, "You're not off the hook yet, Railton."

Paul Schillig moved in his chair, turning his face towards Naldo. Fixing him with clear blue eyes deceptively lacking in guile, "Arnie's adrift," he said, as though that told the whole story. "AWOL. Gone native."

Naldo waited for the many sequels. Finally Schillig gave an encapsulated picture. "He was recalled to Washington. I gather Jim Angleton's boys weren't satisfied with some recent report. They wanted to watch his face as he talked to them."

Again, Naldo waited.

"He was in Berlin, as I suppose you know." This time Schillig waited and got no response. "Well, he packed a bag. Nothing spectacular, two suits, shirts, spare shoes. And he took a briefcase. The briefcase contained, to say the least, confidential documents. An Embassy driver went with him to the airport and left him at the departures entrance. It appears he went in. But he did not check in at the PanAm desk, which means he didn't take the flight. They were there to meet him at Dulles. Naturally, Arnie Farthing didn't turn up."

Thank heaven for that, Naldo thought. With luck he would be at their prescribed meeting place. If he played his cards in the right sequence, he would be with Arnie for dinner tomorrow night. As he thought about it, Naldo hardly heard Paul Schillig's next words. Even half-heard they shook him from any complacency, and made his stomach churn. He asked Schillig to repeat what he had just said.

"Someone using one of Arnie's identities flew out on an Air France flight to Paris. Another of his identities went out of Paris within an hour of arrival. He took a Dutch Airlines flight to Amsterdam, and a third cover went on. We've had a description from four people. It was Arnie. He took an Aeroflot direct flight to Leningrad. It was unscheduled." He lapsed, pronouncing it "skeduled." "The flight should have gone direct from LHR." Schillig was careful to use the acronym for London Heathrow. "Just after the flight was airborne the captain asked permission to divert to Amsterdam, on instructions from his superiors. The bastards do it all the time, so everything adds up to Arnie doing a leap.''

"What about Gloria and the kids?'' Instinctively, Naldo's mind shot to the possible repercussions in Washington. By asking about Farthing's wife and children he held off any thoughts of how he would be compromised if Arnie had, indeed, leapt across the curtain.

"Worrying.'' Schillig gave a sigh. "Gloria sent the boys to her sister, Esther, a couple of days ago. We haven't dredged up the whole route yet, but we're pretty certain she sent them to Dulles via France. Then she took a flight to Italy. It puts her in the frame.''

"Jesus,'' Naldo muttered, knowing he had to tread as delicately as a man walking on thawing ice. He could not believe that Arnold had been turned; could not face the labyrinth of deception which might follow.

"I don't think He's going to help us now,'' Schillig said.

"Did he have much . . . '' Naldo started to ask.

Schillig frowned, then said, "As chief of Berlin Station he had the lot: names; cryptos; CI ops; CE ops; what we knew; what we didn't know; who'd been doubled; names of targets. Damage assessment'll go on for months. We're going to have to break camp in Berlin . . . ''

"If it's true.'' Naldo was surprised at his own positive manner.

"Meaning *you* know something we don't?'' Maitland-Wood asked.

"No, but meaning that I wouldn't blow Berlin until there've been talks with Jim Angleton.''

"Why do you say that?'' For the first time Paul Schillig looked really suspicious. He also fired the question fast, from the lip.

"Because Arnold was—is—a pro. He's under Angleton's discipline. Just as I suspect you are, Paul.''

Schillig unwound his long body. "I was authorized to pass on the information. Langley said you people have need-to-know.''

Naldo thought, I bet they did. "And are you going to break camp?'' he asked, looking up at the tall American.

"If orders come through, then the Berlin boys'll do all that.''

"Hang on.'' Naldo also rose. "Mother's fed you this story. You got any collateral? Any *real* evidence apart from a lengthy coded signal?''

"That's real enough.''

"No, it's a signal. Don't tell me signals never lie, Paul, because we all know they do. You received a signal in high-class cipher, your eyes only, I presume.''

"Naturally.'' The American sounded gritty.

"It gave you some bare facts, which you cannot check, right?"

"It gave me facts. I believe signals like that when they come out of Langley. It was high-priority stuff."

"And we all know Langley, Paul. They can be as devious as the Ks at times."

"Watch your mouth." Schillig took one step towards aggressiveness.

"No, I'm just giving you an alternate, Paul. The signal gave you information—for you and you alone, okay?"

No response.

"Information for Station Chief, London, right?"

Schillig gave a little nod.

"And it also said, pass all this on to the Brits, while you're at it? Just like that? *Eyes Only,* but let the Brits have it as well? And we all know what you think of our Service. You think we dribble like a tap that needs a new washer. Seriously, Paul, don't you think that a signal as rich, and so full of anxiety as this one, would instruct you to cover your mouth with sticking plaster?"

"I only know what I know. The signal authorized me to pass it to C."

"So you passed it to his deputy, the ADC, and one controller who, if I read Mr. Maitland-Wood correctly, is not really to be trusted. Why did you guys want me to hear this anyway?"

"We thought, Naldo," BMW at his most pompous. "We thought you might be able to throw some light on Arnold. You're very close."

"We *were* very close. Worked together; played together at one time. We're related by marriage. That's all. I'd like it put on record that I for one do not believe Arnie Farthing's sold out, gone over, or slipped through the curtain. I believe this entire thing from Langley is part of an elaborate operation. What's more, I want nothing to do with it." He sounded very convincing. In his head and heart he was as sick as a cat.

Schillig left shortly after Naldo's final outburst, and it was Tubby who escorted him to the door. When Fincher returned he was carrying a flagged buff folder. Maitland-Wood took it from him and began to browse through the file within. Finally he looked up at Naldo. "I suppose I should really keep you here all night," he said. "But I'm inclined to think you won't do anything stupid."

"Thank you for your confidence." Naldo lit a cigarette and blew smoke towards BMW.

"I see here that you have four current identities running excluding your real one."

Naldo thought for a moment, holding one hand up and counting on his fingers. "You've got a good filing system. Yes, four and my own. Correct."

"Those identities are withdrawn as from now. You'll tell Tubby here exactly where the idents can be located. He will then come with you and bring each one back here. I presume your own papers are at your home?"

"Correct, plus one of the identities."

"Max will go with you both. If you had any thoughts of, perhaps, following, or even trying to find, your friend Arnold, that will discourage you. Tubby and Max'll leave you at home once the idents have been collected. We'll send a car for you at seven-thirty tomorrow morning, and do the Eccleston Square house. That all right by you, Naldo?"

"Perfectly." Naldo smiled broadly. "I'm not going to run anywhere, Willis. There's too much to be done here." In the back of his head he thought of the fifth identity which nobody knew about, kept against a sea of trouble such as this.

"Shall we go, Tub?" he asked, wanting to move. What he had in mind would keep him very busy if he was going to put a lot of miles between himself and London before the car arrived at seven-thirty in the morning.

EIGHT

1

"I'd rather be waiting till after dusk, if that'd be all the same to you m'dear." The man was big, and seemingly ageless, with a great barrel-chest, broad shoulders, thick muscular arms, and massive hands. His face was weathered by wind and sea spray, hair gray and cut short, almost to the scalp. He wore jeans tucked into high boots and a roll-necked woolen jersey that had once been navy blue. His name was Barzillai Beckeleg and he lived in a small, remote cottage, hard by the sea between the Lizard Point and St. Keverne on the South Cornish coast. Nowadays he made a living from his lobster pots, and a daily boat hire, or pleasure trips, in the summer, with one or two devious bits of sailing thrown in. He owned two boats: one a small smack which he used for the lobsters and fishing; the other a converted German E boat which he had bought for a song in 1946, refitted, painted eggshell blue, and registered as *Overlord*. It was this latter boat he used for the hiring, day trips, and the nefarious business on the side.

Naldo had known him during the war. Beckeleg had often worked with the Special Operations Executive, and SIS people, taking agents from the Helford River and ferrying them to the coast of Brittany. Dear dead Caspar had been full of stories about the man, though he never repeated his true name.

"If us was to leave now," Beckeleg said, "we'd be caught in the open sea in daylight, and them customs and coastguard bastards're worse than the bloody Jerries these days." He gave Naldo a heavy wink. "You'm gonna be all right yere. Safe enough in my little cottage, Mr. Provin. I be goin' to Truro anyhow, this morning. Be back late afternoon though, and you'm not be havin' to worry 'bout me. I bent gonna tell no one you'm 'ere. Rest up, that's my advice, m'dear. We'm gonna leave tonight. After the moon's gone."

Naldo really wanted to be away and in France by late that same day.

123

He had approached Beckeleg's cottage on foot, in the cold darkness, after a night of hide and seek during the long drive from London to this place, lying almost at the point where England was tipped suddenly into the Atlantic at Land's End. He had watched the small white building, just above the rocks, and approached only when he saw the lights come on, and a wisp of smoke eddy and reach for the sky from its chimney. Even then, he had moved with stealth towards the door. Now it was almost seven in the morning. They would have been looking for him, he calculated, since around midnight, maybe even before then. "It means you'll be making the trip back in daylight," he said, still trying to seduce the wily old man.

"Ah, let me worry 'bout that, Mr. Provin. Might even stay over in France a couple of days. There be a nice young widow woman I sometimes visit in Concarneau, which is where I be a takin' you." He gave another broad wink.

Naldo laughed. "Still the same Barzillai," he said, remembering the tale of how this fisherman had stayed four days in St. Malo, right under the eyes of the German garrison, waiting for an agent. It was said that Barlow, as they all called him in those days, had passed the time with a very pretty Breton girl, young enough to have been his daughter. The agent had reported that the girl wept and clung to Beckeleg on their departure.

"All right, Barzillai." Naldo had no option but to wait, and do as the man stipulated.

"There be rashers and eggs in me little galley there." Beckeleg nodded towards the small kitchen which, like the rest of the cottage, was as neat and tidy as you would expect from a man used to living in the tight quarters of small seagoing ships. "You'm keep your head down, Mr. Provin. And don't worry, now. I 'ave too many good memories of you and your uncle ever to let 'ee down."

Already, Beckeleg had given Naldo tea—strong and sweet, thick enough to stand a spoon in. They talked about what must be done later, and presently the seaman left with a suggestion that Naldo should lie doggo and not open the door to a soul. "I'll give you the old V-sign—ta-ta-ta-TAT—when I get back." He thumped the table with a clenched fist to bang out the Morse V. In the war it had been used in many different ways to keep morale high at home and in the Nazi-occupied countries of Europe. Many had realized, for the first time, that it was the opening of Beethoven's Fifth Symphony. A famous tympanist had made a recording of the V with a drumbeat which became a stirring rallying sign to all when it was broadcast each evening. The sound ran through Naldo's head now, bringing back memories of bad times which, in the light of his present circumstances, seemed good by comparison. At least in those days there was a common enemy. Now you could not tell who was friend or foe.

He cooked six rashers of bacon and two eggs, frying a piece of bread in the fat and eating it from a plate on his knees, his chair pulled up in front of Beckeleg's fire, for the day was cold with more bitter weather forecast. While eating, Naldo thought of all that had happened during the night, from the moment he left the shop to this point of arrival in Cornwall.

2

Naldo could not understand Maitland-Wood's naiveté over the question of his four identities—five including his real one. Identities were what the American Agency referred to as backstops, not simply the Flash-identities used on one-time operations that would not stand up under close scrutiny.

Naldo's idents were the full thing. All of them would hold water under any police or security service microscope. They included everything from passport, credit cards, DHSS card and number, diaries with details of next-of-kin, insurance policy numbers, and the like. Tied to these were travelers checks and currency for use in most European countries, plus pocket litter: stamped envelopes holding letters addressed to him at checkable addresses, ticket stubs, bills, Diners Card receipts—Diners had just opened an office in the UK; credit cards were to be the thing of the future.

A line from one of John Pudney's wartime poems ran silently through his mind.

> *Less said the better,*
> *The bill unpaid, the dead letter.*

From the shop, Maitland-Wood had sent them off together. Tubby Fincher and Max, the nursemaid, who never moved far from Naldo's side as he took them from place to place, retrieving heavy manila envelopes, each containing a different identity. One was in a locker at Waterloo Railway Station; another lodged in a safe deposit box at an hotel in Mayfair, where they knew him as Mr. Harvey Dunglass; a

125

third was in a similar box at The Ariel Hotel, near Heathrow Airport, where the staff spoke to him by name. "Haven't seen you for some time, Mr. Zlapka," the concierge said. Casimir Zlapka was a naturalized Englishman of Polish extraction.

The last identity, Menelaus Nochos, a Greek passport, was kept in Naldo's own study at the Kensington house. Barbara looked surprised and alarmed when he arrived home with Max and Tubby in tow, but Tubby, being something of a diplomat, put her at ease. "Naldo's got to hand over some stuff for fussy old MW." After that she offered them a drink, which they refused, Max standing outside the study door while Naldo took down a hollowed-out book, kept high on top of his shelves, containing the Greek identity. He then unlocked his desk and produced his personal passport. "You won't be taking my Diners, or bank cards, will you, Tub?" he asked with a smile.

"Don't think that'll be necessary, Nald. It's just that the Deputy CSS is concerned lest you do a midnight flit on him." Tubby took the passport. "You won't get very far without this, will you?"

"Wouldn't think of going, anyway." Naldo strolled into the hall and saw the pair out of the front door. When it was shut and they were gone, he leaned his back against the door, closed his eyes, and let out a long sigh.

"You all right, darling?" Barbara came into the hall.

He shook his head.

"Trouble at the mill?"

He nodded towards the telephone. "No strangers today, Barb? Nothing odd?" Their usual routine.

She shook her head and repeated the question. "Trouble at the mill?"

"Can't talk about it, sweetheart," he said. "Best you don't know anything." He moved away from the door and held her close. "Might have to disappear for a while." He stopped her mouth with his hand. "No, you must know nothing about that either. When they come and ask, say I just told you I would be away for a week or two."

"Nald, you haven't done anything stupid?" Alarm showed like an unpleasant insect, squirming deep in her eyes.

"*I've* done nothing wrong, and you must know that here and now. But they *will* come, and they'll put you to the question, like the bloody Inquisition. I'm saying no more. It's safer that way. Where're the kids?"

"Out." She looked troubled. "Emma's spending the night with nasty little Emmeline whatsername."

"Emmeline Major, my bestest friend in all the world. My cellmate," Naldo muttered, imitating their daughter's irritating singsong speech when she was talking of friends. The girl's language, brought home from school, was as arcane as that of Naldo's world.

"Art's gone to hear some amazing and fabulous group. He said he couldn't *afford* to turn down the chance of seeing them live."

"Singing amazing and fabulous songs which go, 'Needles and pins-uh; Needles and pins-uh,' I suppose. They all sound the bloody same, four repeated chords and inane lyrics." Naldo walked back to his study.

"You're a musical snob, Nald. They probably said the same about Schubert's songs," Barbara shouted after him.

"He had an excuse. They called it syphilis." He closed the door and sat down behind his desk.

Did BMW *really* believe that someone like him, Naldo Railton, deep into the secret arts since childhood, would not have a spare identity up his sleeve? The answer was probably yes. It was BMW's breed who had smiled upon Kim Philby for staying on and working late, when all CI officers worth their salt should have asked the obvious question—"Why the hell's Kim doing *that?* Best put some sound in and a pair of footmen on his tail." The Yanks would have fluttered him with the polygraph. The problem now was had BMW put some leeches onto *him?* And, if so, how would he get away with it?

He tapped a spot on the brass corner of the desk and heard the satisfying click as the secret drawer became unlatched. He remembered his father explaining how it worked when his parents handed the house over to him. "Used it a lot myself in the last show," James had said. "Wasn't here long enough for it to be a good hidey-hole in the first war." During the 1914–'18 war, James Railton had gone into Germany itself as an agent. They had caught him quickly and he suffered greatly at the hands of his captors who knew what his connections were in the British intelligence hierarchy.

Why do we all do it? Naldo asked himself now, looking down into the drawer as he pulled it from concealment, then was shocked to realize he was repeating one of his father's comments on the trade: "God knows why we do it. The politicians treat us like dirt; the military have trouble in believing us; the general public think of us as superannuated adventurers; while the novelists make a killing from presenting us as candyfloss killers."

Naldo took out a heavy envelope and the automatic pistol that lay in the drawer, placing them in a row, together with three spare clips

127

of ammunition, on the desk top. The envelope contained his personal secret life belt. His spare identity: French documents showing him as Michel Provin. Indeed, Naldo had built up the identity against a possible problem such as this, or an op that had gone wrong. He began to assemble it soon after the war ended in 1945. By 1953 the identity had grown, and had continued to put on flesh regularly from then on. Part of it was luck, around two percent. The rest, as Shakespeare said, is silence. In 1945, while engaged in trying to trace a missing collaborator, Naldo had come across the name Provin in both the Paris telephone directory and the obituary column of *Le Monde.* That was the luck. Silently through the years he availed himself of specialist knowledge to get a driver's license, passport, and other necessary documents.

He used the identity of Michel Provin at least once a year, an essential action, for he needed genuine visas and immigration stamps in the passports. Michel Provin was now on record in official files in several countries. With these documents, Naldo could move like a ghost through Europe. There was nothing, except his physical description, that could give him away, and there were methods of altering the description at least enough to put even the most dedicated skip-tracers off the scent.

Naldo cleaned out his pockets, placing some items into the concealed drawer, and others to one side for burning. He did not for one moment believe Arnie Farthing had slipped behind the curtain. All the information brought in by Paul Schillig was Arnie's way of conducting a paper chase. No, Naldo thought, Arnie's already there, sitting back, prepared to spend Christmas in the villa that was the dark hole in which they would hide and discuss the strategy of how were they to clear Caspar's reputation, and Dick's if necessary. How were they to make their own situations safe within the intelligence communities? How best to prove the Blunt evidence, whatever it was, as sham? How to reveal the truth about Oleg Penkovsky? Last, but of prime importance, how to cut through all this and put their fingers on the real person whom, by their dissembling, both Blunt and Penkovsky had covered in a smokescreen? There was certainly still some very well-placed penetration agent high in the pecking order, either in the Secret Intelligence Service, in London, or the Central Intelligence Agency, Washington. Possibly both.

As he thought of this last thing, Naldo picked up the small automatic pistol, checked that it was loaded, with a round in the chamber and the safety catch on. Together with the three spare magazines, he slipped it into his pocket. Then he burned the small pile of paper put to one side from his pockets, which he now salted with Michel Provin's litter and documents. Last of all, he took a very large, thick empty envelope from his supply in the desk, crossed to the corner of the study, and opened the small safe which was bolted to the wall, partly camouflaged by the imitation spines of books. From the safe he removed Caspar's metal box, which he unlocked, transferring the thick wedge of papers which lay inside, sealing them neatly into the big envelope. Then he left the box in plain view on one of his shelves, the key still in the lock.

After closing the safe, Naldo took a final look around the room. The envelope containing Caspar's papers was in his hand as he left to go upstairs. In the bedroom he dug around in one of the cupboards, eventually pulling out a gray canvas overnight bag. He laid the bulky envelope at the bottom of the bag, then packed a corduroy suit, brown shoes, two shirts, and some warm rollnecks, spare underwear, socks, and handkerchiefs.

From another drawer he took out two airline toilet sets, with their arrays of shaving cream, razors, comb, and eau de cologne. Downstairs again he opened another drawer in his desk. Inside lay a squirreled collection of hotel stickers and airline tags. When he had been in the novitiate of his trade, they had told him never to discard any piece of ID that might one day become useful. Since then, Naldo had kept everything from theater ticket stubs to airline tags. He chose an Air France tag, tying it to the bag's handle. Lastly he collected a couple of French paperbacks from his bookshelves and stuffed them into the bag. Then he zipped the whole thing and clicked its small padlock in place.

As he was finishing off, Barbara came in to ask about food. "I've made a goulash," she said.

Naldo laughed. "You mean *stew*." Barbara called all stews goulashes. It was fashionable, but as Naldo loathed paprika she could never cook the real thing.

"*You*, Naldo Railton, are a gastronomic cripple. Brute!" She saw the zippered bag and the light went out of her eyes. "So soon?"

He nodded.

"Stay for my goulash?"

"I guess I'll have time. Do me a favor."

"What?"

"Switch the lights off in the living room. I want to see if I have company."

At the door she paused. "This going to be very dangerous, Nald?"

129

"Irritating rather than dangerous. We'll talk over the stew. Just put out the lights."

"*And then put out the lights.*" She quoted *Othello* at him as though trying to keep up her spirits. She was back in less than a minute. "All dark. I'll serve in the kitchen, okay?"

Naldo nodded and went to the front room, closing the door behind him, then standing for a moment for his eyes to adjust. He reasoned that Maitland-Wood, if he had been left to run this by himself, could not have a large reserve of manpower for surveillance. Probably a pair of sentinels front and back. BMW would not have the bodies for more than two pairs, and he would never call in the Watchers of Five on something so delicate. There might just be a van, after all, he had spotted one earlier. His cooperation with the fifth floor might easily have caused the wheels to be removed.

At the window he moved the curtain a fraction, positioning himself to get the best view. The van he had seen trying to park had disappeared, but he caught a glimpse of a cigarette glowing in a doorway directly opposite. As though the hidden man had seen the movement of Naldo's curtain, he stepped forward onto the pavement for a moment. It was a wide street, but the sentinel certainly wanted to be seen. It would discourage Naldo from leaving the house and keep him guessing about any wheels that might be around. Naldo knew how to get out of that one, but there was always a risk. An intelligent guess was still two at the front and another pair watching the back.

On his way to the kitchen, he rummaged in the hall closet and found an old reversible coat and a battered, soft, checked fishing hat. He had worn neither in a long time and thought the hat originally belonged to his father.

Over the meal he told Barbara nothing new, but repeated that she should not show any signs of distress. "Just stick to the facts as I'm telling them to you now. I'll be away for a few days. Maybe a week or two."

"And you're not leaving an address?"

"No. If I telephone and you say, 'How nice of you to call,' I'll know you have company. Otherwise I'll probably keep it brief. They'll be listening. Do *not* ask where I'm calling from, whatever they tell you."

"And what might they tell me?"

"It's possible they'll say I've defected."

Her mouth dropped open.

"That will be either a lie or what they want to believe. You can say that I seemed worried tonight and that I mentioned Arnie a lot."

"Why Arnie?"

"Sorry." He shook his head. "I've been preoccupied, and I talked about Arnie. About old times with Arnie. You can fill in the rest—when you first met Arn and all that stuff."

She raised her eyes to the ceiling. "Two Across. The art of spying. Nine letters E-something-P-something-something-N-something-G-something."

"You've got it."

He went into the hall and dialed the shop, asking for the fifth floor. BMW was still there. "Willis," he said, "as we've got an early start I'd like to come in now. If you've an hour to kill I've some things that maybe you should hear about our American friend."

"Which American friend?"

"The one who seems to have won a gold medal for the high jump. You got a car to spare? One that can pick me up?"

There was only a brief pause. "You can have the spare bed in the DO's room. I'll send my own car. Bates is duty driver. You know Bates?"

"Safe as a rock. I'll be ready for him."

Naldo put on the coat and jammed the hat on his head. "How does that look?" he asked Barbara.

"Elegant. Old-fashioned, maybe even foreign, but piss-elegant."

Through the front room curtains Naldo saw the watcher across the street emerge and give some signal, scratching the back of his head. Then he walked down towards the Cromwell Road.

Fifteen minutes later the black Rover pulled up and tooted twice. Naldo kissed his wife, held her to him for a moment, then picked up the bag and left, hurrying to the car and settling in on the passenger side, slinging the bag into the back. He was relieved to see that Bates, a short, sleek man who always reminded Naldo of a whippet, was alone. "Evening, Mr. Railton. The boss says I've to go around the houses a couple of times."

"Good," Naldo said, taking out a pack of cigarettes. The topcoat was unbuttoned and after he had lit the cigarette he put the packet back into his pocket and wrapped his fingers around the pistol.

They circled the block twice, in moderate traffic. There was no sign of watchers, not even a car with a spotter in it. Spotters usually watched for tails, and Bates would have driven the block looking for an all-clear signal, such as hat on, or hat off, from a spotter had there been one. Naldo thought that Bates was too relaxed to have had any surveillance advice laid on him before leaving the shop. As it was he talked, an endless stream of knowledge. Naldo thought that Bates spent his spare time reading the Encyclopaedia Britannica. "You know,

Mr. Railton," he said, in his undisguised camp manner, "I read one of those Harold Robbins books on my holidays. It's taken a solid month of Jane Austen to get over it. There's some real rubbish published these days."

They were turning into Kensington High Street now, having run around the back of the Cromwell Road, then through Marloes Road.

"I'm a shade more adventurous than Jane Austen," Naldo said, slipping the pistol from his pocket, then reaching out with his left hand, under the dashboard, and pulling out the wires on the communications radio.

"What in God's name do you think you're doing, Mr. Railton? You can't do that! Oh, my goodness. What . . . ? Then he felt the pressure of the pistol in his side.

"Drive nice and easily, Mr. Bates, because I'm just desperate enough to use this." *Never, they taught, never ever place a weapon close to a man's flesh. It means you are too close, and the recipient, if trained, can take violent action before you have time to squeeze the trigger. There is one exception to this rule. It does not apply in a moving vehicle when your target is the driver and nobody else is traveling in the vehicle.* Jesus, Naldo thought, what a walking receptacle of strange information I have become. What a prize idiot. Naldo realized he was pushing the pistol so hard against Bates' ribs that he was causing the driver physical pain.

"Mr. Railton . . ." he began to whine. "But, Mr. Railton . . ."

"But me no buts, Bates. Just drive, within the correct limits, and take me to Heathrow. I've a plane to catch."

Bates swallowed and nodded. "The boss is going to be ever so angry," he said.

"*Very* angry," Naldo corrected him. "Very angry indeed."

As they slowed to enter the tunnel to Heathrow, some thirty minutes later, Naldo whispered, "Don't even think about it, Bates." He had kept the pistol firmly in the driver's side all the way, using the vanity mirror on the sunshield to gauge whether there was another car in tow. Nothing was easy in the sodium lighting, but he was fairly certain they were secure. BMW would only now have begun to get anxious. Naldo's last words to Barbara had been to instruct her on the first call she would receive. "Tell them I wasn't quite ready. Say I delayed Bates and we gave him tea. We didn't think to call in again." This last he added because Bates would certainly have radioed his arrival at the house.

In the relatively small car park, in front of the Number One Terminal, Naldo instructed Bates exactly how he should park, guiding him to a dark corner. Heathrow's great population and traveling explosion was only on the brink of blowing. London's major airport still lived in the late fifties. "They're going to need bigger facilities here," he said casually. "Okay, switch off the engine. Now, just look over there." He pointed out of the driver's-side window, and, as Bates turned his head automatically, Naldo sapped him hard on the back of the neck. Bates tipped sideways and Naldo had to put out an arm to save him from falling against the wheel and hitting the horn.

"Great finesse, Railton," he muttered to himself. "Subtle as a train wreck."

He was not worried about the possibility of being seen. Bates had tucked the Rover tightly into the corner, with the trunk almost against the wall. The few people around seemed to be in and out of the place quickly, either dashing to catch a flight or anxious to get away from the airport's environment. Flying was still a relative adventure for most people.

He used Bates' tie to bind the driver's hands, a handkerchief to gag him, and the man's own suspenders to secure his ankles. Now all he had to do was wait for the moment when the car park was completely deserted. It came five minutes later, and Naldo was quickly out of the car, opening the trunk, then dragging the unfortunate Bates from the driver's seat and dumping him in, closing and locking the trunk with a murmured "Sorry."

He locked the other doors and dropped the keys into a drain as he crossed to the arrivals area, his shoulders hunched slightly, the walk a kind of short-stepped shuffling gait which made him appear older. His manner was one of great uncertainty, constantly switching the canvas bag from hand to hand. He paused by one of the litter bins, dipping his hand in to pluck a recently discarded boarding card from the trash.

With the topcoat still open he slid the boarding card into his breast pocket and shuffled towards the car rental desk, where he asked for a car, explaining he spoke no English. There was a short delay while they found one of the girls who was fluent in French. Naldo was amazed at the way the girl hardly looked at him. Her only interest seemed to be in the paperwork, which she went over several times before being satisfied. She accepted a travelers check, drawn on the Crédit Lyonnais, without pausing for thought.

Within three quarters of an hour of arriving at the airport, Michel Provin, freelance engineering draftsman with a bona fide address in the 13th Arrondissement of Paris, was on the road. He figured the first hour would be the most dangerous, for, initially, he was forced to head back into London, turning off the main roads and entering the slow-moving traffic of Earl's Court. He risked double parking outside the small, late-night Pakistani grocery shop. Inside he squeezed through other shoppers and between the heavily stocked shelves. The shop smelled of cumin, ginger, and a multitude of other spices. The owner stood, paunchy and smiling, behind the counter while his two daughters served customers of all races, colors, and creeds.

"Excuse me," Naldo spoke softly to the Pakistani. "Snow swept over the earth,/Swept it from end to end."

The Pakistani smiled and nodded. "Oh, indeed, yes, sir." He cleared his throat. "The candle on the table burned,/the candle burned." Another, rather supercilious, smile. "If, sir, you would like to be following me please." He led the way to the back of the shop, through a small door and into a lighted storeroom. Big Herbie Kruger sat patiently, reading a paperback, on a wooden chair that looked uncomfortably small for him.

"Sorry to keep you waiting, Herb." Naldo smiled.

"Is no matter for me. I read. The scent in here is nice." He waved a large arm towards the shelves of canned goods and packets. "You did good, Nald. You did very good. They asked me in. Begged me in. I took pictures of the stuff the bugger's fitted Caspar with. Only that. I was right, yes?"

"Oh, you were very right, Herb."

"Almost give me a medal, Nald." Herbie handed over a small package wrapped in blue cartridge paper.

"They'll give you a jockstrap medal when you tell them they're off the hook." Naldo took the package. "Tell them when you like. Tell them they're in the clear. Use it to your advantage."

They talked for a few more minutes. At last Naldo said, "I have to get moving. We never saw each other, Herb. Right?"

"Don't know what you mean. Who hell are you anyway?" Herbie gave his big daft smile and turned his back as though he wanted to be able to say with honesty that he had not seen Naldo go.

As he left the Pakistani grocer's shop, Naldo wondered how Herbie managed to arrange these people. Particularly how he convinced them that quoting Pasternak to a stranger was helping some cause in which they believed passionately. Within minutes, Naldo was heading west, towards Cornwall, with a long night's drive ahead of him.

He stopped just after midnight and dialed his own number. Barbara answered with a tense "Hallo?" And when he spoke she said, "Oh, how nice of you to call." He said, "I'm okay," and rang off.

A couple of miles from Beckeleg's cottage, Naldo junked the car, finding a clifftop far away from any habitation. It ran straight down into churning sea, with no rocks below. Taking the car as near to the cliff edge as he dared, Naldo pushed it, allowing it to roll off with the engine still running. He left the lights on and watched, detached as the twin beams turned over and over like a huge Catherine Wheel. He saw the water burst in a white explosion, and the lights stayed on long enough for him to see the vehicle whirl, spin, and disappear, rear first, under the waves. With luck nobody would spot it for days, for the currents were strong along the coast and the car should be towed out as it sank.

He walked the rest of the way, waiting above the cottage until he was ready.

Beckeleg opened the door at his knock, peered at Naldo in the half-light. "Why, Mr. Rail . . ." he began.

"The name's Provin," Naldo said with a heavy French accent. "Michel Provin." He pronounced it Pro-van.

"Course 'tis m'dear. I'd know you anywhere. You come on in, 'tis a raw morning."

3

He woke with a start, his hand leaping to the pistol. There was movement outside the door, and Naldo realized he had been asleep in the chair for a long time. Then came the tattoo of knocks. Ta-ta-ta-TAT. He was cramped and stiff so that it took what seemed to be an age before he could even stand. Barzillai Beckeleg gave the pistol only a cursory glance as he came into the cottage. "You'm not needin' one of them things w' me around, Nal . . . Mr. Provin," he said with a smile that lifted his right eyebrow. "I got some food for us, 'tis past six. I were longer than I expected."

"Nobody out there looking?"

"If there were, I didn't see none of 'em. Nothin' special round here this time o' the year." He gave Naldo another quizzical smile. "And I don't reckon you left many traces."

"When can we go?"

"That's the trouble with folks today. Rush, rush, rush." Beckeleg set a plastic grocery bag on the table. "We'm gonna have ourselves a nice feast afore we go, m'dear. Got some good steak off'n a butcher friend o'mine in Truro. We're gonna 'ave some steak, with chips an' all, afore we go off on a cold night like this. And I don't reckon on leaving 'till ten or eleven. No moon then, and the sea's a bit choppy. Leave it a while, that's what I say. This ain't a night that's gonna tempt they coastguard and customs patrols. We'll take it nice and quiet, young Mr. Provin.''

In the end, they left at ten-thirty, riding without lights, a force six coming from onshore, and the sea chopping from four to six feet.

The only light was the green glow from the radar screen, and Naldo had to hang on to keep his balance, legs astride as he stood next to Beckeleg. The deck quivered, as though being constantly struck by a giant hand from below, and, in the minutes between, you could feel the thrust from the powerful diesels that drove the sleek craft forward, slicing the whitecapped peaks.

Though the wind, motors, and sea produced a lot of noise, the two men were able to speak and hear in the small forward cabin.

"Is it safe, navigating without lights?" Naldo shouted.

'' 'Tis never safe,'' Beckeleg bellowed. ''Particularly when we skirt the French coastline. Very rocky. But 'tis safe enough wi' me. Us Beckelegs've been sneaking into the Breton ports for many generations. We 'as what you call a collective memory. Instinct. Anyways, 'tis quite a calm night for December.''

They were silent for a while, then, as he put on more power, Beckeleg laughed. ''Ah, we was right scared o' these buggers in the war. Fast. Maneuverable, an' all. Lord that was good sport, sneakin' in and joinin' up with the fishing fleets from Brittany. We knew most on the men and their women from before the war, see, and they were pleased wi' us. We'd sneak in, past these bloody E-boats, get into harbor, and wait to drop the lads, and lasses too. Then wait to take someone out, or just get back ourselves. But, o' course you know it all, Mr. Pro-van. Pro-van indeed. My arse.''

Naldo's eyes had adjusted to the blackness. Now he detected more than spray flinging itself at the screen in front of the bridge. ''Is that snow?'' he asked.

''Snow, indeed. It doesn't last long as a rule out here or near the coast. But they do get it at times.'' Beckeleg suddenly became convulsed with laughter. ''Oh, my God, don't talk to me about snow in these parts. Oh dear, Oh dear.''

''What?'' In the glow from the radar screen, Naldo saw Beckeleg wipe his eyes with the back of his hand.

''I shouldn't laugh, really. 'Twas bloody serious then. But I've never gone near the place since.''

''What place?''

"Well. 'Bout 1943 it were. This time of year. Bit later. Near the New Year of '44. I come over to . . . no, I won't tell ee the name of the port, or you'll get wise. I come to pick up one of your fellows, and they 'ad a freak snowstorm. Eight or ten inches on it. I came in at night and there weren't any Jerry E-boats out. When I got to the house where this fellow was supposed to be they told me I 'ad to get out best I could at first light—this would be around midnight. 'Where's the man, then?' I axed, and they said as how 'ee was holed up in the next village inland. A mile off. 'Ee was afeared of coming into the fishing village, convinced I wouldn't be calling for 'im. I were furious, 'cos t'were a bloody dangerous trip.

"Bugger 'im, I thought. I'll go get the sod. So I sets out to walk to this 'ere village. I'm up to me balls in snow, 'cos it's got worse by this time. Well, I finally gets to the place. 'Tis just one street wi' little houses down either side." He began to laugh again. "We did some bloody silly things in them days. I got no idea where this fuckin' Joe's hiding, so I bangs on the first door I come to. Nobody answers, so I bangs again. Then I hears this moaning from inside and I tries the door. It be open, and there, on the bed in this little room, is a woman in labor. She'm in a turrible state. Naked and with the baby almost there.

"Well, we all on us know the lingo; the kind they speaks along the coast anyhow. I axes 'er if I can help and she'm crying and in a panic. 'Yes,' she says. 'You can get the wise woman.' She means the midwife, but the wise women along this coast know more'n any midwife. 'Where can she be found?' I axes 'er, and she tells me 'tis the last cottage on this side o' the village street. So off I goes, trudgin' through the snow. Well, I gets to the place and hammers on the door. This old crone peers out, real old bat, she is. I tells 'er what's to do and she says, yes, she were expecting as much. Must be the young Fartyarty woman. She gets 'er coat and a bag, then she says she can't walk through the snow. I must carry 'er. So I hikes 'er up on me back and we set off, piggyback like, through the snow.

"So, I get about fifty yards and realize she'm gonna slip oft me back, so I yells to her that I shall have to set 'er down, then get her up agin, more comfortable. There's this wall. A low wall . . ." He began to chuckle again at the thought of it. Naldo, in his nervousness, began to laugh as well.

"So, I turns around, bends me legs, and sets 'er on the wall, nice and shipshape. I steps away, to stretch me back like, then turns round." He laughed again. "Oh, my goodness, talk about turrible things you'm done in your time. I turns round and she be gone. Oh, my Christ, I

137

think, she'm done fallen behind the wall. So I goes to look . . ." He could not continue the story, so doubled with laughter was he. After a minute he regained control. "I goes . . . I goes to this wall and looks over it, and . . . Oh, my God . . . Oh dear . . . I looks over the wall, and it's not a fuckin' wall . . ." He struggled with what was obviously going to be the punch line. "Not a wall, but a WELL. I've popped the old crone on the edge of the village well, and she's lost 'er balance. Must've been bloody deep an' all, that well. Not a sound from it."

Later, he said, "Never been back there since. Never goin' back."

"What about the Joe?" Naldo asked.

"That bugger? That bugger 'ad made it to the fishin' village. Waitin' for me when I got back. 'Ang on there, this is the difficult bit." He concentrated on his navigation and seamanship.

They finally pulled quietly into the old port of Concarneau, with the massive fortifications of the Ville Close rising above them, at just after quarter to five in the morning.

They were not challenged once, and Beckeleg immediately took Naldo to a house off a narrow cobbled street five minutes from the harbor. There, old friends of the seaman, still doused with sleep, made coffee and provided bread and cheese. The snow had not yet hit the coast and the father of the house, a stubble-chinned little man who hopped around reminding Naldo of an agile monkey, drove him to the railway station at Quimper. By early afternoon he was in Paris, and taking another train. That evening, M. Michel Provin booked into the Hôtel Palma au Lac in Locarno. It was raining and cold, here in this usually mild Swiss Canton of Ticino. Naldo stood at his window overlooking Lake Maggiore, watching the lights blurring in the downpour.

He was tempted to telephone, for he knew Arnie was only a few miles away. But that would have been bad tradecraft. Unsafe as telephoning Barbara and telling her where he was.

The next morning was still chilly, but the rain appeared to have passed. Naldo set out early, walking to the pier to catch the ferry. He was going back to many memories, not all of them pleasant.

4

During the Second World War, Naldo's late Uncle Caspar had run an agent with remarkable skills. The agent's cryptonym was *Night Stock*, and his real name was Marcel Tiraque.

Tiraque was a wealthy man who owned a beautiful pink villa, with a lawn that ran down to the lake near the town of Ascona on Lake Maggiore. From this villa, Tiraque had moved with amazing skill into occupied Europe, working with resistance groups and the SOE. He saved many lives and was of great value to Caspar. Soon after the war ended, Tiraque died and Caspar secretly bought the villa in Ascona. Only three other people knew the place belonged to Caspar. They were Arnold Farthing, Big Herbie Kruger, and Naldo Railton. The four men had kept the secret over the years. At one time or another each of them had stayed in this beautiful place, and all had a hand in improving the property. Though there had been many offers to rent, or even buy, this unique house, Caspar would never sell it. There was an understanding, taken in the last year of Caspar's life, that the Villa Carlo should belong to his three survivors, who would be responsible for its upkeep. A local lawyer was given instructions that nobody was to be allowed to view the villa, as the owners had no intention of selling or leasing, and all communications which arrived there were sent to a Poste Restante address in Paris.

The Villa Carlo, Ascona, was the secret dark hole into which Arnie and Naldo had agreed to disappear, and Naldo set out on the short ferry ride from Locarno with high hopes that, by this nightfall at least, they would be making plans regarding what action should be taken to clear Caspar's, and their families', reputations. In so doing they would also dig the ground out from under any possible traitor still in place. For Naldo, this had become an obsession, much as the old legend spoke of King Arthur's obsession with the Holy Grail.

Ascona is a magnet for artists the world over. Its quaint, narrow streets, beautiful views of the lake, and the surrounding mountains, make it a tranquil place for men and women who wish to live in peace and just get on with creative work.

Naldo had always been there in the spring or late summer. He was used to getting his first sight of the town from the lake, awash with sunlight, for the good light there is one of the factors that influence painters: the surface of the water like glass, and the color of the houses making Ascona appear to be a small piece of paradise.

Today, mist and clouds shrouded the mountains, the lake was choppy from the chill breeze, and the town's color seemed to be reduced to uniform blacks, grays, and greens. From across the lake, in the direction of the Italian frontier, came a long roll of distant thunder, and Naldo shivered in his lightweight coat as he came down the gangway and under the wood and metal, white-painted arch with the name ASCONA picked out in black.

He was tired, even after the long sleep at the Hôtel Palma au Lac. Now, as he began the twenty-minute walk along the lakeside to the villa, he recalled a dream from the previous night. He dreamed that he met Arnie, not at the villa but in some strange city. Arnie had claimed he had the power to resurrect the dead, and, to prove it, he had the living figures of Stalin, Lenin, and Himmler walk in the street. Traffic went by, and pedestrians did not look twice at these figures from the past. It ended in a room crowded with the living dead. It was like a scene from some bad horror movie. Arnold had called up Caspar, who laughed in Naldo's face and said, "I fooled everybody, didn't I?" In the dream Naldo had asked, "How?" and Caspar replied, "It was I who made the poison to kill the dog."

As he walked under the soggy palm trees, the dream came back strongly, and with a vivid clarity which was unusual.

The front of the pink Villa Carlo faced the road, a low wrought-iron fence barring the inquisitive, and a pair of gates closed to the pavement. Naldo opened the gates and walked the few paces to the short flight of steps which led to the front door.

He had a key and the lock turned easily. Seconds later he was in the wide, paneled hallway.

"Arnie!" he called. "Arn? I made it." He knew the house was occupied. He could feel the warmth of the heating and smell food.

The door to the main living room opened, and Naldo frowned with surprise. It was not Arnold who came into the hall, but his wife, Gloria, still a very attractive woman who had kept her figure and, with assistance, her long blonde hair.

"Gloria?" Naldo sounded part questioning and part surprised.

She smiled. "Hello, Nald. Arnie said you'd be along."

He knew the secret should not normally have been shared with Gloria. Even Barbara was unaware of the Villa Carlo. "Where is he?" Naldo asked, frowning. "Where's Arnie?"

Her voice dropped, almost conspiratorially. "I thought you knew, Nald."

"Knew what?"

"Arnie," she said taking another step into the hall. "Arnie's in Moscow. I thought they'd have told you."

PART TWO

THE FAMILIES SCATTERED

(1964–1969)

NINE

1

In London, they started on Barbara in real earnest on the third evening. That was the day when two sightings of Naldo Railton were reported from what Maitland-Wood described as "Impeccable sources." The fact that both sightings came from proven snitches, one of them known to the French as a spoiled casserole, their term for bad informer, had no bearing on the matter. By the third day, Maitland-Wood was frantic and would have believed anybody.

"If Kim walked through the door and said Khrushchev was a double, Willis'd believe him," Fincher was heard to remark.

The information was, first, that Naldo had been seen at Heathrow on the night he went missing, and there was evidence he had boarded a flight to Paris. Second, from the spoiled casserole, that he checked in and boarded an Aeroflot flight direct to Moscow.

BMW put Fincher onto checking passenger lists, and those traveling on the Aeroflot flight included a name once used, many years before, by James Railton, Naldo's father. "That clinches it," Maitland-Wood announced. Curry Shepherd, a young officer who had recently been brought in from Berlin to work as dogsbody to the fifth floor, muttered, "Round up the usual suspects."

Maitland-Wood did not give such an instruction. By this time he realized that everything had to be played by the book. For one thing, Paul Schillig had popped around from Grosvenor Square to remind him that nobody in Washington would go public on Arnold Farthing's possible defection. So Willis went in to speak with C, who, from the outset, had been unhappy about all the loose talk concerning Caspar. He could not believe that someone as loyal and honorable as Caspar Railton could ever have betrayed his trust. This he made plain to Maitland-Wood, whom he ordered to get the whole thing wrapped up once and for all. Maitland-Wood did not, at that time, tell C what he and his technicians had discovered in Caspar's Eccleston Square house. He was saving that as his big finish.

When BMW emerged from the meeting, some two hours later, he came with instructions to do two things. First, he was to set up a committee whose duty it would be to determine the late Sir Caspar Railton's guilt or innocence. If guilt was proven, the committee would be regarded as a damage-control unit. Second, and of more immediate concern, he was to find the missing Donald Arthur Railton, and decide upon what action should be taken to either physically bring him back to London, or report on other possible options. C made it clear that the reports should come to him alone. He also wanted the whole business completed within a month, which Willis Maitland-Wood tactfully explained was unrealistic. "We'll need at least a year," he said. "Maybe two."

Willis Maitland-Wood was like a dog with two tails. Committees were meat and drink to him. He spoke briefly to Fincher and then set out to erect the whole paraphernalia of a secret committee of enquiry.

It was cryptoed with much heartsearching. BMW wanted to call it *Buoyancy*, but Fincher objected that this would immediately alert their brothers in Five, who already had a committee with a similar crypto, seeking out a possible penetration in *their* Service. In the end they settled for *Credit*. So the Credit Committee came into being on the fifth floor of the shop, just after lunch on that Friday afternoon.

Maitland-Wood took the chair, Fincher acted as vice-chairman, and they immediately co-opted five other senior officers. They were, Desmond Elms, from the Soviet desk; Indigo Belper, from Legal, and as flamboyant as his name; Arden Elder, the 2 i/c from Warminster, and, therefore, a skilled interrogator; Beryl Williamson, a canny, and very pretty, Scottish lady wrangler from GCHQ; and David Barnard, a smooth, precise master in Covert Operations. Barnard was a man blessed, or cursed, with a deceptively charming manner.

By two-thirty that afternoon, the seven-person team had taken over one of the large secure briefing rooms on the fourth floor. Maitland-Wood set out the parameters within which they should work. They immediately listed their priorities, and voted on who could be safely used to assist in the enquiry. The officers, chosen by Maitland-Wood, all ardently subscribed to the theory, based on the information gleaned from the defector known cryptically as *AE Ladel*, that the Soviets had placed penetration agents at the highest levels of both the American and British establishments, in particular the SIS, MI5, and the CIA. This religion, for it was more than mere acceptance of a theory, they shared with the committee Five had set up for the same purpose. Also, the entire committee, with the possible exception of Tubby Fincher, subscribed to the concept that the Railton family, in Britain, was far gone in corruption and could no longer be trusted. In particular, they wanted to sift evidence and bring forward conclusive proof that, at least since the late 1930s, Sir Caspar Railton had been a penetration agent working for the Soviets. They banned all personnel who had been actively close to any of the Railtons, or Farthings, which narrowed their field considerably. In spite of some contact and crossfertilization, Curry Shepherd, who had proved himself to be a skilled young field agent, was appointed as their postman. "I suppose I'll carry the bad news from Credit to the insolvent," he remarked.

For the initial enquiries, which BMW called "A peep behind the Railton scenes," their first choice was Gus Keene.

Keene was Grand Vizier and Inquisitor in Chief, based at Warminster. A telephone call was made requesting his presence, together with his two most capable associates, in London, at the speed of sound. Faster if possible.

Keene arrived at just after four-thirty and spent an hour being briefed by the Credit Committee, who made it clear they required results as of last Thursday week.

Gus Keene, like most good interrogators, was a former policeman who had also read Law, though not practiced it. He was a dark, gypsy-like man, tall and slim, in his early fifties. Meeting him for the first time you might have said, "Country doctor, or the man who wrote a provincial newspaper's daily naturalist column." He had a cozy manner, smoked a pipe, used to great effect during interrogation sessions, and on the surface appeared indifferent when the talk got around to politics or crime. To their detriment, some people found him a generally diffident man. Keene used indifference as an animal will use its coloring as camouflage.

The pair chosen by him to assist in the work were two of his most promising juniors, and after the Credit Committee had briefed him, Keene met with them in a pub within walking distance of the shop.

Carole Coles was in her late twenties, with a first in Law (Oxon); Martin Brook was thirty, with a second in Economics (Cantab), which shows what you can achieve with an economics degree.

"Simple business." Gus jammed his pipe into the corner of his mouth and nodded thanks to Martin, who had just bought him a pint. "All we have to do is sweat the entire Railton clan. From this we are to form an opinion regarding Naldo Railton's disappearance. Ever meet

145

Naldo, Carole? Smashing fellow. Always said he'd go far. Apparently he has. The so-called evidence is Moscow, but I don't somehow believe it."

"Who's first?" Martin Brook asked. He was inclined to fat, with a round, pleasant, and good-humored face, the main feature of which seemed to be his spectacles with their thick, heavy, black frames, making him look like an eternal student. When he was an undergraduate he had played Trophimov in an ADC production of *The Cherry Orchard*. Friends said he was Stanislavskian and just went on living the part. Any fool could see that he was smitten with the lovely Carole, for he watched her with spaniel eyes and hung on her every word. Carole treated him as a joke: apart from his work, which everyone admitted was high-grade octane.

"First?" Gus asked in reply, taking a puff on his pipe and his face all but disappeared in a cloud of smoke. "Oh, *we* are. You see, old Naldo Railton's fairly urgent, but we have to report on other matters, and that means you two spending a few days in Registry, under Ambrose Hill's eagle eye. You'll be going through every piece of paper any Railton's used within the Service. I think the lads back there," he inclined his head in the general direction of the shop, "would even get you to go through a mountain of Railton toilet paper if they thought it would help."

In detail he explained their role in examining the evidence on the late Sir Caspar. "Tonight, though, I think we'll all go and have a talk to Naldo's missis. Barbara Railton, née Burville. Military family. Married to Naldo for, what? Nineteen years or so? Two kids. Probably knows the trade backwards. We'll have to do the first one on her turf, not ours, and I gather that idiot Deputy CSS has already been there muddying the water." Maitland-Wood had, in fact, visited the house near Kensington Gardens on the night that Naldo disappeared. Barbara had been unhelpful and a touch acid.

Now, Keene said, "I'll do most of the talking. You two watch and chip in if you think we're going for gold, okay?" He did have the decency to telephone Barbara first. She put them off until nine-thirty, but once the trio were in the Kensington house, they stayed until two in the morning.

Keene could not but admire Barbara's stand. "Look," she had said, more wearily than angry. "Look, *I* would like nothing better than to know what's happened to Naldo. He came home three nights ago, tired, and obviously concerned. I thought Arnie Farthing had been stirring it, because Naldo kept talking about him. We had dinner together, he took an overnight bag and left. Said he'd be away for a couple of weeks." She went on to say that, in the wee small hours, Maitland-Wood, Tubby Fincher, and half of Special Branch, complete with search warrant, had arrived. "They turned the house over and told me Naldo was missing. That's all. 'Your husband's disappeared, Mrs. Railton, and we don't like the look of things.' No explanation. No hint about what they didn't like the look of. I've telephoned that bloody man Maitland-Wood twice a day ever since. No joy. Nothing. So, perhaps *you* can tell me what's happening. I just want to see my husband."

Good performance, Keene thought, rating it nine point five on a scale of ten. He knew spies' wives. They were into everything and took nothing at face value. He had no doubt that Naldo had simply told her he would be doing a disappearing act, and she was to play the little woman left in the dark. "Let's talk about Arnold Farthing, then," Keene said.

"Why? I want to talk about Naldo."

"Then we might get some clues by talking about Arnold. How close were they? Naldo and Arnold?"

"He was best man at our wedding. Naldo was best man at his. Knew each other backwards, though they hadn't been together for some time. *I* haven't seen Arnie for years."

"They close enough to come running to each other's calls?"

"That would depend on professional circumstances. They both put Service, Agency in Arnie's case, and country before anything else. Naldo is, presumably, like yourself, Mr. Keene, of an age to feel he was born to Empire. Now he only has his country. I don't have to explain about Arnie, he's very much a 'My country right or wrong' merchant. I suppose most Americans still are. Like we Brits, it'll take time, and a heavy dose of hard leftist politics, for them to grow out of it. The Americans think the hard left's a couple of Congressmen talking liberalism. They've no idea. They're as bad as the Brits who talk about the police being fascist. If you've never had to deal with the real thing, you don't recognize it until it's too late."

It was like playing a hard game of tennis with a pro, the three interrogators agreed afterwards. "Bloody convincing," Carole Coles said.

"Truth or consequences?" Keene asked.

"She's a frightened lady," Martin Brook announced with confidence.

"Thus spake the fat boy of the Remove." Keene puffed at his pipe.

147

"Frightened about what? Frightened for her husband? What we might get on her husband? Or what we could discover once we unleash ourselves on the great Railton and Farthing clans? Or what our dogged, bloody-minded march through the grand old man's paper past, Sir Caspar's motivation, will bring to light?"

Carole Coles smiled. "Probably a bit of all four. Thus spake the trim, elegant, poised, and needle-sharp most wicked girl in the school."

"Well, you got the last bit right," Keene spoke through teeth clenched around his pipe stem. "I'll get her to drop by the shop tomorrow. Give her some of my famous tea and sympathy on our home ground." Keene took the pipe out of his mouth. "You two can go work in the salt mines and commit the secret histories of all the Railtons to your prodigious memories. I never thought I'd see the day when the whole of that family ceased to be flavor of the year."

"Accidents will happen, even in the best-regulated families, as my dear old mother used to say, constantly and to our undying irritation," observed the neat, and dark-haired Miss Coles, winking at Keene. They had been very careful. Not even the Fat Boy, alias Martin Brook, guessed that Gus and Carole had been engaged in a passionate affair over the past two years. "How far do you think Maitland-Wood's stamped his clumsy boots all over the evidence?"

"Quite a bit, I should say. But they've got something out of it. There was an arrangement, set for the morning after Naldo disappeared. They had permission to turn over the late Sir Caspar's drum, though the place is more like an entire timpani section. The family's had that little mansion since the Ark. When old Giles Railton lived there he had the young Winston Churchill as a neighbor. It's in Eccleston Square. The other night, after BMW and his gang left Mrs. Naldo Railton, they gathered seven or eight technicians, the kind who know about locks and hidey-holes, and took the Eccleston Square place apart. Very happy with the result, is Mr. Maitland-Wood."

He went on to explain they had removed a large number of papers, and a pile of thick diaries. "Including those for the years 1935 to 1938," BMW had told him darkly. When met by a blank stare, he had explained to Keene that those were the three years during which Caspar Railton had been out. "Private and fancy free. Spent a lot of time dashing about Europe," again darkly.

"Well, I'm for my bed." Gus Keene finished his pint and rose. "I'll ring the shop in the morning and fix up your trip down memory lane. You staying with your people, Martin?"

When Brook was in London he always talked about "staying with my *people.*" Keene liked to quietly needle him about it. "Well, we've been put up at the Regent Palace, so we can't give you a lift out to Clapham, can we?" He grinned, pronouncing it "Clay-fam." "We should all get an early night. Going to be a busy day tomorrow." He could not have known *how* busy.

On the following day the car rented by Michel Provin was discovered.

2

Another month or two and the car would have probably disappeared for good, broken up by the early storms of 1965 and washed away, as though the vehicle had been neatly dismantled by experts. But, as so often happens, a small team of very hearty young men who had recently formed a Scuba Diving Club in Falmouth chanced to choose that tiny scratch of beach, below the acute drop of the cliffs, to practice some inshore diving.

They had made several dives that morning, traveling along the coast in a small boat equipped with a powerful little engine. In spite of the cold weather, the four men decided this Saturday might well be the last chance of the year. The fact that the water was icy made things more of a challenge. When a pair surfaced and reported the car was down there, giving an accurate description of its color, make, and registration number, they acted like responsible citizens and reported the matter to the police.

By five that evening the local law had retrieved the vehicle, discovered its registered owners, and made contact with the rental firm. In turn, the rental firm told them it had been taken out at Heathrow Airport, by a Frenchman called Michel Provin. The information was circulated and a sharp-eyed sergeant at Special Branch had reported the matter to his superior officer, who boosted it over to the shop because Maitland-Wood had sent out one of those catchall memos regarding strange movements.

At nine o'clock, the girl who had handled the paperwork on the car was interviewed, and failed to identify Naldo's photograph. But the same picture had already gone off on the wires through that little office at Scotland Yard which deals with all Interpol movements. In the meantime, Curry Shepherd was given a brief to check through files. He was looking for any possible cross-fertilized Railton contact within a twenty-mile radius of the spot where the car had surfaced. Late that evening, Shepherd took the most likely name to Maitland-Wood's home, an expensive Service apartment near Victoria Station.

"Better drive down there, then, young Shepherd. See the fellow and report directly to me. Be careful if you telephone. You never know who's listening." Maitland-Wood kept a framed World War II poster on the wall of his office. It depicted two women chattering away on a bus. Behind them, all ears, sat Hitler and Goering in full regalia. The caption read CARELESS TALK COSTS LIVES!

Thank *you*, Curry said to himself. All I need is a trip into the wilds of the West Country. Bugger bloody Naldo Railton.

When he telephoned the shop from St. Keverne the next day his news was that Barzillai Beckeleg was not at home. Locals said he often popped over to France.

"With Naldo Railton I'd bet a penny to a pound." By now Maitland-Wood's entire conversation was studded with dark intonations. Carole and Martin were cloistered with Ambrose Hill in Registry, while the entire Credit Committee busily read copies of Caspar's missing years.

He told Curry to come home. He would send a permanent pair of lion tamers—his words—down to bring Mr. Beckeleg up to town for a chat on his return from foreign parts.

While all this was going on, the cunning Gus Keene was having his private bit of tea and sympathy with Barbara, who, quite unknown to herself, was the subject of much discussion at the Villa Carlo in Ascona.

3

Gloria had been a Washington society beauty when she married Arnold Farthing. She was also that rare type of society beauty who worked for a living. She had held down a job of some importance at State and met Arnie almost by chance, even though they had been, to use the argot, interconnected. The connection was that Arnie's case officer at the time, a brave though snobbish career officer called Roger Fry, had been involved with Gloria Van Gent, as she then was. Arnold got her on the rebound, claimed a new case officer, and even won over Gloria's father and mother, who were both Navy to the bone.

She had taken pains with her looks and body over the years, and Naldo, who had always fancied her, after the manner of most men who want to find out how their best friend ticks, realized that she now looked more stunning than ever, standing in the doorway of the drawing room inside the Villa Carlo.

Any familiar desire had been immediately quenched by her news of Arnie's apparent defection to Moscow.

"You mean that was for *real?*" He felt slightly tipsy, and presumed it was because of the fatigue followed by a long sleep.

She laughed, throwing her head back. Not a forced, melodramatic laugh, but a spontaneous melodic burst, as though something had really amused her. "He said your face would be a picture. Come on in, Nald. You're in the second bedroom. Hope you don't mind. I pinched the big one."

"Be my guest." Naldo felt things seemed so bad that he had no option but to go along with them and show amusement. He put his bag near the hall table, threw his coat across a chair, and followed Gloria into the drawing room, which had huge French windows that led onto a stretch of lawn sloping casually down to the lakeside. A pair of beautiful willows hung low over the water. In summer their leaves would trail in the lake and caress the reflection of the mountains, ripping them apart into a million fragments at the first sigh of a breeze. Naldo looked at the damp grayness now and remembered lying out on the grass, drying from a dip in the lake on some perfect summer day which seemed a million years ago. Arnie had been there, and Caspar. The three of them like children in their private hiding place.

He turned to Gloria. "Arnold told you about this place?" He heard the surprise in his voice, realizing that for some reason Arnie had violated his friendship and trust with Caspar, Herb, and himself, by breaking his vow and telling his wife.

"There *was* a reason, Nald." She was wearing a very short, sheath-like dress which made every movement a challenge to any man's eyes, sitting on the long settee that had been in the house since Tiraque's time. She patted the cushion, bidding Naldo to sit next to her, but he remained standing, offended by her action which, to him, seemed like someone coaxing a pet dog.

She nodded. "If it helps, I've only known for a week. Arn said it was too dangerous for him to call you or Herbie. You *are* the only people who know about this place, right?"

Naldo did not speak. His mind was like a wasp's nest, angry at this woman's intrusion.

"Arnold said you would know the lines that followed these—" She quoted:

"Cypresses dot the lakeside, waiting,
Watching, for the day of judgement."

Naldo answered automatically, speaking as though in a trance—

"When all God's beauty here will turn,
Changed into a view more lovely, as we chant the Dies Irae."

He still did not altogether trust her, for he recalled an old talent of which Gloria was proud. She only had to see a play, read a book, or listen to an unfamiliar piece of music and it became imprinted on her mind. She had a knack that some would call a photographic memory, and she could even recall sentences spoken casually years after the event. The lines were from a poem which Naldo had tried to write, here at the Villa Carlo one lazy morning. He read it to Arnie, in a somewhat embarrassed fashion. Ever since, Arnie had used the one remembered verse as a sign between them, usually carried in the heads of agents that Naldo had never met before. Gloria could have got the verse from several people.

"Arnie gave you those words?" Every syllable had suspicion ground into it.

"The night before he left. He told me of this house. Said you'd arrive here. Gave me the poem."

"How long has Arnie worked for the Sovs?"

Her face puckered, as though she was about to weep. For a second, Naldo's emotions clicked into play. He wanted to comfort her.

"I don't know if he really does work for the Sovs," she began.

"You *knew* he'd gone to Moscow."

"Please, Nald. Please sit down. You're making me very nervous, just standing there. Sit down. Anywhere. Sit down and I'll tell you what I know."

Naldo seated himself in one of the three high-backed leather armchairs which matched the settee, realizing as he settled that this had been his late Uncle Caspar's favorite place when they came here. "Tell it, then." He used the manner of a hostile interrogator.

"You know what it's like being Head of Station, particularly somewhere like Berlin. It's like being a doctor always on call."

It was a good description, and Naldo nodded.

"The signal from Washington came in during the morning. He called me. We had a kind of safe telephone thing, just a few key words.

152

Wagner meant he had to go away for a few days; *Browning* was to let me know he would be back late that night, a cover-all really because it also meant he was dealing with an operation. If he said *Running late* it simply told me the truth, that he would be late but there was no need for me to be concerned. No operation involved. We had Flash signals like *Bluebird.* That was the one he used if he got a sudden recall. He had a *Bluebird* a few days ago and came back agitated."

"I know about that, yes."

Arnold had called her with *Bluebird* in the morning. He had also said tomorrow, and to end the conversation he added *Sacred,* which told her that he expected to be home early. "I felt he had been expecting the recall," she said.

Arnie had returned, at around three in the afternoon, to the house the Agency rented for them, and told Gloria that he thought this was it. The end of his Berlin tour. At about six that evening there was a call from the Military HQ where the Agency had all its cipher facilities. There was an urgent Flash from Washington, in a cipher only the Head of Station knew. Arnie had told them to bring it to the house and, half an hour later, two of his people arrived.

"He took the signal into his den and came out with the paper in his hand: the paper on which he had transcribed the signal *en clair.*" According to Gloria, Arnold had looked like a ghost. "His face was gray. I'd never seen him that frightened before. He said he would have to go out for an hour or two. I remember telling him not to be late. He still had to get some paperwork finished and do his packing. He was due to leave at nine the next day."

"You didn't get a look at the signal?"

"No, not the whole thing. I saw the last word and the sender's initial."

"Which were?"

"The last word was *caution.* It was signed with one letter, *A.* Arnold immediately went back into his den and burned everything before going out."

He was away for an hour and a half, and looked better when he came back. They ate. Then Arnold had taken her into his den. "It was swept regularly, and he'd got the office to line it with those tiles, the ones that absorb sound. I think he had some kind of electronic baffler in there as well. He once said they'd fitted a babbler."

Again Naldo nodded, and Gloria came to the crunch. Arnold had told her he had been instructed to bypass Washington. "You'll have to know," he said. "I've lived a triple life for the past seven years, but

I've lived it under discipline." Gloria asked Naldo if he knew what that meant, and Naldo nodded again.

"You'll hear that I've defected," Arnold had said. "I'm leaving tonight, and I want you out."

"He said I should send the boys home, quickly. First thing in the morning. Then he gave me instructions about what I should do. Where I should go. I was to say nothing about this place, or you and the poem, if I didn't make it."

There was a definite possibility that members of Arnold's staff would catch up with her before she got out of Berlin. He had given her detailed instructions on how to leave what he called a paper chase. She was to book a flight to Rome, but take one to Bonn instead, then make her way into Switzerland. Arnold had told her that a search would begin almost immediately they found he was missing. In the event, Gloria got the boys away, to her sister, and herself to Ascona with no difficulty at all.

"And he gave you the poem? That's all?"

"The poem and some messages. He sent an apology to you."

"For what?"

"He asked me to say sorry about the Russian team in London. It was meant to cause some alarm among your superiors. To prepare for what had to be done. That make sense?"

"Yes." Naldo thought of Maitland-Wood putting him to the question after the incident with the *Boyevaya* near Trafalgar Square. Again he saw the men in his mind, and heard BMW's voice: "You deny having worked as a double agent for us, and the Soviet Service? You deny any complicity in running, or servicing any Soviet agent in place? You deny having any preliminary meetings with Russian officers to discuss your own defection?" Naldo forced his mind back to the present. "Anything else?" he asked.

"Arnold said he'd gone ahead to deal with the matter of which you'd talked. He meant something you'd spoken about to each other."

The figure of *Alex,* and the photographs. The ones of Oleg Penkovsky at the Black Sea resort of Sochi, all traveled through Naldo's mind. He saw the snow and felt the raw cold on the night Arnie had laid that on him in Berlin. "Yes," he again nodded to Gloria.

"He said you were to be very cautious indeed. Naldo, Arnold advises that you should keep moving. He said that he might have to give you to the Ks as a bonus. He said you'd understand. The bit of business in London was to set you up, to make your superiors think twice about you. That's what Arnie said. Does it still make sense?"

Naldo nodded yet again. It made excellent sense. He felt that everything was now out of his control. He was balked, not free to return and not knowing which way to go.

"Nald, does that mean we're in danger here?" Gloria sounded apprehensive.

He thought for a moment. "Arnie only said he *might* have to give me as a bonus?"

"Yes. It wasn't definite. He said that, if it had to be, he would try and get a warning to you here."

"How, in the name of Nathan Hale, would he do that?"

"He wasn't specific. You know Arnie, always one to ad lib on the hoof. He said if he could call, he'd use a special ring. Two rings and then a cutoff. The next call had to be picked up."

"Like illicit lovers, yes." Naldo raised his eyebrows. "I can just see Arnie making a telephone call like that from Moscow. I think we can write off anything by way of a warning call from Arnie."

"Well, that's what he said."

Naldo rose and walked over to the windows. On the lake one of the ferry steamers was churning the gray water into white as it turned sharply away from the pier. The ferries always did their turn away in front of the Villa Carlo. "Then we might, or might not, be in danger." He looked at her and smiled. "Who does a fellow have to grope here to get food?"

"Preferably me." Gloria seemed to relax for the first time.

"He tell you where the money was hidden?" Caspar and Naldo had placed various items, including several thousand Swiss francs in cash, under a false floorboard at the top of the house. Gloria said no, and that she had used her own money for food and necessities. Naldo asked about the safety precautions. Arnold had told his wife about these so she could get into the villa. Three years before, Naldo and Herb had come out for a couple of days, it was by way of R & R for Herb, and set up an electronic alarm system, most of which had been filched from Bonn and Berlin.

All the windows and doors were equipped with sensors, and there were several panic buttons, used to set off a house alarm. The whole property, including the lakeside, was ringed with infrared eyes, some of them set neatly into the bark of trees. They were placed at knee height to avoid the beams being broken by small animals, and the width of a human body was needed to activate them so that flying birds could go through the linking rays without causing damage. When the eyes were switched on, a small red light would blink in every room of the house if an intruder stepped through the beam. The main control box, in an understairs closet, would indicate which area had been breached. Naldo thought it best not to go into details with Gloria.

While she was getting the meal finished, he crept up to the master bedroom and deactivated the alarm there. His would be on, as would all the others throughout the house.

Gloria had bought plenty of food and they lunched on a soup she had made from ham stock and vegetables. The ham, she said, would do for a light evening meal. There was also veal, thin escallops, fried in butter, with slices of lemon, potatoes, and a salad. During the meal they talked of old times, Gloria asking after Barbara, and the pair of them reminiscing of years long gone. Gloria had been to see Sara and Dick at Redhill twice in the past year. She had been shocked to find them so frail, and asked who would inherit the Manor when they could not go on.

"My father by rights." Naldo thought of the strain there would be when Dick and Sara had to leave Redhill. Unless special instructions were left in their wills, a lot of family feuding would follow.

The day went by peacefully. Naldo set the alarms that evening, and, when he bade Gloria goodnight, she tried to kiss him on the mouth, thrusting the conjunction of her thighs at him in an explicit offer, and running her tongue across his lips. Naldo held her off at arm's length, telling her gently that it was a kind and pleasant thought, but they should abide by field rules.

The night passed without further incident.

The next day, Naldo went out and bought chemicals and an enlarger from a local photographer's shop. There was a small bedroom, a storage room really, with a sink and water supply. It was at the top of the house, off the landing that contained the false floorboard under which the cache of equipment and money was hidden.

Naldo draped blankets over the window and doors, replacing the naked overhead bulb with a red one. Time, he thought, to develop the photographs Big Herb had taken of the Blunt interrogation material, *Hypermarket.* He had yet to go through the hefty wedge of papers from Caspar's box as well.

It took several hours to develop and enlarge the many frames Kruger had taken of the documents, and the whole job was not completed by dinnertime, though all the prints were pegged and drying in the makeshift darkroom.

On their second night, Gloria was even more pressing in her demands, and when Naldo again told her it was not wise, adding that he did not really want to cuckold his friend, she became angry. "I'm not thinking about you and Arn!" she screeched. "I'm thinking about me. Christ, Naldo, neither of us might ever see Arnie again."

He gave her a short cuddle and whispered that they should give it time. "These first days are the most important," he told her.

Lying in bed, Naldo brought out the pile of documents taken from Caspar's box. The *Hypermarket* extracts would be carefully packed in two separate envelopes and put into the canvas bag, always ready in case they needed to get out fast. He had warned Gloria to be ready to leave at a few minutes' notice.

Caspar's papers were neatly separated into three small folders, on top of which lay a dozen sheets of A4, clipped together. Begin at the beginning, he thought, going through the sheets on top of the folders. Among them was an envelope addressed to JAMES RAILTON ESQ. PRIVATE, CONFIDENTIAL & MOST SECRET. Naldo slit the envelope with the flick knife he always kept nearby, together with the pistol and spare ammunition. Inside there were three pages of neatly folded paper. It was dated 5th January 1964, and carried the Eccleston Square address, below which Caspar had written the words *Destroy after reading* in green ink. The remainder of the letter was neatly typed in single spacing.

The salutation was typical of Caspar—**Dear old James,** it read, followed by **or Naldo, who'll doubtless be reading this if his father's not available.**

Naldo read on, feeling his eyes widen as he scanned the lines:

This is a brief résumé of the contents of my private box which, if you read this, you will have removed to a place of safety. Until now, I have shared with no person my true reason for leaving the Service, and going private in August 1935 to the September of 1938. I do so now.

In the early Summer of 1935 it became obvious to me that the resources of our Service were being used in a disproportionate imbalance. Until that time our main target country had, since the early 1920s, been Russia under its new and struggling Bolshevik leadership. This leadership made it perfectly clear that their intention was a militant communisation of the world, and their political ideology seemed to be at direct odds with that of countries such as Great Britain and the United States of America.

However, by 1935 we were being mesmerised by the

new bogeyman of Europe, the far right wing Fascist Nazi Party, with Adolf Hitler at its head, in Germany. Slowly our targeting priorities altered on a ratio of four to one in favour of Germany as the main bullseye.

True, our brothers in Christ at MI5 were dividing their time on targets as diverse as the Communist Party of Great Britain, and known members of the Comintern, on one side of the spectrum; with The Right Party, The Link, and Oswald Mosley's British Union of Fascists on the other. We appeared to be sandwiched between two ideologies that were both repugnant to any country professing to be democratic, however fragile and flawed that democracy might be.

It seemed to me that both the Communist Party and the Fascist Nazi Party were an equal threat, and, while the physical and geographic danger of an all-out war seemed to be weighted heavily in favour of being activated by Hitler and the Nazis, I felt the long-term disaster would come from Russia and the Bolsheviks. As we now all know, this feeling has proved to be correct. Somehow I knew (not by any superior intellect on my part) that it was totally wrong for the Secret Intelligence Service to put the bulk of its eggs in one basket: the Nazi basket.

I left the Service, then, with a prime object of conscience. To reinforce, with hard fact, my concerns about Russia's long-term plans. In particular, Stalin's blueprint for a World Communist Utopia.

It is easy to say that I am being wise after the event. But we now know that I was right. The world events which took place between 1939 and 1945 played straight into Comrade Stalin's hands.

On my return to the Service in 1938 I attempted to argue with the powers that be in a last-ditch stand. I failed to convince them that the Secret Intelligence Service should increase its vigilance against the Soviets, and, when Hitler turned on Russia in 1941, it was obvious that any mission I had undertaken was doomed, in spite of the intelligence brought to us by early Soviet defectors like Orlov and Krivitsky.

Now we know that, as far back as the mid-1930s, Russia had effectively placed penetration agents into the very heart of the British and American establishments, and it should be clear to all that we still nurture agents, possibly second generation penetrations, within the most sensitive areas of government, military and Security/Intelligence organisations.

The clear indicators, and information I gathered between the Summer of '35 and the autumn of '38 have to be put to some positive use. Therefore, I have planned a small snare in which we might well catch more active penetration agents who are still, *to my knowledge,* operating near the hearts of our two great countries.

The snare will become obvious once it is set in motion, though its aims and ingenuity might not be seen with clarity at the outset. What you, James—or Naldo—must do is sit back and watch when the trap is sprung. With all this in mind I enclose three sets of documents. The first two are diaries covering the events of my life between 1935 and '38. The third are further notes, which will provide a clearer picture of how the trap should work.

I shall be brief in explanation. Diary One is fiction. I have concocted it so that it tallies genuinely with my movements and contacts during those two and a half years. My aims, thoughts, intentions and beliefs portrayed in Diary One are the reverse of truth. What you have is a typewritten copy, *en clair,* of Diary One—the fiction. Apart from this there are three other copies, written in a very simple cipher. Diary One, in its handwritten cipher form, takes up two and a half bound notebooks, which I purchased last year from Harrods. I have seeded the three copies so that someone will most certainly find them, be intrigued, and begin to make enquiries which, I trust, will lead to the snare and uncovering of several penetration agents. Diary One has been left (a) in the Eccleston Square house, hiding in plain view; (b) in my bank, together with some innocuous papers; (c) among a pile of other books and curiosities left, last week, to the Library of the British Museum. I shall die with the certainty that this work of fiction will come to the attention of some gullible members of the Service.

Diary Two is fact. It is also the only copy available so

**guard it well. Make certain, once you have read it
against Diary One, that it can be brought out, together
with the notes contained in the folder marked *Bogeyman*, at the appropriate moment. What more can I say?
You will know the right time to confront whoever is to
be confronted with Diary Two and *Bogeyman*. Diary
Two, as you will see, has a legal document appended.
Sworn by me and witnessed by Mr Leo Morris, a legal
giant and beyond suspicion.**

**Use these papers with care and common sense. You
will snare at least one big fat rodent.**

> *And in such indexes, although small pricks*
> *To their subsequent volumes, there is seen*
> *The baby figure of the giant mass*
> *Of things to come at large.*

> *Caspar.*

Naldo smiled. His Uncle Caspar could not resist a final Shakespearean quote, and the labyrinthine ingenuity of such a long-reaching trap
appealed to Naldo. He read it again, quickly taking in certain facts.
The reference to Krivitsky was interesting. Krivitsky, one-time head of
Russian Military Intelligence, Europe, had fingered a cipher clerk in
the Foreign Office, and, for those who had eyes and ears, he had also
given excellent descriptions which just might have been of the traitors
Maclean and Philby as early as 1939. In spite of Krivitsky's accuracy
concerning the cipher clerk, nobody had bothered to follow up his
more important descriptions.

Still smiling, Naldo turned to the fake diary: Diary One, as Caspar
called it. He saw the date at the top of the page, **Monday 5th
August 1935,** and was about to start reading when the "alert" light
began to flash on the bedside table, emitting a tiny bleating noise, like
a lamb heard far away. Someone had broached the cordon of electronic
eyes around the villa.

Naldo reached for the pistol, then his slacks, which he pulled on,
using one hand as he silently moved, barefoot, towards the door.

On the landing he stood for a moment, his eyes gradually clearing
to night vision so that he could make out dark-gray objects against the
background of blackness. Slowly, he made his way along the landing,
his gun hand barely touching the railing that finally became the banis-
ters.

He had done this before, with the other three who kept the secret of the Villa Carlo. They had gone through standard routine exercises; movement at night around the interior of the house; seeking each other out; they had also done the same kind of thing you practiced on the Warminster courses: sitting in one of the rooms and trying to locate a series of sounds: a door opening, an automatic pistol being cocked on the landing outside; a cough; words spoken in different languages, whispered close to the door. Now it was real.

Every two stairs down, he stopped, listening and hearing nothing unusual. He paused again by the foot of the stairs, then moved left, his back against the wall, watching the small windows flanking the door for any shadow or sign.

The winking light in the understairs closet showed that the beam had been broken at the front, through the main iron gate, and, as he stood there, Naldo saw it increase its rapid blinking, indicating that it had been breached a second time. Then it went out. A person, or persons, had moved through the gate and then gone out again.

He stood, ears straining, for another few minutes, then moved into the hall, going towards the front door, intending to open it with caution and challenge anyone nearby. Almost at the door his bare foot touched something that crackled slightly and slid over the polished wooden parquet. He could see it now, an oblong of gray against the lighter color of the neatly laid wooden blocks. An envelope.

Naldo picked it up, then did a quiet round of the ground floor, checking windows, peering out into the darkness. Nothing. Relaxing, he made his way back up the stairs. The alarm by the bed had stopped bleating and winking. Closing the door behind him, he looked at the envelope in his hand. It was addressed to *Donald Railton Esq. Villa Carlo, Ascona,* in a neat copperplate hand: the type of penmanship you saw only from professional designers and sign painters these days. He picked up his knife, realizing the envelope had a hard cardboard back. It was the kind of thing in which you sent photographs. Indeed, there was a photograph inside. A ten-by-eight glossy which made his heart leap. Staring at the camera, laughing, almost as though she was posing for the picture, was his wife, Barbara. He did not recognize the slightly out-of-focus background, but he knew the set of skimpy underclothes, which was all she wore. They were silk and very expensive, by some Italian designer; she had bought three sets, and Barbara would always wear them when trying to be provocative. Wearing the garments was a kind of tradecraft signal that she wanted sex.

Naldo frowned, shaking his head in disbelief. Then he turned the photograph over and saw there was the same copperplate hand on the back. It read—*I suggest you go to the Rathausplatz in Thun at eight minutes past noon, the day after tomorrow. The photograph should tell you why, just as it tells you who is in danger.* In different writing, which Naldo had known over the years, was scrawled—*Has to be done this way. Arnold.*

Still frowning, his heart thumping, Naldo turned the photograph over again and tried to study the background. As he did so the telephone started to ring.

He had half-expected to hear the two rings and silence which Arnie had given as a contact code to Gloria. Instead the bell went on and on. Slowly, Naldo picked up the instrument and held it to his ear.

The four men who knew of this place had made a rule about telephone contact. The distant caller would speak first. The person, or persons, in the villa would just hold the telephone and listen.

He recognized Herbie's gruff voice immediately.

"Nald." Kruger sounded distraught. "Is okay, Nald. This is secure line. Nald, I'm sorry. I'm very sorry. Had to tell them about the villa. Had no option. They got terrible stuff on Cas. They also got the guy who took you France. No option but to tell them. Get out. Out quick, Nald. If you're there, they'll come for you. One hour. Two maybe at most. Go now, okay?"

"Okay, Herb," Naldo Railton answered, his voice trembling, then, very fast—"Herb, give me a safe number."

Kruger rattled off a string of digits. "Got it, Naldo?"

"Got it." He reached for a pen.

TEN

1

While Naldo Railton was making his way across France and Switzerland, there were a number of dramatic developments taking place in London. First, Maitland-Wood had received a call in the early hours of the morning, at the shop, where he was sleeping until further notice. The police officers who monitored Interpol reports had received word that a man fitting Naldo Railton's description had spent the previous night at the Hôtel Palma au Lac in Locarno. The name Michel Provin, trawled from the car hire company, had hit the jackpot. The passport was French. The description fitted, that was all. The police knew nothing more and asked what action they should take.

"Well, the name fits, but if it's friend Railton, who's already been sighted elsewhere, why would he be in the Locarno area?" Maitland-Wood mused. "Where is Locarno anyway? Lake Como?"

"Maggiore. Near the Swiss-Italian frontier," Tubby supplied.

A thought suddenly struck BMW. He had been through the late Caspar Railton's dossier in detail. Now he recalled something about that area, or at least a connection with it. "Get Kruger over here fast," he ordered Tubby. "None of his dumb-ox stuff or I'll have his arse. I don't care what he's on. I want him here! Now!"

To give Herbie his due, he was not expecting the questions; also he had drunk almost a whole bottle of cognac that night while listening to a recording of Mahler's Symphony of a Thousand. Twice. He was in bed, spark out and stupefied, when they came to pick him up. Also there was a great deal on Herbie's mind, and BMW played a very close game.

"Just want to verify some facts, young Kruger," BMW started in.

"Facts shouldn't need verification." Herbie was a little surprised that he had got the word right.

"Be that as it may, Kruger. You worked with Sir Caspar, and Naldo just after the war . . ."

"All on record." Herbie smiled his daft smile, while desperately trying to get his mind together. Listening to the Mahler and drinking had been an attempt to drug himself into a condition which would eventually bring answers to some serious problems his agents faced in East Germany.

Maitland-Wood then used guile. "It's on record that you've made several trips with the late Caspar Railton and his nephew Naldo. You went to Lake Maggiore in Switzerland, and these visits began in the late 1940s." He pretended to examine the file on his desk. "Locarno, to be exact. Why?"

"You tell me. You got it there, in front of you."

"I want to hear it from *you.* There was a fellow called Tiraque. Lived nearby, didn't he?"

"Sure."

"Where?"

"You must have it there."

"I have, Herbie. But I want to hear it from you. If you went down to that part of Europe, let's say tomorrow, where would you go? And I want a good honest answer that says exactly what I've got written in front of me."

"Thought it was private." Herbie was hoodwinked, caught with his mind in the till. He looked back at Maitland-Wood and knew he had no option. "Villa Carlo, Ascona," he said, and saw the stars light up in Maitland-Wood's eyes.

The following day, the Credit Committee waited for news of the reappearance of either Naldo Railton or Barzillai Beckeleg, suspected of ferrying him to France. Maitland-Wood had sent people scurrying across Europe at the crack of dawn, and was saying nothing about a rumor that Naldo was in Switzerland. So they all got on with reading a typescript of the diary taken from the late Sir Caspar Railton's house in Eccleston Square.

The cipher in which the two and a half books of the diary had been written was a very insecure version of the old Vigenère tableau, and Beryl Williamson, the pretty Scottish wrangler, had the first words in place within thirty-five minutes. After that it was handed over to a team who had the whole thing done, and transcribed, in a twenty-four-hour shift. The team who did this called it a bucket job. They had a joke about round-the-clock work. To them it meant that you got food brought to you in buckets.

After reading the first three pages, Maitland-Wood declared the product to be irrefutable proof of Caspar's treachery, and sat his committee down in different rooms across London so they could digest the entire thing before the next meeting.

"Who'd have thought it?" Fincher muttered, enraged by the contents. "Who'd have thought Caspar would have made such a fool of himself?"

"We'll grill every member of that bloody family!" Maitland-Wood strode across his office, slapping his thigh with an imaginary riding crop. "They've had just one too many rotten apples in *that* barrel. Grill 'em on a slow spit. Roast the buggers. Squeeze 'em until the juice runs out of every orifice in their bodies."

Tubby Fincher did not share in the elation, but C had told BMW to take the matter very seriously. "Get Paul Schillig over," C ordered Maitland-Wood. "This is not coincidence. Young Arnold Farthing's supposed to have leaped over the curtain, now Naldo's missing and we have this dreadful written proof." He pushed the typescript back to BMW, using his fingertips, as though the pages carried a plague.

"I want Gus Keene briefed regarding who he's to put on the rack," Maitland-Wood almost shouted. "That young pair he's brought with him should take a long hard look at this," waving the thick wedge of paper. "We must all be clear about which members of that accursed family still have direct access to sensitive material."

Fincher scribbled on a note pad as he spoke. "Old Richard sees other members of the family, and I should imagine they all talk about current matters," he muttered. "And that means James is implicated. Alexander's in a very sensitive position at Cheltenham, and Andrew's still on the P4 list." The P4 list contains names of lawyers, doctors, and other professional people on call for use by the intelligence and security services. "The Railtons presumably all talk to one another," Fincher added.

"They always have." Maitland-Wood was working himself up into a rage. "They're mentioned in the bloody history books. One of them was a go-between for Anthony Standen, Walsingham's agent. Sixteenth-century stuff. It's said that Walsingham himself was speaking of a Railton when he said, 'If there were no knaves, honest men should hardly come by the truth of any enterprise against them.' Tubby, just see that they're all quietly put on the restricted list. At some point I'll want to talk with the woman we placed there as an extra pension. For now, get me Keene."

"He's interrogating Naldo's wife."

"Well, when he's free I want to see him. He'll have to go through every Railton in the country like a dose of salts. Oh, and get Paul

Schillig over here. We're cutting the Yanks in on this. They have their own problems with the bloody Farthings, who are so interconnected with Railtons that it makes one wonder where all this will end."

It was at this moment the call came in from Cornwall to say BMW's pair of lion tamers had Beckeleg under control, their words, and were heading back to London with him.

"He's kicking up one hell of a stink," the senior of the two men said, on the open and insecure line.

"Subdue the bugger, then." Maitland-Wood had already passed into the uncharted world of a private and personal campaign against the Railtons. That it might do his career some good into the bargain did not once enter his conscious thoughts. Subconsciously, the hidden part of his mind must have been full of vaulting ambition. "They're bringing that bastard sailing fellow, Beckeleg, to London." He turned to Fincher. "Let Keene know I'm even more anxious to see him. Oh, and open up one of the empty safe houses so that we can get Beckeleg interrogated outside the shop."

Tubby hurried away, and Maitland-Wood returned to his journey through Caspar Railton's secret diaries.

The very first two entries set the entire picture for what was to follow. He had already sent down to Registry for the official log, kept on Caspar's movements as a matter of course. Even in the 1930s the Firm was on good terms with the passport control people at the main ports and aerodromes. The diary began on Monday 5th August 1935. The log showed that on Tuesday 6th, Caspar Railton had passed through Croydon aerodrome, booked on the Imperial Airways' morning flight to Paris, Le Bourget. The two entries in the diaries for these dates showed such premeditation that Maitland-Wood almost shook with rage.

In the calm of the Registry reading room, Carole Coles and Martin Brook were also startled by what they read, though this pair, surrounded by files going back to Caspar's induction into the Service in 1915, were shaken not so much by the treachery, but the blatant and wholly insecure manner in which this tough, experienced, and careful spymaster had laid out the facts.

Later, Carole was to say to Gus Keene, "It's almost as though the old bugger has marked a kind of Indian trail that he wants somebody to follow."

"Shouldn't be surprised," Keene replied. "Give us a kiss."

Carole complied, as they were in bed at the time, at the Regent Palace Hotel. Miss Coles then looked at Gus with a soft adoring in her large brown eyes. "Did anyone ever tell you that you look like a souped-up David Niven?" She smiled.

"No. At school they called me 'Monkey' Keene, which I always thought was a comment on my looks."

"Wrong, that's your agility. If you didn't have that leathery skin, and the plumpness around the jowls, you'd look just like a souped-up David Niven, I'd say."

"I feel agility coming on." Keene raised himself on one elbow and Carole turned over on her back, opening her legs. "I shall think of England," she said. "England, and you of course."

But, in the now and present, the ferret in Augustus Claudius Keene—his father had been an obsessive scholar of the Roman Empire—was just starting to probe interesting new ground with Barbara Railton. As he was to put it later, "Suddenly I reached into her drawers and guess who popped out? Our old friend Philip Hornby."

2

They had decided to use one of the small suites on the sixth floor, one down from the canteen, for Barbara's initial official interrogation. It was better than opening up a safe house, which meant a lot of paperwork, and the whole thing could be done with a certain amount of taste.

The arrangements with Barbara were made by telephone, and they sent a car for her. The car arrived not just with a driver, but a nanny: thirty-two years of age, ultra chic, and as tough as old boots. Keene decided that Barbara would be impressed by this, and the way in which the nanny shepherded her up to the sixth floor, occasionally placing a steely hand on her elbow, just to guide her to the comfortable rooms.

The suite was designed for these kind of meetings. There were two rooms. A bedroom—"Just in case you have to stay overnight"—and a sitting room, which was comfortable without being too relaxed: a polished mahogany table with two chairs stood in the center. The table was already set for luncheon. Apart from this furniture, there were two easy chairs, high backed, buttoned leather, with hard arms. They were the kind of thing that made you sit up properly.

Keene used the same type of chair at Warminster. He called them his *lacrimae rerum* chairs, and once, when asked by a particularly dense novice about this title, Gus had replied, "Means they can give you the shits, lad. On the hour, and every hour if the interlocutor is doing his job properly."

The suite's main room was kept at a slightly cool temperature and had one other feature, a large oil painting, very similar to one that Keene had in his "soft" interrogation suite at Warminster. It depicted a graveyard by moonlight. You could only see a very small part of the church itself, but the canvas bulged with tombstones, some new, many very old, cracked, leaning askew and all lit by a gibbous moon which threw the graves into a strange, bizarre perspective. It was an early winter scene, for the trees behind the graveyard were bare, black, and brooding in the moonlight.

It was rumored that Gus Keene had several of these oil paintings, all executed by himself for his own arcane reasons. But there were many rumors about this skillful man: that he recited the *Dies Irae* before starting a particularly difficult interrogation. One officer claimed to have heard a conversation between Keene and a fellow interrogator who explained in detail the finer points of how prisoners in the seventeenth and eighteenth centuries were whipped from Newgate to Tyburn. According to this man, Keene had listened with deep interest, and when the story was done he had calmly asked, "Do you know what kind of whips they used?"

Some of the Gus Keene rumors were true. Others were a slander.

Gus had expected the interrogation of Mrs. Railton to be a difficult and possibly lengthy business. In the privacy of his own heart he also did not expect to get anything out of it. Her attitude on the previous night had convinced him that, whatever Naldo was up to, Barbara knew nothing, had no secrets and, therefore, was as blameless as a newborn lamb. He also knew that, given his sadistic way, Willis Maitland-Wood could even use her as a sacrificial lamb. It was Gus Keene's job to keep her from *that* fate.

On her arrival, Keene bade Barbara sit down, asked if she would like coffee, sent the nanny away to get some and, when they were at last settled in the dreaded chairs, he even asked her permission to smoke his pipe. She seemed relieved and took out a packet of cigarettes. She was to smoke pretty well through the morning session.

"Well, Mrs. Railton, we have to get to the bottom of things, and you're our only real key to what might have been going on in your husband's mind."

She said nothing. Her hand was steady as she picked up the coffee cup, and equally steady as she lit the first of many cigarettes. She took a long pull at the cigarette, drew in the smoke, and then exhaled. "Yes. Yes, we *do* have to get to the bottom of it, Mr. Kane. That's right, isn't it, Mr. *Kane?*"

"Keene." Gus felt an odd nervous twitch in his brain. Attack, one part of him said, but experience and sense told him to make a steady, even confiding, approach. "We talked last night, Mrs. Railton, of your husband's long friendship with Arnold Farthing."

"Yes."

He repeated what she had said about the two men. "At one time, anyway, they were very close. You said you thought Arnold might have been stirring things. Could you elaborate?"

"Naldo talked a lot about Arnie before he left that night. He hadn't mentioned him for some time. Hadn't seen him for some time, come to that. It was odd."

"Then I think I have to let you into some highly classified information. You know, I presume, what Arnold's job entailed?"

"I know he works for the Agency, as they call it. He was stationed in Berlin. Naldo kept on about that as well."

"The Agency?"

"Yes. The Agency and Arnie's work."

Keene nodded, and told her about Arnold Farthing going missing. "He was due back in Washington, but never arrived," he finished. "Nobody's seen nor heard from him since. Unless, of course, your husband heard from him on that last day." He left it hanging, not a straight query, but Barbara felt there was a large question mark, drawn in the pipe smoke rising above Keene's head.

"I . . . I suppose he might have. It certainly stayed in my mind— Naldo's talking about Arnie, that is. I mean, he did go on about him." She looked up at Keene and made steady eye contact. "Where's Arnie gone?" There was some intensity about her question, as though she was attempting to take over the interrogation.

"All the signs are that he's gone East. To Moscow." Keene spoke without melodrama or exaggerated speech. The words came out sounding as though he was telling her that Arnold Farthing had gone to spend a weekend in Tunbridge Wells.

"Arnie?" Her face, and the tone of shocked surprise, were signs that she was either an actress of exceptional talent, or truly rattled. "Arnie, in Moscow? Are you saying he's gone over? Turned, or whatever damned fool word they use?"

"That's the feeling among his own people, and most of those who should know."

"I don't believe it. Not Arnie. Christ, he was so bloody straight it hurt." She lit another cigarette from the butt of the one she had almost smoked. This time her hand trembled.

"They all seem to be bloody straight, as you put it."

"Yes, but . . . well, Arnie was, what do the Yanks say? Gung-ho?" Keene said that, had he been working for Moscow, it would have been good cover.

"Was he under suspicion or anything?"

Keene paused, counting in his head and watching her eyes, then her hands. Six . . . seven . . . eight. "Why do you ask?"

"Well, they don't jump . . . they don't run to Moscow unless they think they've been blown, do they?" She held his eyes steadily.

"That's the usual reason." Nine . . . ten . . . eleven . . . twelve. "I don't know if he was suspect or not. But he *was* called back to Washington, and didn't seem enthusiastic about returning. His wife's vanished as well."

"Gloria? What about the children?"

"They're okay, but you should know that your husband's disappearance is now being linked to Arnold."

She laughed. Loudly and with no false notes, as though she was really amused. "That's tommyrot. Maitland-Wood hurtling to conclusions, I suppose?"

"Him, and others like him. Why's it tommyrot, Barbara? You don't mind my calling you Barbara?"

"Because it *is* tommyrot." She did not answer the second question. "Darling old Nald's so true blue that he could hide in the sky on a clear day. Moscow's nonsense."

"Then why's he disappeared, Barbara?"

"Heaven knows. Personally *I* don't think he *has* disappeared. I think he's up to some op on his own." She frowned, and Keene thought how attractive she looked when she puckered her brow.

"What kind of operation?"

"Oh, Lord knows. Maybe, if he knew about this ridiculous theory; Arnold going to Moscow and all that. Maybe he's just gone to try and talk sense into the man. They *are* close, you know, and since Caspar's death . . ." She trailed off.

"Yes?" Keene sensed he was on a main road. "Since Caspar Railton's death, what?"

She looked down at her hands. "Naldo missed Caspar. We *all* miss him. We knew he was a very sick man, but he . . . well, he seemed indestructible."

170

"Naldo was *really* cut up?"

"We all were. It made a great difference. You could talk to Cas. He was always there. He'd listen and understand. Even our son, Arthur . . ."

"Did *you* ever go to Caspar for advice?"

"Sometimes. You could say things and know they wouldn't be repeated."

"Such as?"

"Oh, Christ, Mr. Keene, you know what kind of things. When you thought your marriage was rocky, things like that."

"You talked to him about *your* marriage?"

"Once. A few years ago I thought we were going downhill a bit. You must be aware of the strain in Service marriages."

"And you were under strain and went to Caspar?"

"Yes. He understood. Gave sound advice."

"What about the state of your marriage now?" The question was not even on his mental list. It came full blown like an incubus leaping into his mind. As he asked it he felt a sense of evil.

"Fine. Great. Super. Marvelous." She paused after each word, an eyebrow tilted, as though she was mocking herself.

"Do I detect a note of uncertainty?"

She stared at her hands again, and he leaned forward, his index finger gently touching the back of her left hand. She looked up at him, her expression one of determination, even arrogance, though her eyes were brimming. A tear slid from her left eye and rolled slowly down her cheek. One tear, he thought, could become a flood.

"It can't be that bad. Come on. Tell me."

She bit her lip, looked down again, and shook her head like a child.

"That's what *my* job's about really," he told her. "I sit and listen. Then I ask some questions to see if I'm getting truth or fairy stories. If I can't tell, then others analyze it for me."

She still said nothing, head down again and shoulders shaking slightly. Was she going to break? he wondered. If so, what was there to break about? "We're just anxious to get to the truth. Reach out to it, even if it's messy, and put it back together. Barbara, we're on your side. We're on Naldo's side. We just need to know if there's anything you can tell us. You know? A candle to light the way."

"And a chopper to chop off my head?" she asked solemnly.

To Gus Keene, Barbara was an unknown quantity. He had read the file, as he had read Naldo's file. The Army and Service wife background made the woman, he thought. Why do tough women break down? Death of someone very close; treachery, mainly sexual treachery. Either way, Naldo or herself. "How's your sex life?" he suddenly said, asking aloud a question that had come into his mind only as a thought.

"With Naldo?" She was in control of herself now. The face, damp and pink-eyed, looked up defiantly again.

"Yes." Where was this heading? "Yes, with Naldo."

"It's always been terrific with Naldo, though I'm pretty certain he's unfaithful as hell. That comes with the job, doesn't it?"

Slowly, Gus Keene nodded. Sure it came with the job. The face of his own wife, Angela, crossed his mind. Can a man love two women? He certainly loved Angela. He also loved Carole. At least he thought he loved Carole. Aloud he said it certainly came with the job.

"That's his business," Barbara muttered bitterly. "He's under more stress. I just thought I had standards for myself. No idea it could happen to me."

Very slowly he asked, "What did you think couldn't happen to you?"

"If I was a Roman Catholic, I guess I'd make my confession and that would be that."

"Pretend I'm your confessor, then. You know what the psychiatrists say about confession: the Catholic sacramental kind, or the Alcoholics Anonymous, or those religions where you stand up and beat your breast and proclaim to everyone in the mission hall exactly what you've done? They say there's nothing mystical about it. Sharing it takes the weight off your conscience."

There was a long pause. Barbara looked up at the oil painting. That was pretty crude and horrible, she thought. All those bloody tombstones in the moonlight. At last she said, "Bless me, father, for I have sinned."

"Go on," Keene whispered, and out it came, the man on the steps of the Connaught; then again in Harrods; the apartment in Hans Crescent; the adultery; her pleasure. "I really enjoyed it. I didn't love him, or anything like that, but there was a day or two when I saw it as a kind of escape. I was aping Naldo's secret life, I suppose. I seemed to think it could be a kind of hobby." She giggled. "That sounds terrible, a hobby."

"It's how a lot of people view it. Only they're not always so honest. They don't own up to it like that." This was classic. They warned of it, had seminars on it. The wives of spies so often take their revenge on secrecy by building a secret life of their own. It happened all the time.

"I thought it would add another dimension." She gave another little splutter. "It was a change."

"Can you tell me this man's name?" It was a standard question, though he did not expect to get anything spectacular. Once he had the name he would ask what the fellow did for a living. The Seekers and Burrowers would take a walk around his life. It was amazing what they could do, the right question to the right person and, bingo, you had a new perspective.

"He's called Hornby," she said. "Philip Hornby."

Gus Keene's eyes widened, and his throat went dry. "Jesus," he said without the word crossing his lips. He took a deep breath. "And this place you went to? Hans Crescent, you said?" He could almost hear his own questions like words coming from a long way off, but her answers, the number of the block; the flat; and telephone, stayed where they hit, deep into his brain.

Finally he cautioned her. "If this man telephones you again, or tries to see you, I suggest you get in touch with someone here. Preferably me, but I'm elusive. Tubby Fincher'd be your best bet. But it's essential that you don't stay alone with him again."

"Oh, my God. Is it . . . ? I haven't done something that would really harm Nald, have I?"

"Let's hope not," he murmured, then aloud, "No. No, that's not it at all." Liar, he thought inside his head. It was unusual, but there were times when the Ks were plain bloody stupid. They had run three men called Philip Hornby in England. Not concurrently, of course, but they had allowed the Hornby Legend, as they called a deep, long-term cover, to be run by three completely different people, all of them doing the same job.

Whatever man was called Philip Hornby was answerable to the Ks. They used him as what they termed a Raven. Ravens were the reverse of Swallows. Ravens were seduction agents. Trained to it. They were usually put in to compromise mousy little women, often with heavy obligations to a parent, and always in sensitive jobs. Ravens would move in and flatter, adopt the same musical, literary, or political stand-point as the target. Immediately there would be a bond. They would become friends, then lovers. Gus had known Ravens who had been run with the same little secretary, or filing clerk, over five or six years. In the end there would always be a burn. The girl would steal "insignifi-cant" documents or facts from the office—"To help us. So that my business will expand, and I'll have enough money to make certain your mother/father/uncle/aunt/crippled brother can be looked after. So that we're free to marry."

It was all standard practice in what the wits called sexpionage, and it was tried and tested. Usually one hundred percent successful. Why Barbara Railton? he wondered. Compromise? To use as a lever against Naldo?

He knew of the Railtons' passion for Shakespeare. It was a legend in the trade. Now, Gus Keene thought of Hamlet and his mother, Gertrude. *Look upon this picture; and on this.* Or would it be, "Listen to this song, Naldo"—

> *O mistress mine! where are you roaming?*
> *O! stay and hear: your true love's coming,*
> *That can sing both high and low,*
> *Trip no further, pretty sweeting:*
> *Journeys end in lovers meeting,*
> *Every wise man's son doth know . . .*

They left it there for the day. Keene asked a few more innocuous questions, to calm her, then rang for the nanny. They took her home in the same car, and Gus Keene sought out the two young members of his team. He would share his news with them before talking to Maitland-Wood. In fact he felt it was his duty to share it with anyone other than Maitland-Wood. Yet he was concerned about Barbara Railton. If they were using some explicit pix of Barbara, probably without identifying the man, to lever Naldo; or even tapes of the act, with Barbara's voice filtered up so that it could be heard clearly, then the woman was not safe. She really needed a twenty-four-hour minder. Preferably a pair of them. With a dog.

When Barbara reached home, she was seen to the door by the nanny, then left. Hardly had she taken off her coat when the telephone rang. In some ways it was the kind of thing Gus Keene was dreading most.

3

Between them, Arnold, Naldo, and Caspar, together with many others, had trained Big Herbie Kruger well, though it was often argued that Herbie was born to the trade and needed no training in the secret black arts. As he himself would say, "Nobody tell me nothing to begin with. In the beginning was me, Herb. They turn over a stone and there I am, all ready, full of suspicion, wise of the streets, and brimming over with the tradecrafting like overfilled beer stein."

When they had said he should operate between Bonn and London, they advised him, "Only come to the shop when you're told to, Herb. Otherwise, just stay in the Annexe. Safer that way. Right?"

"Right," said Herb, looking puzzled. "What is Annexe?"

It was a good question. The Annexe was not easy to find, being halfway up a narrow, unmarked *cul de sac* which runs off Whitehall, heading in the direction of the Victoria Embankment. Annexe was, in truth, too grand a word for the place. The street door was unmarked.

Immediately inside the front entrance, to the right, lay a small office, complete with desk, four chairs, and three telephones. An automatic switchboard sat on the desk, and the room was used by a junior, during the times they let Big Herb work with a junior.

Behind the anteroom was the main office. This had space for only one desk, one chair, and a filing cabinet. The room beyond was a small bedroom, with a bed permanently made up, a tiny bedside table, and a wall clock. There were also things like an electric kettle and a tray with teapot, cups, etc. A sink was hidden by a curtain in the bedroom. When there was a junior, he was allowed into the bedroom to make tea or coffee.

When Big Herbie Kruger first set eyes on this dingy suite of offices he stood in the main area remarking that there was no room to—his words—"sling a dog." Once alone in the place he checked the three telephones. They both ran through the auto switchboard and, he reasoned, would be undoubtedly insecure. Most of the Firm's telephones were linked to recording devices.

On his second day, Herbie went and talked to a girl he knew in Security. "On the quiet, if you see my meaning, Josephine," he growled, doing his lovable cuddly bear act. "I need fumigating, regular. The place is beyond repair. Anyone in the know could have it spiked, ten minutes maximum." He meant, of course, that Josephine should see to it that the Annexe was regularly swept for eavesdropping devices, spike microphones in the walls, and other irregular hardware of that ilk.

Josephine, a big-chested, bubbling girl who liked Herbie enough to give him what he called "A little slapping and tickling on the side," was eager to oblige. On all counts. It turned out that while the telephones were certainly linked to the authorized machines at the shop, the remainder of the place was clean as a police whistle.

On his next trip into London from Bonn, Herbie telephoned a man whom he knew from drinking in his local pub in St. John's Wood and asked him out for a lunchtime beer. In fact, this meant several beers. The man had absolutely no connection with either the Firm or their brethren of Five. Herbie had checked thoroughly. He knew the man only as Eric. Though again, using the many deceptive arts he had learned, Herbie was in possession of Eric's full name and his family history. Eric worked for what was then known as the GPO, and the GPO were the people you saw if you wanted a telephone installed, something that could still take a long time in central London in the 1960s. Certain facts of life never change.

"I pay the bills and everything, regular as inside the clock, Eric," Herb said. "But I need the bloody thing last month. All my office phones are monitored so we can't make calls outside in work time."

Eric now learned that his large friend had a lady, and the lady had a husband. It was necessary for Herb to have a private telephone, installed with great discretion, and operating on an ex-directory number. Herb had gilded the story. His lady friend worked for the same Company as himself.

"Say no more, squire," Eric told him. "Leave it to me. Do the job myself." And true to his word, Eric turned up one morning, before, to use his somewhat crude words, "Sparrow fart." He had a new telephone installed, with an ex-directory number, billed to Herb's home address in St. John's Wood. All kosher, except that the Firm had no idea. A telephone that does not exist, except as one that shows as ex-directory in St. John's Wood, cannot be bugged. This was the telephone Big Herbie had used to ring Naldo at the Villa Carlo, and it was this number that he gave for emergency use to Naldo.

Later in the day of that early-morning call from Herbie, the same telephone rang, connecting Herbie with Naldo Railton, who lay on the bed of his pleasant hotel room at The Grand Hôtel Victoria-Jungfrau, Interlaken, Switzerland.

From the moment Naldo saw the photograph of his wife, with the message requesting his presence in Thun the day after tomorrow, he knew that both Gloria and himself were under surveillance. He was also concerned because the photograph endangered his wife's life. He was under threat, supposedly from Arnie, or friends of Arnie's, because they had that picture. The everyday, normal man-in-the-street would find it hard to believe that people could take a picture of his wife, clad only in silk underwear of dubious taste. In Naldo's world it was not unheard of, and it bore a message. Do as you're told or something much worse than a rather sexy picture will this way come.

After Herb's telephone call, which brought with it a line of communication, Naldo Railton felt a little happier. Not a lot, but he knew what had to be done. He woke Gloria, told her the bare minimum, and instructed her to get her things together in short order.

In turn, he repacked his canvas bag, now containing not only Caspar's papers, but also the entire contribution of the necessary sections of *Hypermarket*, courtesy Eberhardt Lukas Kruger, which he had developed and printed the previous day.

Together, Naldo and Gloria locked up the villa, set the alarms, and left town on the first bus available to take them to Locarno. From there they took a train to Lugano. Before lunchtime they had registered as M. & Mme. Provin. It was only necessary for Naldo to show *his* French passport at the desk of The Splendide Royale, Lugano's de luxe caravanserai. By now he knew the name would be on some list which would ring bells in quiet Swiss police stations, but he did not intend to stay in any hotel for long. Naldo himself was at The Splendide Royale for the best part of fifteen minutes, leaving by one of the trade entrances and heading for the station to catch the first train to Bellinzona which, by luck and no planning, carried him on to Andermatt where he had a half-hour's wait before catching a direct fast train to Interlaken.

He had spotted two of the surveillance team on the way to Lugano. After that, nothing. He had no worries about Gloria, who was very wise to the ways of Naldo's and her husband's professions. She would keep to the room at the hotel, feigning that her "husband" was in the bathroom when room service brought meals. It meant the surveillance team could be bewitched for twenty-four hours.

Naldo had chosen Interlaken because it would take him less than an hour by train to get to Thun. The trains to Thun were frequent. He had no option but to keep the appointment, but he would not take either Caspar's papers or the *Hypermarket* documents with him. They would have to be mailed to somewhere safe. In the meantime he would go through them in detail, in order to be prepared for anything that might follow. But first he had to make sure that Barbara and the two children were taken to safety, and there was only one way to do that.

On the fifth ring Herbie's private, and unknown, telephone was picked up. Herbie grunted at the distant end.

"Herb?"

"Thank God. Nald, I waited for a call. I fell into real tiger trap. Stupid. You okay?"

"Yes. At the moment." He then went through the action he was forced to take the following day: the meeting in Thun.

"You want me come out? You want help? I come, wherever you are, Nald. I come so fast feet do not touch the ground."

"It's better you help from where you are." He gave Herbie rapid instructions which included the code word he would use to Barbara

177

meaning he was well, and that she must do as she was told without question.

Herbie would have to shift gears and do some very fancy footwork. Naldo wanted Barbara and the children protected. To be hidden in plain sight, where nobody would even think of looking for them. Nobody must be alerted.

"I do it all, Nald. I get on it now. Then I call back . . . Where?"

Naldo gave him the hotel and room number. "Any problems, ask for Mr. Provin," he said.

"Leave to me. I fix. I'm good fixer, Nald, you know that."

"You'd better be, you fat idiot."

"Inside every fat idiot is thin idiot trying to get out." Herbie hung up before Naldo could say more.

Praying all would run smoothly, he went back to Caspar's diary, which he had spread out on the bed. He found it very hard to concentrate, one ear cocked for the telephone and Herbie's answering okay which would mean Barbara, Arthur, and Emma were safely stowed away.

He waited five hours.

ELEVEN

1

It had been just after the war, sitting one night in some safe house outside Frankfurt, that the now dead Caspar Railton had given Herbie Kruger, then a lad in his teens, advice that the large German was never to forget.

"If you get on in this business," Caspar said, "there's a golden rule. Gather around you people you can trust, but who aren't in the trade itself. You need good drivers, electricians, plumbers, people with skills. Make sure they're honest, and be certain they're not booby-trapped."

"What is boobytrapped?" Herbie remembered asking. He smiled now as he thought of it. Caspar had gone on to explain that, in the trade, you soon got a nose for the right kind of outsiders. "You have to pull them at home and in the field. They're especially useful at home, where the shop doesn't know about them. Appeal to their instincts of loyalty. Tell them you might want to use them for a special job one day. Make them believe that what you ask them to do is for their country, whatever their country is, and that only *they* can do it."

This had been advice which Big Herbie had followed down the years, as a monk will follow a pattern of religious meditation.

By now, Herbie had a whole private and personal team upon whom he could rely. Each one was handpicked. They would ask no questions, and expect no wages. Eric, the telephone engineer, was one of them though Herbie did not have to work on *his* personal love of country. Eric was a bit of a rogue, acquainted with people who would do him over if he stepped out of line, so he kept his mouth shut on every subject under the sun.

Using the telephone that Eric had installed for him, Herbie now made contact with another private recruit. This man loved driving, was good at it, and remained silent on matters conveyed to him by

Herbie. He could also be trusted to carry out instructions to the letter. He was called Tim Matyear—of Huguenot stock, as his name indicated. A tall, muscular man in his early forties, Matyear, because of certain family matters in past history, would rather die than fail his country. An admirable trait when one considered that both the work ethic and true chauvinism were now both condemned as unfashionable.

"You just caught me, Noddy," Tim said when he answered the call. He knew Kruger only as Noddy. "I was going up West with the wife. Going to see what the bright lights are like, you know how women get at Christmas, thought I'd give her a treat. Regent Street looks a picture with all those angels."

"Sorry, Tim, your country is calling. I have work for you."

There was a long silence at the distant end. Then—

"I can take the wife tomorrow, don't worry about it."

With great care, Herbie explained exactly what Tim had to do, from the telephone call he was to make, to arrangements for picking up his passengers.

It was Tim at the other end of the line when Barbara answered the ringing phone, as she returned to the house near Kensington Gardens after her session with Gus Keene.

"Mrs. Railton?" Tim asked.

"Yes." She was flurried and out of breath.

"My name's Pegler. I've just got back to my office. I gather you need a car in the morning. For your children, it says here. Ten o'clock to take them to, I can't read my wife's writing, is it Haversage or Maversage, not sure which, or where it is? Have I got it right?"

The trigger words clicked into place in Barbara's mind. "Pegler"; "can't read my wife's writing"; "Maversage." These, plus the "ten o'clock" added up to "Be ready in an hour, with your whole family. A car will pick you up."

"Yes," she answered, suddenly going very calm. It was as though Naldo was speaking to her. "Yes, ten tomorrow morning. Just my children. It's Haversage. Redhill Manor. They'll point the way when you get there. We're going for Christmas, only it looks as though I shall have to follow on. I've still got business in London."

"Right, madam." Tim was a natural for the job. "If they're there, with their luggage, I'll be with you on the dot of ten in the morning."

"Thank you very much. I'm most obliged. I'll see they're ready." She hoped to heaven that Arthur and Emma were at home, and not rocking around swinging London tonight. With relief, Barbara heard

180

them coming down the stairs. She recradled the telephone and turned to face them, finding that she was automatically asking Naldo's usual questions—"No odd messages? Nobody been in? Telephones? Gas Board? Electricity meter reader?"

"No calls. No visitors. What's up, Ma?" For a second, in the hall light, Arthur looked like Naldo when she had first met him.

"It's family business," she said calmly. Emma was on the landing behind Arthur. "Pack some warm clothes. Essentials only . . ."

"Aren't we going to Redhill? I thought . . ." Arthur began.

"No questions, please, chickens." She had not called them chickens since they were very small and they reacted to it, knowing instinctively that something was wrong.

"Where're we going?" Emma asked. There was a hint of accusation in her voice.

"I don't know."

"But . . ."

"*I do not know!* But it's on your father's instructions. You'd better be clear that there's some danger. I've no idea what, but just get ready, and prepare for possible unpleasantness."

"Dad's not like that bastard Philby, is he, Ma?"

"Watch your language, Emma. Certainly not. How could you think of such a thing?"

The listeners, who had been on twenty-four-hour watch since Naldo had disappeared, noted the telephone call, passing the information to the supervising officer, who in turn sent it up to the fifth floor.

"She seems to be playing it straight," Fincher said. "The kids're going to the Manor tomorrow. It's bloody cold out tonight, shall I call off the house surveillance?"

Maitland-Wood looked at the transcript of the conversation. "You run a check on this Pegler fellow?"

"Car-hire firm. Up-market. Mayfair. Straight."

"Get the dogs out of the cold, then. I'm off to have a chat with this bloody Beckeleg boatman."

So it was that the two novices who had been detailed to watch the back and front of Naldo's house were withdrawn some fifteen minutes before the black Rover pulled up. The driver, in uniform, got out and was starting towards the door when Arthur and Emma came out, shepherded by Barbara. There were three suitcases, two of them carried by Arthur. Barbara did not wear a coat. She supervised as the luggage was stowed away and the young people settled into the back of the car. To anyone interested, it was as though Barbara was seeing her family off on a holiday. Only at the last minute did she seem to remember something, returning to the house, hands hugging her shoulders in the chill of the night.

Inside the house, she activated the alarms, grabbed a small parcel already prepared and lying on the table in the hall, switched off the lights, and seemed to allow the door to close by accident. She opened the car's front passenger door and appeared to be having a short conversation as the driver switched on the ignition. Only at the last moment did Barbara slide into the passenger seat. The door had hardly closed before the Rover was off, picking up speed.

But there was nobody from the shop to see. Nobody to report back to the Firm. Maitland-Wood had dropped his guard, and in those crucial minutes, Naldo's family had been whisked away. The error was not discovered until the morning, and by then they were already installed in a small family hotel in the quiet village of Axbridge, close to Cheddar, in the West country, lying below the folds of the Mendip Hills.

The only people to note the exit of Naldo Railton's family from their Kensington home were a young couple indulging in some heavy sexual groping in a Mini some fifty yards away. They were due to be relieved by a small van which was to park below them, at one in the morning. The driver of the van would lock his vehicle and go away. The two-man team would stay in the back, observing the house through two-way mirrors, disguised as glass panels.

As it was, the moment Barbara leaped into the Rover, so the young woman slapped the driver's face inside the Mini and got out, quickly walking back up Exhibition Road. The Mini's engine started and it drew away, some three cars' distance behind the Rover.

Tim, the driver, did not spot any surveillance on him during the drive to the West country, but the Mini's driver was a cautious, intuitive man, who knew the roads of England almost as well as he knew the fastest route from the Patrice Lumumba University to Turgen Square, a spit and a stride from Dzerzhinsky Square, Moscow. His skin was black and, at one time, he had hoped to become a doctor. To that end he had gone, with many other so-called Third World students, to Moscow with the promise that he would study medicine. Instead he had been one of the first graduates of the Lumumba University where he learned, not medicine, but the science of guerrilla warfare, the making of bombs, the arts of terrorism, and the way to strike at the heart of the capitalist powers.

The driver had been such a promising student that they had kept him on in Moscow and taught him other skills. On that night he was also helped by two other cars.

The girl who had been with him in the Mini walked quickly into Kensington Gore and crossed the road. She passed the luxurious façade of the Royal Garden Hotel and turned right again, through the police-guarded gates leading to Kensington Park Gardens. Within five minutes, Ludmilla Kirsanov was making her report to the Second Secretary (Trade) in a sterile room in the Russian Embassy basement.

"They have all gone," she spoke in Russian. "But Sammi is behind them. It would be best, Comrade Secretary, to have other of our people out."

The Second Secretary nodded and smiled. "They are already out. Sammi is using his radio. He makes an excellent Jamaican freelance taxi driver on the air. We have them well covered."

"May I go, then, yes, Comrade Secretary?"

"You have done well, Kirsanov. Very well. Sleep now."

2

At almost the same moment as Naldo's family was being spirited out of London, Carole Coles was making her observations regarding Caspar's discovered diary to her lover, Gus Keene, in bed at the Regent Palace Hotel.

Earlier, she had stopped for a drink with their other partner, Martin Brook. He was also at a loss concerning the late Sir Caspar's revelations. "The man was a pastmaster of deception." Brook gazed into his beer. "You've only got to glance at the restricted file to see how he operated through the years. Damn it, he left the Service because he considered we were neglecting the Russian target, and, after the war, he broke that unwilling defector Rogov."

Gennadi Aleksandrovich Rogov was an NKVD (precurser of the KGB) officer who had been lured into the West shortly after the end of the war. Caspar had been mainly responsible for the interrogation of the man whom he had finally broken. Out of the entire business Caspar Railton had written a handbook on KGB tradecraft that was still standard and required reading on the induction course at Warminster.

Brook wore a puzzled look. "There's something not quite right about the whole thing. Certainly the diaries appear to show great familiarity with the Sovs, their operational methods, cryptos, drops, the works. But why would someone like Sir Caspar, who was so careful in his own work, be so slovenly in covering his tracks?"

Carole agreed. "The Father Confessor will have to go through this with his tweezers. If I didn't know that BMW and his crew, including C, were taking the matter so seriously, I'd say it was a hoax."

And, as all these things were happening, so Naldo Railton, nervous to hear that Barbara was safe, carefully examined the documents in his possession at The Grand Hôtel Victoria Jungfrau, Interlaken.

The *Hypermarket* material was straightforward. Just as Oleg Penkovsky had slandered the Railton name by directly suggesting that his cover was blown by an agent of influence working under the cryptonym *Dionysus*, so Blunt had, in a couple of sentences during one of the recent interrogation sessions, provided backup mentions. Like Penkovsky, a few years before, he had directly implicated the Railtons and Farthings.

Naldo read the transcript. The dialogue was like two men chatting, exchanging gossip, in a club. The interrogator was relentless but pleasant. "Anthony," he began the relevant passage, "we have a very strong lead on possible people still working for the Soviet Union within the Service. That is, within both services, Five and SIS."

"Really?" Blunt sounded bored and languid.

"Yes, *really*, Anthony. And by what you've already told us, I want to run a few cryptos through your mind. Think of it as a game. Put the right name to the right crypto."

"Peter, I've told you a hundred times, I've been out too long. The Russian Service had no more use for me. I agree, there are indications that they had someone, probably much better-placed than I. I was low grade. You *must* know that."

"Yes, we know it, but we don't completely buy it, my dear fellow. We're pretty certain that you *did* know one or two people who were active. Let me give you one pair of cryptos. *Dionysus* and *Croesus*. Heard those before?"

When he read the words in the transcript, Naldo's stomach turned over. *Dionysus* and *Croesus*, the names used by Oleg Penkovsky in that last, seemingly frantic, message to London saying he thought he was blown.

He remembered Arnold Farthing, quoting verbatim from the decrypted signal, in the Berlin safe house, as the snow fell outside—

"**. . . Since the late 1930s there has been an agent of influence within the Secret Department,**" Arnold had quoted. By the Secret Department, the Russians meant the Secret

Intelligence Service. **"This man is now retired, but I believe I have met him. I do not know his real name, but he belongs to an aristocratic family which has links with the world of secrets going back for centuries. The man's cryptonym is *Dionysus*. His dossier was Sovbloc Red . . ."** That all figured. The family with links going back for centuries, and the dossier marked Sovbloc Red. The Sovbloc Red stamp appeared on SIS officers' dossiers if they were known to the Soviet intelligence services, and those of their satellites. Caspar's certainly carried Sovbloc Red. **". . . and the dossier suggests that he still provides high-octane material via a relative who is known as *Croesus*. This man might be a son. Further details are that *Dionysus* was seriously wounded in the First Great War. *Croesus* is a Sovbloc Green. Also a member of the same family is what we call a *shifr odtel*."** That fixed it. Caspar had been branded by the words. Inevitably, Caspar was *Dionysus*. Who, then, was *Croesus* if he had a Sovbloc Green, signifying he could be used on covert assignments? Himself? Yes, though he had worked very close to the Russians, Naldo had not yet lost his Sovbloc Green stamp. And a member of the same family was a *shifr odtel*—a codebreaker, a cryptanalyst. The loathsome runt, Alexander, Caspar's younger son.

Naldo recalled the signal had gone on to implicate an American family who could only be the Farthings. His mind filled with fury as Blunt stalled, recovered, and stalled again. He was, Naldo thought, a consummate artist in what the Russians called *Dezinformatsia:* just as Oleg Penkovsky had been. Now Blunt put the boot in.

"Yes." There was a note that Blunt had sounded vague. *As though he was searching back through dozens of names, hundreds of acquaintances,* the note said. Then Blunt spoke again—

"Yes, those were active cryptos. Identification's difficult, I'm trying to recall who brought them up. The Russian Service was very careful about interconsciousness."

"Your last case officer, perhaps?"

"Perhaps. It isn't easy, you know. I recall *Dionysus* being mentioned, and *Croesus,* come to that. *Croesus* was definitely a penetration. There was talk of them being related. Father? Son? Nephew? I really can't remember it. Oh, do let me rest from all this."

"A little more, Anthony. Just a little more. Think about *Dionysus* again. Was he long-term?"

185

"Very." No hesitation, the note said. "Oh, very long-term. As long as Kim or the others, I felt."

"Interconscious with Kim and Guy Burgess?"

"No." Again very firm. "No, but senior. Very senior indeed. I cannot recall Kim, or Guy, ever mentioning a crypto like *Dionysus*, or even *Croesus*. It came from a quite different source." The transcript marked a long pause, as though Blunt's expression was altering. Then, *"Dionysus'* situation in the Service went back to the '14–'18 war, I know that. I mean his history in the SIS, or Five, whichever. I'm pretty sure it wasn't Five. One remark I do recall. My control said something about 'that one-armed and one-legged *Dionysus.'* But he also talked about someone who had been recruited in Shanghai, but that was Five. Could even have been Roger Hollis himself. But I'm almost certain the cripple was SIS. No, positive, and *Croesus* was certainly a relative."

That did it very nicely, Naldo thought. All the backup anyone needed. Right from the fucking art expert's mouth. Blunt was leading them all along false trails, lighting long fuses to distant witch-hunts.

He was already well into Caspar's diaries when Herbie called back to say Barbara and the children were out of London and on the way. They would be in the Axbridge hotel within the hour. Herbie recited the false names under which they had booked in, and the telephone number. All this information, together with a little Flash identity material, credit cards, a few letters and the like, had been handed over by Tim Matyear.

With great relief, Naldo went back to the diaries.

3

Caspar had been careful to use two different methods so that the diaries could be distinguished one from the other. First, the transcript from Diary One, the concocted work originally in cipher, had been typed on a modern electric machine. Probably, Naldo judged, an IBM golf ball. Diary Two, the real and unciphered work, had been done on a much older manual machine. In the package of notes called *Bogeyman*, Naldo discovered the two affidavits giving legal proof. Witnesses, dates, times, and indisputable evidence that the two works were genuine. One true, the other, in cipher, false, and put together in order to mislead someone senior in the SIS, and so prepare what Caspar referred to as a "Tiger trap. A pit with sharpened stakes, covered with fronds and bracken, into which the unwary would fall, no matter who it might be."

The rest of the night was spent tracing those three years of Sir Caspar's double lives. By six o'clock in the morning, Naldo had placed extracts from each of the diaries side by side, marking and interleaving them.

The diary that Caspar had seeded, to be found if necessary, appeared to provide conclusive proof that he had already been recruited by the Soviet Service before his resignation, while the other, real, diary told a very different story. The tone was set in the first two extracts from each.

The entries for 5th and 6th August 1935 read as follows—

DIARY ONE—For the consumption of those for whom the trap had been set:

Tuesday 5th August 1935
Today I left for good. Consummatum est. For several weeks now, since the long talk I had with the man who calls himself <u>Redruth</u>, I have been going out of my way to be difficult, picking small quarrels with senior officers and, twice, with C himself. Today, things came to a head at the morning briefing. I blew up after remarks concerning the Nazi target, particularly a stupid query from a young officer just posted to Prague who had complained that his senior in passport and visa control had not been able to give him any advice on how to proceed with his real work. There was a similar one last week from our new nominee in Berlin.

In front of everyone C said that I was taking it all too seriously and that these things happened. I remarked that we should be acting professionally and we might as well ally ourselves to Stalin, in Soviet Russia, who appears to be doing a good job in removing the dead wood. My implication was that <u>we</u> had a great deal of dead wood.

C asked me to withdraw the remark. I refused and resigned on the spot, leaving without saying goodbye to anyone. I simply cleared my desk and went home, taking with me some extracts from our Most Secret notes on the conduct of officers working in overseas embassies.

Tonight, C had the gall to send a young junior, a pompous little ass called Maitland-Wood, to ask if I would reconsider. My answer was 'Certainly not.' Good.

Finis. Farewell, a long farewell to all my greatness.
But another greatness calls. Tomorrow I meet Redruth in
Paris and it will now start in earnest. I wonder what
Pa would have thought?

Wednesday 6th August 1935

The hell is not being able to confide in anyone.
After a lifetime of knowing and debriefing field agents,
I realise the dangers and terrible loneliness I now face.
Last night I spoke at length to Phoebe about being
disillusioned with the Service, but was careful not to
show absolute disloyalty. Nobody must suspect, and the
danger lies within the family, as it has always done. I
said to Phoebe that, before we try to start a life of
retirement, I would need a short rest. I fear that I
shall need these 'short rests' quite frequently now
that I am to serve a new master.

This morning I flew to Paris, and booked into an
unlikely hotel near the Place de l'Opera. The Hôtel
des Deux-Mondes, which, I suspect, is a whores' paradise,
for they appear to have some rooms which are leased by
the hour. At four minutes past seven this evening I made
contact with Redruth in the Café Balzac. He hardly
spoke, so we observed the local ground rules. He left a
copy of Paris Soir on the table which I picked up to
read when he had gone. Inside was a slip of paper
giving me the address of one of their safe houses in
Paris.

At the safe house, which lies off the Avenue
Kléber, on the top storey of an apartment block, I met
Redruth as arranged. He had another man with him who
said I was to call him Dubois. I think he is a French
national, but he speaks perfect Russian.

We stayed until dawn, and it turned out to be a
long debriefing session. I gave them the names of all
our overseas agents in the Embassies, and also the
identities of the local agents. At least those I knew
about. They were more specific in their demands. They
need from me a complete list of both the Five and SIS
Order of Battle, which I take to mean the organisation,
with names of all who run Departments. This, as I told
them, would take a little time. I would have to sit
down and write out the entire thing from memory. I

also pointed out that I was not completely au fait with Five's operational organisation.

Their questioning was very thorough, and I am in no doubt they are testing me, quite rightly, to make certain I am no double. Both of the men spoke of Stalin in the most glowing terms. <u>Redruth</u> said that he really is weeding out the poison ivy within the system. I cannot but have a high regard for all this. Lenin maintained that early Communism had no chance of work-ing without the co-operation of the West: free trade and the like. Stalin maintains that, to work, Communism must have a leader, someone firm at the helm. He is undoubtedly the man.

I performed their tasks, and wrote a detailed list of the way in which the SIS is organised. Also what I knew of Five's setup. Both are friendly and well-disposed to me. They say someone will be in touch in a matter of three or four days. This is impressive, for it means they will have been able to check what I have told them in a very short time. I shall wait impatiently.

The true diary, typed on an old manual, probably the ancient Royal Naldo had seen many times in The Hide, told a very different story.

<u>Tuesday 5th August 1935</u>
Well, I've done it now. Lord forgive me, I can only hope I get away with it. For several weeks I have engineered rows, been cantankerous and a generally difficult person to deal with. It appears that we are shifting our sights. More and more I see meagre cash, and even more badly-trained officers, going into the field. All the time the accent is on infiltrating the Nazi Party.
It is quite right that we should do this, but <u>not</u> at the cost of action against the Soviet target. C and his cohorts see the Communist Party of Great Britain as the only threat and are happy to leave them to Five. Our own people are gradually being withdrawn from their areas of influence. I think the policy is appalling. The Foreign Office are

said to be certain of some non-aggression pact
with that peasant madman Stalin. I am not so sure.
True, Stalin will sign a pact with either
ourselves or the Nazis. It will, though, be signed
for one reason only: so that Russia has a little
more time to prepare herself for what, inevitably,
must come: a clash between the USSR and the Nazi
forces of darkness.

I have no doubt that, before this decade is out,
we shall see Europe in flames again and I could
weep when I think of the slaughter. The situation
in Spain daily grows worse, and it may be that the
first shots of a new war will start there with the
cut and dried issue of Fascism versus Communism,
or something similar. In the meantime it is folly
to use all our resources on Hitler and his gang.
They will be the first cause, but the last must be
Communism, and Stalin's brand appears to be the
worst possible, most barbarous, way. If I am not
allowed to fight Stalinism from within the
Service, the best I can do is go out and fight it
for myself. In the end I shall, if lucky, return
with the hard information concerning Stalin's
aims and intelligence plans.

It is only a month since I met the man who calls
himself Redruth. He is so damned obvious in his
approach, and it did not take many minutes to
realise that he was testing the water. Three weeks
ago I let him believe that I was interested, by
making one or two vaguely disparaging remarks
about the Service and the weakness of our
country's liberal democracy. He has bitten, and
told me he will be in Paris for the rest of this
month.

When I went into the shop this morning, I was very
much in two minds about the whole business. It is
impossible to talk with C and some of those around
him. If I shared my plans with any of them I would
be turned down flat. The Soviet target is to be
left to Five. In the middle of the Tuesday meeting
a sudden chance came my way and I was able to cause
an almighty eruption which led to a straight

190

battle of bitter words between C and myself, in front of everyone. This will be my only chance, and it appeared to be Godsent. I blustered out, wrote a letter of resignation and cleared my desk.

Now, the plans of the past year can be put on my own operational footing. I am free of the Service, yet I serve it still and, what is best, I shall serve my country more loyally than ever.

C tried to make amends, but it was a half-hearted affair. He sent that ignorant little ass Maitland-Wood, hardly out of nappies, to plead his case. I sent him packing and then told old Phoeb I had resigned. She is bewildered, but will see the point in due course. I have told her I must get away to rest for a while. Tomorrow I shall seek out Redruth in Paris. At least we have his real name on file, and I have made certain that Five know exactly who he is, though I am loath to name him even in this true representation of my actions. Maybe, as time passes, the moment will come.

Wednesday 6th August 1935

I am having second thoughts. This account is being written after my return from the Paris trip, though I shall try to set things out on the days they occurred. Today I flew from Croydon, hating every minute of it. I just cannot understand how Dick and James enjoy the business. The Imperial Airways De Havilland aeroplane was well appointed but noisy. I booked into this really terrible hotel near the Opera. It seemed best to stay away from my old haunts, though I took a walk around and was accosted seven times in broad daylight. Some of the women are attractive, though I wonder how they would take to my false limbs. I laughed aloud when I thought of a mild joke. I could hear one of the tarts in some bedroom saying to me, 'Just unscrew it and throw it over here, chéri, and I'll take care of it.'

At about six o'clock I telephoned the number Comrade Redruth had given me. He sounded overjoyed, and there was absolutely no element of secrecy or tradecraft. He gave me the name of a

café and we met there shortly after seven. Almost
immediately I realised that I have few qualities
required of a field agent. I do not lie easily. The
fellow went on and on about Stalin and the
wonderful things the bastard is doing for Soviet
Russia. He maintains that Communism requires a
strong hand at the helm. 'Comrade Marshal Stalin
is our strong right arm, not just a hand,' he said.
It sickened me, knowing what I do about the camps,
and the terrible slaughter which seems to go on
daily at this man's whim. The fool will denude his
army of leaders and his rule appears to be designed
to cut away any decent Communist with true ideals.
Stalin is after a puppet state, like Hitler. Of
course I had a lot of the old line thrown at me.
'The only way we can curb the menace of the Nazi
Party is by joining forces and turning all Europe
against this Fascist horror,' Redruth said. All I
could do was agree.

Then, with no further preamble, he came straight
out with it. 'Are you prepared to help us in the
struggle?'

I had to say, 'Of course, but how can I help?' It
stuck in my craw, for I knew this man was, in
reality, asking me to join in the Stalinist
struggle. He said I would be a great assistance,
being already a powerful member of the British
Secret Intelligence Service. His face was a
picture when I told him I had resigned. He said we
must talk in more privacy, and gave me an address.
I was to follow him, leaving it for ten minutes
after he made his own exit.

At the house, which was one known to our Embassy
people last year, a second man was waiting. I
recognised him instantly as Pierre Dubois, of the
French Embassy in London. 'Well, Caspar,' he
greeted me. "Never did I expect to meet you under
these circumstances.' I managed to joke about it,
though it was soon obvious that I was undergoing a
test. Both men agreed that I could still be of
assistance to them. Dubois even suggested that I
swallow my pride and return to the Service. As this
is my intention in any case, I told them I would

have to consider it. They then asked many
questions, mainly foolish little things that
could be easily checked. I used common sense and
told the truth. They asked mainly about the
organisation of the SIS. Names and so forth. Also
names of our officers in Embassies, working as
Passport and Visa secretaries. There was little
point in holding back. They almost certainly had
the information already. In the end, they said I
would know more by Friday. I wait with some
anticipation, for, if I am accepted, there is a
strong possibility that, sooner or later, I shall
get my hands on the intelligence I seek. (a)
Stalin's blueprint for Europe. He certainly has
one. For all the reign of terror and
denunciations, the man is mad with power, and the
very fact that the Comintern exists at all is a
sign that he is working towards a Europe, possibly
a world, dominated by Communism. I wonder if it
would be his brand, or the real thing. Both are
bad. His is the worse of two evils. (b) Discover
unknown agents at work in Britain. I have no doubt
there are many.

Naldo read quickly, and with immense interest. The diversity between the two documents was fascinating, the first giving a picture of
Caspar as a completely dedicated agent for the Communist cause; the
second showing the truth of what he was doing. If anyone took the
first, fictional, diary seriously, then there was indeed tragedy ahead for
both Caspar's memory and the Railton and Farthing futures.

During that very first week in 1935 Caspar Railton was recruited as
an agent of the NKVD, as it then was. In the record of truth, he
continued to set out his real aims, while in the fictional Diary One,
Caspar made clear every move. He carefully dovetailed both accounts.
Should anyone ever wish to check his movements they would never
find a deviation. His forays into Europe were always taken as short
breaks, sometimes Phoebe accompanied him, and there was no doubt
that, mixed up with a whole lot of chickenfeed, Caspar had been
forced to provide certain facts. He was careful to record each item he
passed on: usually names of agents the Firm already considered to be
compromised; the many doubtful people who had insinuated themselves into the networks of the SIS across Europe. Often he tested the

Bolsheviks by providing names of those who were thought to be working both sides of the street; or those considered to be borderline cases. The Firm would know, sooner or later, who was real and who false.

It was also clear that the Russians had, long ago, divined that British Embassy passport and visa control officers were in reality SIS people. Caspar saw no reason to muddy the water on this point, and confirmed several names. He also gave them the true information that the Russian target had been downgraded. He made no mention of Five's renewed efforts to penetrate the CPGB and the Comintern.

In the fiction he was utterly dedicated, not to Communism in the mold of Lenin or Marx, but in the hideous bloodletting of Stalin's society, with its purges, show-trials and ensuing barbarism. In the diary of fact he showed just how difficult it was for him to retain the fiction.

In many ways the fictional diary should have spelled out the truth, for he was very careful not to take geographic risks. His business with the controller allotted to him was carried out either in England, France, or Switzerland. He made no move to cross into Russian territory, though on several occasions they tried to tempt him. By the end of 1935 he was fully operational, with the cryptonym *Dionysus*. The crypto which stuck across the years. In fact it became even more clear, as time went by, why both Penkovsky and, later, on Kremlin instructions, Blunt had fingered Caspar. By the early spring of 1938 Caspar had the relevant information he had set out to gather. Soon after his return to the Service he went cold on his controller, who was quickly arrested and expelled from the country. Within three years of war, the NKVD must have suspected, if not actually known, that they had harbored a double.

Why, then, Naldo asked himself, did they not simply liquidate Caspar? Many traitors to the Stalinist, and later other would-be Soviet dictators' causes, were simply executed. The NKVD had a special squad whose duty was to carry out these "executions," going to the ends of the earth. This was the élite unit originally known as Smersh—*Smert Shpionam*, or Death to Spies, made into popular fiction by Ian Fleming, some of whose James Bond books Naldo had read with amusement, particularly for their high content of "in" jokes. The unit was far from amusing though, operating under that particular name between 1943 through 1946. Its name had altered over the years, but it still existed as a special core of men and women whose job it was to carry out what came to be known by the KGB as "wet affairs," operations associated with the spilling of blood. One of their first assignments had been in the field, murdering huge numbers of Russian people who had been overrun by the German Army. It was enough for these poor people to have been forced to live, cheek by jowl, with their brutal enemy for Smersh to execute them as traitors.

It was soon quite clear why Caspar had not paid an early price for his treachery to Russia. The men who had recruited him managed to keep his true identity a deep secret, so deep that, when they finally discovered the truth, they were too busy hiding it for the sake of their own skins to be bothered with denouncing Caspar. In the thirty months or so that Caspar worked undercover in Europe, he came into contact with many names that were to become both famous and infamous in the annals of the SIS, during and after the Second World War.

In particular he was constantly in contact with a Russian legend: Spatukin, the man who at long-range controlled the bulk of the KGB's planted penetration agents. During the late 1930s, when they first made contact, Spatukin, if that was his real name, was only in his late twenties, a boy wonder of counterintelligence work. Caspar wrote of him—

He is of medium height and looks more American than Russian. The rumor is that he is the son of an illicit relationship between a White Russian Princess and an American businessman. Whatever the truth, he has sharp features which do not appear Slavic in any way. His hair is dark, yet the complexion is clear and pink, very healthy-looking with black eyes. He speaks English, French and German as fluently as his native Russian, but I feel uncomfortable in his presence. He can, like all good agents, sit very still, not moving a muscle for long periods. He can also hold his tongue, a trick we have all learned, for it makes others imagine they must fill the silence with their words. The dark eyes can become disconcerting. I personally feel that when he is looking at me he does not trust me. He boasts that no photograph of him exists so all I can do is try to describe the features. As I have noted, his nose and chin are sharp, pointed, the chin with a small scar where he once put his teeth through the fleshy part below his lower lip. Dark eyes, as I have said; very still. They flick towards someone who speaks and remind me more of a snake's tongue than

eyes. I notice a tendency for him to turn his eyes
onto a person without moving his head. His hands
are also worth noticing. Long, with square palms,
elegant fingers, the nails trimmed very close.
Rarely does he use his hands to make gestures, and
there is a minute scar, about an eighth of an inch
across, on the back of his right hand, just below
the middle finger. In normal conversation his
voice is soft, pleasant, even musical with almost
a lilt to it, even when speaking in his own tongue
or German, not the two most musical of spoken
languages. Some of this might stem from the fact
that he is an intelligent music lover,
particularly partial to the music of his own land,
with a great interest in new composers emerging
from the Revolution. Spatukin is most dangerous, a
young man, younger than I, and already blessed
with power. He still has a long way to go, and
blessed with an ambition which he will never allow
to carry him into excesses that might leave him
unprotected among the old guard, or those who
influence Stalin.

In March 1938, Caspar wrote in the factual diary—Diary Two—

Monday 7th March 1938
So there we have it at last, the full aims of
Soviet Russia. At this moment they are, as I always
thought, playing for time. I know they bargain
with the Foreign Office on one hand, and with von
Ribbentrop in Berlin on the other. As I have
maintained over the years, whoever becomes their
ally will be used so that they have the chance to
prepare for what must come. At the meeting with
Redruth, Spatukin, and the Soviet General
Bulanov, Deputy Chairman of NKVD, last week,
everything was made clear. Bulanov cannot last
long. Uncharacteristically, he talks far too
much. He claims to have Stalin's ear, and there is
little doubt that the man is a go-between,
carrying the Marshal's instructions to the NKVD
Chairman, Yezhov, whose days are also numbered. If

I am to believe all Bulanov says, Stalin's
Communist ideal is a complete undermining of the
Western liberal democracy by active stealth. When
the war with Germany comes, which it is bound to,
sooner rather than later, the fact remains that
many Soviet activists are already in place. I have
picked up several pointers. There is at least one
in the SIS. There are several in the diplomatic
service, and within the Foreign Office. Redruth
and Bulanov boast about people with cryptonyms
like Elli and Homer; Basil and Timon. They know
details of my old Service, and of Five, down to
minutiae that Five's telegraphic London address
is Snuffbox. They are aware of so many things I
have never given to them, that there can be no
doubt of treachery on a Tudor scale.

The Russian Service is playing to win, and while
we neglected to watch, and keep ourselves posted
of the movements of activists, they were already
doing their work, recruiting and burrowing. From
what I have learned, I believe the establishment
of Great Britain and its Empire is riddled with a
thousand cancers, men and women whose allegiance
is neither to Britain nor the Soviet Union, but to
the evil that is Joseph Stalin. When he finally
goes, they will side with whatever brand of this
powerfully emotive political ideal appeals to
them.

It is true to say that Britain is lost, and
probably the rest of Europe. Maybe not in our
lifetime, but certainly, I would say, by the end of
this millennium. The strength of the Soviet Union
lies in its capability of taking punishment. A
thousand strong men can die, but there are another
thousand waiting to rise up in their places. It is
the same with the penetration agents with which
they have infected political parties, government,
civil service, trade unions, the Intelligence and
Security Services, the Military and Police
Forces. We might well catch a few, but there are
dozens more to take their place, and, within a
decade or so, others will have been converted. I

have no doubt that the same is true in the United States of America. Some, I am certain, are very young. Others older, but certainly not wiser.

All the information I have gleaned will be set before C for instant action. I trust he will go directly to the Prime Minister who will pass it on to the President of the United States. Nobody has time on their side any more.

Would that it had been that simple. It became all too obvious, once Caspar had returned to the fold and rejoined the SIS, that C, and those at the top, were much more concerned about the events taking place in Germany than any stories, however devastating, that Caspar brought back to them as hard intelligence. In his notes, Caspar Railton wrote, in the summer of 1939 from his place back in the Secret Intelligence Service—

I have given up trying to push my cause. There is little point. If C and the politicos will not listen then I must try and help wherever I can. Today I have asked C if I might go out, like an Apostle of Christ, into the highways and by-ways of Europe and compel them to come in. He appeared to understand what I was asking, to recruit far-sighted people in France, Belgium, Holland, and other European countries, so that we might have some kind of active intelligence-cum-sabotage arm available in the heart of Europe on which we can fall back, should Hitler and his Legions strike suddenly. I have left all my notes, together with names, cryptonyms, intelligence digests, information gathered, and hints for *Croesus* to press my case further with C and, if necessary, the Prime Minister, Lord help the poor old bugger.

As he read on, so the sun rose, and Naldo looked out of the window to see the Jungfrau swathed in mist and early snow. He was tired, like some traveler who had gone for miles. He thought of Arnold, and the meeting he must attend that day in Thun, and the lines of Robert Frost, so often quoted by Arnold that they were almost hackneyed—

> The woods are lovely, dark, and deep,
> But I have promises to keep,
> And miles to go before I sleep,
> And miles to go before I sleep.

He returned to the two diaries and the notes, reading on, against time now, for he would have to catch a train at ten o'clock if he was to get to the pretty, and paradoxically awesome, little Rathausplatz, in Thun, by midday.

A girl came in with the breakfast he had ordered, her large blue eyes opening in amazement at the unruffled bed, and the mad Englishman sitting with his pile of papers, eyes ringed through lack of sleep. He smiled at her and made a joke in German. She nodded politely and scurried out, as though afraid this tall man would rape her.

Naldo drank the strong coffee, as his eyes hurtled down the pages, and then stopped, suddenly, like a car braking hard to avoid a head-on collision. There, in black and white on the now dry, yellow-edged paper was the identity of *Croesus* and the whole reason why Caspar's long, hard, fruitful years in the wilderness, posing as an agent for the Soviets, had borne no fruit within the SIS. *Croesus,* for whom Caspar had himself provided the crypto, or code name, had deliberately blocked the lengthy true diary, and the very full pile of notes. It was obviously clear to Caspar when he wrote the words which sprung from the page now. Once he had trusted *Croesus* with his life. Now, Caspar had been forced to set a trap for him, and a trap that, even with all this evidence, *Croesus* would fail to understand, for the devious way Caspar had set the spring would make even *Croesus* feel safe. But it was certainly all too obvious to Naldo. So obvious and horrible that he retched. The person named *Croesus,* trusted by Caspar Railton, confidant and loyal to the Service, was a true double. This person had not played the traitor, as Caspar had. *Croesus was* the traitor, and Naldo felt dizzy with sorrow, for he knew that *Croesus* could still be active. If he was not, it was quite possible that the role of *Croesus* could be passed down, like some title, within close family. So, only one of three people, all of them interconnected within his family, could be the *Croesus* of today.

Naldo just made it to the bathroom. The new knowledge made him physically ill and he vomited for twenty minutes. He wondered if Caspar had been so sickened by the knowledge that he had not possessed the strength to point the finger, preferring to leave this trap. Naldo retched again.

When he came back into the room, his mind was made up. There was no time for hesitation now. He must go to Thun and, if necessary, do what Caspar had done. How else could he clear his uncle's name, and bring the flawed and contagious *Croesus* to book?

TWELVE

1

While Naldo Railton was in The Grand Hôtel Victoria-Jungfrau, Interlaken, waiting for the news that his wife and children had been moved safely out of London, other men were gathering for a meeting three thousand miles away, at the CIA headquarters, Langley, Virginia.

It was evening, and they met in the French Room, the DCI's conference office. Nobody could remember why it was called the French Room.

Essentially these officers were there in order to set up a damage-control committee. They would assess what needed doing, which agents and case officers required warning, what operations should be closed down, following what they believed to be the full-scale defection of Arnold St. John Farthing.

Among those present were the Head of the Soviet Desk and his staff; the Controller Counterespionage, with his entourage; Controller Security; three senior men from Covert Operations; the British liaison officer from the Secret Intelligence Service, MI6, who was there under protest; and four members of Counterintelligence together with their chief, James Jesus Angleton.

The DCI looked grim. He had spent a very unpleasant hour at the White House explaining the situation, as best he could, to the President. The President had, among other things, called the DCI an "amateur with a paper badge that read the word 'Secret' clear for all to see."

"I've invited MI6 Liaison into this meeting," the DCI began. "I understand he has something to tell us."

In a pained and shaken tone, the British officer went over recent events. How the late Sir Caspar Railton had become suspect; how other members of his family were under suspicion, and how, at last, one of them had, in his words, "Been flushed and had run for cover."

"By which, I presume, you mean he's disappeared with some icing off your own secret cake," one of the Covert Operations officers said.

200

"In a word, yes," the Brit nodded sadly, adding that Naldo Railton had been a particular friend of Arnold St. John Farthing. In turn they all knew both men had close links with the now departed Caspar Railton.

There were questions about Railton's immediate family. Missing. Counterquestions about Farthing's immediate family. Missing, but for the two boys, who were safe with an aunt. They asked the Brit what his Service was doing about minimizing damage, should it be proved that Naldo Railton had, in fact, "Gone over," as they said. "Gone over" had a slightly less harsh ring to it than "defected," just as "passed over" is nicer than plain "dead."

The Brit said he suspected the family was tainted. As far as he knew, all members of the Railton family who had contacts with the SIS were to be interrogated.

"Then I guess we should do the same," Controller Security said sharply. "I've dug out the files. We have one of Arnie's relatives here, inside Langley, Clifton Farthing on the Soviet and Eastern European desk. And there's a worrying situation with another couple who have links with both the Railtons and Farthings." He was speaking about Hester Railton, Caspar's daughter, who was, to use the current American slang, shacking up with Luke Marlowe, a direct Farthing descendant.

"They're just about into everything, those two," Security said. "Activists if ever I saw them. The Bureau's got a file a mile high on them: black rights; human rights; nuclear disarmament; peace protests; marches and demonstrations all the time. Twice they've been picked up on suspicion of carrying drugs. Cleared on both occasions. I guess the Bureau should pull them and make them sing all over the backyard down on 10th Street. What about this Clifton Farthing?" He looked towards the Head of the Soviet Desk.

"We've no complaints. He's almost too good to be true. My country, right or wrong. Superb material."

"Sounds like we should shake his tree then," from Security.

There was a silence, as though the angel of death had passed through the room. It was broken by a cough as Angleton lit another cigarette. They all looked towards him.

"Well, Jim, you're the expert. What measures should we take?" the DCI asked.

Angleton smiled. "With all the respect in the world," he said, "I feel we've wasted enough of our friend's time." He nodded towards the SIS liaison officer who, taking the broad hint, looked at his watch and withdrew.

"Well, Jim. What should we do?" the DCI asked again.

James Angleton inhaled smoke, then blew it out in a long thin stream. "We should," he said with a slight smile, "do nothing."

The silence that followed was charged with several million volts of static.

Someone tried to speak, the voice beginning angrily, but Angleton's quiet, measured tones cut through, knocking any possible barrage of verbal artillery to one side until he had the floor again. "We should do nothing at all. Gentlemen, I have certain indisputable facts to place before you. You will undoubtedly ask why you were not apprised of these facts sooner, and my response is, because in the work of counterintelligence the stronger your cards, the more essential it is to keep away from mirrors. For some years now we've been running a little scam."

The DCI looked up, sharply and angrily. Angleton returned the look with a pleasant smile. "We do have Special Group's approval, sir. A little before your time. I've never bothered you with the details." All Covert Operations with a budget of more than $25,000 had to be approved by Special Group. Angleton, in an almost offhand manner, said the operation had already cost them over two million dollars. "Incidentally," he continued, "Clifton Farthing is *not* here at headquarters at the moment. I have him out doing a small chore for me. Now . . ." He began to tell a long and complex tale. Some of those present could hardly believe their ears, but, by the time James Jesus Angleton had completed his story, every man in the room looked dazed and bewildered. If the Head of Counterintelligence was telling them the truth, there *was* nothing for them to do. Except, perhaps, wait.

2

Just before dawn, Gloria Farthing, Arnold's wife, left the suite which she was supposed to be sharing with Naldo, under the names M. & Mme. Provin, in The Hôtel Splendide Royale, Lugano. It was not yet light and she made her way carefully down the service stairs used by the maids. In a closet she found a coat and headscarf, belonging to some young woman who had probably just come on duty. She did not particularly like the coat, which was green and of some thin synthetic material. The headscarf did not go with her shoulderbag, but she had no choice. The bag contained almost everything she needed in order to survive—her own passport, a second American passport in the name of Mrs. Margaret Teasdale, credit cards, currency, and travelers checks.

With the headscarf tied tightly in place, and shoulders drooping in a slouchy walk, Gloria left by the rear staff entrance.

Time passed, and eventually the watchers of the surveillance team, who had waited through the night, decided it was time to collar Naldo and Gloria. There would be commendations in it for them, so, at about ten in the morning, they walked into the lavish foyer and asked for the Provins' room number. One of the men went up while another called the suite from an in-house phone. There was no reply and, when they alerted the management, the passkey was used. The suite was empty. The cupboard bare. Reluctantly, the team leader used a telephone in the duty manager's office. Mr. and Mrs. Provin's account was settled by credit card. It was the least, and the most, they could have done.

By this time Gloria was heading towards a crash rendezvous made after one short call from a public telephone in Lugano railway station.

3

Naldo Railton washed, shaved, dressed, and carefully packed his canvas bag, leaving all of his Uncle Caspar's papers, neat in their folders, on top of the few clothes. He was experiencing a mixture of fatigue and despair, thinking of the great affection he bore for every member of his old family, and the past pride he had so often felt. To Naldo the great Railton clan was a microcosm of Britain itself. True, they had certain advantages and privileges, but these were gradually being eroded by the political temper of the times. Yet there was history within the family: history, service, loyalty, treachery, wilfulness, good deeds, work, and a great sense of the things the late American President had summed up in his words, "Ask not what your country can do for you; ask what you can do for your country." Those had been stirring words for the United States, and they had been words followed by many a Railton in Britain for centuries.

Naldo thought of the long-dead members of his family, and his genuine love for those who lived on. For his father and mother, James and Margaret Mary; for Dick and the once untiring Sara at Redhill. For his cousins, his sister in her convent, and all his kinfolk everywhere.

At the writing table he searched through the leather stationery folder and found a postcard with a drawing of the hotel on it. He addressed it to his father and mother, then wrote the greeting, knowing his parents' love of music and how, over the years, they had communicated by it in a strange, almost psychic way—

> Music can noble hints impart
> Engender fury, kindle love;
> With unsuspected eloquence can move,
> And Manage all the man with secret art.

The quote was from the eighteenth-century poet Addison, and Naldo had known the words for most of his life. They would contain a hidden significance for James and Margaret Mary. He rummaged through the drawers in the writing desk, eventually finding two plain sheets of paper and one plain envelope which he addressed to Peter Ferguson Esq. care of Poste Restante at the Trafalgar Square Post Office in London. Working quickly, Naldo reached into his memory for a cipher that would work, then wrote a coded message at speed, checking that it said all the right things, gave all the correct instructions. At the end he wrote one line *en clair*—

What is best in music is not to be found in the notes.

N

Herbie would understand, for the quote was from Gustav Mahler, and they had both joked a lot about advice on interrogation given by Gus Keene at Warminster. One of Keene's maxims was, "Don't listen to the words, hear the music as a whole." Now, Naldo had to pray that Herbie still cleared the Ferguson box regularly, for Herbie was the one person with whom he could arrange some kind of contact in the days he was pretty certain now lay ahead of them.

Naldo looked around the room. He thought briefly of how his father had been held captive in terrible conditions in the first war, then, with great affection, how Caspar had gone, of his own volition, to do what he thought best for country and Service. He was determined to avenge the slur being cast on his uncle, and cry havoc among his enemies.

Naldo went downstairs and paid his account with cash, for he had exchanged travelers checks at the hotel in Locarno.

He went outside and walked in the general direction of the Interlaken West Bahnhof, stopping off at a stationer's to buy a large padded envelope and parcel tape. At the post office, with its slung posthorn sign, he filled the new envelope with all Caspar's documents and papers, carefully sealing it with parcel tape. He then addressed it to Bernard Carpenter, at a convenience address in Slough, registering the package and marking it to await collection, safe in the knowledge that, fire, flood, bomb, or act of God apart, the envelope would still be there for him to collect in twenty years' time if need be. He then put the matter out of his mind.

He also posted the card to his parents, and the letter to Mr. Ferguson, before heading for the station again. At two minutes past ten o'clock, Naldo boarded the Berne train which would, less than an hour later, deposit him in Thun.

4

As Naldo's train was sliding out of Interlaken station, so the Credit Committee met on the fifth floor of the SIS headquarters. In waiting, sitting around the anteroom reading old copies of the *National Geographic,* were Gus Keene and his two juniors. In a corner, young Curry Shepherd, his blazer looking slightly the worse for wear, sat meditating on the relative merits of death by garotting or a slow boiling in oil, both of which he contemplated with BMW in mind, the DCSS having called him from a warm bed, next to a warm and loving woman at the dawn's early light.

Willis Maitland-Wood was in a foul temper. For one thing he had just learned that, having tracked Naldo across Europe, his own searchers had been misled and lost their quarry in Lugano. He was also tired, for he had spent three hours uselessly with the old sailor Barzillai Beckeleg.

At six in the morning, Willis went home, called Curry out of bed to await instructions at the shop, and dozed fitfully, waking eventually in deep depression and feeling as though he had drunk himself stupid.

"Well!" As chairman, BMW addressed the committee. "I presume you've all had time enough to read and digest the late Caspar Railton's decrypted diaries."

There were nods, and murmurs of affirmation along the table. "There are facts," BMW continued, "of which you should all be apprised before I ask what conclusion you came to after reading this extraordinary document of duplicity." His eyes roamed over their faces: Desmond Elms, small and wiry with sharp features and glittering eyes that made you think of *The Wind in the Willows;* the impeccably dressed David Barnard, from Covert Ops, not a hair out of place, and the face and eyes placid; Indigo Belper, in a pink vest which did not go with the striped suit, a watchchain, out of place, hanging from buttonhole to breast pocket. Belper fiddled with his copy of Caspar Railton's diary and looked ready to quote case law; the petite and pretty Beryl Williamson, looking very solemn, as though someone had just asked her a question which had to be answered slowly and with great care; Arden Elder, from Warminster, who gazed at his copy of the diary, then flicked his eyes towards Maitland-Wood as though the chairman was going to add some necessary, and missing fragment to the work. Lastly, the wraithlike Tubby Fincher averted his eyes, almost wilfully refusing to meet those of Maitland-Wood.

"Donald Railton," the chairman continued, "has gone missing."

"Who?" from Arden Elder, who then gathered himself together. "Oh, yes. You mean Naldo."

"Has gone missing," Maitland-Wood repeated, "and I don't mean by accident. Yesterday, after we knew for sure where he had gone, a surveillance team followed him. He was in the company of Arnold Farthing's wife, Gloria. As you know, confidentially, Farthing is also missing and there have been traces. Traces which point to him having crossed into the Soviet Union.

"Donald, Naldo if you must, has neatly given the surveillance team the slip. Because he was accompanied by Gloria we can presume, though not *assume*, that they are about to join Arnold Farthing. Naldo's wife, Barbara, was assisting us, under interrogation by Gus Keene. She also disappeared, with their two children, last night."

"In other words," Barnard had a half-smile on his face, "the dirigible has ascended and our lords and masters are in the profound ordure."

"You might say that," BMW all but barked at him.

"We're *all* in trouble, that is what you want to say, yes?" Desmond Elms, who spent so much of his life reading from Russian transcripts, had a tendency to speak English with certain inflexions of Russian syntax.

"We are on the brink of a major scandal, yes," Maitland-Wood snapped. "We cannot disguise the fact, any more than we can disguise the truly terrible contents of these diaries." He touched his own typewritten pages. "There has been a very minor leakage. One newspaper has got onto the American side of the matter. We have D-Noticed it for the time being, but, unless we come up with quick answers, questions will be asked in the House and we shall find the wrong people going public on this. I have certain ideas, which I will put to you in due course. Gus Keene and his people await our instructions. C has ordered us to take whatever steps require taking . . ."

The first interruption came, at this point, from Belper, the lawyer. "I would like to know, if we are presumably all agreed on the evidence as it stands, what steps we *can* take. If this," he lifted the pile of typescript, "is proven and conclusive evidence, then the damage control will be considerable. Add to that the possibility that two very senior officers from our Service and the American Agency have both been penetrations for some time, the damage is heavy. What it *means*, Willis, is that practically every operation since the end of the war is compromised. What *it means* is that almost every case officer and agent we have working within the Sovbloc is also compromised. *What it means* is we're scuppered, sunk."

Everyone began to speak at once, and BMW had to bring the meeting to order. For him, he was incredibly restrained. As yet they should not make judgments on the younger Railton, or Farthing. The pair had always shown renegade instincts. They had to await developments from that quarter. While they waited, it was essential for them to make some very definite decision regarding Caspar Railton's secret diary. For his part, the news here was bad. He saw nothing but deception and intrigue in Caspar's actions, therefore everything he had done since his return to the Service in 1938 should be examined in the light of this overwhelming evidence.

Each member of the committee had his, or her, say. All but one were in favor of treating the secret diary as genuine, and taking steps to examine what damage resulted. There was one dissenting voice. Tubby Fincher rose to his feet and spoke for almost ten minutes, saying he felt the evidence was, in the main, slim. It was against all the tradecraft practiced by Caspar during his long and loyal career. In a word, he felt they were being duped.

Maitland-Wood was furious. "How duped?" he shouted. "We were already led to this conclusion by the evidence and warnings from *Alex.*" Even now he would not speak Penkovsky's name aloud, though the world knew of it.

"You know what I feel about that." Fincher held his ground.

"There're also the words of our latest catch."

"Five's latest catch," Fincher corrected him. "And I wouldn't put too much credence on him either."

In the end, it was decided that Keene alone should be invited in to discuss possible interrogations.

As Keene was being summoned, so a signal was brought in from C's office. Maitland-Wood read it quickly, not believing what he saw. The signal had come in an undetectable squirt of complex cipher, direct from the DCI, Washington. Decrypted, it all but told C to call off any action against both Arnold Farthing and Naldo Railton. C's own scrawl on the paper instructed BMW to keep the matter to himself until they could talk, later.

It took Maitland-Wood a minute or so to compose himself, and when Keene came in, he asked, rather shakily, some thought, if this master interrogator had read the diary. Keene said he had, his voice reflecting his thoughts, which were soon to be aired.

Like Fincher, Gus Keene quite simply told the Credit Committee that he was unconvinced. "None of it rings true of the man we all worked with," he said. "This is not so much evidence as a false confession. The kind of thing the police are faced with every day. Only in Caspar Railton's case, one would have to assume that there is a reason for it. Certainly I believe he met the people he claims to have met. That he sold out to them is another matter altogether. Yet there has to be a reason. I believe it's this committee's duty to investigate the reason rather than the assumed guilt. I, for one, cannot accept that Sir Caspar Railton would have blazed such an easy trail for us to follow had he been telling the truth under oath."

The argument went back and forth for some time. In the end, Gus Keene was asked to speak with James Railton, Alexander and Andrew Railton, and Dick Railton-Farthing. Their wives would probably require interviews also.

Once more, to the committee's surprise, Keene made another suggestion. He would prefer to speak with Caspar's widow, Lady Phoebe, before he carried out any further questionings.

Reluctantly the Credit Committee gave its permission, with Maitland-Wood adding a rider. As the German, Kruger, had been a particular friend of, and was influenced by the entire trio—Caspar, Naldo, and Arnold—Keene should also, as he put it, have a dig around *him*.

"There'd be no harm in it," Keene said with some diffidence.

5

The small enclosed square in Thun which contains the town hall, or Rathaus, had always seemed to Naldo to be like something out of a horror film. Not that there was anything sinister or horrible about it. Quite the contrary. The Rathausplatz is "Quaint." As Naldo's father once said, "Quaint with a capital K."

At a little before noon, Naldo entered the square and once more marveled at its quaintness. The streets leading into it were cobbled, as was the square itself. The Rathaus was just too good to be true, ultra Swiss, with its cleanliness and pristine-painted look, the shutters open and the signs of Christmas across its blank face. It was, Naldo now thought, its blankness that made it like some unreal chocolate-box painting. If there was anything sinister about the little Platz, it was the castle which towered high above it.

Standing among the cloistered arches which run opposite the Rathaus itself, Naldo looked up at the castle, realizing that, depending on weather, or mood, it could either be straight out of Disneyland, or some unreal backdrop to an early Frankenstein movie.

Today, though, Naldo did not smile for he, of all people, knew that here, in this unreal little square, he awaited his destiny. As his eyes moved slowly around the square, watching each point of entry for the contact to arrive, he was conscious of all that had led to this point.

In the beginning there was Caspar's funeral and the secret approach through Herbie. He recalled the Berlin meeting, with its attendant horrific truths revealed: Penkovsky, the magnificent hero of the Western Intelligence Community, the dream source, shown as an unreliable witness. A manipulator through which the West was saved from the holocaust of nuclear war, when, in reality, the holocaust would have been in the Soviet Union. Penkovsky, the man who had, at the end, fingered Naldo's dear dead uncle as a traitor. Penkovsky, who was executed, yet still magically lived on in luxury by the Black Sea. Penkovsky, who could help clear the air.

Then the full revelation of Caspar's two diaries and his notes. For those who had eyes to see, the true treachery was clearly revealed, and Naldo, being a Railton, had seen the flaw, and felt the bacteria plunge into his own bloodstream. Time had to pass, so that he also could recover from the sickness and recuperate enough to fight the disease that had been spread, to the point of ruination, from within his family.

He thought of Arnie's place in all this, and hoped he was right in the deductions he had made. He thought of those he was leaving to face whatever music had been arranged for them. In particular he thought of Big Herbie.

Two men, out of place, wrongly dressed and furtive, came into the square and loitered. Another pair, one of them a woman, came in, walked to the center, and took a photograph of the Rathaus, then the woman whirled around and snapped off three quick frames of Naldo, who stood quite still waiting.

"Glad you made it, Nald." Arnie had materialized behind him, arriving with no sound, probably during the seconds Naldo was distracted by the photographer.

"You knew I would, didn't you?"

Arnold moved in beside him, pointing up at the castle. "Wouldn't like to serve any time in there," he said casually and both men laughed.

As the laughter died, Arnold spoke very quickly. "They have no sound equipment on us, and I'm not wired. Well, I am, but it's faulty. Trust me."

"Of course."

"They think they've been running me for the past five years," he said, his voice low, and the words coming out very fast. "I was put on a hook and they bit. The problem is that very few people back in the real world know it. The Blunt stuff made me panic and run, if you understand."

"Perfectly. I have more, Arn. A lot to tell you about Cas."

"Later. You have to be clued in, and there's no time."

"You've been running me, right?" Naldo almost smiled.

"Astute, Railton. Most astute. Your crypto's *Beaver.* You've given me a lot of stuff on the U.S. bases in England, mainly security details and types of forces, names of squadrons and units stationed there. Everything *you* know about. You also gave me *Fontana, Dredger,* and *Matador.*"

"My, I've been busy." He was amazed by what Arnold had said. "You're a close devil, Arn. I ran those ops, and knew your Service was involved. I didn't realize it was you personally."

Fontana, Dredger, and *Matador* were all operations which looked as though they had been blown by a penetration agent. It was how they had to look, for they were interconnected and their success depended on the Russian and East German services thinking they had been disasters.

Arnie smiled at him, making clear eye-contact. "Funny what you learn when you start browsing," he said. "Ready to get the bastard?"

"*Alex?*"

"Who else? *This* is the only way I could get the pair of us near him. You ready?"

"Let's go."

210

They walked, comfortably, across the square, the four minders taking station, one walking point, another backstopping, the remaining pair quite close behind Arnold Farthing and Naldo Railton.

High in a room overlooking the Rathausplatz, Clifton Farthing took a dozen more fast frames of film, freezing the departing convoy as it left. He turned to the other man who had been monitoring the long-range sound equipment, and nodded. The man walked over to a telephone and dialed a local number, then handed the instrument to Clifton.

It rang four times before being picked up at the distant end. *"Heartbreak* is running," Clifton Farthing said into the mouthpiece.

In Thun, the shops sparkled with Christmas treats, and Naldo wondered, for a second, how long it would take.

He was not to know that this would be his last taste of the West for several years. When he returned, the world would have become a different and even more dangerous place.

6

A week later, out of habit more than any operational necessity, Big Herbie Kruger moved through the streets of London, observing all foreign rules: checking constantly that he walked alone. Eventually he found himself in Trafalgar Square. He entered the Post Office and asked at the Poste Restante desk if there was anything for Ferguson. "Peter Ferguson," he said and tried not to show surprise when they looked through the letters and told him yes. "From Switzerland, Mr. Ferguson," the girl said, thinking this was an odd name for someone who spoke with Herbie's accent.

He had to show ID, which he always carried tucked away in the back of a wallet. Peter Ferguson's driver's license.

The letter burned a hole in his pocket all the way back to the Annexe. Then all the way back to the flat in St. John's Wood. There, behind his own locked door, Herbie opened Naldo's ciphered letter, smiling at the Mahler quote, then studying the rest of the message, which seemed to be about how the correspondent, a Norman Ferguson—hence the signature "N"—had bumped into their Aunt Jane in Lucerne a month earlier, and how well she looked. There followed a long description of how things were in Switzerland and when Norman expected to be home.

211

Within ten minutes Herbie was unbuttoning the cipher, knowing that his face was looking more gray as each word was unfolded, for the true message read—

IT IS POSSIBLE I SHALL BE MISSING FOR DAYS, MONTHS OR EVEN YEARS. TAKE NOTHING YOU HEAR ON FACE VALUE, BUT I THINK I SHALL BE IN MOSCOW WHERE I SHALL NEED SOME FORM OF COMMUNICATION. TRUST NOBODY BUT YOURSELF WITH THE MESSAGES, IF AND WHEN THEY COME. IT MIGHT BE A LONG TIME BUT PLEASE ARRANGE TO REOPEN BOX TWELVE AND HAVE IT CHECKED EVERY THREE WEEKS. IF MESSAGE ARRIVES ACT ON YOUR OWN INITIATIVE AND YOURS ALONE. DO NOT INVOLVE ANY OTHER MEMBER OF MY FAMILY AND ESPECIALLY ANYBODY, REPEAT ANYBODY, ON THE FIFTH FLOOR. NALDO.

THIRTEEN

1

When Katherine Stear left the Secret Intelligence Service in 1961, nobody in either Personnel or on the fifth floor had any sinister plans for her. Kate Stear had come into the Service in the 1930s as a trainee cipher clerk. Her file had been shunted around and, at one point, lost altogether, so it was almost by accident that, in 1940, they realized she was a fluent French speaker. So, early in 1942, having done the necessary courses at the Abbey, and in Scotland, she worked two tours with SOE in France, before being badly blown.

Always lucky, Stear was about to be taken in for a third time, when the compromise was discovered. Thereafter, she worked in Covert Ops (Planning), then, for several years in one of the shop's cipher rooms. Towards the end of her official career, Kate did a bit of nursemaiding. In the early 1960s they offered her a nice little retirement stipend, looking after three London safe houses, but Stalks, as she was known to most people, said she had done enough.

Early in her career some idle wrangler had pointed out that if you used her initials, KL—Katherine Louise—her name was an anagram of "Stalker." From then on she was known as Stalks, and it was as Stalks that she took on the housekeeping job at Redhill Manor.

Richard and Sara Railton-Farthing had advertised privately, through the Service, for anyone with organizational experience and ability to take over the running of Redhill. Stalks was the ideal choice and she settled down happily, becoming almost one of the family in a matter of weeks. She had two assistants with no Service connections but with some nursing experience. Both Richard and Sara planned well ahead, for they knew in the late autumn of their lives that Redhill would continue as a family concern only if they kept an eye on their future declining years. Deep in their hearts, they hoped that Naldo would eventually retire and take over the burden on behalf of the whole family.

Stalks was twenty-two years of age when she first joined the Service, five foot four in her stockinged feet, trim and, as one officer put it at the time, as tasty as a ripe melon. It was well-known that she had been embroiled in a disastrous love affair with a young member of the Service who had later been murdered by the SS in Austria. She never got over it, though there was talk of her carrying on a liaison with another, unnamed, senior officer. But, by the time she went to work at Redhill, she had become a plump, apple-cheeked, happy middle-aged lady.

Stalks was a natural for Redhill, partly because she was a whiz at organization and liked hard work, and partly because she understood the family. She had experienced the strains and stresses on both sides of the counter, from the worry of making life or death decisions at a distance, in the relative comfort of London, to the stomach-knotting, bursting terror of servicing dead-drops or handling difficult agents, and watching friends get taken by the opposition. There was an affinity between her and the entire Railton clan, so it was not unnatural that she felt that old deep sense of nervous indigestion once more when, in the first week of January 1965, she received a polite, though firm, invitation from Willis Maitland-Wood to visit the shop.

> We would like you to come in next week, on the 10th, at around 11am, but feel that you should make some other excuse to the family who employ you and hold from them the fact that you are going to talk with us—

So, BMW wrote, and it was this "excuse" which brought back all the old fears. Willis was telling her to lie, which meant that Willis was into something unpleasant concerning the Railton family. She had a pretty good idea about where the unpleasantness lay, and she would rather not share it with the godhead on the fifth floor.

Stalks loved most of the Railtons, and the Farthings she had so far met. There were exceptions of course, but she had, unquestionably, never liked BMW, and did not, therefore, take kindly to either his invitation or suggestion. Yet, from experience, she knew that life could become difficult if she did not comply. So she bit on the bullet of conscience, made the excuse, and traveled up to London on the agreed date, presenting herself at the shop just before eleven A.M.

When she arrived at Maitland-Wood's office a further surprise awaited her. Willis was not alone.

"Hello, Stalks, nice to see you again." Gus Keene sat in a corner chair, reloading his pipe.

"Well, to what do I owe this honor? C's food taster and the Grand Inquisitor himself?" Her voice was cheerful enough, but she felt her heart banging at her ribs, and the unpleasant taste of bile in the back of her throat.

"Sit you down, Stalks. Glad you could make it." Willis MW was full of friendly zest. Too friendly, she considered.

"You commanded it, Willis, and I obeyed." She sat, gathering her Windsmoor coat around her and placing the handbag—black leather, a Christmas gift from Richard and Sara—beside the chair. Keene was doing something noisy with his pipe, sucking in hard with a box of Swan Vestas matches laid across the bowl.

"How're the folks who live on the hill?" Keene asked with a chuckle.

"Bearing up, considering the kind of Christmas they subjected themselves to." If he was going to be frivolous, then she could be equally so, and would match him.

"And what sort of Christmas was that?" Keene had got the pipe going now, and he leaned back in his chair. A man ready for a good gossip. Willis, while still present, seemed to have disappeared into the wallpaper. Stalks remembered that he was uncharacteristically good at that trick.

"Mr. and Mrs. Railton-Farthing take too much on at Christmas." She looked at the ceiling. Someone had once told her not to look interrogators in the eye all the time. If you did they inevitably thought you were lying. "They have this damned silly family tradition. Everyone has to be at court for the Christmas celebrations, and they do themselves proud. But it's too much for them these days. Gets out of control; every family has its little ups and downs, most especially if they all get together for the winter solstice. Full house, Christmas dinner, with everyone done up to the nines, long gowns and penguin suits; a tree and presents ceremony. They all arrive and behave like children. That is, when some are not behaving like pigs."

"Not everyone was present this year, Stalks, were they?" Keene, she noticed, was not looking at her as he spoke.

"No, that's for sure, and it only made matters worse."

"In what way?"

She paused, then asked if she was legally bound to answer questions about the family who now employed her.

Willis began to say something, but Gus Keene overrode him. "I suppose not. Not at an informal gathering like this. But you know the score, Stalks. Everyone in this fair land is bound by the Official Secrets Act, though precious few of them realize it. Some of us are further bound because we've signed a piece of paper which says we've read the damned thing. I'm not being difficult, old love, but we could get nasty and make it official.''

"I see." She certainly did see. "So might I ask the purpose of this *informal* gathering?''

"Ask away." Keene gave her his avuncular smile.

"Take it that I've asked.''

"Right." Keene drew in on the pipe. "Naldo and Barbara were in absentia this year." Statement of fact, not a question.

"Yes.''

"You know why?''

"No, but it was bloody difficult because young Arthur and Emma *were* present. They were also bloody unhappy and plagued everyone with questions. They missed their parents dreadfully.''

"So do we all," Willis said, as though he really meant it.

"And were young Arthur and Emma given any satisfactory answers?''

"I heard Richard saying they mustn't worry. Oh, and they had cards, letters, and gifts from their mother and father.''

"Happen to notice where they were posted—the cards and letters, I mean?'' Keene cocked one eye at her as if to say that people like Stalks do not lose the habits of a lifetime.

"Southend. Letters and cards both. Richard had a long letter as well. It contained a check to buy the presents, a job which I eventually did in Oxford.''

"Southend as well?''

Stalks nodded.

"Well, that's as likely a place as any. You have a theory about where Mum and Dad had got to?''

"It's pretty obvious they've gone AWOL. I'm treated like family. Most of them expressed alarm, and not a little despondency.''

"Most?''

"Not that pompous excuse for a lawyer, Andrew, or his nasty little brother, Alex. Their wives were concerned. Richard and Sara were nearly out of their minds with worry, as were James and his dear wife. But they would be, wouldn't they? Son and daughter-in-law vanished. They had the big German chap, Kruger, with them for the festivities. He was also worried, but he did try and liven things up. Party spirit. Nice man. Full of music. Good at his job, I shouldn't wonder.''

"I shouldn't wonder either, Stalks. They mention me, by any chance?'' Keene removed his pipe, tapping the stem against his teeth.

216

"I got the impression they were all going to see you at some point." Stalks appeared to relax for the first time. "It didn't bother Richard and Sara. Nor James and Margaret, but it worries the hell out of Andrew and Alexander. Caspar's widow's still too distraught to make any sense of it, but it's spooked Andrew and Alex."

"So it should. Kruger?"

"Oh, you've talked to him already. I suppose you're seeing him again. He really couldn't care less about you, Gus. Herbie's that kind of bloke. Straight. Does his job and brooks no funny business."

"Ah." Keene was still a little annoyed at the way his first session with Kruger had gone. Herbie had denied all knowledge of what had happened; owned to having lunched with Naldo at Gennaros, but denied either seeing or talking with him since. He also pointedly said that if anyone could believe Naldo had gone over they must be flat-earthers. It was a term he had obviously just learned because of the way he used it indiscriminately. "People who only listen to Bach are flat-earthers," he had announced during the interview, apropos of nothing. Keene was to try again, in a couple of weeks, but did not fancy his chances. As for the short interview with Phoebe, the poor woman was half out of her mind. Who would have thought Caspar's widow would have gone near crazy with grief? She had once been a trained nurse, and always appeared very down to earth. "Tell me about the wives," he said. "Alexander's wife, for instance."

Stalks would have sworn that she saw a lecherous glint in Keene's eye.

Alexander's wife was very young, and a recent acquisition. Tall, slender, blonde with dark roots, vivacious and with an aura of sexual promise that was enough to make any redblooded male turn to fantasies.

"Maiden name was Butcher," Keene mused aloud. "Delia Butcher. Sounds like something from a novel. I always think of Delia as one of those women who dress up for men. You know, strict nanny or jackbooted torturer."

Stalks thought that Keene was shrewd as well as lecherous. She had, on one occasion over Christmas, seen the inside of Alex and Delia's bedroom. The wardrobe door was open and gave her a new insight into Alexander Railton's private life. "You might be right," was all she said for now.

"You know something, Stalks. I can always tell with you. I'm right, aren't I?"

"Each to his, or her, own taste, as long as they don't do it in the street and frighten the horses, as they say. It could be *her* particular kick, you know, not Alex's.''

''But you rather think it's him, yes?''

''I don't really know. I'm aware that they play sexual games, but who of us hasn't in our time, Augustus Claudius?'' It was her turn to cock an eyebrow, and Keene suddenly recalled a night, not really all that long ago, after some successful operation when he and Stalks had been alone together. He could hear his voice echoing from the past. ''Talk dirty, Stalks. You always look such a lady. Talk dirty.'' Aloud, he asked, ''Would he stray?''

''Who? Alex?''

''Who else?''

''Why should he? I think he's found his fantasy. Or, rather a whole flock of fantasies.''

''Doesn't mean a thing, and you know it, Kate Stear. Alex is in a sensitive position. Sometimes doesn't get home for a week at a time. Would he seek the services of specialists?''

After she had thought about it, Stalks had to say yes he might.

''But Delia was sorry for Naldo and Barbara?''

''Concerned. Worried, yes. Barbara's become a chum, it seems. I think she's the only Railton who takes Delia seriously.''

''And Anne?'' Anne was Andrew's wife. Spiteful people said he had married her for her name, because Andrew and Anne Railton sounded nicely upper-crust. There was money around as well, and Andrew was never a sluggard where hard cash was concerned.

''Anne?'' Stalks nodded. ''Nice. Comforting to James and Margaret. Helpful to Richard and Sara. Treats me like a servant, of course.''

''Of course. Unless you're descended directly from royalty, or own something trendy and very expensive, like a pop group or a nightclub, you're peasant class. Anne was brought up that way. But you like her, Stalks?''

She gave a thin smile. ''I'm sorry for her, and, yes, yes, I do like her. Anne's such a bloody snob and all the others take the . . . ''

''You were going to say, take the piss out of her, Stalks.'' Keene chuckled again and pulled on his pipe. ''Bad influence, working with people in this Service for most of your life.''

She nodded. ''Anne tries really hard, but she's such a mousy little thing, and has absolutely no style. She has a magnificent body when stripped, by the by. I've seen it. In my servant capacity, of course.''

''Of course,'' Keene added.

''But she's so bloody foolish, and such a slave to that bugger Andrew." Stalks scowled. "Sometimes I find it very hard to believe that two superbly nice people like Caspar and Phoebe could have such idiot sons. Oh, yes, Anne said . . . " She stopped abruptly.

Keene coaxed, "Anne said what, exactly, Stalks? It's why you're here. Family gossip."

"Anne had the vapors because Andrew's apparently been removed from the P4 list."

"And did Alexander also gripe?"

She hated herself for it. "Yes. Says he wants an explanation. He's been cut out of some of the more sensitive areas at Cheltenham. Going to ask you straight, Willis." She moved her head slightly towards Willis' desk.

"Good," Keene answered on the DCSS's behalf. "We'll be able to tell him that he's a possible security risk. Kinky goings on with the ladies and all that. What else did you learn from your prying, with your eye to the keyhole and tooth glass to the wall, Stalks?"

She thought for a moment, then said to herself, "What the hell, they'll get it anyway." Aloud she told them there were already family squabbles about the Eccleston Place house. "It's Naldo's, but there's nobody to live in it. Andrew's livid."

"And what else? Was it, in spite of the things you've mentioned, a good Christmas?"

"They tried, for the sake of the kids. Andrew's children were there, almost out of school now, young William's going to be like his father, he's an absolute prig. Naldo's Arthur put him in his place, though. Fists flew."

"Perish the thought. Fisticuffs at Redhill as the Yule log burned bright. Give us all the dope, Stalks. All the juicy gossip."

"They went through the motions of enjoying themselves. Delia was furious with her husband. His gift was definitely not appreciated."

"And it was, what?"

"One of those new Sony portable television sets. The label said it was so she had something to watch in bed. He added a crudity concerning the way they performed sex and it didn't leave much to the imagination. It was quite uncalled for."

Even Willis laughed.

"Nothing else?"

Stalks shrugged. "If you don't count what I suspect was a bit of incest between William and Emma—is it incest with cousins?—and Big Herb getting rolling drunk on Christmas night. Oh, and a knock-down-drag-out fight between Andrew and his uncle James, that was

219

about Eccleston Place incidentally. No, a good family Christmas." She grinned to indicate sarcasm. "Turkey, ham, mince pies, plum pudding, crystallized ginger, sausages, champagne, brandy, fourteen kinds of wine. Ooh, my! Ooh, my! Ooh, my!" Stalks did her world-class impression of Mole from *The Wind in the Willows.*

"Ooh, my! indeed," Keene said sagely. "And the talk about Naldo and Barbara?"

"There was no talk about them, as such; and I've told you, it was obvious that they've gone missing." She gave a pert little smile. "Oh, the Railtons who count do not believe for one moment that Naldo's a traitor. Nor Barbara for that matter."

"So?" Keene nodded.

"Nor, I should add," Stalks gave him her biggest rosy-cheeked smile, "do any of the senior Railtons hold with the current theory on the late Sir Caspar."

"What current theory would that be, Stalks?" Keene looked at her hard, but got no reply. Stalks returned to Redhill under a kind of discipline. "If there's any sign of the missing pair, letter, postcard, telephone call, you're to let us know instantly," BMW told her.

On the following morning, Gus Keene had his first interview with Alexander Railton.

2

They met in almost farcical secrecy, in a rather opulent safe house the Firm kept for delicate matters just off St. James's. There were even code sentences to be exchanged on arrival and, once inside, Alexander Percival Railton almost went berserk.

"I was told Willis Maitland-Wood was to meet me here *with* you. I insist on seeing him. There are questions I must put to him."

Gus Keene, accompanied by Martin Brook, thought Alex was going to stamp his small foot.

Indeed, Alexander's size went totally against genetics. All the Railton men produced in their own image, in spite of their chosen wives' genes. They had sons about them who were tall, long-boned, fine-looking, and with one distinctive feature, patrician noses that flared slightly at the nostrils. Railton men who sired females found the daughters all took after their mothers.

Like his great-grandfather Giles, whom he had never met, Alexander

220

was the exception, and Caspar, though he never said a word, was sad at the physical shaping of his son, overcompensating by being more generous and affectionate to Alexander, though the son showed little respect for his parents. Alexander was short, just over five feet, with dark unruly hair and an odd, strutting gait which bespoke arrogance, not an unknown quality in small men.

Certainly he was brilliant, a superb mathematician with a distinct bent towards electronics, who had graduated into the field of clandestine communications during the Second World War. It was natural that he would become a senior officer at GCHQ, and he had risen there, happily concerning himself with codes, ciphers, and analysis.

Even when he had met, courted, bedded, and then married the fair Delia Butcher, at the relatively late age of forty-two—Delia was twenty-six, in 1962—Alexander seemed to continue to be wrapped up in his work. He had no really close friends at GCHQ, but those who knew him best said that with marriage he had become less tense, and certainly seemed to look younger and even dress differently. If it had been a woman, people would have said "mutton dressed as lamb." With Alexander, friends admired the new, fashionable cut of his clothes.

Yet, now, throwing this small tantrum in the house off St. James's, Gus Keene's instinct told him this was a Railton who could turn out to be a painful thorn in his flesh. He had absolutely no desire to interrogate the unpleasant, moody little man, but he started right in with a certain amount of aggression.

"Mr. Maitland-Wood can be called." He placed a hand gently but firmly on Alexander's shoulder, propelling him into the room they planned to use. "You may talk to him when he's free. In the meantime, Mr. Railton, I require words with you."

"And who the bloody blazes do you think you are?" Both words and voice betrayed the terror under the bluster.

"You know very well who I am. The name's Keene, Mr. Railton, and that's really what I am, and you know it. Keen as mustard, keen to get on with my job, keen for results. As for the bloody blazes, I'm your senior three times over. In some matters I can even override the great C himself, so I would suggest you keep a civil tongue in your head, come in here, and answer a few questions." Without even pausing for breath, Keene told Martin Brook to get BMW on the telephone. "Tell him a Mr. Alexander Railton from GCHQ is kicking up a stink and appears to crave a boon."

Gus Keene guided Alexander into a chair, pulled another close, and started in as though he was dealing with an obviously hostile suspect. "First off, you can tell *me* what you want to talk about to *Mr.* Maitland-Wood."

"You've still not really said what you want with me. This is undemocratic. You're treating me like some guilty suspect in a murder investigation." Keene's actions and manner did not appear to have dispersed any of Railton's arrogance.

"What do I want with you?" Keene roared, and his roar could be considerable when he put his mind to it. "You'll soon know what I want. For starters, what was it *you* wanted to ask the DCSS?"

"A private matter."

Keene took out his pipe and began to light it as Martin Brook returned to the high-ceilinged room they had christened the inquisition chamber. "Says it's a private matter, what he wants the DCSS for." Keene did not even move his head.

"Oh yes?" Fat Martin said cheerfully.

"Has not yet learned the new lesson. For members of the Railton family there are no such things as private matters."

"This is outrageous," blustered Alex Railton. "I want a lawyer. My brother. He'll soon put matters to right."

Keene puffed contentedly. "Oh, no. My brother's bigger than your brother, Alexander." He leaned forward. "Shall I tell you a secret? If *you* fail to cooperate, we have the right to cast you into durance vile and throw away the keys."

"Above the law, are you?"

"In certain respects." Keene paused. "In *certain* respects, yes. People in this Service, and those under discipline to this Service, which means you, have been known to go missing. Some have never been found."

"He's right, you know, Mr. Railton," Fat Martin added cheerfully. "I would advise you to tell Mr. Keene what he wants to know."

"It's a very personal matter." Some of the bite seemed to have drained from Alexander.

"Such as why certain files have stopped crossing your desk at Cheltenham?"

Railton scowled, opened his mouth, closed it, and scowled again.

"Because if it *is* a question of classified files being withdrawn from your previously considerable orbit, Mr. Railton, I *can* be of help."

"How so?"

"I can help by getting your answers to certain questions. Questions, first, about your cousin Naldo."

"Donald." Alex spat the word. "I might've known it was mixed up with that sneaky bastard."

"Naldo, *and* your father, Alex. We have to know some things about Sir Caspar as well."

Alex Railton remained silent, so Keene went on. "Tell me, Alex, when did you last see Naldo?"

"If you *must* call him by that babyish nickname, I last saw him at my father's funeral."

"You spoke with him?"

"No. Well, just in passing, I suppose."

"And the time before that?"

"When my father died. I came in from Cheltenham. It was a very difficult day."

"Yes, I can imagine."

"What with Father's death and my mother in such a state . . . "

"And the house . . . ?" Keene did not complete the sentence.

"Oh, Andrew saw to the alarms, and locking up the place with Donald . . . Naldo. The keys were left with Mama."

"You go back into that house, Alex?"

"When?"

"Anytime after your father's death."

"No. No, I haven't been back since he died, not to Eccleston Place."

"You're absolutely certain."

"Positive."

"When were you last there, then, Alex?"

"Eccleston Place? Easter. Last Easter, '64"

"Really? Then how come your fingerprints were all over the place when Mr. Maitland-Wood went in the other morning?"

Willis Maitland-Wood had made a statement soon after they had taken Naldo from outside the Eccleston Place house. While he had ordered a surveillance team to keep an eye on the house, he had *not* authorized any surreptitious entry. The first time any of his technicians had entered Sir Caspar's former residence they had done so with him, and Tubby Fincher, on the night Naldo had disappeared. Gus had asked him, "Why didn't you deny all that to Naldo at the time? When he accused you, Willis?"

"Giving him a bit of rope. Seeing where it would lead," was all Maitland-Wood had to say, except for his constant repetition of facts. Nobody had gone in on his authority. Apart from Naldo, who did not have his authority, and apparently did not legally require it. In turn this could only mean that either Naldo was lying, which was unlikely, because of the evidence of the sprung traps he had laid; or someone else had paid the house an unauthorized visit. The fingerprints pointed towards Alex.

Alex Railton looked as though he was in shock. *"My* fingerprints?" his voice cracked.

"Yes, Alex. Some smudged; some perfect. Your prints."

"But in the meantime there are a few other questions. Do the cryptos *Fontana, Dredger,* and *Matador* mean anything to you?"

"Of course."

"There's no of course about it. Only a limited number of people knew about those little games. But I gather you handled the communications on all three."

"Yes. Three among many."

"You discuss them with Naldo?"

There was a long silence. Then, "I was given to understand that my cousin had need-to-know."

"Quite right. He ran all three of those ops, and all three went down the drain. Yes, he had need-to-know. You discuss them with him?"

"Yes. Under operational rules. But yes."

"Good. He come to you or did you meet somewhere?"

"We met. We met halfway. Twice. Year before last, and last year. Once when *Fontana* and *Dredger* were running. Then again when *Matador* was in full swing."

"Where? Where did you meet?"

"Where would any Railtons meet if they wanted a halfway house? Stratford-upon-Avon. Same place both times. The Alveston Manor. Lunch."

"You lunched alone, I take it?"

"Yes. He left his goon in the car outside."

"What goon, Alex?"

"That bloody German goon of his. Kruger."

"Kruger's not his goon, Alex. Kruger has his own parish. His own parishioners." Now Keene was puzzled. Big Herbie Kruger was in no way connected with either *Fontana, Dredger,* or *Matador.* Those three interlocking high-risk ops were Naldo's. Run by him, targeting East Germany and Russia. Though they might well have been better off with Herbie's specialized knowledge. There had been specific instructions to keep Herbie well clear, according to Maitland-Wood.

"Kruger's a drunken oaf," Alex said with little conviction, and

Keene recalled Stalks' information about Herbie getting very drunk at Redhill over Christmas.

But, if Alex Railton was telling the truth, Herbie *was* involved. Naldo flouting instructions? Alex Railton denying the Eccleston Place matter? These were new sets of numbers in a vast elusive equation which Gus Keene was beginning to find more puzzling. He continued with the first interrogation session of Alexander Railton, probing at the Eccleston Place fingerprints, then leaping back to the amount of information passed between Naldo and Alex concerning *Fontana*, *Dredger*, and *Matador*.

It became increasingly obvious that, as far as Eccleston Place was concerned, Alex Railton would not crack until the evidence was laid out one piece at a time before him. As to the other matter, he was able to give dates and times, as well as the rough details of what had been discussed.

Maitland-Wood arrived a little after six, and spent an hour with Alex Railton, carefully explaining to him that C, himself, had given instructions for classified material to be shunted clear of Railton at GCHQ.

"You're accusing me of treachery!" Alex fumed.

"Not at all." For once BMW had himself under control and behaved like the true professional he could be when he took pains. "I'm sorry, Alex, but you look like a security risk to us."

"Because of my damned cousin, and the follies of my father?"

"Mainly because of your own follies, I fear." Maitland-Wood had always felt respect for Alexander's work. He might not have removed him from sensitive areas if it had not been for the intimated evidence of Stalks. BMW was a prude, who regarded the slightest sexual deviation as grounds for caution. In a way, Gus Keene had to agree. There was always the threat of blackmail, using Delia Railton as the recipient of "sneak previews" as they called the kind of photographs with which Alex could be badly burned. In the end they sent him away, only slightly crestfallen, with a date to carry on the interview during the following week.

"I want all the pretty pix from Eccleston Place," Keene told BMW. "Even with the evidence I don't know if he'll admit to anything. There's a very strange smell emanating from that quarter, Willis."

BMW grunted, and Keene continued. "You *have* been frank with me about those three ops of Naldo's, Willis? I mean nothing went on that I should really know about?"

"You have everything you *need* to know." Maitland-Wood was brusque, and Keene had the distinct impression he was hiding something. Need-to-know was paramount in the procedures of their trade, for it provided a whole series of cutouts between planners, the case officers, controls, and agents in the field. Need-to-know was the set of locked Chinese boxes that kept everyone in the right place with just enough information to allow the show to be run smoothly.

Keene shrugged. "Then I'll have to talk to Big Herb again," he said sadly.

"Yes," Maitland-Wood snapped. "Yes, Gus, you do that. Do it fast. I don't trust the bugger."

3

Not to put too fine a point on it, Big Herbie was making love to the bubbly Josephine from Security when the telephone rang. Josephine, who was no newcomer to sex, found the large German to be one of the best lovers she had ever pulled into the prone position.

Herbie was fun and sexually inventive. In the grace and favor house they had provided for Herbie, in St. John's Wood, she found him tender and very satisfying. When the telephone rang they were both mounting towards a pleasurable climax, making love to the third movement of Mahler's First Symphony.

This was a relatively new experience for Josephine. She often had fantasies about getting it in a warm bath, or out by some riverbank on a sunny day with nothing between her bare buttocks and the soft mossy earth. Not only had she never had the experience to music, but also she had never even heard of Gustav Mahler. At the time, Josephine's musical education consisted of the lyrics to most of Perry Como's and Andy Williams' hits.

It did surprise her that she seemed to have heard the tune before. For Herbie it was excellent. The First was not his favorite symphony, but the third movement, with the *Frère Jacques* melody turned into a slow funeral march, was good for the rhythm of copulation. He was becoming more and more involved in the music of Mahler, and, while the chubby, bouncy, and bubbly Josephine was, naturally, uppermost in his mind, Herbie recalled that the Maestro had written of that symphony, "All the floodgates within me were thrown open at one sweep."

Herbie's and Josephine's floodgates were about to be thrown open when the phone rang, and Herbie was quite unable to answer it until the act was completed. Josephine was a noisy girl who reached orgasm to the accompaniment of a wild scream. She was still being noisy when Herbie panted, "Ja?" into the instrument.

"Herb? It's Mr. Keene. Gus."

"Ja–hu–hu, Mr.–hu–hu, Keene–uh. Gus–hu."

"Ahaaaaaaaa!" Bubbly Josephine went on in the background.

"You all right, Herbie? What's that caterwauling?"

"Hu, one–hu, moment–hu, Mr. Keene. I have some avant garde music on the player here. Hu–hu. One moment, please."

He jammed the sheets into bubbly Josephine's mouth and she grabbed them gratefully, silencing herself from what had been a singular pleasure. Herbie consigned Mahler's First to oblivion, then went back to the telephone. Gus Keene was laughing. "Kruger, you old ram. I just worked it out."

"What you work out, Mr. Keene?"

"What you're up to."

"Up to? I listen to music."

"The food of love, Herbie."

"Ja. Give to me the excess of it, that pain again."

Gus Keene could not make up his mind whether Herb was deliberately misquoting Shakespeare, learned from a Railton probably, or having him on. "Need to see you, Herbie," he said grittily, having decided that Kruger was, in fact, taking him for a ride.

"Sure, Gus. Tomorrow morning do? First thing, or later, which is going to be best for you?"

"Neither. I want to see you now. The place we met last time, off St. James's. Within the hour, and that's an order." He hung up, smiling at the thought of Big Herbie sorting out the problem of the rest of his evening.

Kruger arrived at the safe house within three-quarters of the allotted time. He was also, for him, dressed neatly. True, the suit looked as though it had been run up by a tailor's apprentice with a bad drugs problem, and the tie lurched to the right of his collar in a disastrous swing. Apart from that, he looked good. The shoes matched for one thing.

Gus had brought in a large pile of sandwiches, or, to be exact, Carole had been sent out for them, having completed her stint in Registry for the day. There was fresh coffee and they fed Herbie as they plied him with questions. Carole had wanted to talk to Keene and Brook about the day's archaeological dig, which made her even more convinced that something was very wrong with Caspar's cryptic diary, but Keene said it could wait, filled her in on Alex's reticence regarding Eccleston Square and his new story about the three blown operations, *Fontana, Dredger,* and *Matador.*

"You keep a diary, Herb?" Fat Martin started in.

"Diary? No. Is very difficult. Also very insecure, very unsafe. You start keeping diary, you end up in the pokey for Official Secrets."

"How do you keep track of work, then?" Keene asked, passing him the plate of sandwiches for the sixth time, while Carole Coles poured fresh coffee.

"Usual. Official log. Kept in lock and key always."

"Where?"

"Private safe. Annexe."

"Good. I want you to be careful about this, Herb." Keene put on his clean-cut, straight-talking look. "You good at remembering dates?"

"Pretty. Give or take a month, yes."

"And if we gave you some dates and you couldn't remember what you did on those days we could trot across to the Annexe and find out."

"Sure, Gus. Why not?"

"Conversely, if you tell us what you were doing on such or such a day, we could check it in the log?"

"That's how we all do it, sure."

"Okay. Try these for size." He gave Kruger the two dates, one in '63, the other last summer, when Alex claimed to have met Naldo in Stratford.

Herbie thought for a moment, then looked up with a big grin. "Sure, Gus. I remember those days. Easy, because they're connected, right?"

"You tell me."

"Sure. I went to Stratford-on-Avon with Naldo. Shakespeare's birthplace. Swan of Avon. Naldo call him Billy the Kid. Funny, uhu?"

"You see anyone else?"

"Yeah. Naldo saw that little cousin of his. That Alex. Naldo tell me Alex is a little shit. I remember. They had meals both times."

"But you didn't?"

"I made packed lunch and sat in Naldo's car. Better really. Naldo was worried about Alex. There had been fuckup . . ." He looked sheepishly at Carole. "Sorry. Cockup. Screwup there had been with communications on ops he was running."

"Ops *you* knew about?"

"Sure I knew. I was part of operations. Adviser capacity."

"What were the ops, Herb?"

Kruger frowned. "You have right-to-know?"

"Call Mr. Maitland-Wood if you like."

There was a long pause during which Gus Keene waited for Herbie to chicken out.

"Think I'd better," Herbie finally said. "They were bad ops. Black. Had a double meaning."

Keene nodded briskly towards the telephone, and Herbie dialed the shop. From the St. James's end, they knew he was put through to the DCSS at once.

"I got Mr. Keene here." Herbie showed no particular awe. "He's wanting to know stuff about the ops Naldo ran last year and year before. The black things. I was adviser, you got me?"

BMW said something, and Herbie replied, "Mr. Keene and his people want me to talk about them, those three operations. Is okay or not?" BMW said something else and Herbie held the instrument out to Gus Keene.

"Apology to make, Gus." Maitland-Wood sounded genuinely contrite. "Those three operations were, and are *very* sensitive. I told you we instructed Naldo to keep Kruger out. I lied to you. Kruger was advising. Specialist knowledge and that kind of thing. He doesn't know much. We kept him at arm's length, but you can question him about what he does know. After that, I think we'd better talk. I'll give you the full strength. Okay?"

"Thank you." Keene put the phone down, showing a certain amount of irritation. He disliked being led up the garden path by senior officers who were supposed to brief him.

"Tell us what you know, Herb. He's okayed it."

"Ja. So he told me, ja. You know the cryptos?"

"*Fontana, Dredger,* and *Matador.* Right?"

Herbie nodded. "Okay," he said. "They were interlinked, but with a difference. I don't know who planned them, but the operations were bloody ruthless. We had fewer sources than we would have liked close to the Ks in East Berlin. Well, in East Germany really, and Moscow as well. Object of those three caperings was to get someone close. Get a national from the East recruited to work close to the Ks, then make himself invaluable so they'd take him to Moscow, okay? We had the man. Ideal. Wonderful. Best there was. Problem was how to dangle him without it looking obvious."

"That's always the problem."

"Sure, but there's one proofooling way. Nobody likes it, because agents die from it."

"Yes." Keene was really saying, "Go on."

"What you do, Gus, is dangle several. In this case four of them. Three fakes and a real one. When the Ks discard the three fakes they choose the real one. Like magician making you take King of Spades, yes."

"Yes." Keene felt the disgust deep in his stomach. What Herbie was saying was that the Firm had deliberately sacrificed three underpar agents in order to get a penetration in, which was tantamount to murdering three of your own men. "What you're saying is that *Fontana*, *Dredger*, and *Matador* were three phony passes. The real pass was a separate thing?"

"Nearly, but not quite. First two were no-goods. *Matador* was the key for whole thing. *Matador* gave them two choices. One good and one bad. Drove Naldo half crazy, those ops. He didn't like losing agents."

"You didn't mind?"

"Weren't my agents, Gus. I was watching the backs of my people already there. I didn't lose anyone." He gave a huge shrug of the shoulders. "This game you need to have strong stomach. I learned that in the camps, and as a kid in the war. Didn't like it, but was necessary. Naldo surprise me. Was bloody squeamish."

Yes, Keene thought, I bet he was. Carole Coles had gone a chalky color. "How did they tip off the Ks, Herbie?"

Kruger did not look at any of them, and his usual boisterousness seemed to have ebbed away. "I suddenly got severe loss of memory, Gus."

Keene nodded. He wondered how men like Naldo, or more especially the operational planner, managed to live with this kind of thing. Like some time-lapse photographic sequence, he saw it all: Naldo briefing four German nationals, pledged to the West, trained, brave men, with Naldo in full knowledge that three would never make it. In his mind he pictured Naldo smiling and slapping each of them on the back. Naldo alone with each man, in secret, maybe for days going through the briefing routines that were worthless except for the chosen one. He nodded at Carole, Fat Martin, and Herbie. "I'm going out for a while. We'll talk about this again. Some other day, Herb, okay?"

On his way back to Swiss Cottage, Herbie found a pay phone, dialed a Berlin number, and put a lot of loose change into the box that swallowed money like a hungry gannet.

"Fienhardt," announced the voice at the distant end.

"You know who this is?" Herbie asked in German.

"Ja."

"Checking on that little job. Anything new?"

"No. It was looked at two days ago. Nothing."

"Okay. I call you again. Two, maybe three, weeks." Herbie hung up. Fienhardt was one of his occasionals in West Berlin who knew plenty of people in the East. He thought Herbie was into smuggling icons out from Russia and he had a number of special friends who ran messages for him in Moscow. The friend he had last used to check out what Naldo had called Box 12 had reported in his clandestine letter to Herbie that Box 12 was still empty as of forty-eight hours ago. Next time he would use another friend. You could not be too careful when it came to smuggling from the East.

4

Clifton Farthing got back to Washington two days before Christmas, several weeks before Gus Keene started to work on Alexander Farthing and Herbie Kruger. He drove out to Langley in order to make his report on the opening stages of the operation they called *Heartbreak*. His Chief of Section said he could leave the film in the safe and complete the report in the New Year. "Go home. Spend time with your wife, Cliff," the older man told him. "Have a good Christmas."

Clifton did a mental double-take. His immediate superior was not known for showing feelings for wives and families.

After the holidays were over, Clifton drove in and took a week or so doing the *Heartbreak* report. After it had been presented, he was told that they had taken him off the operation. His Chief of Section, a short, bulletheaded former FBI man, said his specialist services were needed. He was off the Soviet and Eastern Bloc desk.

Within twenty-four hours Clifton was being briefed for work in Southeast Asia. Vietnam in particular. "We need men with your experience more than ever now," his new boss said. "We're pushing more and more people over there and things are getting worse all the time. I guess Vietnam is going to be the place where we show the Communists where they get off: and tell the rest of the world not to kick us around, eh?"

Clifton nodded obediently, but felt a gnawing pain in his guts. He

231

did not see it as an easy job. They told him that he was to make a field analysis of the Vietcong's intelligence organization. "We plan to exploit them," the operational planning staffer said. "Cut off their agents, and it will be like cutting off their balls. The entire apparatus of the Vietcong's intelligence networks will be unmanned. It's the intellectual way to win this little war before it really gets off the ground."

Clifton did not like to ask him how to find the Communist agents and apparatus, any more than he liked to ask how castration could be intellectual. He had spent a lot of time around the Vietnamese and, to some extent, had an inkling of how they thought and acted. He wanted to ask, "How do you find their balls if they have them hidden away in their guts?" but he knew what the answer would have been: "You cut each one of them open and find the damned things."

There were going to be a lot of innocent Vietnamese cut open to find one Vietcong spy. When he left, Clifton almost shrank away from the horror he knew must come, even if he did his report correctly and with care for the innocent. He mentioned it to one colleague, who simply said, "There're going to be fewer innocents in the world in a year's time anyway."

Clifton wondered if he would have been better off going where Arnie had gone with the Brit. As the aircraft flying him out tilted upwards and set course, he thought about the tall Brit whom he knew was related distantly by marriage. Under his breath he asked, "I wonder who's screwing him now?"

FOURTEEN

1

Naldo dreamed that the nuclear holocaust had taken place. The earth was changed into a great wasteland. He and Arnie were left alive. They seemed to move across countries and continents as though possessed of magical powers. Naldo looked at Arnie and saw that his friend's skin had become infected with great brown blotches.

He examined his own hands and arms and saw he was also covered with these hard growths, some the size of saucers. The blotches were like large scabs, crusted and hard. He squeezed one and liquid ran out.

When he next looked, Naldo saw a small, twiglike object starting to sprout from one of the huge crusts that almost covered his entire body. He saw the same was happening to Arnie. They were growing branches. From the branches, buds and leaves began to sprout and they could no longer move with the magical speed they once possessed.

"You know what's happening," Arnie told him. "We're turning into trees. Soon we will not be able to move at all. We'll put down roots. The roots will seek out water and creatures will begin to live in that water. In a thousand years or so, birds will nest in our branches and the whole cycle of life will start again. This is to be our reincarnation."

When he woke, Naldo was sweating, terrified by the dream, and relieved to be himself. He even went to the little bathroom of the apartment which he shared with Barbara and examined his skin to make sure he was all right. The dream had been so vivid he needed reassurance.

When they had arrived in Moscow, Gloria was already there. It had taken them a week to be brought out of Switzerland, then into East Germany. The team who traveled with them were snatch experts, trained to move secretly in Europe, able to alter their identities so that they became other people, with new papers and lives, in a matter of minutes. Years later these same people, and many like them, helped in the training and movement of Communist-financed terrorist groups. But for the present their one job was to bring Arnold and Naldo to Moscow. They knew nothing except the fact that their charges had worked secretly for the cause in the West. This gave Arnold time to brief Naldo further in his own story, or Legend as the Soviets would have it. Naldo was to be grateful for this instruction during the year to come.

They constantly changed passports and trains, while the final portion of the journey was made by air. Just the two of them, Naldo and Arnold, with the four KGB people and the aircrew in a military plane that creaked and bumped alarmingly. They landed at a Soviet air base near Moscow and there Gloria was reunited with Arnie. Their children had been left with Gloria's sister, Esther, in Connecticut.

Barbara arrived a month later. She told Naldo how a letter had been brought to her at the Axbridge hotel, saying that she should go by bus to Weston-super-Mare. She was met at the railway station by a young man wearing a very smart coat over a badly cut suit. Arthur and Emma had been picked up and taken to Redhill Manor by car, where they were left at the entrance to the long drive. She had spoken to them from a flat the KGB took her to in London. It was Christmas Eve, and as soon as the holiday was over, they gave her a false passport and she flew to Amsterdam where an Aeroflot plane had made an unscheduled landing to take her on board. She could not understand how she had gone so easily through the passport controls without being recognized.

"Naldo, is this for *real?*" she asked, looking around the cramped, dingy apartment they had been given on Leningrad Avenue, in a pink ugly building almost opposite Factory No. 2, the watch factory. Their neighbors worked either at the watch factory or the nearby tobacco factory. "Are *you* for real?"

"Yes," said Naldo, carefully pointing to the light fittings and the telephone that never rang, cupping his hand to his ear to indicate there would be listening devices in the apartment. "If you don't like it, Barbara, they'll let you go back to England—I think." While he spoke, Naldo wrote on a pad of paper, *No this is not real. The conditions are real but I'm doing something else. Be very careful.* Most of the time they talked aloud about the children and other members of the family, or daily trivia. Important conversations took place on paper, which was burned afterwards in the potbellied stove or ignited and flushed down the lavatory, together with two or three sheets directly below the pages on which they wrote. At that time in the mid-sixties life in the small apartment was almost primitive. The tap water ran red with rust and the food was poor.

A woman KGB officer came each morning to take Barbara out and look after her while shopping, and to help her with the language. They only went to local shops, never into the heart of the city. Two KGB surveillance men were on duty around the clock to see that they did not go out by themselves. They were virtually prisoners in the apartment, but a car with smoked glass windows arrived at seven-thirty each morning to take Naldo to "work."

Work consisted of long interrogation sessions, described as debriefings. He was not allowed to see Arnie, and did not even know where his cousin lived. Certainly he did not see him in the big offices at No. 2 Dzerzhinsky Square.

The weather was bitter. Neither Naldo nor Barbara had ever been so cold and they could not stand being outside for more than half an hour at a time. The cold bit deeply into their lungs so they could hardly breathe, while inside they rarely moved far from the big old wood-burning potbellied stove. The KGB watchers occupied a street-level apartment directly opposite the building where Naldo and Barbara lived, and there was always a car nearby. Naldo reasoned that it would be a long time before they could be trusted to move without bodyguards.

He wondered if any of this was worth it, either for himself or Arnie, and their families. At home he would be branded as a traitor, while all they desired was to save his Uncle Caspar's reputation and the honor of their families. In the end he saw their two families as microcosms of their countries. Both the families and the countries were being eroded by change and decay. At the same time things that they believed in: honor; allegiance; decency; the law; essential knowledge between right and wrong; the freedom of the individual, were being ground down under new political ideologies, or presented in a propaganda drive aimed at making countries believe that weapons, and the warfare that could be waged with them, would be for the sake of the individual. Hypocrisy, waste, lack of caring, the idea that the State owed you a roof, work, and money, had crept like a dozen cancers through the bodies of their once great nations.

Now, Naldo did not care what happened to either Barbara or himself. He knew he must do what he had set out to accomplish, even if politicians, civil servants, or the omnipresent man-in-the-street might scoff at him for being idealistic and old-fashioned. So he went meekly to Dzerzhinsky Square each day to undergo the interrogations that were camouflaged as debriefings.

The four people assigned to him behaved impeccably, and with friendliness, putting him at ease, asking their questions as though this was merely a routine matter. In overall charge was General Ivan Ivano-vich Pliner, who asked Naldo to call him Ivan on the first day. "And I shall call you Donald, yes?" He had a square open face, almost the look of a peasant, though there was a hardness around his eyes which seemed to say, "I am a long-serving officer. What I know, I know."

"My family and friends call me Naldo." He had caught the trick in time.

"Ah, yes, I had forgotten." The General smiled, showing two gaps among his bad teeth. "As a child you could not say the name Donald. I remember now, this is in your dossier." It was a hint, Naldo suspected, that they knew a great deal about him.

Ivan Pliner was assisted by two majors, Andrei Novik and Semen Gorb. Both were tall young men, in peak condition, strangely similar in looks, high Slavic cheekbones and silky blond hair. They treated Naldo with grave respect and asked if he would care to exercise with them. "The Chairman has given permission for you to use the gymna-sium and the swimming facilities as long as one of us accompanies you," Semen Gorb told him. "There are set hours for you to use these places."

"So that nobody can lay eyes on the British traitor?" Naldo asked with a smile.

Both men appeared greatly shocked. Oh no, they assured him. It was for his own protection. The Comrade Chairman was anxious that nobody should speak about his presence in Moscow. "When the time is ripe," Novik said, "the entire world will know of the bravery of you and your companion. There will be a press reception in your honor, and you will explain your motives to all."

Naldo asked when this would be, and their answer came in the form of another question. For a complete record would he tell them of his motives? Why had he, a member of the British bourgeoisie, and an officer of the British Secret Organs, passed secrets to the Soviet Union?

He lied convincingly. "First, I believe that all peoples will eventu-ally be bound together in one aim and one ideal," spreading his hands, his elbows tucked into his side and arms extended in a gesture which said, 'My body is your body. We are all one people.' " Aloud, he said, "Personally, the sooner that men and women of all nations understand there is only one way to go, the better it will be. I helped gladly, and will help again. I became sick and disgusted, after the Great Patriotic War, by the phony socialism and the challenge of the old capitalist ways; the double standards of my country, and America's duplicity. I could see the only thing to do was look to the East and embrace the full fervor of the revolution."

236

Though Naldo had been in Moscow for only two months, Novik now dropped a hint. "It is possible you will be asked to return and carry on the fight," he spoke gravely. "Who knows?"

"I thought the world was to be told of what I have done?" Naldo thought the statement very odd.

Semen Gorb quickly stepped in. "I have heard the Comrade General say that it might be good for us to issue a statement saying you had been apprehended on a charge of espionage. We would pretend you were in one of the camps for political prisoners. Eventually they could exchange you for another of our people held in the West. It is a perfect cover for you to carry on with your deception."

Naldo wondered if they would really *pretend* that he was in a camp on the Gulag. It was much more likely, he considered, that they would put him there if they became suspicious of his motives. It was at that moment he decided to send Barbara back home.

Nobody played the old interrogation games of hard and soft, even though General Pliner always gave a cheerful impression that they all knew everything about Naldo anyway, so these sessions were simply a matter of filling in a very few gaps.

The fourth member of the debriefing team was a woman. Major Katarina Lunev was obviously either very well connected, within the Russian *Nomenklatura,* or had been specifically set up for Naldo. "You must call me as my friends like, Kati," she began her introduction one marrow-freezing morning when even the car ride, with the heater going full blast, had failed to warm him. She spoke English with an American intonation, and was later to tell Naldo that she had spent several years in the Russian Embassy in New York. She had enjoyed New York, and, at their first meeting, said she found the way of life in America pleasant. "The food is good. Also I have bought many nice clothes and luxuries while I am there. They have so much and yet so little. While I like it in America, I see so many impoverished people and so many with great riches. There is unfairness. Here we try to be fair. Jobs for all. Homes for all. Care for the sick and aged."

Naldo thought of the Russian women he had seen that very morning, shoveling snow from the pavements, clad poorly against the cold, their feet wrapped in sacking. "All people here are not as lucky as you, though, Kati." There was perhaps a hint of criticism in the way he said it, for two red spots of anger flushed to her cheeks. "People here do the jobs best suited for them." Her tone became snappish. "If a man or woman shows intelligence and aptitude, they will have a better job. All have equality, though this cannot apply where intellect is concerned. My work is not all comfort, you know."

237

He did not want to irritate her, so he rephrased his words, making it clear that even in a country that was truly socialist, like the Soviet Union, it was necessary for the better minds to hold more important jobs.

Kati could never have been called beautiful in any accepted sense, her face was too thin, but with good cheekbones, set very high. She had a large nose and her upper teeth were long, touching her lips when she smiled. But it was a wonderful smile, which spread to the big dark eyes that widened when she showed either surprise or amusement. Her hair was coal black and a shade rough in texture, while her eyebrows always seemed to need plucking. Kati's main asset was her body. She was tall, slim with breasts just a shade too large for the rest of her frame. All in all she was inexplicably sexually attractive, though even an expert in these things would have been hard put to explain why.

Also, at thirty-two she was a widow who claimed her husband had died in a tragic air accident.

Semen Gorb told Naldo that her former husband had been an Air Force general, which explained some of the privileges. "Much older than she," Gorb explained. "He died in helicopter crash. Very sudden. Never really explained. It is said he did not get on with the Chairman, so . . . " He raised his eyebrows in speculation. Naldo noticed that none of his "debriefing" panel ever referred to the head of the KGB by name. They would say "the Chairman," and nod, as though they knew something would soon happen to put the man out of business.

The daily routine resolved itself into a pattern, not immediately discernible, but it was there, under the surface when you looked for it. There was always one part of the day during which he would be kept waiting, sometimes for an hour or so, on other occasions merely for fifteen minutes. After a couple of weeks Naldo realized it was always done at a time of maximum inconvenience: when he had been asked to hang around for a couple of minutes before going to eat, or to be taken around some specific department within the headquarters complex, at that time still confined to the old All-Russian Insurance building, backing onto the Lubyanka. There were outstations of course, but in those days the larger extra facilities were only on the drawing board.

The so-called debriefing was methodical and expert, to the extent that Naldo found himself being constantly surprised. In the field he had known KGB professionalism, but it had always been tinged with a sense of inferiority. All the Western intelligence community talked as though the Russian Service was big on brawn and small on brains. Here in Moscow, Naldo began to feel that, possibly, the British and U.S. services had taken KGB inefficiency for granted.

There were no question and answer sessions. Instead, they would sit around in what he soon recognized as a contrived relaxed atmosphere, and talk. Naturally the talk revolved around the information Naldo was supposed to have provided for Arnie. But there was always an air of general chatter, in which any questions were deeply buried. All four members of the team were at pains to point out the exceptionally detailed knowledge they possessed about the Secret Intelligence Service, from its basic structure to names, and the mannerisms, foibles, strengths, weaknesses, and efficiencies.

During these conversations, which often went on at great length, one or another of the team would leave the room, without explanation. When that person returned, Naldo observed that a new line of questioning would start within fifteen minutes or so. From this he judged that they were not only being monitored by recording apparatus, but also by another, possibly more knowledgeable, officer.

He took great pains to constantly ask about his friend, and former controller, Arnold Farthing. He was told Arnie was well and looked forward to being reunited with his friend and colleague as soon as was conveniently possible.

At night, Naldo would be returned to the apartment block to find Barbara looking frozen and harassed. Her hair, until then, had retained its deep blackness and, from the first days he had known her, she had worn it cut short, like a black cap. Now, during that freezing winter, the black sheen disappeared and turned gray. For the first time in all their years together, she had let her hair grow to shoulder length.

The apartment smelled of cabbage. In Moscow at that time there were few culinary luxuries. Barbara managed to get bread, cheese, cabbage, beetroot, on good days potatoes and fish. On really good days she obtained steak: a tough, stringy, sweet-tasting meat that she swore was reindeer. Naldo hoped it was not dog.

In the cold of the night they huddled together for warmth, and made love with the intense passion they had experienced in their younger days. When he was able, Naldo would write down instructions for her to memorize and, once she had them pat, he would dispose of them in the same way he got rid of all their most secret conversations. In this manner he told her the realities: that he was posing as a defector in order to put right wrongs that affected their country and family. He also told her that she should go back to the West and be there for the children, and to take out the truth to his superiors. He would not be staying long in Russia.

However, he added a warning, saying she should keep certain true facts from a short list of names. Three of the names were heavily underlined and her eyes widened with both sadness and horror when he explained the reason for this. All three were connected by inter-family ties. All three were at the top of his knowledge of treachery. *One of these three,* he wrote in front of Barbara, *can never be trusted. You must warn others off, and never speak the truth to them. As far as these three are concerned you do not know the full truth. For their knowledge only, I am as bent as a corkscrew.* He smiled at her as he wrote these last words: raising his eyebrows in a comical grimace.

Barbara made it clear that she did not wish to leave him, but would do so only if he assured her he would be returning soon. Her love and loyalty to him remained undiminished. She had thought briefly about admitting her own infidelity on that one ghastly occasion, then decided against it. What purpose would a confession serve at this juncture?

As for Naldo, his view of women stemmed directly from Barbara. She had been his rock, his anchor to reality when, for so much of the time, he spent the better part of his life in a world of illusions, tricks, fake boxes, and the art of deception. For him, Barbara was the real world when he returned from dabbling in that dangerous and, for the most part, fictitious land they called the secret world. In spite of his own moments of physical infidelity, which he regarded with as much emotion as a man might regard the passing pleasure of a good meal, he adored his wife.

Barbara was like all women, but held the most special place for him. Naldo thought of women not as the weaker vessels, but as the bedrock of human life. For him, women were there to counterbalance the follies of men. They added color to the drabness of the male; gave strength and intelligence to the stupidity of his own sex; gilded the style of life by their very presence; enriched the world in ways a man could never contrive. In short, Naldo regarded women as much more than the equal to men. In his philosophy, man could not exist without women. Mankind would be lost without their best qualities, and he was certain that while men could never survive without women, it was a sure thing that women could survive and live quite easily without men, except to impregnate them and continue the human race.

The so-called debriefing sessions became more and more delicate. But Naldo had two small advantages. First, Arnold's trust. The American had obviously built up a firm relationship with the Russian Service over the past few years. It was quite clear they trusted him, but did they trust Naldo? Probably almost, but not quite, though Arnie as an ally was a definite advantage. Second, Naldo had a great deal of experience in interrogations and debriefings. He had seen grand masters at work, and knew what the KGB team would expect. All defectors, even those who came with goodwill, tried to retain something. They held things back until they were on safe ground. They also made up answers which they considered their inquisitors wanted to hear.

Naldo structured the whole of his interrogation in layers within his mind. He was the receptacle of many true secrets and these he buried deeply. They would never surface unless the team resorted to full frontal violence, the water, electrodes, and rubber hoses, which was unlikely; or the system the Ks referred to as chemical, injections of "soap," as sodium pentathol was known, or other so-called truth serums, like scopolamine.

So he gave them items they probably already knew, adding in small, uncheckable lies of his own. Some of operational value, others merely the tittle-tattle of the shop. He gave no names he thought might be compromised, only tiny morsels that, on the face of it, sounded good. In the early days he threw in some of the intelligence about squadrons and units of the United States Air Force based in Britain, then, slowly, he drifted into the shop itself. Throughout the first months he switched the subject and showed reticence about the interlinked triple operation about which he knew they badly wanted cross-references.

He could hold out only for a short time, and by spring, as the snows and ice started to thaw, the debriefings had zeroed in to the bull's-eye of his supposed secret work for the Soviet Union: the three operations called *Fontana, Dredger,* and *Matador.*

The team spoke quite openly of the cryptonyms, as though they knew every move, each meeting, and the planning details on an almost day-to-day basis. Naldo was heartened as the questions continued, for it was obvious they knew only the parts of the operations they were meant to know. They were aware of the three possible agents who had wandered into their sights. They even named them. They outlined to him their own analysis of each subject, how they had almost been fooled by the third one, an East German political analyst called Schütz. "I gather our people were about to make the final approaches and begin his training when they had the message from your friend Farthing," Pliner told him. Then he looked up and smiled broadly.

241

"Later we discovered it was you who had provided the information. Three times. Three really good agent material. All or any of them could have been recruited. But *you* gave them to us. Tell us now about how you manipulated Schütz?"

Naldo, in his mind, saw the little bald-headed Heinrich Schütz, in the Berlin safe house they had shared on and off over more than a year.

2

Schütz was one of those natural, gray men in the world Naldo and his colleagues inhabited. The old adage of the secret world was that a gray man would have difficulty in catching a waiter's eye. Schütz was just such a man. Naldo's problem with him was that he appeared to be a gray man with bad nerves.

The other difficulty was that he, Naldo Railton, had the responsibility of making the final choice from two such men, Heinrich Schütz and another middle-aged man, Joseph Brunner. There was little to choose between them. They were both the right age, they had kept their noses clean, were accepted as Party members in East Berlin, and they were both academics respected in their own fields. Schütz, the political analyst, who had spent the final two years of the war in one of the death camps because of his public analysis of the Nazi Party and his, never proven, leaning towards the left.

Brunner was about the same age, a bald, short, historian, accepted as a Party hack, who did the lecture circuit, urging his students in Poland, Czecho, and Germany to accept the current line of history as demanded from Moscow. Brunner's nerves appeared to be intact, though Naldo wondered if he had fallen too deeply inside his cover. A year ago there had been a memo from London suggesting that he should be pulled out for a long period of R & R, then put at a desk.

Sometimes, London advised, the man with bad nerves had more of an instinct for survival. The choice was horrific. No agent runner, control, case officer, call them what you will, likes to lose an agent, yet there are times when you have to walk away in the knowledge that you are abandoning a man or woman who has put his, or her, trust, confidence, future, and life into your hands. Naldo had already been forced to do it twice, during *Fontana* and *Dredger*. Both of the people concerned in those two operations had always been marked as expendable; both were hooked, dangled as bait, and rejected. One, a woman called Hanna Düse, had gone missing, never to be heard of again. The other had made it back by his fingernails. The final operation, *Matador*, would be the clincher. They had to deliberately pick one man, who would be blown by an American penetration agent, and then choose someone whose whole legend stood up.

When it came to the final choice, Naldo went against his instincts. Brunner would be the one to come out of it alive. For weeks he instructed both Schütz and Brunner, each without the other's knowledge, and the instruction of the men differed in subtlety. Schütz's already frayed nerves were played upon, as a man will clean the plastic casing off electrical wire, leaving the wire bare so that a connection can be made with it. Brunner's confidence was bolstered, and his weakness was probed in an attempt to remove it as a surgeon might remove a growth.

Naldo hardly slept for the six weeks he had been given for the final phase of the job. He suffered a recurrent nightmare in which, with no warning, he was sent off in place of Schütz. In the dream he would look in the mirror and see he had become the little bald German, so that he knew what would happen.

In the end it worked like a charm, though there was a nasty ten days when it looked as though the Russians had wholly taken the bait on Schütz. On the eleventh day the body was found, dumped near the SIS headquarters in Berlin. Six weeks later they heard that Brunner was receiving special treatment. A short time before Caspar's death, Naldo had the first taste of the product. Brunner was in and running, working between Moscow Center and the DDR.

Now, in Moscow, Naldo went through each move in the preparation of Schütz, adding little details for the record—how Schütz had been turned, and what specific targets they had given him. "We wanted names," he told Pliner. "There had been a call from my Service and the Americans for details of changes among the Russian personnel in the East. That's what they needed."

"You think, yes, from the names they could have built an analysis of what we were doing?" Pliner, stoop-shouldered, and carrying a little too much weight, raised his dark eyes and gazed speculatively at Naldo from under his bristling eyebrows. "You really think names would have been enough?"

Naldo shrugged. From what he had seen in Registry at the London shop, the files on KGB field officers were good, he told the General. "Each has a page or two on his specialist work. You get the names of a couple of good agent-runners so you assume they've something going for them in West Berlin. Extra Russian cipher clerks mean 'listen to the traffic with greater care.' It must be the same for you."

The General gave a little nod and said they also wanted names. Arnie had given most of the Americans. The General did not know the Agency had taken to reversing names and faces, playing tricks and giving false expertise so that a CI man could very well be an expert on strategy, and thus was able to read the runes from the new military units stationed in the satellite countries. Naldo gave them the two main Berlin safe houses he had used for the three operations. They would almost certainly have been closed down and put on the market as soon as he disappeared.

It was immediately after this particular session on *Matador* that Naldo asked if his wife could go home. They had played several little charades for the sake of the listeners. Word games which became heated, knock-down, drag-out domestic fights. By now the listeners must have had a good idea that all was far from well in the Railton apartment opposite the watch factory. Naldo had even noticed that Kati was taking more interest in him, asking concerned questions, saying he looked under strain or very tired. "Family problems," he would say as though naive to the way the apartment was spiked. His look of fatigue came almost solely from the high amount of sexual activity, which they covered by playing a cheap radio loudly. They did not know when they would see each other again, so sex became the salve for the yet to be inflicted wound.

"Ivan," Naldo said to the General, "I have a favor."

"If I can grant." Pliner went on writing notes in longhand, making a crude pretense that there was nothing in the way of recording going on.

"My wife."

"Yes?"

"She is unhappy here. She misses the children. Also she is disenchanted with me."

"She did not know of your activities before you ran to us?"

"No."

Pliner's shaggy eyebrows went up and down, like some crude imitation of Groucho Marx. "So?"

"So she wishes to leave."

"To leave Soviet Union?"

"It will make my life easier. I go home to World War Three each night."

Ivan Pliner made a noise that was half laugh and half grunt. "If she does not like . . . Then, I suppose we have no reason to keep her. You do not discuss work with her?"

"Of course not." They certainly had nothing on the tapes.

"I do what I can."

"If you can do it, I would hope it would be without drums and trumpets."

Pliner smiled, nodded like an old sage. "Naturally," he said. "Your people have not even posted you officially missing. The rags that pose as newspapers in your land have not even a nose. Is that right, a nose?"

"A sniff, probably," Naldo corrected. Barbara would need time before the SIS inquisition got to her.

That night, in the midst of a fake row to keep up appearances with the sound stealers, Naldo wrote more instructions for Barbara. *Before anything happens officially you must get to . . .* He filled in a name and Barbara smiled for the first time that evening. *You just say to him that a friend wonders if he remembers the night they invented champagne,* he wrote, lifting his head and smiling before saying loudly, "I've asked General Pliner to get you home. This *cannot* go on, Barbara. It's interfering with my work."

She told him loudly to do something anatomically impossible with his work. "I hated it in England. I hate it even more here, you bloody traitor."

"How can I be a traitor when I simply follow my conscience?"

"Fuck off, Naldo."

Three days later, when he was brought back to the apartment, Naldo found Barbara was gone. No note. No explanation. Her clothes had also disappeared. Twenty-four hours later he was worrying in case they had her in the Lubyanka or one of the camps. It would not take much to sweat Barbara.

During the following week, Ivan Pliner told him that his wife was back in London. It had taken a few days to get her out, but he could telephone her if he so wished.

It was another four days before Naldo was sure she was out. Ten times the call was placed to his London number. It made the connection five times and there was no reply. Finally, on a Saturday morning, Barbara picked up the telephone. "I've been to my lawyers," was all she said. "You'll be hearing from them, care of Dzerzhinsky Square."

This was what they had arranged. They would even go through with some kind of legal divorce to keep the play going until the last act.

By June, Naldo was moved into a better apartment, on the Smolensk Boulevard in one of the modern blocks which seemed despairingly at odds with the decorative older buildings nearby; the old Morozovs' house, and the small Nevitsky palace, now, respectively, the Party Committee headquarters and a school for delinquent children. He was given more help, and allowed to go out without any obvious watchers on his back. They still said he could not see Arnie yet, but on the first Saturday of this new freedom Kati Lunev suggested that he might like a visit to the Bolshoi.

Naldo had never been one for the ballet, but he had heard people enthuse over the Bolshoi's performances. In any case, this was a chance to test why Kati had been assigned to the team.

Inside the plush and gilded theater, she talked of other great performances she had seen. Also of last year's visit by the Royal Shakespeare Company. "It was the Paul Scofield *King Lear*." Her eyes glowed. "Every woman in Moscow is in love with Paul Scofield, and I was lucky. I went on the first night and shook hands with him at the reception." She lifted her elegant hand as though showing him an icon. "It was wonderful. Oistrakh led the standing ovation. He is so huge and when he clapped, his arms moved right out as though he would embrace the Scofield. I wept." She gave him a little smile and he patted her hand. "The hand that touched Paul Scofield," he said.

The ballet was *Giselle*, and Naldo thought the sets looked old and tatty, and the performance seemed mannered. But what would he know?

They had dinner at a restaurant in a side street off the Arbat. Half the diners were already very drunk when they arrived, and the slothful service was matched only by the food which made any indifferent English meal seem to be a gastronomic delight. As yet Moscow had not accepted the fact that tourism could benefit their economy. They were still suspicious of any foreigner. Dissidents, subversives, and all foreigners were possible enemies of the State and the cause, so they were treated as such.

During dinner, Kati flirted, and threw tourist information into the gaps in conversation. "The composer Scriabin lived in the next street. You know Scriabin?"

"Not personally but I've heard his music." Naldo smiled, but the joke was lost on her.

"Now it is museum. Personally I prefer modern music. I am very fond of the Shostakovich 13 Symphony, you know? Where he had put the Yevtushenko poems to his music? *Babi Yar, Yumor,* and the others?"

Naldo nodded. He remembered some papers crossing his desk at the shop, wondering if they could do anything about the musician and the poet, Shostakovich and Yevtushenko.

After a long pause she made the move, reaching across the table and running her hand over his. "You are lonely without your wife?"

"She is divorcing me."

"General Pliner tell me. You must need a woman."

"Sometimes," he said quietly. "But not yet."

She said nothing more, but her eyes looked troubled and he wondered if she would receive a tongue-lashing from Pliner for not seducing him. Good, hope she does, he thought. But, by the following Saturday, when she showed him around the Kremlin, Naldo relented, took her back to his new apartment, kissed her twice and felt her respond with her sharp tongue penetrating his lips. Either she liked him very much, or she was well trained, he considered.

Kati made love as though this was the first occasion she had been let off a tight rein in her entire adult life. "There was a time," she told him later, "when I would have done this for a crust of bread."

Naldo wanted to say, "Isn't that what you're doing it for now?" but he controlled his tongue, just as he curbed his mind while taking her. Yet his mind was not held back for long. Here was a woman who knew what bed was all about, and she surprised Naldo by her inventiveness.

"Ask anything of me, Naldo," she whispered. "I will do whatever you wish. You think me slut, yes?"

"No," he lied as tenderly as he could.

In the silence of the night, disturbed only by Kati's steady breathing, Naldo wondered what he was doing here at all. He wanted to be home with Barbara and the kids, and, now that the interrogation was over, they seemed to be playing the fool with him. First he had been given small tours of inspection. The sheer size of the Russian Service was awesome, and he recalled his Uncle Caspar once saying, "Never underestimate the buggers. They hold a couple of cards we can never play." Now he understood what those cards were. First, weight of numbers; second, and most important, the KGB was still the most necessary part of the whole regime, for it had been forged out of the revolution and was required to support what was still, in reality if not in fact, an illegal government which had taken the country by force. The hierarchy remained paranoid with suspicion, of people at home and governments abroad.

Kati began to press him to let her stay with him. Live in the apartment. He saw the action as a clever surveillance move. The round-the-clock watchers could be called off. Naldo resisted as long as possible, but, in October there was capitulation. By then it appeared that they had accepted him, giving him the rank of Colonel and the Order of Lenin, but not yet allowing him to see Arnie, though he heard his American cousin was now also a colonel in his own right, and hung with every honor and decoration the grateful Service could award.

They put Naldo in the department within the First Chief Directorate that dealt with illegals, picking his brains about English characteristics, in particular the kind of education that might put people in line for a pass from the SIS or MI5. Naldo saw no point in lying or prevaricating. He reasoned they knew it all anyway and were using him merely as a testing ground. Indeed they put possible legends to him for approval or comment, asking questions about how the two British services had changed since the war.

Did they, the faceless questioners asked, continue to make passes at people still in the universities? Were the redbrick universities now the true stamping ground of the coat-trailers and auditioners? Did they still spot men and women who were borderline cases when taking the Foreign Service Examinations?

God knew, Naldo thought. He had taken no part in recruiting for years. The questions arrived at his desk each day in the revolting institutional-green-painted room, with a window that looked straight out on Dzerzhinsky Square: a high-ceilinged office with heavy furnishings, almost Germanic in their dark and solid build.

Each evening he would return to the apartment and Kati, in fact he had grown quite fond of her: nothing to do with love, though they rutted shamefully and he discovered that Russian girls can have odd sexual preferences like bondage. He supposed that, in Kati, it was the counterside of guilt. Unless she was an exceptionally skilled actress, it would seem that she really adored him and, now they both had privileges, more luxury goods flowed into the Smolensk Boulevard. Kati was always giving him little surprises, gramophone records of English composers' works. One weekend she provided the Walton First and his Belshazzar's Feast. They played them all that weekend, even as they made violent love. Kati hardly ever seemed to be on duty anymore, and only appeared in her uniform, or at least part of it, when she wanted to play sexual games. She was Naldo's trained housekeeper, making sure he did not slip out to fill some dead letterbox, or meet a contact. He was certain she went through his meager mail, for it was always very long in arriving.

By early autumn there had been exchanges between Barbara's solicitors and his own, an SIS P4 firm who acted as though he was still in

England. He reported the facts to General Pliner, who gave a secret smile and said, "Is good, yes?"

One Monday morning in early November, just as the cold was starting to edge itself into his bones again, Naldo's office door opened without the usual warning from the young officer who acted as clerk/minder.

"Hallo, Comrade Colonel, how's the world treating you?" asked Arnie Farthing, all done up in boots and greatcoat, a big fur hat in his hand.

Naldo rose, smiling. "Arnie . . ." he began, then moved towards the big man with his battered face, and embraced him in Russian fashion. Behind Arnold Farthing he saw another man: sleek, immaculate, with one of those shining well-barbered chins you usually associate with wealth in the City.

"Brought someone to meet you." Arnold looked into Naldo's eyes and he could not tell whether it was a sign of warning or one of triumph.

The door was closed and the newcomer smiled. He was much shorter than either Naldo or Arnie, with sharp features and thick graying hair that had once been black like his eyes.

Naldo took in the small scar below the man's lower lip, and, as he reached out a hand, saw also the tiny scar on its back and knew he had met this officer before, in Caspar's real diary.

With a minimum of gestures, General Vladimir Spatukin introduced himself, taking a chair and sitting. Naldo hardly saw him move. It was like a cinema jump-cut, standing one moment, then seated, perfectly still, the next, looking up speculatively at Naldo.

Arnold broke the ice. "General Spatukin is to be your immediate superior at the turn of the year," he said, and Naldo definitely detected a note of warning. "I have been helping him with the possibility of new illegals in the United States, which should not be difficult now they are so hopelessly entangled in Vietnam."

Naldo had heard all the news there was to come out of Vietnam, and felt coldly worried for America and its youth.

"It is possible I shall go there for a few weeks to see the reality," Arnie continued easily, and Naldo wondered, not for the first time, if his American cousin was exactly what he sold himself as. By now he trusted nobody and wondered if he was becoming as paranoid as those he worked with and for.

"Go to Vietnam?" Naldo knew he sounded like a halfwit.

"Why not? Already we are getting samples of the latest American equipment. I shall be doing some analysis on it in the spring. Vietnam will be warmer than a December and January in Moscow. What news of Barbara?"

Spatukin cut in, speaking perfect English, with the hint of almost a French accent, "She is divorcing him, is she not, Comrade Colonel Railton?"

Naldo nodded, looking into Spatukin's eyes. He remembered his uncle's comment about the eyes. *Like snake's tongues rather than eyes.*

"I knew others of your family, Comrade Colonel." Spatukin's thin mouth hinted at a smile.

"Yes. My uncle, Caspar."

The Russian nodded. "A sound man. I also knew the other. The sexual deviant." The smile broadened and Naldo's stomach turned at the next words. "I did not think I would live to become the father-in-law of another Railton."

"The . . . ?"

"You are living with my Kati, my daughter. She has had one bad marriage, but says she'll be happy with you. It seems you are the apple of her eye, her once and only love. I can only trust that she is as near and dear to you . . ." He paused, then picked up the poem from which the last words had been taken, slightly changed—

> *"In every feature*
> *As the shores are close to the sea,*
> *In every breaker.*

"There, it is not usual to hear men in KGB fouling their lips with Boris Pasternak's poetry, but there is excuse for me, because I knew him, like I knew your Uncle Caspar in a way."

He moved his eyes towards Arnold, and Naldo recalled the other thing Caspar had written about Spatukin flicking his eyes towards people without moving his head. "So," he said quietly, "I look forward for news of your divorce, so we can have a real Russian wedding." He paused, the smile friendly. "Now, though it is raw and cold outside, I think you two boys should go for a walk in the park while I hold the fort here." He gave a minuscule nod of his head, inclining it towards the door.

Naldo could only think of Barbara and his house in Kensington, and his children.

FIFTEEN

1

They had spoken to Barbara for two days, right there in the Dzer-zhinsky Square building, before telling her she could return home. At first they asked about her relationship with Naldo, then it was detail. Could she identify the people who brought her over? No. What would she say to the SIS inquisition? Tell them my husband's a bloody traitor, then ask for a lawyer to deal with the divorce. You will not change your mind? Why should I change my mind? If you change your mind we shall find you, Madame Railton. There is no place on earth where you can hide from us.

After the frighteners came the soft lads. Two of them with good physique and light-colored hair. She thought of them as the twins. How could they make life easier for her? Just get me out of your dirty, sloppy, disgusting country. But we can still help you in England, Barbara Railton. No, thank you, I can help my bloody self. That's all, folks.

They laughed and then explained how she would go. Two pass-ports, a wig, and a pair of severe spectacles. It would be better for her that way. A passport in the name of Rourke. Brenda Rourke. Republic of Ireland paper. There was an address in Malahide. Photo-graphs so she could describe the place and some small details. Let-ters in her desk; clothes in the wardrobe. They even had a legend for her: assistant to a publisher's distributor in Swords, not far from Dublin airport. She would leave Moscow on a Finnair flight to Hel-sinki. Helsinki-Paris. Paris-Dublin. Drop out of sight for three days in Dublin. The hotels will not ask to see your passport. Then Dub-lin-Heathrow with Aer Lingus, and no questions. They could guar-antee it.

She did not believe them, but it all happened just as they said it would. She missed Naldo like the very devil, but followed his instruc-

251

tions, taking a cab home, then, that night, going to a secure line and dialing the number, saying the words, "I've a message from a man who asks if you remember the night they invented champagne?"

Big Herbie laughed loudly. A belly laugh, and the sound waves came as a reverberating shock through the receiver. Barbara flinched and held the instrument away from her ear. Naldo had said there was no reason to think, at this stage, that Herb's home telephone was being monitored. If it was, they had a fallback, a cover story.

"Sure I remember. How could I forget? Who forgets his first champagne? It was Paris, 1948, still a child. They got me pissed as arseholes, excuse please the language." Big Herb's growl made Barbara forget her sadness for a moment. She was strung out like piano wire and thought she might snap at any time.

"Tell him I see him at Earl's Court Underground at six tomorrow night, okay?" Herb growled, still chuckling.

"Okay," she said, hanging up and doing the arithmetic. For Earl's Court read Baker Street, with the ghosts of Sherlock Holmes and Dr. Watson for pipe-dream, fictional comfort. For six tomorrow night make it one hour from now. The fallback was Waterloo at an hour and a half after the meet was broken. Following that, Naldo had written, *God help you both. The Ks will have hounds after you, not to mention the boys back at the shop. It has to be done correctly otherwise nobody's going to believe you.*

Between the bouts of sex and the faked rows, Naldo had taught her the elementary rules. *You have to think of it as an epidemic,* he wrote before burning. *Imagine anyone onto you has got the killer disease, and you catch it, ring o' roses and all. Tishoo-Tishoo, all fall down. Black Death. All surveillance is the Black Death.*

She did three doubles on the Underground and changed taxis twice, walking for the last half mile, and was as sure as anyone who has not done it before could be sure, that she had no tails. No cars. Nobody on foot. She came down past Madame Tussaud's and thought about the Chamber of Horrors and the execution panoramas: the ax and the gibbet, the rack. All for traitors as well as murderers. But traitors were murderers also. *My bloody family seem to have cornered the market in treachery. Deception runs through our history like haemophilia ran through the bloody Romanovs.* He had looked gravely at her as he burned the paper and whispered, "We're all a lot of bleeders," softly, so that the tapes would not hear.

She loitered outside the station, then saw a black cab flash its lights once. It had the FOR HIRE yellow and black TAXI sign lighted, so she flagged him down.

In the back, Herbie opened the door and pulled her in. "Round the block three times," he said to the driver, and made him take a fourth for the insurance. Then, looking at Barbara in the diffused light of the cab, "Jesus, Barb, you change your hair."

She had removed the wig and dumped it in a litter bin after making the phone call. "My hair's changed *me.*" She looked away so that the large German would not see the tears.

They went to Herbie's office in the Annexe. It had been deloused that morning and was clean. At this time in the evening there was a tape on the telephone and that was all. He left her there and went out, returning with some brandy and some cheese sandwiches.

"Sorry, no champagne, they ain't invented it yet." He gave her his big daft grin and sat down on the far side of the desk. "Okay, Barb, what's the story? No way I can keep you hidden for long."

She kept absolutely to the scenario Naldo had given her. There was special-interest stuff at each level, though she did not tell him that. "The American Agency will deny," she said after giving the broad outline. "They're running it very close, and Nald doesn't even know if the DCI is in the picture. The rest of the stuff is very hot." And she told him about Caspar's two diaries. "The one being dissected by the Credit Committee is the phony, but it's also a trap. It should lead them to one of three people. I can't say who, not to you, Herb, and not to the committee. Naldo says they have to find out for themselves. Put two and two together and come up with the right name. Even he's not sure. He called it a game of 'Find the Lady,' only it's 'Find the Jokers.' And it's family. Three contestants. One certainly still active. Another *maybe* still active, certainly concerned." Then she went on with the important message for Herbie's ears only.

"Could be a year, two, more even. Might only be six months. But he'll contact you first. You and only you. You're to be his way back. He said you'd play the honest broker. Keep clearing Box 12. That make sense?"

"Sure it make sense. God hope I'm still here. In England. Then he tell me where both diaries have been stashed, eh?" Herbie looked grave, no flicker of a smile. "What is crypto for these bastards? We know this?"

"One's *Croesus,*" she said, and the saying of it made her feel sick, just as it had caused Naldo to vomit when he had worked out the full strength in the Hôtel Victoria-Jungfrau, Interlaken. "One of the three Railtons. A double from way back. Lying dormant like a snake under a rock." Christ, she thought for the hundredth time, how the hell can Nald bear it?

"Credit Committee know the crypto *Croesus.*" He was not smiling now. "Gus Keene know it. They ask me. Blunt knew also."

Barbara nodded.

"You got to turn yourself in, Barb. You know that?"

"Yes," very quietly. "Yes, but I'm going to do it the way he told me. In fact, Herb, you're going to turn me in."

"So? I put you in chains, Barb? Take you with the cuff links?"

"Handcuffs, Herb." She had caught the habit from her husband. "No, you're to call Gus Keene and say I'm here and I want to come in, but I'll only speak to him. No Credit Committee. No supernumerary confessors. I'll give Gus *all* my sins and some of Naldo's as well. You'll do this for me, Herb? It's what Naldo wishes."

"Sure," he said, and then asked if she had anything else to tell him.

She nodded, and spilled the really secret stuff Naldo had said she *must* get into Herbie's mind: the trigger phrases, signal words, and two map references. When it was over, Herbie said he understood, repeated it all back to her, then picked up the telephone to dial Gus, who was in Warminster.

2

As far as the Credit Committee, and the general investigation into the strange carryings-on of the late Sir Caspar Railton in the 1930s were concerned, things remained very active indeed. The committee met, once a week, sometimes at the shop, but often in odd rooms of even odder houses and apartments scattered throughout London.

Each week, after the meeting, various members of Credit repaired to the Registry, armed with index numbers of files and dossiers. Already they had managed to check every movement Caspar had made during those fallow years of the 1930s. Any time he stepped out of the country had been followed through, and all dates matched. "Not a foot wrong," said David Barnard, sleek as ever and, as a counterintelligence officer of no small standing, with a sneaking regard for Caspar's choreography. He had an attitude to Caspar's journeys which was similar to that of a banker looking at a dodgy account, and, to prove it, had drawn a chart to cover the period set out in the diary. It was like a ledger, and his double-entry system appeared to have paid off, which was more than one could say about any backup confirmation from Lady Phoebe.

Gus Keene and his two assistants were spending long hours with all interested Railton parties, and their interrogation of Lady Phoebe was possibly the most harrowing any of them had experienced. Caspar's death had wrought terrible changes in the elderly lady, in her heyday so extrovert, sharp, and blatantly well-organized. It was as though her mind, her memory and intellect, had all passed from her at the moment of Caspar's death.

Now, Phoebe lived in a land of make-believe. She wept and laughed by turns, and on some days spoke to everyone as though Caspar was alive. Twice, while Keene, Carole Coles, and Martin Brook questioned her, she waved them aside and told them they would have to ask Caspar. "He says I'm never to keep a diary." Her eyes were feverish. "Cas always says diaries can bring trouble. Never keep them. He doesn't and neither do I."

It was the one speck of magic dust the team took away with them.

"Sir Caspar cautioned against diaries. That was a voice from the past, genuine," Carole said in the car, and the others agreed.

"Therefore," Keene said, half-an-hour's silence later, "Sir Caspar kept a diary for a purpose, and we know that purpose couldn't have been to incriminate himself. QED. Quite Easily Done as my old mathematics teacher used to quip."

"Unless he wanted to make a clean breast. Plead guilty after they had interred his bones." The fat Martin Brook was unconvinced.

"Don't be more of a bloody fool than you already are, Fat Boy." Keene was off again, his mind striding through possibilities. "We're all agreed that bloody diary's too good to be true. Yet there has to be a reason for it. Why, why, oh bugger, why?"

They had several sessions with young Alex Railton, who continued to deny he had been near the Eccleston Square house, against all reason, for the evidence was there and they told him so.

"If you won't admit to it, Alex, then we'll have to regard you as hostile and, therefore, possibly a person with things to hide."

"I have no thing, or things, to hide," Alexander snapped back. So they then became very hostile indeed, making threats to have him removed from GCHQ and really sweated.

"Do that and all hell will be on your backs," he retorted, as though telling them the trail would lead them to great embarrassment.

"For God's sake let's do him," Brook had angrily pleaded. But Gus would not hear of it. "More fish to be fried. Let's gather some rosebuds while we may, then hang them around his nasty little neck."

It was a hard time they had of it with brother Andrew, who also threatened litigation on a large scale. Unhappily he was a very experienced interrogator himself, and knew a lot of the tricks. Keene even went to BMW and voiced his opinion that Sir Caspar's pair of male children should be taken by force. BMW roughly ordered them to hold their fire. "Bad enough being landed with the Confessions of Saint Caspar. Don't want to go off at half cock with his bloody offspring. Leave well alone for the time being."

Gus was not going to argue. The time would come, he considered, when all would see sense, or sense would finally prevail. So they took themselves off and had a long day's journey into the early hours with the old folks at Redhill. It was not productive. Neither were the three days they spent with Naldo's father and mother, who both looked, and obviously were, tired and worried sick. James seemed to have become very feeble physically, though none of them could deny his sharpness of mind, for he answered every question pat, as though someone had fed them to him before the team arrived.

"So we do it all again," Gus Keene announced, and they set to with new queries and several tributaries of reasoning. Much good did it do them.

Back at Warminster, Gus called them together in order to riffle through the piles of nonevidence before them. Then, one evening, the telephone rang at Gus' private number and there was Big Herbie at the other end saying he had someone with him who wished to surrender only to Gus, and please would he not tell any of the big guns on the fifth floor, and especially no member of the Credit Committee.

Gus sent Arden Elder off on a wild-goose chase to Oslo, where they already had a low-grade defector pleading for someone to talk with. He then gathered Carole and Martin around him and the trio set off, in one of the Service cars, a Rover with smoked windows, for Whitehall and the Annexe.

3

Gus housed Barbara in what they all called the hospitality suite: in reality a very safe area away from the Warminster main house. It was a purpose-built brick building with no windows, but a pleasant interior with all mod cons, including room service, provided by two stalwart members of the Warminster staff, who could have been deaf-mutes for all the response anyone got from them.

"You'll want to rest, Barbara. You don't mind my calling you Barbara?'' Gus had given Carole the job of settling their unexpected visitor into the quarters. "Woman stuff," he said, patting Carole on her neat little bottom, an action they both rather liked, particularly when it was surreptitious.

"You can call me Minnie Mouse if you like." Barbara was edgy and in one of her touch-me-and-I'll-scream moods.

"Okay, Minnie. Waddya wanna do next?" Carole did her impression of Mickey Mouse. She had others, including a fabulous Streisand, and a rather good Shirley Bassey, which she usually did in private for Gus.

It broke the ice-maiden attitude that Barbara had cultivated from the moment the three inquisitors had arrived at the Annexe.

"She talk to nobody but you, Gus. Also, until you've talked, I would not mention this to anybody else, and by anybody this I mean. Not Willis, Tubby, C even. And certainly not that crazy committee they got to say Caspar was fucking double." They were in the outer office and Herbie had shut Barbara away to rest in the next room once he had called Gus. "Is deadly secret," he said.

"But she's talked to you, Herb. Yes?" The eyebrows rose.

"Not exactly. No."

"Come on, you fat fraud. She landed up on your doorstep."

"Listen." Herb laid a finger alongside his nose. "Between the two of us only, okay, Gus?"

"Always." Keene lied. "You know you can say anything to me. Wouldn't repeat it to a soul."

Herbie cozied up to Gus Keene. Whenever Herbie did that, Gus thought it always spoke of intimidation. "Look, old sheep . . .''

"Horse."

"Sheep, horse, what's the difference? Listen well. That lady has come in from a very cold climate. I tell you for once only. Barbara didn't want to come. But she did. It is to bring truth. She and Nald cooked it between them . . .''

"The truth?"

"No, her getting out. She tell me only what is good for my eyes, right? Nothing. Okay. She has things only for your eyes also. You screw this one up and you answer direct to me, Gus."

"I'm a little senior to you, Herb."

"Go take a flying jump. Senior makes no difference. This is the real world. The bloody Ks warn her. You got to keep her in pearly for long time."

"In what?"

"That's what she say. 'Herbie, not even the fifth-floor boys. Naldo says Gus has to keep me in pearly.' ''

257

It took a full minute, by way of devious logic, for Gus to work out that he meant purdah.

Now, he waited in the big house, concocting ways and means in case Barbara really had got something big and the world was going to explode around him.

"What you reckon?" Fat Martin asked from his place by the window.

"Instinct tells me Naldo's trying to do a deal. He wants to come in. Realized his mistake and doesn't like it over there with the babushkas and snow inside during a long hard winter. But my instinct could be very wrong. I can't buy Caspar as a Soviet penetration, and I've never seen Naldo as a willing defector. Herb could just be right. Maybe she has something bloody important, and maybe we are to be the keepers of the holy book." He opened his mouth to say something else when Carole Coles came in, all of a rush, with red cheeks.

"She wants to talk now," she puffed. "No rest. No sleep."

"A little chicken soup?" Gus asked.

"You've been talking to room service," she grinned. "Chicken soup and a big juicy steak. Red wine. Said the house red would do fine."

"Anything would do fine if you've just spent several months in a winter Moscow. Two days, they tell me, is quite long enough."

"Are we going to let her talk now?"

"Naturally. First rule. Let it all come gushing out. See if we can give her absolution after that."

They all trooped out towards the hospitality suite.

Barbara had taken a shower and was dressed in a white terrycloth bathrobe. Her hair was swathed in a turban made out of one of the hand towels, and the deaf-mutes had delivered the food. The air smelled as though someone had taken a shampoo in a steak restaurant.

"Come in." She sounded bright.

Maybe too bright, Gus thought. "You want to keep us up all night, I understand?"

"I want to give you the headlines. I think there'll be plenty of time to write the whole story later." She crumbled bread into her soup. "Forgive the manners, I'd forgotten what real bread was like until I got into Dublin. I ate like a pig for three days, and I fancy going on like that. It's only . . ." She stopped short, and Gus quickly looked at her. The brightness had been a pose. Now great lashing tears were hitting her cheeks and forming rivers of pain.

"Only what, love?" Carole was exceptional when it came to tears. She had her arm around Barbara's shoulders, and Barbara was making a wet rag out of Carole's clean white blouse.

258

"Naldo . . ." Barbara sobbed. "I want him back." Then, like a child, "I want Naldo back . . . I want him . . . Didn't want to come out alone . . . Please get him back in one piece. Please."

"Take your time, Barbara," Carole cooed as though to a frightened infant. "Just take your time, then lay the news on us. If it's for real, we'll get him back. Just tell us."

4

Jumping forward several months, skirting the debriefing of Naldo Railton in Moscow, together with his burgeoning relationship with Kati, to the arrival of Arnie with General Spatukin, there was news laid on Barbara's husband.

Naldo walked in the Park of Culture and Rest, Dzerzhinsky Park, with Arnold. It was cold and their feet crunched in the frost of snow. Heads down, with the fur hats pulled over their ears, and hands in the pockets of their greatcoats. Two old friends sent out for a walk in the park by a very senior KGB general.

"They got sound on us?" Naldo asked out of the corner of his mouth. Not even a lip-reader could have deciphered.

"We're clean and on our own." Arnold looked up, glancing around to see only children running or sliding among the statues and bare trees, their mothers watching. "Not a hood in sight," he said.

"Why?"

"Why not? How they been treating you, Nald?"

"They let Barb go."

"I know. I vouched for her after listening to the tapes. I have their complete trust."

"And I haven't?"

"Oh, you have. They're very impressed. You did very well, and I managed to piggyback you. Together, Naldo, we've convinced them, but don't drop your guard, they're suspicious devils."

"Spatukin?" Naldo muttered.

"What about him?"

"He must know I'm dodgy. Caspar walked out on him. Left him to carry the can. He was Caspar's control, and my uncle didn't like him much."

"*He* liked your uncle. He also likes us, and I think that was because of Cas."

"How?"

"Cas turned the bugger."

"What?"

"Cas ended up controlling him. Kept him in cold storage against the time, then handed him over to us. Just after the Rogov business in fact. I got to lay the news on you, Nald. Spatukin is with us. I'm off to Vietnam in two weeks. There I hope to make certain contacts. Get the ball rolling. Once I'm back, it'll be Spatukin who'll provide the long weekend passes for us to visit Sochi and look up your old buddy Penkovsky."

"Jesus!" Naldo could hardly believe it. Then the horrors hit him. He thought of all the ruthless pain and trouble that had gone into the three operations run in order to get Brunner forced on the Soviets in East Berlin. He thought of the dead. Of plump little Schütz, dumped from the car; of the woman, Hanna Düse, who had never returned; and of the one who had come back and would never operate again. The one who wakened with night sweats and nameless horrors. Naldo had packed the whole thing away in his mind, or he would also waken screaming. "No one thought of letting us know, or even giving us a slice of the take?" he asked quietly.

"Not my department." Arnie did not glance in his direction.

"You let us . . . You let *me* go through those three charades, two dead and one blown forever just to get some low-grade stuff, when you had his nibs sitting here in Moscow Center?"

"He doesn't oblige very often. Besides, your people were desperate to get someone in, and it helped with the cover we were building for myself."

"Jesus, God!" Naldo reflected on the difficulties they had running Brunner anyway. The Ks had taken him into their Service, given him a modest training, promoted him two notches, and then let him run errands between the Center and Karlshorst. It took a fortune to support him, ten days to collect a letter, and that only gave them names of the latest KGB officers promoted in Moscow. Once, in the few months they had run him, Brunner had provided quality material and London had come back to say they already had it from the Kremlin watchers. And all the time, General Spatukin was passing on tasty tidbits to Langley. Whether he obliged often, every week, or once a quarter made little difference to Naldo's feelings.

"Why should Cas pass Spatukin to your people? Why not keep him for his fellow Brits?"

"I thought you had figured your uncle. By the time we did the Rogov thing he was already a very disillusioned man."

"And maybe he knew something nobody else knew. That the penetration in London was really bad."

"Quite possibly."

"And now Spatukin wants me to marry his daughter?"

"Quite possibly," Arnie repeated, not looking at him this time. "Insurance I should imagine. If he can't get out you can always take his daughter along for the ride."

"Barb's going to love that," Naldo spoke with great bitterness.

5

In the present, inside the hospitality suite at Warminster, Barbara had no way of knowing of this future little sideshow. They all sat around and watched her eating, Martin Brook writing down her request for books. When she had finished, and offered each of them a glass of the house red, Barbara sat back.

"There are things I have been instructed to tell you before you ask anything else. I'm going in headfirst and just pray you're not stupid; pray you don't run to the headmaster or his nasty little committee with it. All I ask is that you hear me out. Then you can put the questions back to me." She smiled, and her crimson-ringed eyes lit for a second. "It concerns active penetration agents here. Now. It also concerns a fake diary. You ready?"

"We're all sitting comfortably," Keene smiled back. "Now you can begin."

SIXTEEN

1

Give them the logic first, Naldo had instructed her. So, for starters, Barbara told them the things they knew, or could check. The suspicions, the intruders at Eccleston Square, the operations called *Fontana*, *Dredger*, and *Matador*. She gave the names of the agents involved. Who lived and who died. Then, as he had also suggested to her, she told of their version of the way in which Naldo had slipped out of sight; of the secret arrangement he had with Arnold Farthing, and what had happened when he arrived at the villa in Ascona. She did not know anything about the photograph, but Gus Keene did, and already he had begun to think of ways and means in that direction.

"I don't know how Arnie made contact," she said. "All Naldo would say was that Arnie sent him a message which could really not be resisted."

The talks that she had been party to with Gus, before slipping out of England herself, seemed to have been forgotten. At the time Barbara had been worried that her one act of infidelity might have put her husband in jeopardy. Now she could not make the simple connection.

Oh, Christ, Gus thought, Naldo played the gentleman. He did not want to make her feel bad, so he stayed deaf, blind, and dumb about the picture of his wife copulating under the eye of a camera, or grinning, half dressed. He was certain the photographs existed, and that would have been the obvious way for Arnold to have hooked him.

"Wherever we lived in the world we always had an escape route," Barbara continued, oblivious to Keene's slight sigh. "A system if we had to get out fast. There was always a way. Naldo was cautious. He arranged things as best he could for London, and I asked why. He simply said, 'No reason, but *always* think of the worst.' Naldo knew of his enemies, and felt it was prudent."

Only then did she sidetrack and get to Caspar Railton's diaries. As she spoke she remembered Naldo's written words to her in the dingy flat across the road from the watch factory. *If Gus is the man I think he is, give him, and those he trusts, the fact that there are two diaries and nobody will interrupt until you've told the lot.*

It worked almost like a charm, even though there were some pertinent interruptions. "I don't suppose anyone knows that Caspar left *two* diaries?" she said clearly, dropping her voice on "diaries." "One was for the consumption of Service brass and possible penetrations. The other is the real thing. Like a coin. Two sides. But the real truth is, like the queen's head, on one side only."

Someone out there put 400,000 volts of electricity through the room. Barbara felt a new alertness in the listeners.

"I knew it! I knew it!" Carole Coles looked as though she would stand up and do a little jig of triumph. "It was all too easy. Nobody keeps a diary of events they want to hide. Not in this game."

"In old age they do." But even Keene sounded elated. "When they're afraid they're going to forget things. Elderly spies have died on account of cheating by taking notes."

"Were these diaries written in old age, though?" Fat Martin had a wide grin on his face.

"Possibly." Gus looked at him as though he had the intelligence of an ant.

"If I could . . ." Barbara began.

"Of course. We're being very rude." Gus gave her a little bow, a gesture which said, continue, put us right.

"The diary contains some kind of trap. That is, the diary for consumption by the Service. What Naldo says is that there was one firm and old penetration right at the heart of things. This person, cryptoed *Croesus,* might still be active. If not, the job is passed on to the next in line, like a baronet. It's deep family stuff. Caspar didn't name them, but Naldo says if analysts ferret around in the fabricated diary, they will stumble on the truth. He also says that he believes Caspar was too emotionally involved to put the matter straight before he died. Naldo says you have to take a good look at three people, one of whom is still active. The others . . . ? I just don't know."

"When you talk of Naldo saying things . . . ?" Gus began.

"I really mean Naldo wrote things, often at great length. The Ks had sound on us in that ghastly little apartment, but he went over every square inch and found nothing to give them pictures. We knew where the sound-stealing stuff was and played up to it. For Naldo's safety it really had to look as though I came out of my own free will, in disgust, thinking he had been turned. It has to go on that way. I shall even get a divorce.''

"The two versions of the diaries," Gus began again.

"No, I *haven't* seen them." She smiled, her eyes still damp as they talked. "Naldo has not told me where they are, but it seems that, when the crunch comes, they can both be obtained. He's anxious that the princes of the Service should follow through on the logic of the concocted diary only at this stage.''

Gus stopped her again. "There are two things that worry me about all this. I'm told the diary being examined by the Credit Committee checks out with every move Caspar made in the 1930s when he was out of the Service.''

"They dovetail," she replied quickly, anxious to put him right. "Naldo says it's a remarkable job. All the dates and meetings in *both* diaries took place. The names he gives are for real. It is the spirit of the diaries that differs.'' She explained that the fabrication showed Caspar as an agent doubled back by the Soviets. "In the other version he blows all that to pieces; shows how he was not doubled at all, but was doing things for the right reasons. He was collecting intelligence, looking at Stalin's grand plan for Europe, and the Soviet Service's part in it.''

"Then why," Gus asked softly, "didn't he put the whole of this thesis to the powers that be when he returned to the fold?''

"He tried to do just that and got nowhere. In his papers he claimed to have used someone he preferred to call *Croesus.* After he failed to make any impression he left the job to *Croesus* entirely. Caspar felt that, during World War II, the Soviet target just remained dumped. It was his reason for getting out in the thirties anyway. He couldn't work from within, and he felt very strongly about the whole business. He was bitter. Disillusioned. So he left it to someone else to plead his cause. Remember, Gus, the spirit of the times was *hands off the Soviet target.''*

Keene nodded, speaking almost to himself, "And *Croesus* failed to deliver, even when we belatedly put the Sovs back in our sights.'' Then, louder, he asked, "But what about Arnie and Naldo? I know the Ks, they don't take in defectors unless they're pretty certain of them. They're more paranoid than we are. Arnie Farthing and Naldo Railton seem to have just walked in and were accepted with open arms.''

"Part Two of the story," Barbara said quietly, as though she was still not quite convinced about what she had been instructed to say. "Nald maintains it is all deniable, but you can prise it out of the right people." She nodded at Keene. "That's one of the reasons that this part is for you only."

Everyone remained very still, waiting for her to speak. "Somewhere, among the many covens run by our Cousins at Langley, there are two operations. Both are deniable, both buried so deep that he is uncertain about the DCI himself knowing of them. The first was called *Heartache*. This was a ploy to dangle a very senior field officer and play him directly to the Ks. It took five years or so before they bit completely, but when they did, *Heartache* continued to give the Sovs the same high-quality intelligence he had provided for a long time."

"Why?" Keene interrupted.

Barbara answered the question without even pausing in the narrative. "It had a dozen prime objectives; a sort of rolling operation which could be made use of at the right moment, as far as we can judge. Langley, Naldo thinks, has already got a contact very close to Moscow Center. He said you already know, from defector information, that the Center claims to have all our services well and truly shot to pieces: penetrations in Five, the SIS, and CIA. *Heartache* was a ploy to discover more, to snatch names, or, in the end, to do something even more sinister."

"Do we know who Langley's man is in Moscow Center?"

She shook her head. "Naldo only had Arnie's word for it. A kind of throwaway, a hint even. We don't know if he's well-placed or very low-grade."

"And *Heartache?*"

"Is Arnold." The room went even more still. "God knows what backup he's got. Precious little, I should imagine. Someone highly placed at Langley, with a very involved, complex, Byzantine mind set the thing up and ran Arnie solo."

"So what about Naldo?" Afterwards they would have been hard put to say who voiced that important question.

"It appears that things began to close in. Suddenly the reasons for *Heartache* changed. Arnold met Naldo a few days after Caspar's funeral. He told him that Railtons and Farthings were under suspicion. He also told him one other known secret. A secret big enough to make the SIS and the CIA look like gullible idiots if it ever comes out."

"Idiots?" muttered Fat Martin.

"*Heartache* went into a new phase coded *Heartbreak*. It appears that *Heartbreak* was intended to get rid of the threat that hangs over both services."

"What kind of threat, Barbara?" Keene leaned forward. There was

265

still a little wine in the bottle and he poured the dregs into a glass and swilled it down as though taking a magic potion.

"Naldo wouldn't tell me, but he did give me one story. He said there are some things, skeletons, that no intelligence service, no country even, would ever make public because of embarrassment. He said that a CIA agent had resigned and gone on a hunt for the truth about the Kennedy assassination. Apparently this man got at the truth, which had something to do with the Vietnamese. The proof was brought back to Washington and they shredded it and burned it. What Naldo said was, a country could live with the idea of a lone nut killing the President, but it would be too hard to live with the idea of a squalid revenge killing."

Keene nodded; Carole looked blank; while Fat Martin seemed intent on catching flies in his mouth.

"Naldo said that, in the end, *Heartbreak* meant Arnie going into the East, running as a blown defector, to put right this embarrassment, whatever it is."

"Get this straight." Keene's brow creased. "The embarrassment has nothing to do with the Kennedy assassination?"

"Absolutely not. He used that as an illustration. There is something still lying around in Russia that could cause red faces on both sides of the Atlantic. I did get the impression that it had something to do with President Kennedy, but not with the assassination. It was something so embarrassing that the history of it should never be put right. *Heartbreak* is now the end product of Arnold Farthing's long dalliance with Moscow Center, and, because Naldo was, and is, a party to the truth, he became involved. It appears that Arnie had used him."

"Used Naldo?"

Barbara let out a long sigh. "*Used* him, Gus. You don't mind if I call you Gus?" She parodied the way the whole team were being so polite to her. "Arnie used names. People in the trade. They were his own agents. His network for the Ks, and Naldo was set up good and proper for it because of those three bloody, and I use that word advisedly, operations: *Fontana, Dredger,* and *Matador.* You must've been cleared for that triumvirate of idiocy, Gus, because you've already mentioned it."

Keene nodded, inclining his head towards his two assistants to show they were all clear on the ops mounted at great cost, of life and finance, to put one barely productive agent adjacent to KGB sources.

"You'll recall, then, that our dear Cousins in Christ at Langley were cut in, and they offered their services to drive the no-go dangles into the net. To tip off the Ks about which offers they should not accept."

Another nod.

"It was Arnie who tipped the Ks on all three occasions, giving them a clear equation from which they could only choose one man. A man called Brunner, I gather. I also understand he hasn't been of much use."

Keene looked as though he had very suddenly had a thought. "Barbara, how come you're cleared for all this? Yes, the whole business has been a disaster, and was never a well thought-out operation from the start. But how come you're cleared for it?"

"I'm not. I'm not even part of your bloody Service. I'm the messenger girl. Naldo cleared me off his own bat, because someone had to bring the truth out and I'm saying nothing to your damned Credit Committee. I want locking away here with an armed guard, six dogs, and a padlock on my drawers. I also require a good divorce lawyer who'll keep his mouth closed, and my home telephone number routed here. Right?"

"Right. And I'm supposed to do what?" Keene looked bewildered.

"*You* are to lead Credit to the right conclusion. *You* are to find the jokers. One, possibly even two, out of these three." Barbara produced a slip of paper from the pocket of her robe and handed it over to Gus Keene, who took it and read the names. Like Naldo and Barbara before him he felt the nausea rise into his throat. "Jesus Christ, no!" he whispered, looking at Barbara's hand, which was beckoning to take the paper back from him.

"I've got used to the idea," she said. "It doesn't make it any easier, but I've got used to the obvious one. I can also make an intelligent guess on who to choose from the other two. It's the prime mover that takes some getting used to, but when you think about it, the whole damned thing becomes obvious." She paused, as though for an intake of breath, then added, "By the way, Naldo says you can trust Herbie."

There was silence for a while, then Keene nodded, raising his eyebrows in a gesture that was meant to be one of both acceptance and sorrow.

2

"So, let's take a vote. *Can* we trust Herbie?" Keene looked from Fat Martin to Carole Coles.

"There seems to be nobody else," from Fat Martin.

Carole said, if Barbara was moving them towards some deeply buried truth on Naldo's instructions, then, at least for a while, they should keep her happy and do as she asked.

"By happy, you mean trust Herbie?" Keene was just testing.

"Who else we got?" Fat Martin was looking out of the window. They were in Keene's office inside the main house. Summer rain fell heavily onto the lawn and hushed itself through the trees.

"Summertime, and the living is easy," Carole sang. She had quite a nice little voice and could carry a tune. Her old grannie had always said, "You should go on the stage with that voice."

"Bloody easy," Keene commented. "But as you rightly say, murdering the English language, who else we got?"

"So, do we go on sweating Barbara?" Carole joined Fat Martin at the window.

Gus gave the instructions. Yes, they had to keep Barbara under wraps and go on pegging away at her. "I must caution everyone regarding my dear old second in command, Mr. Elder of the Credit Committee. If he gets a whiff of Barbara, we're in trouble. Okay?"

That was something they took seriously, and Gus began to draft a memo to all. Hands off the person in the hospitality suite. Nobody but the qualified room service, plus his team, were to go near. No sneaky peeps, no questions. On pain of getting chucked out minus pension and any other insurance.

"So," when he had completed the order, "we go on with Mrs. R; we also have to run through the entire Railton clan; and have a word with Herb. Herb first, I think."

They caught him unawares as he was leaving the Annexe for the night, and they all drove to a house Gus used quite often, and not on the normal books at the shop. As Chief Inquisitor he ran this place out of the Warminster funds and had yet to be caught.

"Just a little help, Herb," he began.

"A little help for you, Gus? This is often a lot of grief for the one who helps."

Gus smiled and nodded. Carole fixed the drinks, and the Fat Boy stood looking down into the street. The house was in Soho and a sea of umbrellas floated below. It had rained for twenty-four hours.

"You have friends in that nice complex in Langley, Virginia?" Gus asked.

"Some." Herbie tilted his palm, accompanied by similar head movements. "Depends on which offices you want."

They had talked about that on the way up to town. "If it's deniable, the things called *Heartache* and *Heartbreak* have to be Counterintelligence. Those people can bury operations until the end of time."

To Herbie he now answered with the acronym "CI."

"Oh, yeah. Real pushover." Herb laughed.

"Well?" Carole asked.

"Well, what?" Herbie snapped back. "You want for me to call Jim Angleton on an open line and ask what he's got running? Sure. Easy. Make my mark and get boot up the arse from everyone."

"Isn't there a more discreet way of doing it? Anyone at Grosvenor Square who'd know about a deniable CI op?"

Herbie appeared to be wrapped in thought, only Gus, who had eyes and ears for these things, detected a tiny change in manner, indicating that Herb had hit on a line of reasoning.

"Don't know." Herbie was still wrapped in his magic thought cloak. "What's the question?"

"Deniable operations running against the Sovs. One called *Heartache* which went on for around six or seven years and then changed, last winter, to *Heartbreak.*"

"You want this unofficial? Big operations?"

"Let's say operations so quiet that you can't even hear a pin drop."

"Shit! Well, might not work, but is one fellow. Old friend from way back when I worked with Nald, Arnie, and Cas, just after war."

"It concerns Arnie and Naldo. In a way it concerns Caspar as well."

"Then why not ask bloody Credit people?"

"Because they're rogue elephants, or hadn't you noticed?" Fat Martin said quietly.

"Sure, you know Willis tried to sick a P4 lawyer onto Naldo before he bought himself wings?"

"Who?" Gus Keene tried to sound disinterested.

"Ohh." Herbie shrugged. "Legal and General. Lofthouse. Know him?"

Keene knew him, and had tried to have the man taken off the P4 list at least twice. "Nobody else, Herbie? You're sure?"

"Yeah, sure, Gus."

"Now, how about this Agency fellow, Herb?"

"So. A guy who worked Covert Ops and CI, way back. Before Langley. Guy called Marty Foreman. They put him out to grass, okay? Here, London. Grosvenor Square. Might not know because he's getting on, but still has eye to the ground always."

"So try Mr. Foreman, Herb."

"What if it goes wrong? I point him at you?"

"We know nothing. Didn't even ask." Gus smiled sweetly.

"Okay, spell out what you didn't ask."

"We didn't ask if there was any truth in a couple of ops, working under the same flag. *Heartache* and *Heartbreak.* Concerned Arnie going over the wall. Confirmation that there were such operations, that's all we want."

"I try him. If I come back with arse in sling, you know the answer's yes."

"We'll give you a call tomorrow. Payment comes now. How about us all going for a nice Indian."

Gus knew a little place at the Kensington High Street end of the Earl's Court Road. Nobody could ever remember its name, but they called it "The Ring of Fire" for reasons not hard to figure out, particularly in the dark reaches of the night.

Herbie ate a double chicken vindaloo with dry vegetable curry, washed down with twelve halves of lager, and they left him in St. John's Wood crying curses on all who criticized the works of Gustav Mahler.

He got back to Gus, in Warminster, at four the following afternoon. "First one existed," he said, sotto voce. "Second one exists now. Noisy as the grave."

"You sure?"

"He wanted to know if it was something to do with Naldo. I tell him, yes. I say future of Naldo at risk. Then he gives me the two names back and tells me what I told you. Nothing else. He say he lose his pension if anyone checks back. Okay?"

"That'll do very nicely, Herb. Thanks."

"Don't mensh, old sheep."

They spent the day with Barbara, breaking down her time in Moscow into segments and showing her faces from what they called their "holiday snapshots."

"Now," Gus said. "Now we do the difficult bit for a week, then Barbara for another few days, then another difficult bit."

"Where do we start?" This was late and Carole was wrapped around him, as Gus had told his wife he would not be home much for several weeks. His wife did not know that Gus had, of late, become disenchanted. He knew she was seeing a personable young insurance salesman, which meant the days were numbered and he had to make decisions. "You ever hear an old song, Carole . . . ?"

"Plenty, from old people like you."

"Droll. This one goes, 'There's no one with endurance like the guy who sells insurance.' "

"Can't say I know it." Again she asked where were they going to start.

"We'll toddle off to Haversage in the morning. Fat Martin can go on

270

asking questions of Mrs. Naldo Railton. We shall put the bite on the old folks who live on the hill."

"You don't really think . . . ?"

"I don't know what to think anymore. Not since Barbara showed us the three names. Fun with Dick and Sara at Redhill can't hurt, though."

In truth Gus was terrified of what he might find under the stones as they made their progress through the minds of the Railton family.

Almost at the same time, across the Atlantic, two FBI officers were knocking on doors in the Williamsburg area and asking questions about a couple calling themselves Hester and Luke Marlowe. Hester being Caspar's only daughter, Luke being the son of one of the many Farthing aunts.

Gus and his team would spend all summer long talking to Railtons and their wives. The Agency and the FBI would be doing the same to Farthings still alive in the United States.

The final results, from both sides, were discussed at Warminster at just about the time that Naldo walked in the Park of Culture and Rest, which was also known as Dzerzhinsky Park. More, within hours of that quiet conversation in Moscow, during which Naldo learned that Spatukin was a double, and they would soon be putting paid to Comrade Penkovsky, the Credit Committee, in their wisdom, decided to prepare a lengthy document, for heads of Five, the SIS, and the Prime Minister's office, not to mention their illustrious Cousins at Langley. This document, it was agreed, would categorically state that the late Sir Caspar Arthur Railton had been a pawn of the Soviet Service since the late 1930s.

Also, on that very night, the flamboyant legal eagle Indigo Belper actually telephoned the spy-watcher at a national daily newspaper and whispered, "Willie, *have I* got a story for you."

3

At Langley, Marty Foreman, being a loyal and trusted member of the Agency, went straight to see his old and reverend chief only two days after the pass made at him by Big Herbie in London. Marty had always given the false impression that the London posting was a backwater to retirement, so he had not even suggested to Kruger that he was returning for a parish council meeting in Washington.

"The Brits're onto us," Foreman said. Long ago he had been a street fighter, and would probably have ended up in jail had not, first, the Office of Special Services taken him to its bosom during World War II, and, second, when things settled down, the CIA had given him his head.

"You say anything?" his chief asked.

"Kruger knew the names, *Heartache* and *Heartbreak.* He said it had to do with Naldo Railton. Matter of life or death. I confirmed the ops were known to me, but indicated I had no details. I don't think it'll go far up the line. My guess is that Gus Keene's running his own little investigation, and there's a rumor that Mrs. Donald Railton's back from the delights of Moscow, breathing fire and about to perform a long-range prickectomy on Naldo. I guess that's how it's seeped through."

"So why won't it go further, Marty?"

"Because wily old Gus Keene, he of the smooth tongue and thumb-screws, has Barbara Railton locked away and ain't telling nobody—know what I'm saying?"

"Well, they're witch-hunting the Railtons, living and dead, like some of our boys, and the FBI're doing the same thing to Arnie's kith and kin over here. I guess when entire families have been involved in the trade over a few generations they tend to throw up the odd rotten apple."

"In the case of our British Cousins, there's bound to be deep concern. If a Railton's doubled again, they'll have no need to eat their stewed prunes each morning. Family jinx; family weakness. We know how Arnie's doing?"

"He's playing it real close. Poker minded, but I guess he'll do what's needed."

"Always covered his back and front, both, did Arnie. So, no intelligence from him?"

"We know he's trusted. We also know he's going off to Vietnam. I'm hoping we can fix up a meet. His kinsman Clifton is on his way back there now."

Marty nodded, looking anxious. "Any of that lot expendable?" he asked, looking at the ceiling.

His chief stared hard at his hands, the words coming out in a whisper—"Yes. Arnie'll take his chances forever and a day, naturally, though we'd try and get him, and Fido, back if they blow." Fido was their name for Spatukin.

"So, then there is one?"

"Just so. Arnie's got Naldo incensed about old comrade *Alex.* He'll fix the details, but I'd say Naldo will do the blowing away. You can't kill a guy twice, but, if it goes wrong, then Naldo'll have to be sacrificed. I guess Naldo's been expendable from the start.''

"Shit," Marty said under his breath.

"Name of the game.''

SEVENTEEN

1

Gus Keene had promised Barbara that he would not pass on to the Credit Committee anything she told him. He was as good as his word. But he had said nothing about talking to C. So it was to C, Chief of the Secret Service, that he went with the utmost discretion.

As it turned out, C had just given his deputy, Maitland-Wood, some very strong and binding instructions regarding the long document which had been prepared by the Credit Committee, and so was in no mood to be inveigled, bluffed, or generally have wool pulled over his eyes.

"This document," he had said to BMW, after reading the two-hundred-page conclusions of the committee, "should, to my mind, be burned. However, because it's official, and was called for by myself, I cannot disregard it. We'll keep it in Registry, under lock and key. *My Eyes Only.*" This last almost shouted, for C was worried by the whole business. He would soon face an angry Prime Minister, for he was duty-bound to report the committee's findings, and nobody wanted another scandal. Also he was more than displeased with the committee's conclusions, for reasons which had come directly from his Cousins at Langley, and, out of loyalty, had to be kept to himself alone.

In his office he greeted Keene with a curt nod towards a chair and the words, "I trust, Gus, that you are not bringing me another crisis."

"Depends, sir, on what you consider critical." Keene sat, and there was a long silence, at the end of which C told him to get on with it. Gus did just that, telling all, except for the three names he had glimpsed on the slip of paper shown to him by Barbara. Even then he covered his tracks. "I'm only part of the way down the road with her." He looked up at the ceiling. "I gather, though, there are three likely contestants, one of whom could be long-term and possibly still active. If not, he might well have passed on the mantle to others."

274

There was no window in C's office, and he had turned off the tapes during the long pause following Keene's entrance. Now he rose and walked over to the picture which occupied the place of honor directly behind his desk. It was a large, and very fine print of Hieronymus Bosch's "The Garden of Earthly Delights." C gazed at the reproduction for a good five minutes, as though trying to find the answer to the meaning of life within this strangely modern bizarre painting which he could hardly believe had been executed in the 15th century. Then he began to speak in a low voice—

"I know about Naldo," he said. "Naldo and Arnie both if it comes to that, but you didn't hear it from me. Okay?"

Gus nodded.

"Even here, at the top of the world, I am also subject to certain disciplines," C continued. "I cannot even talk to the PM about that side of things, and I thank heaven the Press haven't got wind of it. Also, I have viewed old Caspar's diary with grave suspicion from the moment it came into the office. I knew Caspar very well. Damn it, I know the whole family very well. Some of them I'd find difficult to trust with my laundry, let alone classified information, but Caspar was another matter. The bloody diary just doesn't ring true. Caspar knew our world inside out: he knew names, ops, history, and tradecraft. Cas was a walking encyclopedia. He'd never have committed anything to paper without reason. Certainly he wouldn't have told the world he was a long-term penetration, if that was the way of things. Your tale of two diaries makes a lot more sense. Incidentally, did Barbara tell you where the other diary can be found?"

"Alas, no."

"Then you'd best keep on at her; and go through the other members of the family like the proverbial dose of salts."

"We've already had various cracks at them." Gus looked concerned. "It's like trying to grab water in a sieve."

"Your best people then. Let them have a go."

"My two best people've been with me from the beginning."

"What do they make of it?"

"Like you, and myself. They don't believe the diary's for real. I fear Maitland-Wood and his colleagues've been so mesmerized by what they see that their thinking's impaired. At the first sight of that diary they thought they had the holy grail. All the answers to a lifetime's problems sewn up and tied with a pink ribbon."

C nodded. "If the answer to a difficult problem suddenly appears, one is inclined to accept it as gospel. Saves work; solves many hours of thinking. The police do it all the time, then wonder why they get their fingers burned in court. People become obsessed by obvious evidence. They tend not to question the passages that don't make real sense. You just work away on Barbara. Go through the others, again and again if you have to. Call on me if you need support. In the meantime we keep everything, especially the results of the damned Credit idiocy, to ourselves."

"Silent as a dumb Carthusian, chief." Gus left the shop feeling happier than he had done for some time. He had not calculated on Indigo Belper and his tongue which had wagged to the Fleet Street spy-watcher.

2

Things took a while to even start bearing fruit. The spy-watcher who, for the record, wrote under the byline David Watson, had tried to make a few more enquiries but there were hardly any takers. He obtained only one new piece of information during this first pass. A Foreign Service contact agreed that the SIS was running a tight investigation called the Credit Committee, and they had found the late Sir Caspar Railton guilty of being a Russian penetration. It was outrageous, of course, for anyone in the Foreign Service to even whisper this to a man like Watson, but there was a lot of drink taken, and the FO man had telephoned the next morning, pleading with the newshawk to forget what had been said. "No way," Watson had told him. "No way, but your name'll never surface." He then went to his editor and told him the entire story. The editor said, "Write it," which he did. But, by the end of the day, there was a D-Notice slapped on the whole thing, and the Foreign Office contact had handed in his resignation. They reported this last fact, but the D-Notice meant they could not publish the gravy.

The editor told Watson to keep probing. "Use every source you can think of. Let's get a tame MP to ask a question in the House, then the fur'll fly. This sounds a good, long-running piece. You may even get a book out of it, Claud." Watson's real name was Claud David Watson, hence the use of David as his byline. He considered Claud Watson, or C.D. Watson, inappropriate.

Eventually the fur did fly. But not until very much later. In the meantime Gus and his people began a systematic heavy interrogation of every Railton they could lay their hands on. "Just the usual ploys,"

Gus told Carole and Martin. "You go over it once. Then you do it a second time. After that, again and again: like the young lady from Spain, if you know that disgusting limerick."

So Gus gave Carole and Martin instructions concerning Barbara. They were to sweat her. "Start gently. Go right back to her very first Railton contact—which would be her first meeting with Naldo, I should imagine. Then home in on Caspar. Begin long sessions. Go through her memory. Every meeting she ever had with Caspar. Every word she said. Everything he said. You know how to do it, so do it well. They always think they can't remember, but *you* know it's always there, locked away on the mind's tape recorder. Just tease it up to the surface. Start with family occasions and then ripple outwards. About a month's heavy going should do it."

"You don't want much." Carole raised her eyebrows.

"The lot, my dear. I have heavy duty to do as well." And, so saying, Gus took himself off to Haversage where he lodged at The Bear Hotel, overlooking the market square, hired a car, and then made his telephone call to Dick Railton-Farthing at Redhill Manor.

Gus spent a week in Haversage, delving into old memories with Dick and Sara. He was open and honest with them. "It's really about Caspar," Gus began. "You know what's been going on?"

"Some damned fool investigation. Trying to prove old Cas did a double on them. Madness," Dick retorted.

"They have pronounced him guilty as charged," Gus said softly. "That's not for public consumption. But, locked away in the vaults, there are two hundred pages that say he was guilty as hell."

Dick took a deep breath and coughed, the wheezing, racking cough of old age. "Gus, I don't know you all that well, but you can take my life on it: Caspar's no penetration. Why, old Cas was . . . "

He coughed again as Sara hobbled into the room, leaning heavily on two sticks. Gus had seen the photographs of her as a young woman, and knew she had been stunning in her day. Now, age and sickness were upon her and, for a second, as she stood in the doorway, Gus pondered on what seemed to be the unfairness of life.

"Old Cas was what?" When she spoke, Sara's voice was not that of an old woman, for it still held the mirror of her youth.

Both men must have looked guilty, so she repeated the words, her voice even stronger. "Old Cas was what?"

Gus nodded at Dick.

"This is Service stuff, my dear. Service. Classified . . . "

"Classified, my foot!" She looked at Keene, and, for a moment, the smile was that of the beautiful young thing she had once been. "Mr. Keene. I've forgotten more secrets than you'll ever know. Now, what about old Cas?"

"Actually, one of my reasons for coming down here was because neither of you are true, born Railtons, and I need help."

She laughed again. "My dear Mr. Keene, when one marries into the Railton family the past is forgotten. I once heard Caspar himself say the Railtons are worse than the Church of Rome. When you convert to that Church it is said you become more Catholic than Catholics born. The same is true of the Railtons." Her smiling eyes flicked towards Dick. "Wouldn't you say that's true, my darling?"

Dick coughed again, grinning and nodding vigorously.

"So what is it about Caspar?" she asked.

"There's been an investigation," Keene started.

"Oh, phoo! Of course there's been an investigation, and brainless idiots like Willis Maitland-Wood and Indigo Belper have found him guilty of treason. We all know that. His wretched sons, the appalling Andrew and Alexander, can speak of little else."

"Then I trust they don't speak of it outside the family." Keene sounded stern.

"What d'you think they are? Cretins, that's for sure. Adult vocal hooligans. Unpleasant specimens. Yes, I grant you all that, but family business stays within the family." Again the smile. "You'd be surprised at what secrets are held in this house, Mr. Keene. Real secrets, not the rubbish about Caspar—or poor old Naldo, for that matter. We never speak of these things outside. We're old-fashioned, I suppose, but we're silent as the grave. Just like Caspar who lies there and cannot fight back."

"I'd like to help you fight back." Keene let the sentence lie between them until she spoke again.

"Your reputation is that of a tough interrogator, with few scruples."

"Maybe. But I really do want to help you. About Naldo as well as Caspar's memory."

"If I ask why, you'll doubtless say you'll help by putting us all to the question." This time she did not smile.

"It's the only way I know."

"Ask then. We'll soon know whose side you're on."

So Gus started his lengthy probe into the past, jogging old memories, hearing stories of Caspar's youth, collecting snippets along the way. He stayed in Haversage for nearly two weeks, then broke off to deal with other business, returning to the case of Caspar Railton again and again,

278

visiting Naldo's parents, James and Margaret, and spending many hours talking. It was an odd investigation, for it continued over many months—which grew into years—and he heard things he would never have guessed about the Railton family. The older folk talked of plots and burns and treachery; of misuse and disinformation over the years. By the end of it all, Gus Keene supposed he was the only man outside the family who had seen some extraordinary documents, kept safe in a vault at Redhill, which told a tale of unmitigated treason.

At the same time, Carole and Martin plugged away at Barbara until she was completely dried out, to use the jargon. Then they shifted to the unwilling Alexander and Andrew.

It was early in 1966 that they came to one particular conclusion which led them to think that, as Carole put it, "The smart money should be on Alexander." They had turned up more on him than was healthy, and most of it seemed decidedly dubious.

3

"The randy devil likes little girls." Carole Coles said it without humor. There was nothing remotely funny about a man of Alexander Railton's age and status having a yen for little girls.

"How little?" Gus could guess the answer was not going to be pleasant, but age certainly came into it. Bad enough to have a suspect like Alexander working at GCHQ, even though his sting had been severely drawn in that very little classified material ever crossed his desk. Worse if he turned out to be what Gus always spoke of as "a devious."

They were in the office Gus had been given at the shop because he was up from Warminster a great deal of time these days.

Fat Martin looked dubious. "We don't know," he said, looking at the floor. "To tell you the truth, we don't really know if the guy's quirky at all . . ."

"Oh, come on!" from Carole.

"Stop bickering," Gus snapped. "Let me hear the full fairy tale."

"We haven't got the complete fantasy if you want the truth," again from Fat Martin.

"There is strong evidence." Carole stood her ground. "Look, Gus, we did a bit of a naughty."

Gus Keene sighed, then shrugged and said they had better tell all.

"This began with old Stalks." Carole took a deep breath. "Remember, she said Alexander might be a little, well, on the iffy side. We've been getting nowhere with anybody. You've seen the transcripts. Barbara's been totally cleaned out. She adds nothing new. Friend Andrew is a pompous prat, but he knows how interrogations work. He's been damned difficult but he'd win in a straight fight. You could say he's cooperated fully. Then I remembered all the stuff you brought in from Stalks—the hints that Alex Railton had a quirky sex life with his wife."

Gus nodded. Under his breath he muttered, *Delia Railton, née Butcher.* Aloud he said, "I rather thought that was merely a bit of SM or leather suits and things. Bondage even."

Carole shook her head. "It's little-girl stuff. Gym slips, white stockings, blue serge drawers. That's how Alex gets his rocks off with Delia."

"And how have you come by this fascinating, and probably useless, information, Carole?"

"Well. First . . ."

"We burgled his place to get a look-see," Martin grunted.

"Great." Gus managed to suppress his real anger. "You walked in and just had a look around?"

"We took some pictures."

"Oh, good. If there's anything we can use, how d'you propose I clear it?"

"You could backdate an okay." Carole's voice betrayed the fact that she knew Gus would do nothing of the sort.

"How expert was the break-in?"

"Very. It's a straightforward Yale which took American Express."

"I mean are they likely to suspect you've been nosing around?"

"No way. He doesn't know we took pix of his cavortings either."

"What cavortings?"

Carole delved into her shoulderbag and produced a large envelope from which she took a pile of grainy prints. Gus turned each over, his face deadpan as he looked at Alex Railton and his wife playing sexual games in their living room. She was dressed in the full schoolgirl gear, with her hair in plaits and the pair of them doing extraordinary things to one another.

"So he likes to see his wife dress up and they play fantasy games." Gus threw the pictures onto the table. "For all you know, it could be *her* kick."

"No." Carole had another envelope in her hand.

"How did you get those?" Gus inclined his head towards the photographs on the table.

Martin muttered things about shrubbery and a gap in the curtains, plus some camera jargon.

Gus sighed, reaching for the other envelope. "Ah," he said, looking at the prints. "Regular little surveillance team, you two. What about the questions and answers?" The second set of pix showed Alex Railton on the move, round and about Cheltenham. He sat in a car, watching a children's playground; there was one of him offering a bag of sweets to a small throng of girls—all between around ten and fifteen years old, and wearing similar school uniforms to the one Delia wore in the other photographs. There were several of him sitting in a snack bar which appeared to be frequented by young girls; and others of Alexander loitering—playgrounds, streets, parks, school gates.

"Dynamite, eh?" Carole smiled.

"Depends. I asked you where the question and answer routines went to while you were playing at jolly James Bond?"

"They went nowhere, Gus," Martin answered. "Absolutely nowhere. We hit the bugger with everything. He still won't admit to having been in the Eccleston Square house, even when we showed him all the evidence—and that's been going on for months now. The same with Andrew. Barbara's the only straight one, and she's bloody miserable."

"So we thought we might dig a bit." Carole looked pleased.

"And what am I expected to do with these?" Gus gestured in the general direction of the photographs.

"Couldn't you loosen his memory a bit? Spot of pressure on the right nerve?"

Fat Martin muttered the word *Blackmail* under his breath.

"Neither of you has yet learned about Andrew and Alexander Railton, have you?" Gus looked dangerously angry. "Neither of you really know anything about the Railtons as a family. Andrew and Alexander would be the ones who'd shout 'Fire! Police! Ambulance!' if we tried that kind of stunt. Tried to burn them. None of these," he tapped the pile of prints, "are going to help us one iota." He sighed again. "In fact they prove simply that he is probably a bit on the quirky side. If there's a case of child molestation in the area, we can tell the cops where to start looking. That's all, and I should imagine that Alex Railton's future freedom is seriously at risk. He's more likely to be pulled by the cops, then we've lost him forever and a day."

"People like that are a security risk. You know it, Gus. We know it." Carole had two red spots flushed high on her pretty cheeks. "Have *you* got anything from the folks who live on the hill? Or Naldo's parents?" She saw Gus Keene's face as she said it. She had been his mistress long enough to know that hard, evil-eyed look. "Christ, Gus, you *care* about these people, don't you? You really care about blessed Sir Caspar's reputation, and Naldo's conscience. And Barbara—all of them. You probably care about their American relatives as well. Gus, they're just a load of ingrate stuck-up snob shits. Over-privileged, over-wealthy, and over here. I don't like breaking the law to get stuff like the dirt on Alexander, but that's how we work, isn't it?"

Keene stood, like a statue, unmoving, only his hard eyes and the set of his mouth betrayed the terrible anger. "Sit down. Both of you. Sit down," he almost whispered.

"Those two families are like a secret Apostolic succession," Carole went on, disregarding all the signs of anger building up in Keene.

"You're so wrong." Gus was still in control of himself. "Those two families have had a few people in the trade—our trade—but only a few. There are Railton and Farthing doctors, politicians who know nothing of intelligence, lawyers—even a Farthing dentist, and a Railton who runs a charity. But, yes, Carole. Yes, I do *care* about those who have been, or are, members of the intelligence and security communities. You want to know why I care?" He did not pause for an answer. "I care because our profession is honorable . . . "

"Second oldest, and just as sordid," Carole sneered.

Gus nodded. "Yes," he barked. "Yes, we're whores, and like whores we provide a necessary service. Not to individuals, but to our country. We do the dirty jobs: the jobs the Press call stinking and underhanded. The politicians shout and rave and accuse us of operating as though we're above the law. We have to operate that way. You know it. I know it. God save us, Carole, you and Martin have just done it, and you felt it was necessary. Okay, why do we do it? Because we believe in freedom of thought, of speech, and of movement. Our way of life, like the American way, is imperfect—of course it is. But would you prefer the Soviet way? Or *any* totalitarian way? No, you wouldn't. Here we can criticize the government in public; here we can read what we like and more or less print and say what we like. Try doing that in a totalitarian state—Communist or Fascist. We *can* do it, which makes us vulnerable as hell, so we're the people who put a ring around our vulnerability. So don't ever talk to me about our job being dirty. It's meant to be dirty, it's meant to sail close to the wind, it's meant to cripple and maim people's minds . . . "

"What about the moral issues?" Carole snapped. "I feel filthy some-times."

"Moral issues?" Gus was in full flood now. "What moral issues?"

"Opening up people's private lives; becoming peeping Toms; listen-ing at keyholes . . ."

"Which you've just been doing. Okay, not nice, but we would not be carrying out our charter if we didn't poke around a bit. Supposing the Prime Minister goes on a trip to a totalitarian country—the Soviet Union or Argentina, say. Suppose he goes missing for a couple of days. Do we sit on our bums? Do we hell. We put the PM under the microscope. We put Trade Union leaders under the microscope if we have to, or some far-right-wing idiot. It isn't nice, but we do it, just as we pull military and economic intelligence out of the sky, or from some little turncoat who doesn't like the way he's forced to live. We do it in the name of an imperfect freedom; and don't ever tell me, Carole Coles, that it isn't a job that has to be done. You do it, or you get out. Understand?"

They had heard it all before, of course, and they had used the same arguments themselves when other people had a go at the intelligence and security services. But they would go on questioning the morality. It was good, they would say, for their souls.

4

Gus spent the next four days with Naldo's father and mother, James and Margaret Mary. Though they both looked tired and old, the wily Gus knew better than to put down his guard. These were old Railtons, who knew where many bodies were buried. This was no time for tea and sympathy, so, even though the talks appeared to be informal, and were often conducted over tea and cakes, he read between the lines, like some intellectual who could read the subplots of Shakespeare's plays between the lines of blank verse.

They went through Caspar's work during the first war, then he zeroed in on the period when Caspar had resigned from the Service.

"Didn't see much of the old horse then." James sucked his teeth and took another bite of cake. "You see, I was out of it as well, as you *must* know, Gus. I didn't see eye to eye with the management either. It's all on record. Personality clash, I think they called it. Load of balls, that. I just couldn't take on a job they wanted me to do. Supposed to be impartial, the Service—and Five, of course. The job wasn't impartial, it was for the good of a political party, not for the good of country. They lured me back, of course, but I was out for almost the same length of time as Caspar. Didn't see much of him, though. Always popping off abroad. We spent most of the time living it up, didn't we, darling?" He turned to his wife.

"If you call going to concerts and recitals in London living it up," Margaret Mary laughed, light and high-pitched. "That's what we did. That and the odd trip to Bournemouth. Mr. Keene, it was wonderful. For the first time in our married lives I didn't have to share James with the Service."

"Only with the family." For a second there, James sounded very young again.

Gus thought, I bet you didn't keep a diary. Then he put it into a question.

"Diary? I should think not. Ah." James looked as though he had suddenly realized what Keene was getting at. "Caspar. Caspar's bloody diary." A sip of tea, his hand steady as a rock. "Bloody fool. Thought Cas knew better'n to keep things in writing."

"And what about your son, Mr. Railton? What about Naldo?"

Margaret Mary sighed, just audible, in the background. "You know better than that, Gus." James put down his teacup. "I don't have all of it, but he's operational, isn't he?"

"He's missing. Probably in the USSR."

"He's also guardian of Caspar's diary." A wolfish smile on James' face.

"And you know things about that, don't you, Mr. James?" Gus was doing his cozing-up routine.

"I'll tell you what I know. Things I wouldn't tell people like Willis MW."

"Should you . . . ?" Margaret Mary began.

"On one condition, Gus, because I believe you've probably guessed some of it already; just as I believe you'd keep a solemn promise to leave my name out of anything that goes to this bloody Credit Committee."

"Naturally, though, I might have to report directly to the Old Man."

"C? C knows it already." James then went on to tell of Caspar's request concerning the removal of certain items from Eccleston Place, and the setting of traps within the house to make certain nobody else went in unannounced.

Gus went back to the shop and looked up James' dossier in the Registry. There was nothing at all about his time out of the Service except one exit from the country. Nineteen thirty-seven, the Dover-Calais ferry, and a train to Paris where he had disappeared. Margaret Mary did not go with him. Nobody had any thoughts on reasons. No marginal notations like those in Caspar's file. What did you do between the wars, Daddy? Gus asked himself. Then he went back and asked James about Paris.

"Oh yes. Thirty-seven, or was it thirty-eight?" the old man said as though memory was failing him.

"Nineteen thirty-seven. June. Out for a month," Gus supplied.

"Yes. Yes, I remember. Proper little gadabout, wasn't I? Fancy them watching ports and aerodromes, as we used to call them. Did the same for Caspar, did they?"

"I suspect they had a little list of all the old team. Immigration would make notes and send them back."

"Funny, I thought everyone was getting a little slack about that kind of thing."

They talked for an hour and Gus only realized later that James had said nothing about his reason for going to Paris. Some other time, Gus thought.

On his way into the shop he saw certain faces: people leaving as though they had been in for the afternoon, as they had—Indigo Belper, David Barnard, Arden Elder, Beryl Williamson et al. The Credit Committee still met once a month.

"Not disbanded?" Gus asked C. He had come in to give the Chief the full strength about Caspar's approach to James, and how James had fielded it and passed the catch to Naldo.

"I keep them on the go." C was looking at Bosch again. "Keep them at it, in the hope they'll see sense."

Out of interest, Gus asked him about James' dossier, admitting he had not been able to pin James down about Paris.

C gave what passed as a laugh. "You won't either. Old James is a sly dog. *I* know what he was up to."

"Oh?"

"James loves his wife dearly, as we all do. But there was someone else at that time. Worked in the secretariat. Nice little thing. Blonde, called Alice something. James was spending time with her before he went private. The Paris trip was a bit on the side, Gus. June can be a wicked month in Paris. Don't know how he squared it away with Margaret Mary."

285

"Alice?" Gus mused.

"Alice . . . Alice Pritchard. Married quite well, I think. Someone in the trade. Wartime thing, of course. She still lives. Yorkshire, I believe. He died. Bomb during the blitz. Forget his name. Might've been Ross. Yes, Len Ross. Agent-runner. Spain, Portugal, that kind of lark. Leonard Cyril Ross. Toddled to and fro from Lisbon mostly, then got himself killed in the blitz. Poor old Alice."

Gus made his excuses and left. The Old Man had a good memory, he thought. But is it good enough?

So, the months went by and other things occupied the minds of Gus, Carole, and Fat Martin—Ireland, and the constant battles against the PIRA, who had become very active again, trying to lead the North on its inevitable journey towards the Kremlin, cloaking its activities in old clothes of spite and vengeance; problems in the Middle East; clashes throughout the world. They went on doing their jobs, and, every few weeks, when there was time to spare, they returned to the problem of the late Caspar Railton, and the current devious ways of certain members of the Railton family.

5

Once the legal papers arrived in Moscow certifying that his marriage to Barbara was over, Naldo could not escape from the situation in which he found himself. Now, both Kati and her father, old Caspar's friend of the 1930s, General Spatukin, began to put the pressure on. If he wanted to maintain the fiction, Naldo would have to marry the girl.

"Comes with the job, Nald," Arnie told him, walking in one of the parks, out of sight and sound from surveillance. By now the months had pulled them into the summer of 1967. "They'll not believe they have you, body and soul, until you pass that little test."

"They believe you?" Things were taking much longer than Naldo had calculated. Three years had gone by and he hated, not only Moscow, but the strain of working in this kind of cover.

"I think so."

"You haven't taken that long-promised Vietnam trip yet." Naldo had allowed suspicion to run away with him. He jumped at shadows, saw surveillance teams wherever he went, imagined they were still stealing sound from his apartment.

"Anytime, my old son. Here, a week can mean a year, and a day can mean an hour. You've learned that, haven't you?"

"You getting *anything* back to Langley?"

"A little. The Vietnam thing's been laid on from Langley. I meet an agent face-to-face. No surveillance from the Sovs. We exchange information. I give what I have, I get some chickenfeed back to keep the Ks sweet. I have a line into the Embassy, and I guess that can be firmed up." He said all this without even looking at Naldo. Then—"As for you, Nald, you've given precious little but some expertise. They'll expect a commitment."

"Then I have to do it? I *have* to go through a farcical marriage with Kati?" Naldo asked the air around him, not expecting, and not getting a reply from Arnold.

"After you've done it, the General will be more disposed to arrange the matter we really came for," Arnold finally said.

"*Alex*'ll be dead of old age before we get around to that."

"I think not, Nald. Spatukin's too set on us all getting out in one piece, and by *all* he means his daughter as well."

"Barb's going to be more than happy to see us, then." Naldo tried to smile.

A month later he saw Arnie Farthing again, and General Spatukin, together with Madame Spatukin and all Kati's sisters, cousins, and aunts in their finery.

It was done in the usual manner for the Soviet Union—not that Naldo wanted any religious blessing. Like any other Russians, they went through the process at the Wedding Palace within the Kremlin— a singular honor, obtained by the General himself. Kati dressed in white, as was the custom, and they stood under a chandelier on the red carpet in front of a picture of Lenin and the Soviet Emblem, exchanging their rings and making the usual vows.

Afterwards, everyone embraced, they drank champagne and ate chocolates, and then went on to a feast at Spatukin's large apartment, where everyone, except the bride and groom, got very drunk and ate far too much.

There was music and dancing, while every now and then the guests would shout *Gorko! Gorko!* and, to cheers, the couple would embrace and kiss.

They left early, to lewd comments and nudges. Back at the apartment, Kati went straight to the bedroom and stripped to her underwear, which was pure silk and had been brought in from Paris by one of her father's couriers. "Now I make you real wife. I make you very happy," she said. And she did just that, in a variety of ways that brought extreme pleasure to Naldo.

On the following morning, they flew Arnie out of Moscow and into Hanoi. The day after that, with two Soviet guards, and a posse of Vietcong, they moved up towards the battle zones. It took three days on foot, and eventually they rested in a complex labyrinth of underground tunnels.

Arnie examined the maps with his KGB bodyguard and pinpointed the reference. "I'm to go alone," he told them in Russian. "I don't want my contact frightened off."

"Those are our orders, Comrade Colonel. We stay here. You go alone."

"Good. Just see nobody follows. I could be completely compromised." At dawn he left, through a disguised exit, taking an hour to make his way carefully through the foliage. Aircraft passed low overhead, and to his right Arnie heard the sound of a firefight as U.S. troops met in skirmish with the VCs.

Finally, checking his compass and the map, Arnie lay on the damp ground and waited. He wore jungle fatigues, boots, and helmet. From his belt hung a 9mm Makarov, strapped into its holster.

Clifton appeared on the dot of seven-thirty, coming out of the damp rising mist and walking with care. Arnie rose and went to him.

"You've left your people behind, I hope?" Arnold held out his hand and gripped Clifton's big paw in his.

"There ain't nobody here but us chickens." Clifton smiled. "I hope to God you're alone."

"Not even a leech. Talk naturally, though, just in case some idiot's decided to disobey orders. Next time we shake, I'll pass stuff to you. It's red-hot. How's it all going?"

"Crazy." Clifton looked dejected. "It was a crazy idea in the first place. Operation Blowtorch, they called it. Now it's Operation Phoenix. We have a lot of teams working the villages, and we promise immunity to those who tell us the truth."

"You're actually doing that?" Arnold was genuinely surprised. He never thought they would go through with it.

"There're going to be a lot of unhappy people by the time it's over." Clifton spoke low, his eyes on the ground. "We tell them to point us to the VC spies, and they point at anyone. I figure a lot of old scores are being settled. Three-quarters of the people we're pulling in swear they've never had anything to do with the VC. A lot of innocent people're getting the chop."

"War's like that." Arnie frowned. "Best be getting back. Any instructions?"

"Just carry on. Oh, yes, is the Railton okay? They wanted to know that particularly."

"He's having himself a ball." Arnie smiled. "You got stuff for me?"

"A lot. Nicely prepared. They'll take it like salmon takes a good fly. The real stuff'll be out of date by the time they do anything. The rest is chickenfeed."

Arnie nodded. "My stuff's all Grade A. Exchange the papers clean, Clifton, otherwise we just might not get another chance."

They shook hands and Clifton palmed the twenty pages of thin paper that Arnie had folded into a tiny ball. Arnie took the stuff Clifton had brought in full view. If they did have someone watching it would look as though only Arnold had received anything. "See you next month," he said.

Three days later, Arnold was back in Moscow, and they assigned him and Naldo to work together in Department T—Scientific and Technical Intelligence Collection. They spent most of their days at the so-called Research Institute, near the Byelorusski Railroad Station, where U.S. equipment, discarded in battle, or stolen by the VC, was brought for testing.

"I go once a month, now," Arnold told Naldo, in a safe spot—in Gorky Park. It was autumn, and the first chill of winter was on them. Soon the place would be full of skaters and chestnut sellers.

"You want someone to carry your bags?"

"When it happens, I'll let you know."

"Well, for Christ's sake give me some warning. I have to set up the get-out."

"Begin now," Arnold told him. "Even if it's going to take two years, start now."

6

Box 12, the dead-drop Naldo had given to Herbie, was, in fact an old street trader—flowers in summer, seeds and herbs in early winter, before the intense cold drove people indoors. She did it for the money, and would not breathe a word because she thought she was working for the *fartsovshchiki*, the dealers, and peddlers in black-market, countereconomy goods. She had been operating for years, and knew only two code words. One for the drop and another for the pickup. She was paid well in certificate rubles with which, through a third party, she bought legal luxuries.

She was at her usual place, selling the last flowers of the year, when Naldo approached her and bought a bunch of sorry-looking sunflowers. In Russian he asked if anyone had been looking for Gramophone Gennady. She nodded, and he slipped her a small envelope, together with some rubles, which was a chance, as she was paid regularly out of the Embassy.

A week later, a German engineer, in Moscow for a conference and talks on building a new sewage works, approached the same old lady who, by this time was into fir branches, which most people could get themselves, but people often bought out of pity. They helped to brighten up the place and cost little enough. Soon the old lady would be driven indoors by the bitter winter. The German asked if she ever saw Mikhail, the one with two fingers missing. Again she nodded, and the engineer bought some sprigs of fir. They were passed to him together with Naldo's envelope.

Four days after this, the envelope was sitting on Big Herbie's desk at the Annexe. Herbie unbuttoned the code and read through it. "Naldo gone fucking mad," he muttered to himself. "This is impossible, even by the spring. Shit!"

Then Herbie sat down to work out how he could get around the tremendous difficulties of Naldo's request. There was only one way. He would lie to C and get him to set up the op. It was the only way. They would need a submarine at least, and a guide to get four people off the Black Sea coast. Even C would jib at it. Certainly the Royal Navy would spring several leaks.

The year moved on. 1967 turned into 1968. Naldo did as he was instructed, kept to the sham of his life, and felt as though he was struggling through each month, carrying a heavy load. 1968 gave way to '69, and, in April, Arnold made his monthly trip to Hanoi.

Each month, as the war progressed, he met Clifton Railton at a different RV. The reference figures were passed through the American Embassy, and nobody questioned how they arrived there in the first place. The whole operation had been well-planned from first to last, though now Langley was getting jumpy.

On this meeting, Clifton had a message by word of mouth. He did not know that the paper Arnold would hand to him was clean as a baby's conscience. For Arnie, the risks involved in the monthly meetings had become too dangerous.

"Mother wants you out," Clifton told him. "She wants you out now. I am to take you if it's safe."

"I want out." Arnie did not smile. "I want out yesterday. Today we'd be mown down like corn. They're on my back. I'll have to figure a way next month. Okay. Just take what I give you and get the hell out. Next month, if I don't turn up I've either bought the farm or I'm out, okay?"

Clifton nodded sadly. They shook, and the papers were passed. Up until now they had been good—mainly intelligence on Soviet supplies to the VC.

"See you," Clifton said, turning his back and walking away.

Arnold took his time. He undid the strap around the Makarov, withdrew it from the holster, and shot Clifton twice through the back of the head.

"We go in one month," he told Naldo when next they were able to talk. "You will get leave as from May 10th. The General is making arrangements for us to travel to Sochi on May 12th. We'll have a day to set it up. Then, 'Bingo.' Don't say anything to Kati yet, okay?"

Naldo's heart lifted. It meant they could take care of *Alex* on the night of May 13, 1969. Who said revenge was a dish best taken cold? Whatever happened, it would be one back for dear Caspar.

PART THREE

THE FAMILIES DESTROYED

(1969–1989)

EIGHTEEN

1

"Herbie, it can't be done." C had heard many idiot requests in his life, but Kruger's petition really took the biscuit.

"It's a necessary op." Herbie floundered.

"Listen, my dear fellow." C took on the mantle of a benign uncle. "You want me to mount a deniable snatch operation, without the knowledge of anyone else on the fifth floor, which entails putting a sub into the Black Sea and taking four people out. Can't be done. For one thing the Navy wouldn't wear it, even if it could be carried out from a surface ship doing a hospitality trip into Istanbul. I'd have to know more about the four in question before I even put it to them on that level."

"Can't tell you no more, Chief." Herbie looked frantic.

There was a long pause. C trusted Kruger. To the extent of even investigating the possibilities of nominating him for Deputy CSS (BMW's tenure would run out in a few years). The Foreign Office had not taken kindly to the idea. The post, they said, could be held only by a British national born.

"Herb, listen to me," C finally said. "How would you feel in my place? You know how things work. Someone comes in and asks for a major snatch—a bring-'em-back-alive operation in the Black Sea. Right off the coast of the Soviets' favorite playground. Four people, who are nameless. If the op goes wrong, we're all caught with our pants down. Sure, we might do something limited, running out of Turkey, but it's a long shot. If they're yours, why can't they come via East Germany? That's the way you always do it. That's your bloody fiefdom."

"These four won't be in East Germany."

"Then you have to give me some background. You *have* to say who they are."

Herbie looked around the room, as though he could sniff the microphones. "We on tape?" he asked bleakly.

"You want the tapes off?"

"Only if it's sure. One hundred-fifty-percent certain."

C opened a drawer in his desk. Inside lay a small console of six switches. The switches had been wired onto a piece of hardboard, and it looked like a do-it-yourself job. C clicked through the lot. "There. Two hundred percent." He smiled.

"Okay. I say it once. Once only, special for you, Chief. Is two Russian nationals. One big KGB boil and daughter. Is also Naldo . . ."

C was not given to profanities or expletives. "Shit!" he said.

"And is also Arnie Farthing. Please keep under your hat, Chief."

"Oh, God save us!" C came from behind his desk and began to pace the room like a caged beast. "Look, I know the facts. I know about Arnie Farthing and Naldo, but I'm also under discipline, so I didn't say that. Understand?"

Kruger nodded.

"How in hell has all this happened, Herbie?"

"Naldo went off on his own op. I don't know what is about. But serious. I know serious, just like you know Naldo don't do a runner on us. Naldo play doubles."

"Bloody mixed doubles." C looked and sounded angry. "Why? Why go off and pull strokes like this? You backstopped him, Kruger. Why?"

"He get pissed off with Willis."

"Give me your version from the top."

"Okay. No tapes?"

"I've told you, *no* bloody tapes. Just give it to me cold."

Quietly, Kruger told him about Arnie's message to Naldo at the funeral. Then the conversation when they had lunch after Railton had seen Arnie in Berlin. He left out the bit concerning the Blunt material, but kept Naldo's fury concerning the Caspar accusations. "He told it me straight. Some defector put boot in on Caspar: That start the talking. That what Naldo believe anyhow. Next thing I know, Naldo's gone and I get message via an old drop. I am to use one of our Moscow postboxes, one we don't use much anymore. Then, yesterday Naldo leaves message in Moscow box. Two Russians, one American, and himself. Somewhere near Sochi on Black Sea. Most urgent pickup. Snatch. Date and time to follow. But he reckons around three, maybe four, weeks—12th, 13th, maybe 14th May."

"I should have you damned well hung, drawn, and quartered, Kruger. You knew Naldo was off on an unsanctioned . . ."

"I knew nothing, Chief. I do him favor. Put him next to Arnie. Then he goes walkabout. Bloody Willis frighten him off. Willis is bloody Dennis."

"Dennis?"

"Ja. Dennis the Menace; character in kids' comic. I sometimes read for my English. You know?—Desperate Dan eat cow pies; Lord Snooty and friends. Good for me to practice, ja."

C grunted. "Herbie, it's me you're talking to. You can leave out the funny stuff. It probably goes down a hoot with the probationers, but not with me. Right? So it's to do with Caspar?"

"Yeah. Yeah, so I think. Bloody Credits Committee, and Caspar. What I do about getting Naldo out, Chief?"

"I don't think *you* can do anything. Come to that, I don't think I can make it happen either. Just keep in touch. Any time of the day or night. Tell the duty officer London's Burning. Got it?"

"London's Burning." Herbie nodded violently.

"That'll get to me fast." He stopped pacing to stand next to Kruger. "I've told you, there's precious little I can do to get Naldo out. If they're still on, then you'll just have to tell them to try and make it through Turkey. They'll have to get themselves out."

"Long walk to Turkey."

"Then tell Naldo to get his hiking boots on. All four are beyond my help now, but I'll still try. Oh, and Herbie . . ."

"Ja?"

"Not a word or I'll cut your tongue out."

"Don't know what you're saying, Chief."

2

Naldo and Kati were having dinner with the Spatukins, in their large apartment in an old building on Kutuzov Prospekt. The place had nine rooms and had been given a major face-lift sometime in the late fifties. The meal was almost sumptuous, and the ladies withdrew after the pudding, following the old Western etiquette, leaving Naldo alone with his "father-in-law."

He had worked close to the General ever since he had been moved, with Arnold, to Department T, and had even come to like the man. He had mellowed since Caspar's first descriptions of him, in the late 1930s, yet Naldo could still spot the younger man behind the older man. Spatukin was able to remain very still, like a snake waiting to strike; at times he was also very silent. He sat there, saying nothing and waiting for the others to speak first, his eyes darting around the room without moving his head.

Now, over the dinner table, sipping brandy—obviously the General did not like port—he *did* turn his head towards Naldo. He smiled, then lifted a finger, pointing to the ceiling and making a circling movement, then touching his ear.

So, Naldo thought, the General himself is afraid of sound stealing, even in his home.

"Arnold tell you about my offer?" Spatukin's English was excellent, the accent was not Russian, but more of a French intonation.

"Which one, sir? You have made many kind offers."

"I thought we should have a holiday. A few days in my little dacha near Sochi."

"Oh, yes. Yes, he did mention it. Wonderful, if we can get away."

"I'll arrange it. Unfortunately Nina will not be able to get away. But I hope Kati will come with us. About the middle of next month. May is good down there; before it gets too hot. My God, it is terrible in the summer. Far too hot then. It will be good for you to get out of Moscow."

"Also we can talk in peace about some of the work . . ." Naldo began.

"No. No. And no!" The General smiled without even looking at Naldo. "We go there for a small holiday. You English have a saying, all work and no play, eh?"

"You're right, sir." Naldo felt uncomfortable. The conversation had become stilted. If he had been a listener, his ears would be fully pricked up now, and the dates would have been jotted down. He turned the conversation onto the latest piece of equipment that had been ferried in from Vietnam, the M79 grenade launchers.

"The modern slingshot," the General laughed, and Naldo had to step in and talk for a while about the technical statistics of the weapon. He could hear himself giving chapter and verse on the launcher and hoped it did not sound as though he was too eager—trying to prove himself. All the time the General sat, staring ahead and nodding occasionally.

When he got Kati back to their own apartment he asked if her father had mentioned the trip next month.

"Why didn't you tell me? Mama said you knew."

"I wasn't certain we would get away. It appears your father's fixed things."

"He can fix anything." She threw her dress to one side of the bedroom. "He can fix anything, except me, my darling Naldo." She leaped towards him, and he felt his body react. It was odd, Kati stirred him so quickly. It was as though he was a young boy again, yet to complete the act with her he always had to imagine it was Barbara.

Later that night he lay in the dark and thought of Barbara. His real wife. Only a month and he might well be back with her, and that would be a relief. With Kati he had to pretend all the time: not that it was much of a pretense when she got him roused, yet he still had to have Barb's body in his mind, behind the closed eyes and the fencing tongues.

He dropped into sleep imagining he was back in the house off Kensington Gore, lying quietly beside his wife. Could she forgive? Yes. Yes, she must understand. Anyway, he could always mention the photograph. That would bring tears before bedtime.

The next morning Naldo took a devious route to work, passing the old woman who was Box 12. He bought a small posy of flowers to put on his office desk and asked the question. There was a crumpled piece of flimsy paper wrapped around the posy.

In his office he thrust the paper into his pocket and took it to the toilets with him, sitting in the bare cubicle and unbuttoning Herbie's reply before burning the paper and flushing it away. At lunchtime he sought out Arnold and suggested a walk.

They went through the Byelorusski Railway Station and out into Gorky Street, with the statue of Gorky looking old and dirty, even though it had only been there since the early fifties.

"My people can't get us out," he told Arnie without any dramatics. Inside he had already felt the clutch of panic. He had imagined that Herbie, with his contacts in the East, could have fixed something, even if it was only a fake fishing boat to carry them along the coast to Turkey.

Arnold's voice was very level. "Don't worry about it," he said, turning and smiling. "It can be done from this end. I've discussed it with the General. He can fix papers, and we can use his car. Official delegation, driving to Ankara. That do you?"

"Risky. The place'll be swarming . . ."

"Trust Spatukin," Arnie said sharply. "He's our one big hope." He laughed, and Naldo suddenly wondered about Gloria.

"How's Gloria getting out?" he asked, fast, as though Arnold had become suspect.

"How d'you think? She's off in a couple of weeks. I have approval for her to visit the kids, in Paris."

"Won't your friends in Washington snatch her?"

"No way. It's sewn up, Nald. Stop worrying. Get a message back to Herb or whoever's running your side of things. We should be crossing into Turkey—probably at Batumi—late on May 13th."

Naldo bought another posy on the following morning. His message to Herbie was short, and read—*Expect to make it on our own. Probably crossing into Turkey at Batumi sometime on 13th.*

Herbie flashed C, who breathed a sigh of relief. "That, we can handle," he told Kruger. I'll set the wheels in motion. We need people there to see it goes smoothly."

By the following day it had all changed.

"We're going to crash out in Spatukin's chopper." Again they were in Gorky Street at lunchtime. It was a warm spring day, and people sat on the railway station steps, eating rolls of black bread filled with salted herring, or goat's cheese if they were lucky. Others simply ate the bread. Food was still a luxury in Moscow. Long queues formed as soon as there was a hint of some delicacy.

"Is that his decision?"

"He told me to let you know. He figures directly after you get *Alex*. That'll be the night of 12th."

"*I'm* to do it?"

"Who else? The bastard sold Caspar down the river. He was your uncle. We both felt it was your job."

Naldo smiled. "Good. I thought there might be an argument. Who's going to fly the chopper, and which way do we go?"

"Spatukin's doing the flying. His personal pilot's taking us down, on 11th. That'll be a full day's trip with stops for refueling. Kati is going by train, ahead—three days before us. You get briefed. We do it just after dark on 12th and go straightaway. The General says he'll plot a course straight over the sea, flying very low. Your folks'll have to clear the way for him. We'll try to make it near a place called Sinop, bang on the north coast."

"The General's chopper . . .?" Naldo began.

"You're not going to like this, Nald. It's an elderly Ka-18. Been around a long time, but Spatukin's apparently a very good pilot."

"I'm not so concerned about him. What's his official pilot like?"

"Terrible." Arnold had the decency to smile.

The next morning Naldo purchased more spring flowers. Late that evening Herbie put out a London's Burning call for C.

3

C spent a week having talks with people in the Foreign Office. As far as the shop was concerned the Old Man was taking some leave. In truth, C wished he was on leave, because the Foreign Secretary himself was unhappy about the whole business.

"You say this thing's got to be contained, yet we're going to be forced to call off the Turkish Air Force. That'll get back to the Sovs faster than sound," he grumbled.

"Not if you give me control of it, sir." C always made a habit of calling the Minister sir. He said any officer in the SIS should by rights genuflect to the PM as well. The Foreign Secretary and the PM were the only people in London who could give them support when it was most needed.

Reluctantly, the Foreign Office said they would take the PM's instructions as binding, once C had spoken. He went over to Downing Street that night and put his case. A high-ranking Soviet defector, and one of his own men, not to mention a member of their Cousins' Service. After three hours of questioning and cross-questioning, the Prime Minister agreed. That night C telephoned Herbie at home, something unheard of, and told him it was a "Go." "Now all we have to do is work out our own cover and detail the best people to be there. I'm told this place on the coast, Sinop, is supposed to be a fun city, as our Cousins would say. Used to belong to the Greeks, centuries ago."

"Sod Greeks," Herbie grunted. "I go, Chief. Send me. I greet Naldo."

"It's not a question of *greeting* Naldo, Herbie. You have to think logically about this. It's a question of arresting Naldo. In the Service's book, Naldo Railton's a defector until he proves otherwise. So you certainly do not go to Turkey."

"Okay, but don't worry, Chief. Naldo come up smelling of violence."

"That's what I'm afraid of. I think you mean violets, Herbert." C became very formal. "You keep every orifice in your body closed. I want nobody to be aware of what's going on."

Nobody became aware until it was all over, and it was to C's credit that, to the very few people involved, the operation was dubbed *Violet*.

Over the next few weeks C saw several people, in secret, mostly at night. The British Ambassador, and the local SIS Resident, came into London for twenty-four hours from Ankara. In a small restaurant near Trafalgar Square, C had a quiet dinner with the Turkish Ambassador, and, two nights later, met the Air Attaché from the Turkish Embassy.

On May 8th, two quite senior field officers, coded *Menelaus* and *Thersites*, left for Turkey (later, in open seminars at Warminster, C was criticized for using unsafe cryptos—both names being taken from Shakespeare's *Troilus and Cressida*. Some felt this gave the game away regarding the operation having some bearing on the Railton family, whose God was the Bard).

The stage was set and they had even put a man into Sochi, just in case.

At seven o'clock on the morning of May 11th, General Spatukin's fat little Ka-18 helicopter took off from Moscow's Military Air Facility. Their flight time, including stops for refueling, was nine hours, so, with the hour's time difference, they should arrive at Spatukin's dacha around five that evening. "Just in time for sunset over the Caucasus," the General had said, as they drank coffee in the officers' canteen. "You will like it, Railton. You'll like Sochi very much. There's still some building going on. We started to enlarge the resort in '61, but there's now something for everyone. Particularly ourselves."

The next day later a small number of people in Turkey and London began to get the familiar feeling of butterflies in their stomachs. One of them was Herbie Kruger.

C had told him not to expect anything until around six in the evening. There was a four-hour time differential between London and Sochi. If anything happened before six, they would call him in. Otherwise, Herbie had been asked to be in C's office at six-thirty.

When the red telephone rang in the Annexe at four minutes to five, Herbie knew before he picked it up that there was trouble.

"At zero, scramble the line." He recognized C's voice. "Five . . . Four . . . Three . . . Two . . . One . . . Zero."

Herbie pressed the button. "Okay?"

"No!" It was the first time he had ever heard C really flustered. "I want you over here now, Kruger. We have a major disaster on our hands."

"What is . . . ?"

"Tass has just broadcast a Flash report. There's been a shooting among the private dachas at Sochi. They've arrested an Englishman on charges of espionage. He's been named. Donald Arthur Railton."

NINETEEN

1

The arrival in Sochi was spectacular. The helicopter came in over the mountains just as the sun began to set, so that the view was that of a town bathed in blood.

Sochi is probably the most popular of all the Black Sea resorts, and has particular relevance to the Soviets, for its growth in importance has only come since the revolution. In all it is only a little over one hundred years old. Before the mid-nineteenth century it was almost a village, and called Shatche. There was a military stronghold, Fort Alexander, and in Roman times the waters of the local springs were known to have healing properties. Even today, people crowd into the town to take the waters, as they do at spas throughout Europe. Sochi is a place of rest and healing.

In 1937 the serious development began, and was interrupted by the Great Patriotic War, during which there was much fighting, and more heroism in the area. Only in 1961, eight years before, had the development continued, adding an entire new area known as Greater Sochi.

As the helicopter dropped towards the wooded foothills, Naldo saw the long stretch of seaboard, and the town reaching back towards the mountains of the Caucasus, laid out with broad streets, houses, and apartment blocks that were, incredibly, quite elegant. As they began to descend, other things could be seen: sanatoria, parks, gardens, hotels, and villas. No wonder Sochi was a much-loved place. Naldo thought it reminded him a little of Nice on the Côte d'Azur.

The dachas, which are holiday homes for those counted among the *Nomenklatura*, were shielded from the road which ran down into Greater Sochi, each little estate lying in grounds that were carved out of woodland.

The woods, mainly of tall firs, remained intact close to the road. Tracks, large enough to take a vehicle, were the only sign that, behind

303

the deep screen of trees, there were places barred to the full-time residents of Sochi, or normal visitors and holidaymakers.

The fat little Ka-18 skimmed over the treetops, then slowed. The trees seemed to break apart, revealing a large clearing. Below them now, there was a lawn the size of a tennis court, bordered by gardens with paved walks, and trellised bowers.

The helicopter settled gently onto the lawn, behind the dacha.

The house itself faced them: three stories high, made from clapboard and surrounded by a wide, decklike porchway. The lights were on and Kati, who had left three days earlier, came out onto the deck as they disembarked.

Inside, the rooms were paneled in pine, designed in a Scandinavian style. From the pictures on the wall, to the linen, cutlery, and furniture, the house could have been the second home of some capitalist baron. It reeked of privilege, and Spatukin showed them around with pride.

Naldo was shown to the room he shared with Kati, and after Moscow it was like a five-star hotel. There was a huge circular bed, something he had only seen in recent copies of *Playboy* magazine. By the side of the main bedhead a console of controls jutted upwards, from which he could remotely activate the door lock, television, radio, and the drapes which covered two large windows looking out onto the lawn. The bathroom was filled with the latest in American sanitaryware, with many extras: well-lit mirrors, an electric shaver and toothbrush, a large circular bath and a shower.

Naldo showered and changed into comfortable lightweight slacks and shirt. He had brought, on Arnie's instructions, a pair of black soft training shoes. Now, feeling relaxed and excited at the prospect of what was to come, he went downstairs.

Dinner was already prepared and waiting for them. There appeared to be three servants, not counting the helicopter pilot, who disappeared almost as soon as they landed. Later that evening, Naldo learned the servants, and any of the retinue of a visiting official, lived in a small but comfortable dacha well away from the main house.

They ate in classic style, huge portions of smoked salmon, caviar, and cold meats, with *pirozhki,* delicious small pies made from rich sweet pastry and filled with cabbage, boiled eggs, salmon, rice, and mushrooms. The wines were Georgian, for Sochi lies close to the Georgian border, sweet, heady and breathtaking. Naldo wondered how the ordinary Muscovites were faring that evening.

When the food had been cleared away, and the servants gone, Spatukin drew them all around the table. "Kati knows why we're here," he began. "We do it tomorrow night. Well, *you* do it, Naldo Railton, but we are all involved. It is impossible for one to carry it out alone. I suggest that, to begin with, we take a short ride tonight, so you can all see the target."

Outside, on the gravel at the front of the house, stood an American jeep, Great Patriotic War vintage, restored and lovingly maintained. "We get the spares in through Finland," the General said. He then explained that their target lived—"very securely"—in a dacha similar to his own.

"But his is strongly guarded," he warned. "They have it surrounded by a high mesh fence, and there are always two guards on duty—KGB border troops who come here to the local garrison, as a kind of rest from the tougher areas, like the East-West border. The entire place is floodlit during the dark hours, and normally you cannot get near to it without being challenged. Tomorrow, I have made arrangements, but we'll come to that later."

They drove down the track from the General's dacha and turned right onto the main road. About five miles up the slightly inclining road, he slowed the vehicle. Already they had passed two other entrances to dachas—"Nobody is down here at the moment," the General said. "Only ourselves and the target." So, *Alex*'s dacha lay about a mile into the woods, three dachas down from Spatukin's residence.

Even from the road you could see the floodlights, sending a shaft of brilliance up through the trees. "Tomorrow night, at about nine-thirty, we go up that track," Spatukin told them as he turned the jeep back in the direction of his own dacha.

More wine was brought, and they sat, conspirators, around the big pine table in the dining room. Spatukin had some maps and paper spread around him. He passed Naldo a plan which was obviously *Alex*'s dacha.

"Tomorrow, I have arranged for certain things to happen. We leave here at exactly nine-fifteen in the evening. Under normal circumstances, we would drive up the track and would be halted here." His finger moved down to a point which was roughly twenty-five yards from the gates in the mesh fence. "We will reach that point at exactly nine-thirty, and at nine twenty-five there will be a power failure."

He looked around the table and smiled. "Also, when the two guards disappear to find out the cause of this failure, they will accidentally leave the gate in the fence open. The house lights will not be affected, but our little car will be right in the dark. You, Naldo," his finger stabbed out, "you leave us at this point. We will have the vehicle turned around and pulled close into the trees for the return journey. The floodlight system which protects the gardens and track will be out for half an hour, as will the telephones. So, the lights go out as we approach. You leave and go straight to the gate, here." His finger again jabbed the plan.

"The house lights should guide you, and my intelligence is that the target will be in the house, together with a young woman. Nobody else. They should be just completing their evening meal. Your friend, Naldo, keeps to a fairly strict timetable. He breakfasts at nine, exercises at ten, lunches at one in the afternoon, dines at nine and—forgive me, little Katya—fucks between ten-thirty and midnight. If it is a warm day—and the reports are good—he will be dining here." Again the finger. "Usually, on warm evenings, like tonight, they eat with the windows open. If they are closed you will go straight to the front door and ring the bell, hard and loud. He will, of course, think it is one of the guards." Spatukin paused, then spoke with emphasis. "Whichever way you go, it is essential that you make sure the man is dead. You also kill the woman."

"But . . ." Naldo began. He did not think of shooting Oleg Penkovsky as murder. The girl was another matter.

"You kill them both," the General commanded. "It is absolutely essential to the whole of this operation. I'm leaving a mess behind in any case, but you don't want the alarm raised sooner than it has to be. Nor do you want anyone in the house to be able to describe you with accuracy. It must be done quickly. You go in and do it fast, then you get out fast. We have to be up the road and into the helicopter before anyone realizes what has happened."

The General gave a humorless laugh. "I want to be airborne and out of Russian airspace in double-quick time. We all rely on you."

He asked if there were any questions.

"What do I use?" from Naldo.

The General looked across the table at Kati and nodded. She rose and walked over to a built-in pinewood sideboard. Opening a drawer she brought out a long box, made of wood with some kind of black covering. She placed the box in front of Naldo, who opened it. Inside, nestling in velvet, was a short Walther P5; a long, stubby, noise-reduction system; and one magazine, filled with eight 9mm rounds.

"A gift from us all." The General smiled. "Kill them both, Naldo. Use all eight rounds if you have to, but blow their heads off. I mean that, literally. It would be best to make certain no local police or doctors have a chance to identify them. Him in particular."

Naldo did not even acknowledge what was an obvious order. Reluctantly, he realized that the General was making things operationally sound. In the General's shoes, he would have given the same instructions. Without even looking down, he took out the pistol and stripped it, just to encourage them, he thought. Luckily the P5 was one of eight automatic handguns that Naldo could strip and reassemble blindfolded. As he reassembled it now, his fingers checked that the whole thing was in working order, running the ball of his thumb over the firing pin, to check its length, finally cocking the mechanism and doing the unthinkable—the one thing no weapons instructor would countenance—pointing the weapon at the floor and pulling the trigger to hear the pin thud home. He would have plenty of time to check and recheck the pistol, but he wished to indicate his own professional attitude.

"It'll do the job," he said at last. "Now, sir, can you get us out?"

Spatukin showed no surprise. He talked for ten minutes on the route he planned to take, on the tactics that he would employ—as high as possible until they were over the sea, then down to wave level to avoid radar search. He went into questions of speed and wind; how he was going to get local details from the nearest air-traffic-control center, at Novorossiisk, before they left for Penkovsky's dacha. The helicopter had already been refueled, and the pilot told to go into town and enjoy himself for four days, then call in for further instructions. "I have made sure that he will be well looked after." A vulpine smile from Spatukin. "He will imagine that his own particular charm has drawn the lady to him."

Arnie laughed, but both Kati and Naldo did not even smile.

When Naldo seemed satisfied, the General went over the plan again, then again, with questions.

They drank some more wine, and a little brandy. At around midnight, Spatukin announced he was going to bed. "I have left instructions that we are not to be woken until late. I think we all require rest."

Alone, in their bedroom, with only the P5 for company, Kati dragged Naldo onto the great circular bed. He had absolutely no desire to make love to her, but, as she persisted, touching, kissing, undressing and manipulating him in the way she had learned, Naldo became aroused. For a time she rode astride him and came quickly to her own series of fast little multiple orgasms. Then she disentangled herself and took him in her mouth, using tongue and teeth to bring him to his own ejaculation, which he thought was going on forever.

An hour later it happened again and this time he took her from behind, his hands cupped hard around her breasts as he thrust both of them to their separate apogees.

Later, as he lay in the dark, Naldo wished it had been Barbara. But that was impossible, so, if anything went wrong tomorrow—no, it was today now—at least he had the satisfaction of knowing that his last sensual encounter had been good. In the morning, he felt relaxed, at peace, and ready to avenge his uncle.

He spent the morning making sure the weapon was in first-class condition. He checked the eight rounds of ammunition, weighing them in his hand and, finally, going down to ask the General's permission to fire one round in the garden.

Spatukin was uncertain, hesitant, asking if seven rounds would be enough for tonight. "I'll have both of them with four," Naldo told him, and, having gained permission, he went out, chose one round at random, and blasted a tin can from a low wall at twenty paces.

Everyone seemed impressed, and from that moment on, Naldo carried the loaded weapon everywhere. Safety on, and the magazine in place.

They ate a light lunch, and an early dinner, none of them very hungry. At eight forty-five Naldo went to the bedroom and changed into the clothes he had been advised to bring with him. Black pants, a black cotton rollneck, and the black training shoes he had worn on the previous evening. He gave the pistol one last check, then screwed the noise-reduction barrel into place and went down to join the others, carrying the weapon close to his side.

2

Spatukin drove with almost exaggerated care. There was no moon, and only one other car passed them along the road, heading in the opposite direction. The night smelled of pine and that dry scent that comes after a hot day. As they had gone out to the jeep, Naldo was conscious of the night noises starting to close in.

For a moment or two on the previous night he had stood on the deck outside the dining room and heard the low sound of owls, and watched the flicker of black against the darkness, as bats displayed their radar, and performed fast, complicated maneuvers in Spatukin's garden. He felt the bats and other predators of the night were very close now.

The blaze of lights from the target dacha went out just as they turned onto the track. Spatukin killed their headlights, dropping into first gear. The jeep seemed to make a great deal of noise.

From ahead there was a shout, then another. The two guards calling to each other, Naldo hoped. Then they came around the final bend and the dacha was in full view, ablaze with interior lights which reflected onto the surrounding decklike porch, but no further.

Naldo's eyes, well adjusted to the darkness by now, could see the tall wire mesh, and the door in it, half open.

"Go!" Spatukin whispered, and he did not hesitate. Do it now, he thought. Do not even give it chance to react against your conscience. Kill. Kill for dear loved and dead Caspar. In a crouch he ran from the jeep, through the gate and across the lawn, springy under his feet.

There was movement from within the dacha, a figure in the dining room, standing and stooping. As he drew near, Naldo saw that the man was pouring wine into a crystal goblet set in front of a dark-haired girl. The big French windows were wide open, and it took only four strides and a jump to reach the deck, then another two steps. The pistol was close to his thigh, the safety off. Almost silently, Naldo Railton appeared in the center of the open windows.

The man looked up, his face showing interest, not fear. For a second, Naldo supposed that he thought it was one of the guards, then Oleg Penkovsky realized what was happening and opened his mouth to shout.

He did not look much older than when Naldo had last seen him in Paris. He certainly looked more fit. It was undeniably Penkovsky and, in the fraction of a second that gave him target identification, Naldo thought recognition crossed the Russian's eyes.

"This is for Sir Caspar Railton," he said softly, extending his arms and squeezing the trigger twice.

Oleg Vladimirovich Penkovsky's face disintegrated in a bloom of blood and tissue. No cry, no sound, just the two thumps from the pistol and then a body standing for a second with no face before it curved backwards, hands clutching in reflex. The Great Agent of Conscience was dead.

Naldo did not see him fall. Neither did he see what the girl looked like, or even if fear showed in her eyes. He turned his arms, not moving his body, and squeezed off the next two shots. He knew the job was done, for he saw the mist that had been her brain hang for a second, like a halo above her chair. He was out of the room and heading across the lawn again before what was left of her hit the floor.

Across the lawn. The gate. Open. Step through. Then the lights came on. Night was suddenly day, and there was noise. It sounded like a pair of submachine guns. Three quick bursts.

Spatukin was already out of the vehicle, standing, as though waiting for Naldo. He gave a little cry, his arms going up and a well of blood springing from his chest.

Arnie was out by the time the General fell, but Naldo only had eyes for the obscenity of Kati's body falling from the rear of the jeep. He had his pistol up and was in a crouch trying to identify the firing points, but Kati's body slowed him down. She tipped face downwards, and fell to the ground, her skirt catching on the vehicle. She must have tried to stand and jump, he thought, for she lay in a spreading pool of dark liquid, facedown, her skirt rucked up showing her buttocks; and by the time Naldo's brain had registered that, Arnie was also dead, his body terrifyingly still, slumped against the vehicle's hood and blood making a river, splitting into a delta on the metal.

It took less than three seconds, and Naldo felt his whole body stiffen, waiting to receive his share of the bullets. Then there was a blow to his wrist, knocking the P5 onto the earth at his feet. Almost automatically, he looked down and felt the next strike, to the back of his head. He thought he was throwing up as he hit the ground and entered a world of darkness.

He did not know how long he had been out. He did know that he could not move. There was pain in his head and a terrible thrumming noise. The world seemed to be tilting and vibrating under him.

Again, Naldo tried to lift his body, and this time he knew he was strapped down, with his ankles and wrists chained in some way. He tried to speak, and a face appeared above him. A woman. Then he felt his sleeve being rolled up, and smelled the antiseptic before the sharp prick in the arm.

As the world went away again, Naldo realized what the thrumming noise and the vibration were. He was on an aircraft.

3

He had no sensation of time. It was as though he had been floating for days on a raft, in terrible heat. His mouth was dry, and he now felt a very bad pain in the back of his head. He tried to lift his head from the pillow, and this time he could move, only he knew the pain was real. As real as the rough cot they had laid him on, and the bright light far away, covered by a grille in the ceiling.

After three tries, he got his feet onto the floor. The cell was not a dank dungeon, but almost clinical, with white, glaring tiles, though the door was strong and made of metal. Almost on cue, as though they could read his mind, the door opened. The officer who came in wore the shoulder boards of a captain and he was flanked by two private soldiers, each with an automatic rifle.

"How are you feeling?" The officer spoke in an almost kind manner, as though he really cared how Naldo felt.

In his present state, Naldo obeyed his reflexes. "I've felt better. Bad head. Throat . . ." He stopped, not because of any realization of his predicament, but because his throat *was* dry. Bone dry.

"We'll get you something to drink, and then some food, perhaps." The captain smiled pleasantly and went from the cell, leaving the two guards staring at him. They were young, only boys, Naldo thought. They seemed overawed.

The captain returned with an orderly who carried a tray, and a little brisk man in the white coat of a doctor. Before they passed over the tray, the doctor examined Naldo's eyes and looked into his ears. Then he probed the back of his head, asking, in English, "Tell me where it hurts. Here? Or here? Which hurts most."

"About the same." That was all Naldo could get out. The doctor nodded and motioned to the orderly, who placed the tray on the cot. There was some black bread, a bowl of thick *borshch*, and a pitcher of water, together with a glass. Everyone stayed in the cell while he drank, asked for more water—which they brought—and then ate the bread, and drank the *borshch* with the provided spoon. As he ate, so it came back to Naldo. There was no particular feeling about the death of Penkovsky or the girl. The pictures uppermost in his mind were of Spatukin, Arnie, and Kati. He could not get the sight of Arnie's blood sliding down the hood of the jeep, or Kati's briefly clad buttocks revealed in death, from his mind.

"You feel better now?" the captain asked.

"A little more human."

"Good. Before we fly you to Moscow, which will happen in the morning, I am bound to make a charge against you. You are Donald Arthur Railton?"

"You must know that, yes."

"You are a member of the British Secret Intelligence Service?"

"No. You know I have not been so for several years. I am KGB."

The captain gave a sigh. "We had hoped you would not have been foolish." He still spoke evenly. "You are a member of the British Secret Intelligence Service, sometimes known as MI6?"

"No."

"Very well. I will record that you deny this. Do you also deny acts of espionage against the USSR? In particular acts of espionage within the KGB, where you attempted to place yourself as a defector?"

"I deny them. I deny any act of espionage."

"Oh, dear." The captain frowned. "We had hoped to save you the difficulties you will encounter in Moscow."

"What are the particular charges?" Naldo asked.

"Acts of espionage against the State. Posing as a member of the State Organs."

"Not murder?" Naldo asked.

"Why should we charge you with murder? You are a spy. You have spied, not murdered."

Naldo saw Penkovsky vividly in his mind, the face disintegrating; and the girl with the crimson halo. He had not dreamed that, any more than he had dreamed Spatukin, Arnie, and Kati shot before his eyes.

"So, no murder charges? Just espionage?" He felt sick again.

"It's enough." The captain sounded genuinely concerned. "This is very serious, Mr. Railton. You should really consider your position. Plead guilty and maybe they'll make it easier on you. Tell everything and you might even be exchanged."

"I've nothing to tell." They would use drugs, disorientation, every trick in the book, Naldo thought. What the hell. Penkovsky was dead. Caspar avenged.

4

The special effects man from *Mosfilm* was packing his bags as General Spatukin came down the stairs. "Realistic, yes, but also very messy," the General said.

"I'm sorry, Comrade General. I did warn you that the blood would stain and soak everything."

"My God, I thought I really *had* been shot." Arnie Farthing, wearing slacks and nothing else, came in from the porch. "That spring harness has bruised my chest." He went to the foot of the stairs and called up, "Katusha! Get out of that shower and come down so we can drink."

Kati appeared at the top of the stairs; she wore a terrycloth robe and was winding her long hair into a turban. "Ugh!" she said. "Can you get us jobs in films, Comrade Technician?"

"I thought you were a great actress." The *Mosfilm* man smiled.

"You would!" The General's bark was obviously worse than his bite. "You would think she was good, lying there showing her knickers to everyone."

"Papa." She came down and kissed him. "Wasn't it all worthwhile? We got rid of that little shit Penkovsky with no fuss. After all the problems he's caused."

"Yes. We don't have to lie about him anymore. Yes, even getting fake blood all over a good uniform is worthwhile. Come, let's have a drink."

TWENTY

1

"You realize that even your own people have denied you. Don't be foolish, Donald Railton. Just tell us the whole story. We are fair here in the Soviet Union." He was tall, slim, very good-looking in a French manner, and spoke English without a trace of accent. He did not even look Russian, just as Spatukin had not looked Russian. Neither of them had the Slavic facial bone structure. At one time or another, Naldo thought, as a kind of aside, both Spatukin and this man must have been field agents. Scratch a KGB man who did not look Slavic and you would find a field officer.

Of course they would deny him. They would anyway, but ten times as vehemently when they considered he had made the jump over the wall of his own volition. Naldo wondered how they, and the Langley Cousins, had taken Arnie's death. He had suffered nightmares over Arnie, Spatukin, and Kati during the long haul back to Moscow.

They had been very gentle with him: making sure there was always reasonable food; giving him a lot of rest; making certain he was medically fit. Well, of course they would. They had to make him look fit and well-fed at the show trial. He still couldn't understand about Penkovsky. He had said as much and they had laughed. "The traitor Penkovsky is long dead, Railton. Shot within hours of his trial. It's old history." After the last time it had been spoken of, they had sent in a psychiatrist who, among other things, asked, "Why do you imagine *you* shot the traitor Penkovsky?" They sounded genuine enough, and he had not worked out the simple answer to that one as yet.

At least he knew where he was now. Moscow. The Lubyanka. At first he thought it was Lefortovo, the KGB prison. But this was certainly the Lubyanka. You could smell it. Death from other regimes, and the unexpected bullets after the confession. Naldo had always been susceptible to places, houses, buildings. This one was full of ghosts. Most of them were screaming. But the same would apply to

314

Lefortovo, he suspected, though there had been recent rumors that Lefortovo was undergoing refurbishing of some kind.

Well, he thought, what can they do? Kill him? Possibly, and who knew about death, except that you lived with it every day of life? Keep him locked and chained up with little food and no comforts? His father, James, had suffered just that, from the Germans, for quite a time during the First World War to end all wars. He knew the stories, and believed them. In one prison they tried to break his father by leaving him hungry for days and then feeding him poison that attacked his bowels and stomach, so that he fouled his cell and became so weak he could hardly move. Then they made him clean the cell and left him for some days before feeding him emetics and purgatives so that he had to go through the whole process again. If his father could live through that, then certainly Naldo could.

The one thing that worried him most of all was the interrogations. Brute force had been long replaced by psychological tricks and drugs. Naldo was terrified of betraying his country, even though his country thought he had already betrayed it.

He lost all track of time. When the slim, good-looking officer came to him again, Naldo thought he had been in the Lubyanka for around two weeks. They took him from the cell and into a small room, bare but for a scrubbed table and two chairs. He realized, as they sat him down, that he had his back to the wall, and there was a slit in the wall behind him. Covered up from the outside but there nonetheless. There was paper and a pen on the table, from which they had never properly got rid of the bloodstains.

So this was one of the famous Lubyanka cellars; one of the rooms of confession. The prisoner wrote it all down and signed it, then, from nowhere, a bullet took off the back of his head. It was the old routine. The interrogating officer would excuse himself for a moment and the shot would come from the slit in the stone behind the prisoner's head.

So I'm going to die, Naldo thought, and at that moment, the Russian who looked like a Frenchman came in.

"Mr. Railton, good morning." He sat opposite, his eyes straying to the paper lying on the table. "We would, naturally, like a full confession from you. Just the bare facts will do—that you are a member of the British Secret Intelligence Service; that you penetrated our intelligence service; that you are guilty of crimes against the State."

"I write it all down and then you shoot me."

The man laughed. "Oh, no, Mr. Railton. That's the old-fashioned way. I think we want you alive."

"So that my confession can be read at the trial?"

The Russian smiled. "There will be no trial. How's my old friend Kruger?"

Now it begins, the voice echoed in Naldo's head. This time he could not say who spoke, Caspar, his father, or Big Herbie.

"I don't know anyone called Kruger," Naldo said with an infuriatingly wide grin: almost an imitation of Herbie's daft smile.

2

In London, the real problems started ten days after the news of Naldo's arrest. The Sovs had made certain that everyone knew, including the newshawks in Fleet Street, not to mention the American Press. There were two long communiqués via Tass; the first gave bald facts, that a British spy, one Donald Arthur Railton, had been arrested in a Black Sea resort after a gun battle. The way it was worded, Naldo came out as a latter-day gangster. The second communiqué was more detailed. Railton was in custody. He was a long-term British penetration agent who, for many years, had given the Soviet intelligence service tidbits of information. In 1964 he had entered the Soviet Union saying that he had been forced to run from probable arrest. The entire thing had been a British operation from the start.

The press release went into a lot of detail, saying that Railton's story was believed for a time, then it was discovered that he was consorting with anti-Soviet elements. Railton had been on leave in the Black Sea resort of Sochi when the KGB had cornered him just as he was about to pass vital intelligence to the West. Railton had fired on a KGB team. Fire was returned, but finally Railton had given himself up. Happily there were no casualties.

The Press had a field day. David Watson, the spy-watcher who had his information regarding the Credit Commission directly from Indigo Belper, submitted the Caspar Railton story to his editor once more. They had it set and ready to start running when a D-Notice crunched it to pieces.

"Only one thing for it now, Claud." Watson's editor was determined to get the scoop. "We must get one of your tame MPs. Questions in the House. Right? Told you to do it before. Right?"

"The times were out of joint. Nobody would play."

"Well, do it now, Claud."

Watson went off and fixed lunch with a backbencher who owed him a favor or two. On the following Monday the backbencher put the

Foreign Secretary to the question. "We have all seen the reports in the Press regarding a Donald Arthur Railton, who has been arrested in the Soviet Union as a British espionage agent. Does the Right Honourable Gentleman deny Railton was working for our intelligence service?"

The Foreign Secretary made the usual evasive reply. He had been advised that Mr. Railton had long retired from any activities connected with the Foreign Office.

"Would the Right Honourable Gentleman agree that Mr. Donald Railton was a nephew of the late Sir Caspar Railton?"

The Foreign Secretary said he believed this was so.

"Then has the Right Honourable Gentleman any statement regarding the late Sir Caspar Railton? There were rumors that the Foreign Office had held an enquiry after Sir Caspar's death. The rumors maintained that Sir Caspar had been a long-term Soviet penetration agent, and it was said that this had been proved."

This was not a matter for the Foreign Secretary to comment on at this time.

Speculation in the Press was followed by more questions. Two weeks later the Prime Minister made a statement. During 1964, information came to light that the late Sir Caspar Railton had been working in the Foreign Office for a number of years as an informant for the Soviet Secret Service. A committee had been set up to examine the evidence. It was on record that the late Sir Caspar Railton might well have been a Soviet agent. Certain irrefutable facts pointed in that direction.

So the cat was out of the bag, and the Press used a tremendous amount of ink on the story. One publishing house contracted Watson to write the definitive book on the subject. Then, towards the end of June, Alexander Railton was arrested, late on a Tuesday night, for contributing to the moral delinquency of a minor.

Gus Keene was at Warminster when the news came through, and he sent Martin Brook straight to Cheltenham. Alex Railton was being held overnight in the local pokey and was to appear in front of the magistrates at nine on the next morning. The police were not letting him go, even though they were under pressure from a local solicitor. Pompous Andrew, it was said, had driven straight to Cheltenham.

Martin telephoned Keene late that night. The arrest had followed a serious complaint lodged by the mother of a fourteen-year-old girl. The mother had discovered what were described as "certain items" (contraceptives, a phallic vibrator, and some extraordinary underclothes) in the girl's room. Under questioning, the girl had told her everything had been given to her by Mr. Railton. The Railtons were friends of the family.

317

"Looks open and shut," Martin said.

Gus was worried. They could put Alex away for a long time. Whatever happened, GCHQ would never employ him again. There had been random surveillance on Alexander since his name was put in the frame. Now, Gus thought, they had lost him completely.

"I had a talk with the local law," Fat Martin continued. "They tell me Alex is outraged; denies everything; shows no sign of agitation or remorse; isn't going down easily."

"Would you expect him to?"

"Suppose not, but the coppers don't sound at all happy."

"See what the magistrate makes of it in the morning." Gus had surrendered to being philosophical about these things. He had enough problems. His wife had left him and a divorce petition was being filed. Carole was anxious to know if her name appeared and was causing Gus some grief. Apart from that, he had several important cases running, none of them easy.

On the dot of nine the following morning, Martin called from Cheltenham. "The event's off." His voice had that tired, disillusioned tone.

"What d'you mean, off?"

"They released our friend ten minutes ago. The local law's withdrawn all charges; Alex left breathing the proverbial fire and brimstone. The girl apparently broke down very late last night and said she had been lying about him. The goodies she had stashed away were bought at a local sexual aids shop with her own pocket money."

"Oh, hell. Now where does that leave us? And how the blazes can a minor get stuff like that?"

"She looks twenty when she's tarted up." Martin sighed at the distant end. "I've seen the pictures. They've also found the receipts in her room, and she's admitted wanting to pin something on Alex. She had a crush on him and he turned her down. Told her she should know better, and that if there was any more of it, he'd inform her parents. So off she went to the local kink shop and bought a load of stuff that she hid in plain sight."

"Little bitch." Gus grunted. "I'll be at the shop all day. Just leaving. Do a report for me and I'll try to get a full surveillance on chummy. Okay?"

"Delighted. Anytime." Martin hung up.

C already had the full story by the time Gus arrived for his monthly meeting. "You look tired, Gus. Everything okay?" he asked.

"I should imagine you know that everything's not okay in my private life, Chief." Gus slumped into a proffered chair.

"What's that got to do with the price of eggs, Gus? You were never the one to allow private matters to cloud your judgment, and I don't believe that's what's worrying you now. Incidentally, young Carole came to see me. Offered to resign. I told her no."

Gus nodded slowly. "You want the truth, Chief, Alex Railton's got me worried. I've only had the bare facts from young Brook, but something's nagging away in the back of my mind. Can't put a finger on it."

"Well, I'm not going to brighten your day, Gus. Clifton Farthing's missing, presumed killed in action, which means Langley has no effective contact with Arnie Farthing anymore. Their Embassy reports no sightings of Arnie since around the time they pulled Naldo."

"Great. Good. Super. Wonderful. What we doing about Naldo?"

C smiled and opened his hands. "What can we do? We know he's still alive. There's been no trial, which probably means he's being dried out. Our closest source says they've moved him from the Lubyanka. He was in Lefortovo for ten days, which is *very* short term for interrogations, then on to one of their clinics. Ironically it's the so-called Outpatients Clinic for Psychiatric Diseases, in Sochi."

"There *will* be a trial though, surely." Gus was not really asking a question.

"Who knows? I suspect they've nabbed Arnie as well—Christ, Gus, I shouldn't be saying any of this to you. I'm not even supposed to dream about Arnie and Naldo—dream the truth, I mean."

"Safe with me, Chief."

"Not the point. We're in enough shit already, what with the PM's statement on Caspar . . ."

"Why couldn't you have denied that, sir?" Gus had lapsed into an almost formal tone.

"Because, officially, it's the truth. I appointed the damned committee. I have to accept the findings. The findings are that Caspar was a penetration, so that's what we're left with. Find someone to carry on a crusade against the findings, give us new evidence, and maybe we can reopen the business. Put down Willis and his gang. Go and do it, Gus."

"I might at that." He looked at his shoes for a long time, as though they held the answers, like crystal balls. At last he said, "I want round-the-clock watchers on Alexander Percival Railton."

"I can try, but what's the object, Gus?"

"I believe he's tainted. You can argue it's because of his poor old father. That and the recent developments."

"What recent developments?"

"Come off it, Chief. They'll turf him out of GCHQ for a start."

"Already turfed."

"That was quick. The police picked him up as he was leaving last night . . ."

"And he's not going back. Not even allowed in to clear his desk. It's all being done for him."

"He going to fight it?"

"Not on your life. The decision was made last night. I am told he was informed this morning. When he turned up at the office. Apparently he merely said he was thinking of leaving anyway."

"I'd still like the surveillance. Even more now. Especially now."

They shifted from the intrigues surrounding Railtons and Farthings, alive or dead, and moved on to other business, which was considerable. Yet something niggled in the back of Gus Keene's mind. Something had surfaced during the routine, random checks they had made on all members of what had become a blighted family. He thought it had to do with Alexander, just as he thought the charges against the man, plus their subsequent dropping, was a put-up job in more than one sense. If C had asked outright, Gus would have told him he thought Alexander was about to do a runner, and he could not have been more wrong if he tried.

"Know what I think?" C asked him just as their session was finishing.

"What do you think, sir?"

"I think," C said slowly, "that they're keeping Naldo for stock."

"We haven't got anyone to trade."

"No, but it's possible someone juicy'll come along. Poor old Naldo, going through the mill over there, and then having to suffer your inquisition if we get him back."

Gus merely grunted.

3

The rumors about refurbishing Lefortovo Prison had been without foundation, Naldo decided. The fact that he was there had been his own fault. First lesson, he thought, never try to be funny with an interrogating officer.

After his denial of knowing Herbie, the officer in question had smiled back, got out of his chair, and called the guards. Within fifteen minutes Naldo was in a *voronok*—a prison van—on his way across the city.

Within an hour he was in one of the ice cells. Below ground, within the prisoners section of Lefortovo, there are isolation cells maintained at low temperatures all the year round. In spring, as Naldo discovered, there was a rime of frost on the walls, and he was ankle deep in water. He had no bed, no toilet facilities, and they fed him a little bread and water twice a day. Apart from that, he saw nobody.

Within forty-eight hours he was reduced to sitting in the water in one corner. A week later it seemed to him that he had been in this cell all his life. In nine days all sense of time and place had gone, the disorientation of Naldo Railton had begun. He hung on to one thing only. Though he soon ceased to remember how or why, he knew that his own father had gone through something like this. After ten days, they dragged him out of the cell. He was placed in a warm bed and given an injection.

When he woke it was in a hospital room: a private room with bars on the window through which the sun streamed. He lay there, floating, it seemed, above the bed. Then people came in. Men and women. One of them said, "He's coming out of it. Fill him up again." Naldo knew what was said, though it was not spoken in English. As he drifted again, he felt at peace with the world. He could not tell if this was a dream or whether he was living in a kind of drunken stupor.

At one point he knew that they had moved him to a different room—one he knew, in Berlin. He carried out highly lucid briefings, and was sad about the people he spoke to as they were doomed. Naldo knew what it was like to be a military commander ordering people to go on a suicide mission. One of them was a woman.

There were other people, different places. Languages he knew, but had forgotten. He saw the men and women passing before him, looked into their eyes and spoke to them. For almost a day he spoke with C, going through operations stretching back for years; then, for a time, he was with BMW, cursing him and saying Caspar was innocent. He even broke all his personal rules and told BMW where both the diaries were stashed, at the postbox in Slough waiting for him to collect, in the name of Bernard Carpenter.

He spent a great deal of time sitting in a house in Berlin with Arnie. He stood by the window and watched the snow coming down outside. Then even that altered. There was another meeting with Arnie. Herb was there as well, only Herb was so young. Herb was almost a child, a teenager.

"Now it begins, old sheep," Herbie said, and Naldo went out into the snow, knowing that, somehow, he had been burned. After that, he only saw a few people he recognized. Some of them were long dead.

They included his Uncle Caspar. After Caspar appeared, a voice in Russian said, "That's it. We won't get any more."

Naldo Railton slept peacefully and woke. He recalled having woken briefly in this room before. A hospital room with bars on the window. He realized the sun was not shining and he felt dog tired, as though he had spent months walking over difficult terrain. Nobody came, so he slept again.

It was morning when they woke him. A nurse, young and blonde, breezed into the room and asked if he had slept well, placing a breakfast tray on a table which could be rested over his thighs. She propped him up on pillows, and said the doctor would be in shortly. He looked better.

"Where am I?" he asked.

"Where are you, indeed! You're where you've been for the last six months, Mr. Railton. Now you eat your breakfast," and she was away with a crisp, sexy rustle of her starched uniform.

On the tray there were bacon and tomatoes, toast, butter, and a large pot of coffee. He ate his first English breakfast for some time—he had no idea how long.

A clean-shaven doctor arrived after his breakfast had been removed by the blonde nurse. He had a Scottish accent and was very hearty. "Well, you're certainly looking better, Naldo. Sometimes these things take a while. I think you reached a crisis in the night. You had Sister Jopmore sitting up with you, most of the time." He began to examine Naldo. Eyes, ears, throat, blood pressure, reflexes, chest. "Aye, you're coming along famously."

"Where am I?" Naldo asked.

"Och, none of your old tricks now, Naldo. You're almost well, man."

He tried another tack. "What's the date, doctor?"

"It's the one after yesterday's date; and the one before tomorrow. Come on, Naldo. It's December 4th. They'll be decorating for Christmas soon. Or would you like to be out of here by Christmas?"

"Only if I can go to Redhill."

"Aye, I don't doubt that. Your father's going to be there. He telephoned this morning, as he's done every morning since you've been in. Sends his best wishes."

The hospital routine went on around him all day. English nurses bustled in and out. He was given pills and an injection. Food came regularly. It was appetizing and well-prepared. By nightfall he had almost come to believe he had suffered some terrible loss of memory.

In the night, he woke, sweating, his mind in turmoil. As his hand moved to the bell, illuminated by the bedside locker, he pulled back and everything returned to him. Everything, including the strange journey that seemed to have taken place, together with its meetings and the people he knew, or had known, from the past.

This was the moment of truth. Now, he was the traitor. He let out a long wail of despair which echoed into the night like some terrible banshee crying, and he saw past, present, and future lying in ashes around his bed.

They tried to keep up the pretense of his being in an English hospital for five more days. On the sixth morning, it was not the chirpy blonde nurse who came in to wake him from a, now drugged, sleep, but the KGB interrogator he had last seen in the Lubyanka.

"Now you can tell me how my friend Kruger is, yes? You've told us just about everything else."

This time Naldo did not give his imitation of Big Herb's daft smile.

4

London was clogged with Christmas shoppers. It got worse every year, Gus thought as he made a painful way over to the shop. Now C wanted to call off the heavy surveillance, and Gus had no answers. C had not said as much, but had hinted at it during a telephone call earlier in the week. The surveillance was giving them nothing new. Besides, it tied up a lot of manpower.

Even the shop was trying to get into a festive mood. Mistletoe hung from corridor lights and there were sprigs of holly over the photographs. Some offices had cards pinned up, and a Christmas tree stood in the main reception on the first floor. Even Willis greeted Gus cheerfully when he arrived on the fifth floor. "Your monthly meeting again, Gus? Time flies and all that. See you at the Christmas party."

"You want to pull the lads off Alexander," he announced to C almost before he had taken his seat.

"Not necessarily." C was brisk and to the point. "The long-term watch on that one hasn't given us the whiff of a fly's fart, Gus. We both know it. But I'm not going to press you. I would rather present you with another possibility." He moved from his desk to a table placed along one side of the office. The table contained around sixty surveillance photographs, each numbered and ciphered with the name of the target. Gus saw immediately that the photographs came not just from the close watch they had kept on Alexander since the spring, and the "little matter of the girl," as C liked to call it. These photographs were also from the random surveillance, about three days and one full night, they were running on each of the Railtons. Gus noticed the first one in the upper row was of Dick and Sara, hobbling together in the rose garden at Redhill Manor.

"What is it you wanted, then?"

"Well." C trod carefully. "I think it would be wrong to withdraw altogether from Alexander. But I *do* think this one deserves a much closer look." His hand drifted towards five photographs of a watch kept on a Railton they coded *Woodpecker.*

Gus looked at each picture in turn and asked why.

"The elderly lady in conversation here." C pointed, then looked at Gus for a reaction.

"We've never had an ident on her," he said, then he saw C's face. *"You* can give us an ident?"

C nodded. "Not your fault, Gus. We've all got other things on our minds, and I know you've been overstretched at Warminster. I had a peep through the snapshots the other evening. Mulling over how we could spread the manpower in a more economic way."

"You mean that's . . .?" His lips were beginning to form a word.

"Yes, and she's been doing an awful lot of traveling around of late."

"You mean we're onto the wrong brother?"

"Precisely. The elderly lady's a naughty, Gus. Don't expect elderly ladies to be doing this kind of thing, and she's probably known him since he was a young lad."

"Then we put the full works on him, and put Alexander into the random category."

"Exactly what I thought. Hope you don't mind, but I've issued orders to that effect." C gave a bland smile. "When's the wedding, Gus?"

"Just before Christmas, Chief." The divorce and its aftermath had gone more smoothly than Gus had any right to expect.

"Good. Glad you all managed to sidestep any Service involvement. Now that's dealt with we can get down to more pressing matters." C walked over to his desk and picked up another flagged file. "Tell me how we're doing with *Bald Eagle,*" he said.

Sod *Bald Eagle,* Gus thought. I want to get my hands on that bastard in the picture.

324

TWENTY-ONE

1

There were eight of them in C's office. Willis Maitland-Wood; Gus Keene; Carole Coles; Martin Brook; a senior officer from Five called Daryl, who was the regular liaison between the two services; one of the most reliable P4 lawyers; and the Head of Special Branch: known to all as HOB.

Each sat quietly as C went through the photographs. He matched places, times, and dates to the recordings: the conversations stolen through spikes, telephonic harmonica bugs, and parabolic mikes.

The first tape was a conversation between the target and a woman, who had already been identified by C.

"I hope you've got it for me," the woman said. You could not tell her age, the voice might have belonged to a girl of twenty or a woman in her seventies.

"Only some of it." The target sounded defensive. "The client's a trifle shy, but he's also on the hook. He brought work out to show me. Samples. I took a quick look, then told him we had to have the lot. He's offering exclusive classified material on the current and future deployment of American missiles here in the UK."

"Documentary evidence?"

"I saw a couple of pages, which I've copied here, that's all."

The woman made a sound of frustration: "Paaah!"

"Hang on," the target said rapidly. "He's tied in tight. He has no room to move. He'll give us all the goods. It's fixed. The man's in the mire without my help."

"*Verdi* is getting pushy. He wants it yesterday."

"Then give him the two pages as an appetizer. The rest will come, I promise you. Tell him to make direct contact if he wants it."

"I think he'll probably do that. He seems annoyed about something. He's not happy with you."

"Tell him to call me."

The tape beeped, and C pressed the pause button. It was a big Revox reel-to-reel machine. "We've put all the most damaging material onto one tape," he told them. "The next section is a telephone call made two days later, that would be the 7th January, to the target's office at exactly 19:00 hours."

"Yes?" was all the target said when answering the incoming call.

"You are alone?" The voice was male; a slight accent, possibly middle European.

"As always at this time of day."

"You recognize my voice?"

"Yes. *Snowball* said you might call."

"I need to see you. Can we lunch tomorrow?"

"Dinner would be better."

"As you wish. Say the Caprice at eight. Book the table in your name."

"I'll be there."

Again the tape was paused, to allow C to speak. "The contact was, in fact, that evening. *Photograph Four*. Target with the man we've identified as Second Secretary (Trade) in the Soviet Embassy, name of Savelev, Vasili Savelev. They dined at The Chesa in the Swiss Centre, Leicester Square, and we couldn't get any sound on them. The conversation was agitated. Later we quietly checked. The pair dine there quite often. Also the target occasionally sees a woman there. The tradecraft's good. We intercepted a booking for the following day at the Caprice, but nobody turned up. A week later there was another contact call. Dinner at The Chesa again. This time we got sound in. Here we go. Extraneous noise has been removed, thanks to the boffins."

On the tape, the same pair greeted one another and ordered their meal. Once it had been served, the contact asked—

"You have the stuff now?"

"No. I'll have it on Thursday without doubt. I've had to get a little tough with our client. He now knows where he stands; I'll have photostats of *all* documents by Thursday evening."

"We'll meet again, then. Same time, and you'd better have the stuff. Center's getting very edgy about you."

"I'm not happy myself."

"Why have they taken you off their list?"

"I've told you. Nothing specific. Only the old stuff. My cousin; my father. Possibly the business in Cheltenham."

"You've detected no surveillance?"

"Nothing. You?"

"We don't think so. Galina and Sammi have swept behind me, and one time they followed you. It seems clean."

"Well, I hardly think they're going to put anything on me. They've been concentrating on my brother. I fixed that one myself. He's got no idea, and he wouldn't know a surveillance operation if they wore placards. Anyway, those people are always short of watchers. They have to borrow from MI5."

"It's possible we might have to let you go dormant for a time." The contact spoke very quietly, but the words seemed to carry a subtext of threat. "We do look to you for the current stuff. Too much work has gone into this burn."

The conversation then moved to trivialities, theaters visited; TV shows watched; even the mention of a concert at the Festival Hall. Towards the end, it was reiterated that they would have dinner on Thursday.

"Right," HOB said. "Do we know who they're burning, sir?"

C nodded. "Cipher Clerk, Ministry of Defence. Name of Stanley. Nicholas Stanley. He has personal problems. Mainly financial, and I suspect the target's got him well buttoned up. Interesting remark about his brother."

"Indeed it is." Gus gazed at the ceiling. "Who are Galina and Sammi?"

Willis took that one. "Galina Kirsanov, thirty, assistant to the Second Secretary, who is, of course the KGB Resident. Sammi's one of their drivers. Black. Attended Patrice Lumumba and was shunted into Special Operations three years ago. Blends in nicely over here. Full name Sammi Omunda. Soviet papers, of course."

"Did your people know there was countersurveillance?" HOB asked.

Willis was about to answer, but C beat him to the draw. "Yes. We had people on the Embassy. They watched all the comings and goings, remained at a discreet distance and kept in touch with the main teams, advised them which way to move, how to avoid detection, when to switch bodies. It appeared to work."

He gave the HOB a slow smile. "Let me go back to young Stanley of the MoD. He has access to the documents described in the conversations. From what we know he'll be taking copies of the entire series out of his office this evening. We know he has an appointment with the target at five-thirty—in the target's office. That's unusual, but I suppose necessary in this case. The target won't want his hands on the stuff for any great length of time. Stanley put in a request for the whole file this morning, and we marked it. One copy only. Every page has

327

transposed words or typos. So it's directly traceable back to Stanley. We have them all."

The P4 lawyer broke in. "Bang to rights."

"So we pull him—Stanley—*after* chummy and his contact, Savelev." The HOB looked satisfied.

C said they should also pull the girl and Sammi. "They're never far behind. I suggest using several teams, and cars very close. We don't want any heroics, or public interest."

HOB nodded. "You realize, of course, that we can only hold the Sovs for a few hours? Less for the girl and the black fellow, more with the Trade Secretary, but only if he has the stuff on him."

"He'll have it, and, if they work true to form, Savelev will leave the Swiss Centre first. The target goes about ten minutes later." Willis was determined to have his say. "If you take my advice . . ."

"HOB knows all the tricks, Willis," C said not unkindly. "I look forward to results."

"I get a small go at the Soviets?" Gus asked.

" 'Fraid not, Gus. Your lovely wife here," inclining his head towards Carole, "can take a shot at turning the girl. No harm in making a pass. And you won't have very long, my dear Mrs. Keene. All three will be PNGd on their way back to the Embassy. Keep 'em indoors until Aeroflot can fix them up. So, quickly-quickly, Mrs. Keene."

Carole was touched. When she was plain Carole Coles, C hardly spoke to her. Now he never took liberties, always calling her Mrs. Keene. "I'll give it a whirl, Chief." She flashed him the smile she reserved for would-be defectors, and Gus, then added, "Might I make a suggestion? Mrs. Railton—Barbara. She's in the Kensington house and we have a very light presence there. I think we should beef it up for the next few months."

"Agreed," C snapped. "See to it, Willis."

"And what about *Snowball?*" HOB wrinkled his nose.

"Anytime, I'd say." C's brow creased. "Anytime after you have the rest in the bag."

HOB gave a curt nod. "And, I presume, *before* we let the Russians go."

"Naturally. Good luck."

Gus lingered, and when the others had left he asked C if he could have what he called "The loan of one officer."

"Who're you thinking of, Gus? I write it on a piece of paper and read your mind, eh?"

"I don't think there's need for that, sir. You know who I want, and I'd like him to liaise with the SB."

"What you mean, my dear Gus, is that you want Kruger in the car, or taxi, or whatever they're going to use, when our man climbs in."

"It'll amuse him, sir, and he's pining for Naldo."

"Aren't we all, Gus? Aren't we all?"

2

The Swiss Centre complex is situated at the northeasterly edge of Leicester Square, where the narrows of Wardour Street snake chaotically into New Coventry Street. The Centre covers a Bally Shoe outlet, plus Watches of Switzerland, a cinema, and an entrance to the gourmet food shop along the Wardour Street side. The main entrance, straight off the pavement of New Coventry Street, allows access to the food hall and has stairs down to three restaurants and a sweet and cake shop. The Chesa, the Swiss Centre's flagship restaurant, is just to the right at the bottom of the stairs, where you are greeted by pleasant girls, either in red uniforms or the national costume of one or another Canton.

They had three people already inside The Chesa—one man dining alone, and a young couple, seated near the table that had been earmarked for the target and his control. A further three women officers, and two men, either waited for dates who would never turn up, or drifted between the other restaurants, trying to make up their minds where to eat.

It was seven o'clock, bitterly cold, and outside the other teams were in place. Among the watchers and snatch squads there was much tension. Everyone knew this might be their only chance.

The welcome party covered all entrances and exits. One of them, in jeans and a short coat, shivered just inside the main entrance, while a gentleman, seemingly oblivious to the temperature, played the bagpipes, just as he did on most nights of the year.

Radios crackled in cars, then from cars to hidden walkie-talkies with earplug mikes. At seven-ten the Russian Second Secretary boarded an Underground train at Knightsbridge. The news rippled around Leicester Square, and downstairs in the Swiss Centre: muttered key-words and short sentences were fed through the earplug mikes. A few minutes later everyone heard that Sammi was right behind him, while the female agent was heading their way by taxi.

At seven-fifteen, the target was en route by taxi. A full team had the cab well boxed in.

The Russian was the first to arrive; Sammi loitered around Leicester
Square, while the Russian girl, whom they coded *Balalaika,* came in
a taxi and took a seat in the far corner of the restaurant where she had
a good view of the entrance and her Resident's table. Everyone admired
her choice of seating, because there were so many blind spots in The
Chesa, which has white stucco walls, curved into a series of arches
down the length; a bar opposite, and more white stucco, all hung with
giant cowbells and pieces of rustic Swiss farm equipment.

The target arrived at seven-thirty on the dot, greeting the Russian
like a business colleague he did not know very well. They ordered a
very light, one-course, meal, and the thick envelope, which obviously
contained the documents, was passed, almost casually, across the
table, in plain view. They were in the restaurant for exactly fifty
minutes, and the Russian left first, going out of the main entrance. The
team earmarked for him got the news from one of the "waiting-for-a-
date" girls.

Savelev turned right, pausing at the corner of Wardour Street with
the car pulling up directly in front of him. He stepped back to avoid
the two men who got out. Then a third man pushed him forward,
almost into the arms of the car's occupants. It took less than fifteen
seconds, and he was sitting with a Special Branch officer on either side
of him, and the car gathering speed, before he even had time to cry out.

"Not too much shouting please, Mr. Savelev, sir," one officer said
firmly.

"You have no right . . ." Savelev began.

"We are officers of the Metropolitan Police, Special Branch, sir, and
we are taking you to West End Central Police Station where we wish
to ask you some questions." They both flashed ID, but touched neither Savelev nor his briefcase. They knew there were photographs of
the envelope being taken and placed in the case.

Five minutes later the target came out, looking for a cab. A passenger
was just paying one off on the corner. The fare must have been heavy
because he fumbled with his change. They had come all of thirty yards
down Wardour Street as soon as the instruction had crackled over the
radio.

The driver nodded to the target, indicating he could get in while this
idiot tried to sort out his money. As the target climbed in, so its
previous passenger followed him, and, with neat timing, the far door
opened for a bulky figure to climb in.

"How are you, Andrew, old sheep?" Big Herbie said with a huge
smile.

"What the . . .?"

"Let's take it quietly, Mr. Railton. Plenty of time to talk at West End Central." The Special Branch man also smiled.

In his mirror, the police driver saw four men latch onto Sammi, and another team enter the Swiss Centre in search of Miss Galina Kirsanov.

"A good lot of weather we're having, eh, Andrew." Herbie smiled.

When they got to West End Central, the Second Secretary (Trade) was already shouting his head off.

Half an hour later they were explaining the evidence to Andrew, who made no comment, but simply kept asking for a solicitor. All the wind and hot air had gone out of him, and he looked like a man who, very suddenly, had discovered the food he had eaten contained arsenic. Which, in one sense, it had.

Savelev was allowed to leave an hour after his arrival. They kept the briefcase and let Sammi out with him. The two men met in the reception area and went through a charade of not knowing one another. Neither realized that the Foreign Office had already PNGd them through one of its solicitors who arrived, in person, at the Embassy with the instructions.

In one of the interview rooms, Carole Keene was explaining the situation to Miss Kirsanov. "It's a one and only chance, Galina. We have to let you return to the Embassy now, in fact. If you go you'll be back in Moscow within seventy-two hours, and they'll never send you abroad again. You know that. I know it. Back to Moscow, or stay here and live a pleasant, uncomplicated life. We'd pay well and give you plenty of work." It was about the tenth time she had said it.

"*Yeb vas!*" Kirsanov spat into Carole's face. She left ten minutes after her colleagues.

"What does *Yeb vas* mean, Gus?" she asked her husband as they prepared for bed, in the early hours of the morning, after Gus had seen Andrew Railton banged up for the night.

"Fuck you!" he translated.

"Oh, good. Now?" Carole gave him her most falsely coy look.

3

They kept Naldo under enough sedation to prevent him from attempting to walk. The standard of the food had gone down rapidly, once they let him know he was still in the Soviet Union. A doctor checked him out each day, and topped up the sedative. Apart from that, he saw only those who brought food, and came to make sure he had not soiled the bed. He was not in Moscow, of that he was certain, because it was now the end of January and no sign of snow showed from beyond the bars of his window.

Once every month he had the pleasure of a day with the slim, French-looking interrogator, who let slip that it was like the Arctic in Moscow. Naldo played the game, pretending to establish rapport with the interrogator, with whom he was now on Christian-name terms. Naldo and Jacob. All very cozy.

The drugs they used to keep him from getting out of bed seemed to allow rational thought. Certainly they allowed deep depression. To combat the depression, which had grown from the knowledge of having betrayed his country under hypnotic drugs, Naldo decided he should try and get his mind going on rational thought. He started by trying to remember the great Shakespearean plays. First, by plot, act by act. Then scene by scene. Last of all, by text. This final mental exercise was the most difficult. He only got a few bursts of language, skipping great hunks and then landing on a long speech that he knew by heart.

Gradually logic returned, and, with the logic he accepted the fact that he was not responsible, personally, for treachery. It was important for him to try reconstructing the vivid recall he had undergone during the hypnotic phase. He went through all he could bring back from his subconscious, knowing that, should he ever get home again, the boys at Warminster would want chapter and verse on everything. He knew for sure that he had blown Brunner. He hardly had to be even half mentally agile to realize that. What anguished him was the huge area of ongoing operations he might have spilled.

He worked on other matters also, figuring out why nobody would discuss Penkovsky, or even admit that he, Donald Railton, had murdered the man. You cannot kill a person twice, and Oleg Penkovsky, it was well known, had gone to his death immediately after the trial. So that was that. They would never admit it. He could never be accused. If he spoke publicly, they would say he was a raving loony.

The word trial began to repeat itself in his head, forcing its way upwards and confronting him with another question: why had they not taken him back to Moscow to stand public trial? The Soviets rarely missed any opportunity to chastise the West with an espionage show-trial. Yet they had not made any move towards this. The answer came during a visit from Jacob in late February.

They had done the usual question and answer routine, which had of late borne down heavily on Arnold Farthing. Why they should want so much information on a dead man was beyond him, but they did, and Naldo gave them tidbits from his own store of knowledge. He asked about Arnie's wife, Gloria, and was told that she had decided to stay in the Soviet Union. He wondered about where they had taken her—what part of the Gulag—and what had been done about the children.

At the end of the February meeting, Jacob was about to leave when he dropped a shattering piece of information into Naldo's head.

"They've arrested your cousin," Jacob said without the trace of a smile.

Naldo looked surprised, and then elated. "They finally got the little shit," he said in the kind of voice described as containing "grim satisfaction."

"I would never describe Andrew Railton as little." Jacob still did not show any pleasure. "A shit, probably. But a big shit, yes?"

"Andrew? They've arrested Andrew? What in God's name have they arrested *him* for?" In spite of his dislike of cousin Andrew, Naldo always thought of him as a somewhat priggish pillar of society. The nastiest prefect in the school. "Why?" he repeated.

"Why d'you think? He worked for us. For years he was a penetration. In the end he let his guard slip. They even got his controller, but he's back in Moscow now. Andrew's coming up for trial in a few weeks. What is the expression? They'll throw the book at him?"

With some satisfaction, Naldo said they would also lock him up and throw away the key.

"We'll see." Jacob gave a minute trace of a smile. "We'll see."

Later that night, Naldo knew why they had not thrown him to the Party wolves in Moscow. KGB were keeping him in stock, against something unfortunate happening to one of their penetrations. Andrew had certainly been one of the three possibilities he had deduced from Caspar's papers. But he could never have been the first one. Andrew was a second-generation traitor. There was someone else. Caspar had known it, and indicated it in his papers.

The thought plunged him into depression again, for he was almost one hundred percent certain who the leading light in *that* act of treachery had been.

4

As the date for Andrew's trial approached, there were hectic comings and goings at the shop. The Legal Department had worked in close cooperation with Special Branch, and C had seen to it that the whole operation was credited to their brothers at MI5. The case against Andrew William Railton was, as they say, open and shut—"More shut than open," one legal brain had pronounced. Andrew, everyone knew, was really for the high jump.

In drawing information in—especially for the damage-control operation that was taking place—various SIS residents were being pulled into London for short briefings. One such was Mark Bertram-Prince, official food taster to the CIA, which meant he ran liaison in Washington.

The British Embassy in Moscow had still picked up no traces of Arnie Farthing since Naldo's arrest. They knew little. Only one further communiqué—the third—had been issued through Tass, following the original shooting and detention of Naldo on charges of espionage. This last communiqué simply said that Donald Arthur Railton was being detained for lengthy interrogation and his trial would be held when all the facts came to light. The Ambassador had pleaded constantly to be allowed to see Naldo, and he was backed up by the Foreign Office, but excuse piled onto excuse. All the Embassy knew was that Naldo was being held at the Psychiatric Hospital in Sochi.

As for Arnie, the U.S. Embassy in Moscow had not had a glimpse of him, which bore out the operational sight-seeing of the British—

Until the SIS liaison officer, Mark Bertram-Prince, was summoned to London. Even then, only a chance remark started people taking action.

Bertram-Prince was a long-serving SIS officer. His experience was large, and he had that particular talent which involves hearing and seeing things not meant for his ears or eyes.

On his second day at the shop, Bertram-Prince spent several hours with C, and, towards the end of the session, he asked, almost diffidently, "Chief, know anything about an operation called *Heartbreak?*"

C said he certainly did know of such an operation, and called in Willis BMW to hear what their man in Washington had to say.

"There's quite a batch of stuff at Langley," Bertram-Prince told them. "And it keeps coming. Mind you, I don't think I'm supposed to know because there's a cloak of silence around the whole thing."

"Do you mean . . . ? Are you suggesting . . . ?" C took a deep breath. "Mark, is *Heartbreak* still running?"

"Very much so. I brought it up because the little I've seen of it relates to a Soviet source. It's all pretty good material. I've only peeped at four or five things but, if it's for real, *Heartbreak*'s feeding them golden eggs."

C and BMW exchanged shocked looks. "When did you last have sight of anything, Mark?" Maitland-Wood put on his concerned voice.

"Last week. A heap of information regarding military economics, with special reference to the Sov's Air Force." He saw the look on their faces. "I said the wrong thing?"

"No. No. No." C's voice sank to a whisper.

Later he talked to Willis in private. "You realize what this means?"

"It means that Arnold Farthing's still active."

"Not only that." C banged the desk with the flat of his hand. "It means that, in all probability, the bloody Yanks sold Naldo out. I want to see Paul Schillig first thing Monday morning, and no buts or sorrys, or recall to Washington tricks. I want to put the bugger through the blender."

TWENTY-TWO

1

"After all this time, you'd have thought they'd get the air conditioning right." Marty Foreman sat in his shirtsleeves. There were wet patches under his armpits and an island of sweat had formed across his back. Outside, the temperature was well below zero. Inside the CIA complex at Langley, swamps and jungles came to mind. People were always going off sick. In winter it was too hot; in summer you shivered with cold.

The stocky, pugnacious Foreman clenched his fists and beat the air. "For Christ's sake, Paul, what can I say? When Arnie first put up the idea of *Heartbreak,* as the final operation, he said he needed human collateral to give him credibility after they took him in. We think he's just about the bravest field agent we've ever had. We accepted the idea of Naldo Railton, and it was always understood, here, that Naldo was expendable. I'm sorry, that's all I can say."

"I bet Naldo didn't know he was expendable." Paul Schillig kept his voice pleasant and level.

"Look, what can I tell ya?" Marty beat the air with his fists again, in an almost emotional act of frustration. "When it started, right at the beginning, how were we to know they'd denounce old Caspar as a traitor; or arrest his son with a third-rate Center-trained controller who knows from nothing about tradecraft. Two guys who hadn't the faintest idea of how to watch their asses. Who knew, then?"

"And who knows now, Marty?" Schillig always tried to keep any anger out of his voice. Many years ago he had learned the art of being nice; showing himself as a reasonable man. Now he was on the verge of revealing that side of him that never appeared in public. "You haven't been hauled up in front of *their* Head of Service and told he'll see to it that every single CIA operative will be vacuumed out of the United Kingdom within two weeks. This damned operation could cost us any special relationship we've managed to reclaim with the Brits."

"What do they know?" Marty Foreman stood and strutted around the room, arms waving as though swatting invisible flies. "They know from nothing, and they're starting to look fucking stupid. The Prime Minister is forced to admit an internal investigation found Caspar Railton to be a long-term penetration, and that after another Railton gets put in the bag by the Sovs. Now yet *another* Railton's going down. They're going to think Railton's a crypto for *all* their officers. Three in a row and that ain't funny anymore. It makes them look like idiots."

"Can it make the Farthing family look like idiots, Marty? I hear you've had problems with *Heartbreak* yourselves."

"Who in hell told you that?" Foreman snapped, and Paul Schillig drew a sheet of white paper from his inside pocket. He had spent all morning with the DCI and James Jesus Angleton getting the piece of paper. It gave him complete access to all the *Heartbreak* material, and the operation they called *Heartache* which had been organized to set it up. Being a disciplined man, Schillig had been through the files: just a quick trip to examine the views. Later he would return and spend hours with them. In the meantime he would get all he could from Marty.

"What d'ya mean by it anyway? Why don't you get off my back, Schillig, and leave the covert ops to professionals?"

Schillig went very quiet. "What I mean by it, Marty, is that I need to hear everything. The whole business, blow by blow. Detail. Minutiae. Whatever you want to call it. Why Naldo was expendable, and what happened. I have to know it, and I have to be able to give reasoned answers. Your own boss, Angleton, has given the go-ahead for you to talk to me. The DCI has said I am to have *all possible* cooperation from CA people, and don't deny you're Covert Action, Marty, because I've known you too long."

Foreman slumped into his chair, hanging his head like a stubborn schoolboy. Finally he said, "Okay, so what d'ya wanna know?"

Paul Schillig sank into the other chair. "Don't you listen to a thing? I want to know the whole score, Marty. I need to know what was going on, what *is* going on. I've got to know how far Arnie's now at risk, and how he gets stuff out. How far's he blown, Marty? They going to throw him into a camp, shoot him, or let him go bananas like Naldo Railton, in one of their hospitals? We have to cut the Brits in, and the word is you've got an operation, deep in the heart of Russia, that's going sour."

"Okay. Okay. Give me a minute, Paul. Get my breath and I'll tell ya."

Then Marty started to talk. "You know how things go wrong. Okay, we realized that there was need to get someone there. Need to put one man right into the Center. We've had a casual there for a long time. High-class, but nervous. We only got stuff from him once in a blue moon, and he refused to work full time. Lots of excuses: lines of communication were difficult; he required someone to hold his hand; the whole thing had to be one hundred percent waterproof—which, as you know, just ain't possible in our profession. So Arnie came up with a great dangle. To be honest we had Clifton in mind to start with."

"Why Clifton?"

"Because he spoke Russian like he was third generation from a peasant. Then we went over it again and decided Clifton didn't really have the balls for it; tended to be a little flaky. We needed to make them an offer they really could never refuse. Someone with a lot of experience and good contacts. Arnie proposed himself, and we began *Heartache*, which was the dangle, and by God it was good. It took Arnie five years. Five solid years in Berlin. A word here; a hint there; he even had a blazing tantrum in a restaurant and walked out on Jim Angleton—right in front of the Soviet Resident. They swallowed him and played him. We even handed them good intelligence. Real pearls-before-swine stuff." He gave a throaty laugh. "Mind you, we invented some of the stuff ourselves. But it was great."

Schillig nodded encouragement.

"They took it all, and, finally they came to that point we all have to face when running a defector in place. They offered him a way out; said if it all suddenly went wrong, he'd have a home in Moscow. They gave him what he was after, on a plate, right?"

"So far. How did Naldo come into it?"

"Naldo was running his own dangle. Find the lady. Trying to get someone close to the middle-ranking Ks in East Germany. He needed Arnie's help. Got Arnie to tip them on who not to touch, so he was pulled in off his own bat. Okay?"

"Up to a point." Schillig looked concerned. "And only up to a point. Naldo asked for help and got it, but he had no knowledge of Arnie's real setup."

"Look." Marty made the gesture with his hands. "You know how it is, Paul. We were bowling along a straight road, motor running nicely, everyone happy, then, crunch!"

338

"Crunch?"

"Another car; another operation runs straight in front of us, like a kid on a tricycle. It was something completely apart from what Arnie was doing, but it did have an effect on Caspar Railton, and then Naldo."

"You like to tell me what it was?"

"Not really. Nobody here says it aloud. It's one I keep away from you, Paul. Maybe the DCI or Jim'll tell you, but I doubt it. Just take my word for it. We were suddenly faced with facts we found unpalatable, and part of those facts could put Caspar Railton in the frame as a long-term Soviet agent. Mind you, Caspar had helped to put himself in the frame, but for other purposes. The thing we don't talk about was in Russia, and had to be taken care of. Arnie saw Naldo—this was after Caspar's funeral. You know how much that guy loved his uncle?"

"I know Naldo was close to him, yes."

"Close? You're joking. To Naldo, old Caspar was father, mother, lover, adviser, friend. He loved the guy more than life—certainly more than his wife and children; more than his Service; more than country." He paused, eyes flashing. "Arnie told him of this thing we don't talk about. Naldo put two and two together very quickly—Arnie was a shade naughty, mind you. He gave him a couple of pushes. But Naldo wanted revenge. It was Naldo who wanted to go into the Soviet Union and take care of this blight; this guy who, in his mind, had tipped the scales and put the boot in on Caspar a long time ago."

"So Arnie said, 'Come along with me, Nald, we'll do it together.' "

Marty shook his head. "No, it didn't even happen like that. The whole business just went out of control. They set up this committee in London to stick Caspar's dead body up against a wall and shoot him. Almost at the same moment, and by pure coincidence, the Sovs started a compromise operation on Naldo's wife. They do that, as you well know. We do the same thing from time to time. Compromise someone and then keep it in a safe to trot out in case you ever need it. Okay?"

"And they needed it?"

"Well, Arnie needed it, but he had no idea they'd jump when they heard Naldo's name. We set up a contact for Arnie—so he could get stuff out of Soviet Russia. That was done slowly, carefully. It's still going on, in fact, but it was time for Arnie to say, get me out. They got him out, and he took Naldo with him. As far as Arnie was concerned it was for collateral. To show them how good his contacts were. Naldo went along for one reason, and *of his own accord*. To avenge his Uncle Caspar . . ."

"And you can't tell me how he . . . ?" Schillig began.

"No. It's the one thing you'll have to get from others. But believe me, Paul, Naldo went to kill a man, and he did just that. All you need know, Paul. Okay? If the Brits want the whole story they'll have to ask Naldo, because we're not giving it to them. Naldo went freely, knowing there was danger, but knowing what he needed to do. That's all they have to be told."

Schillig pondered, looking at the plain carpet as though trying to find a pattern. "As I hear it, you had Farthing trouble, though."

"More collateral." Marty gave one of his shrugs again. "Arnie had to show them he could still get stuff in. Let them see it happen. So, almost on a whim, Clifton became the chosen one. The one *they* would see. Vietnam was on the boil and, when we came to it, Clifton was used. The really heavy stuff still goes out from Arnie through other people. Has done from the start. At the moment he's telling the Sovs that very soon he'll have someone for them right slap-bang in the American Embassy. That's being arranged. But Clifton was a godsend. Arnie told them he needed to meet this contact in Vietnam, and he needed to see him alone, to collect intelligence. Once a month they went through this charade. Arnie told them they mustn't peep, which means they had eyes on him all the time. Every meeting was observed."

"So what went wrong?" Schillig's voice turned cold.

"Clifton went wrong." Marty looked away from him. "Clifton Farthing was an alcoholic, and nobody spotted it, because he never drank in the field. He was the kind that went on benders: you know, three or four days at a time, then nothing for weeks—the Lost Weekend syndrome. It became worse when *Phoenix* got to him. We've made mistakes with *Phoenix*, Paul, but the signs are that, even with the mistakes, the hundreds of clean Vietnamese we've wasted, it's been worth it. But Clifton really felt guilt. As far as he was concerned, he was the big man; he was running as our main courier to Arnie. That was great while it lasted, but we knew it couldn't go on forever, so we went on beefing up lines of communication within Russia itself. And we've put in some very good stuff. Really excellent—dead-drops, letterboxes, Embassy Resident's total involvement, and a full-time contact taking up his appointment next month."

"It all went well, until?"

"Until Clifton began to shoot his mouth off. He got drunk in Saigon; he drank here in Washington; and when he drank he talked. No names, but he boasted of this great operation he was running. Classified stuff; stuff the Sovs would give their right arms for. He did not name names, but Clifton became very dangerous. It would only be a matter of time before he blew Arnie." He paused, unraveled a handkerchief from his pocket, and mopped his brow.

"Then why didn't *you* pull him out, Marty? Why didn't *you* see to it?"

When Foreman spoke he sounded like a man who had just completed a long and arduous field exercise. "It was family."

"Whose family? The Agency; or the Farthings?"

"A bit of both. We couldn't let him go on, and it wasn't wise to have him around, even in a stockade somewhere."

"So someone wasted him?"

Marty locked eyes with Schillig. His eyes were, for the first time since Schillig had known him, full of compassion. "Yeah. Someone did. Arnie did."

"Oh, Christ."

"I've told you: Arnie was getting the heavy stuff to us through the Moscow setup. Took more time, certainly, but it was worthwhile. Christ, Paul, the kinda stuff we get from field agents nowadays helps to back up satellite material. In twenty, thirty years' time we'll have almost bypassed field agents. The technology's taking over, but there will always be things that can only be checked by people on the ground. The Sovs complained to Arnie that he was giving them only a twenty percent yield. The rest was chickenfeed. We knew it; then they knew it. It was the Sovs who told Arnie they were concerned about his Stateside contact. We gave him the instructions. We also told him the truth. Clifton's going to blow you, we said. Waste him, we said, or he'll waste you."

"And that's what he did."

"Sure as God made little apples he did. Arnie's nobody's fool. He knew the Sovs kept an eye on him during the meetings in Vietnam. He told them that *he* wasn't happy. He needed to gain respect and confidence. So he wastes Clifton, and then, as we read it, dropped Naldo in the shit, so that he could come out clean. Clifton was good collateral, as was Naldo. Only Naldo went in *of his own choice.* You must make them see that."

"Okay, but I'm going to need a name. Whatever you say, I need to know who Naldo was after. Just like I need to know why the Brits haven't spotted Arnie lately. Sure, *our* Moscow Embassy can lie, but the Brits . . . Well, they've been looking for him. How? Why?"

"Arnie's in Leningrad is why. He works hard, and the intelligence gets through. I wouldn't say he's one hundred percent in the clear, but it does seem that they really do trust him."

"And for that he had to give them Clifton Farthing, and Naldo Railton."

Marty made a large shrugging motion. "The Brits got Naldo's fucking cousin, Andrew, didn't they?"

"Yes," Paul Schillig said, after a long pause. "Yes, I suppose they did." Then another pause before he said, "What a shitty, dirty, underhanded immoral business we're in, Marty."

Foreman shrugged again. "Beats working for a living. And don't forget, it was Naldo Railton's choice to go in with Arnie."

Schillig returned to London with instructions to tell the Brits all they needed to know. The DCI even gave him complete authority to pass on *all* details of *Heartbreak,* and its current standing, to C.

In spite of Marty's silence, Schillig took Oleg Penkovsky's name with him, though even he found it hard to believe, as did the head of the SIS, who was righteously furious at the liberties taken with one of his best officers. "Your people're behaving like terrorists," was all C said to the CIA Resident. "When's it all going to stop?"

Paul Schillig could give him no answer. A month later, the British Resident in Moscow reported a sighting of Arnie Farthing. "Where?" C asked, and was not surprised to hear he had been seen driving himself into the old building in Dzerzhinsky Square.

2

Andrew's lawyers, distancing themselves from the moral issues of acting for a traitor, pressed for a very early trial. They made sure their client was kept in Pentonville Prison, once known, years ago, as the Tench. They knew that the Warminster interrogators would have preferred to have him on their own premises. That way they would get more from him, and, it followed, would have more evidence to deal out during those parts of the trial that would be "in camera."

Once they had done their job, the legal advisers, who knew they could not win the day, would simply take their money and run. After that, Warminster could have him. In the meantime, Gus Keene and his team, bowing to the difficulties, spent many hours at Pentonville.

Their line of questioning was three-pronged. They were anxious to know how long Andrew had, as they put it, "Been at it." They also tried to establish if Andrew had, at any point, been involved with the so-called treachery of his father, Caspar. Even Gus, who rooted for Caspar, was beginning to have his doubts now that Andrew had been caught redhanded.

The Warminster team had another interesting line of questioning. How, they had to ask, did the Soviets imagine they could get good intelligence from a man who was really only on the fringes of the Service? As a P4 legal adviser, Andrew was on call for his professional services, particularly interrogatory techniques, or to provide cover. P4 people rarely got anything deeply juicy with which to tempt interested hostile intelligence services.

In the few weeks' grace at their disposal, Gus and his people got few answers. They drew a complete blank on the length of time Andrew had been operating for the KGB. As an intellectual side issue they did not get any reason for the treachery. It was not possible to tell whether Andrew had been seduced by political leanings or by the lust for gold.

They were equally unsuccessful over the question of Caspar. "My father," Andrew maintained, "had his work. I had mine. I have no idea if he was or was not a long-term agent for KGB. If he was, then KGB operational policy saw that we remained apart. We were never inter-cognizant."

Regarding the final query, Andrew was relatively helpful. "My controllers always said that a person in my position was more likely to get good intelligence than someone completely inside."

"How so?" It was Gus who asked.

"Their reasoning is that professional men like myself, with strong links into the Service, would have a lot of friends within the Service. Those friends were more likely to drop exceptional information my way. Particularly if I dropped the correct questions." This last seemed to be added as a touch of vanity.

Gus nodded. He knew as well as the next man that Andrew was probably being honest. People within the Service often carry very heavy secret loads, and they need an ear into which they could share their problems. The P4 doctors and lawyers had just such ears, as did former members of the Service.

Oh, yes, Gus Keene thought. Oh, yes, that all figured. They had not yet fitted all the pieces of the Anthony Blunt jigsaw, but he had possessed a very willing ear to "old friends." "The Russians," wicked Sir Anthony had said, "knew I was no good to them after I left MI5, so they let me go." "Really?" people like Gus had said. "They let you go, Anthony? Even though you were still having quiet lunches with your own old colleagues? A wonder you didn't just telephone the stuff to Moscow Center." Until just after the lads came in to say there would be immunity if he owned up, Blunt had been at work. You bet your sweet arse on it.

"I wonder," Gus mused one night. "I wonder why they always met at the Swiss Centre. Presumably, they imagined they were immune— on neutral ground."

Gus and his team still had a long way to go when the nights became shorter, and the acrid smell of fireworks drifted across leaf-strewn gardens and parks. It was November 5, 1970, that Andrew William Railton was brought to the Old Bailey for trial, charged with—as they say—offenses under the Official Secrets Act.

After the first two days of generalization, the court was cleared for most of the time as members of the SIS and MI5 gave evidence. It was a kind of ritual. Andrew William Railton went down for life. In summing up, the judge, referred to "The country you have betrayed, and the honor of your noble Service, and family, you have besmirched."

At Redhill, Sara had laughed loudly. "There's not much honor left." She shook her head sadly. "Neither in country, Service, or family. Especially family. Doesn't that damned judge read the papers anymore?"

Dick merely nodded, and went slowly to the room they all referred to as The General's Study. Sara found him there an hour later, sobbing like a child.

Through his tears, Richard managed to quote from *Hamlet*—

> *"That he is mad, 'tis true; 'tis true 'tis pity;*
> *And pity 'tis 'tis true: a foolish figure;*
> *But farewell it, for I will use no art."*

Sara thought of the words again and again over the next weeks, as Christmas approached. She felt she had no heart to face her fellow Railtons this year, but the annual festivities took place as usual.

Barbara, now back in the Kensington house, smiled also at the judge's unhappy choice of words. Then she also wept: for dear dead Caspar; for James and Margaret Mary, who, she thought, must be heartbroken to see what depths of depravity had befallen the once proud family; for Arnie Farthing, her dear friend; and, most particularly for her husband, Naldo, far away in a hospital she imagined to be vile.

Aloud, she followed the Railton tradition and said to nobody but the spikes with which the walls of her house gave up secrets to the listeners, "Poor Naldo, close mew'd up." And then she wept again until the doorbell rang.

It was Herbie, come to offer some kind of comfort. "We go on little outing, Barb!" he said loudly, twirling his finger and touching his ear, bringing her attention to the mikes.

They went out to Veeraswamy's, that most plush Indian Restaurant, where Herbie ate a chicken vindaloo so that sweat poured down his face, and Barbara was contented with a chicken korma.

"This is good news, ja?" Herbie put down his spoon and fork.

"What?" Barbara looked wild-eyed.

"Andrew going in the pokey, is good news."

"Good, and sad."

"No Barb, is good. Soon, Russians will want him back. You see, they make exchange for Naldo."

She had never thought of the possibility, and her first reaction was, Oh, Christ, the family all over the papers again. Aloud she voiced the opinion that it would never happen. "Both sides would look bloody foolish, Herb. The Railton family is only a tiny, scattered part in all this, but look at the embarrassment they've caused already. Didn't you see the headline in the *Mirror*—A FAMILY OF TRAITORS?"

"Ach, bloody newspaper talking. Who give shit about newspapers, Barb? All print lies. Only good for two things, newspapers."

"What?" She saw his face wrinkle into a gigantic pattern of fun.

"Only good for fishes and chips, and for wipe arse."

"Herbie!"

"Sorry Barb. But it *will* happen. You put a cross on my words. It will happen."

She could not allow herself to believe him, and the next two years seemed, to Barbara, to stretch into infinity, and during that time Gus and his people dried out Andrew as far as he would dry.

After the Lord Mayor's show of Andrew's trial, came the garbage truck of the second trial: that of Alice Edith Ross, née Pritchard, one-time secretary at the shop, secret lover of sly old James, whose adoration for his wife went without question. Alice Ross was the cutout between Andrew Railton and his Soviet control, and it was her voice which had filtered onto the Andrew Railton tapes. She had been known as *Snowball*, though there was not much of a snowball about her appearance. Gus Keene said, "The only good thing is that it proves they must have been running Andrew since the Ark." KGB operations used cutouts only when things were really bedded down. The longer you ran an agent of Andrew's caliber, the more likely there would be a slip. A go-between; a cutout, helped reduce the number of face-to-face meetings Andrew required with his control.

Alice Ross, née Pritchard, was a flashy lady who owned to being sixty years of age, but had almost certainly reached sixty-five. During the hearing she presented a rather pathetic figure: too much makeup badly applied (one newspaper described the slash of crimson which was her mouth looking obscene); her thinning hair died blonde; her fingernails scarlet, the color clashing with the lipstick. Two dabs of bright rouge spotted her cheeks, giving her a bizarre look.

There was a difference of opinion as to whether Alice was really a little crazy, or had cannily put on the eccentricities for the court's benefit. She pleaded guilty; agreed that, in the latter part of the 1930s, she had worked for "A department of the Foreign Office dealing with intelligence matters," which was surely MI6 or the SIS, but nobody would officially own up to the existence of such an organization. Alice said she had become disillusioned with the work and resigned in 1939, only to be shunted sideways into Military Intelligence, with the equivalent rank of captain—Junior Commander—and a small staff at the War Office.

Both C and Gus Keene held their breath when she talked about becoming "disenchanted," for they were anxious that the dalliance with old James Railton did not become public property. "The name Railton's now a sort of living microcosm of the Service," C said. "God help us if another betrayal—if only to wife—comes to light." As he said it, so a ghostly gray thought trudged through C's mind. It stayed to haunt him for a moment, then was gone. This grim and terrifying idea was to return to him again and again until, thank God, it was exorcised by events.

But Alice had either forgotten or wanted to avoid any hint of moral turpitude on her part. So the fleeting meetings and breathless, stolen weekends remained hidden. Instead she told her story blatantly, describing how she had met Russian military personnel during her time with the ATS; how they had politically seduced her, and how she had, in 1944, agreed to work for the Soviet Service. The charges against her were tied into Andrew's case, so nothing else came out in public. The judge seemed to take the business lightly, and once she was found to be guilty he passed a sentence of five years.

The Press were led to believe that Alice Ross was a rather silly woman who did not understand what she was getting into. They also spoke about her departure to serve imprisonment in Holloway Prison. In fact, through an arrangement with the authorities, Alice was taken to the most secure section they kept at Warminster, where the confessors started to work on her life, leading her through the long labyrinth of treason, coaxing names from her, and filling in the blanks.

When Stalks came in to see Willis Maitland-Wood and Gus Keene, at BMW's request, after Christmas 1970, she reported that Andrew's family appeared to be much more relaxed without him at Redhill. "Anne was positively pleasant," she said, "and the kids seemed to be relieved their father had been banged up." She reported that Barbara had made a brave effort to join in, but she was obviously deeply depressed, while young Arthur and Emma were, to use her words, "very supportive. Really went out of their way to be of help." Of Alexander and his "brazen wife," as she called Delia, there was little to talk about. "Alex seems to have become less opinionated. He struts less, and doesn't say much. It's as though his problem's altered him somehow."

"It has," BMW said with a touch of acid. "Alexander's applied to be positively vetted again. Even says he's ready to be fluttered, as the CIA would call it." Fluttering was Agency jargon for the regular polygraph test on which they insisted, though everyone knew there were ways of beating the lie detector.

"Nobody's going to take him back, are they?" Stalks was appalled.

"It could happen. Everyone's short of trained staff. Alexander's just the kind of man we're looking for—if we can bring ourselves to trust him. They're going to vet him, and my money would be on him coming back in: well, at least back to GCHQ."

Stalks also painted a grim picture of Sara and Dick. "Getting more infirm by the minute," she told him. "Strange how age treats people. James and Margaret Mary must be in their late seventies, yet they bounce around quite happily. Alert and physically spry, apart from occasional moments of depression about Naldo. I know Sara and Dick are older, but, when you see them together, you'd think James and his wife were thirty years younger."

As she was leaving, Stalks asked if there was any news of Naldo, and was met with a shifty look and a negative reply.

Late in January, "old Phoeb," Caspar's widow, died, and it was noted by all that Andrew did not apply for permission to attend the funeral. These things apart, life went on much as usual, with all the attendant treacheries, rumors, and betrayals, right up to the summer of 1972, when the Railton family would have hit the headlines again if things had not been kept deeply silent.

Unknown to the world at large, which included the Press and most members of the SIS and MI5, the Soviets had been making overtures since early in 1971. Their offer was straightforward. They were prepared to exchange Naldo Railton for his cousin, Andrew.

No deal, the Foreign Office replied without hesitation. The Minister was adamant and did not even consult C about the rejection.

The Soviets made the offer again six months later, and were once more rebuffed. This time C was brought in. "Play the usual game," he advised. "Let them think we couldn't care less about getting Naldo back. Anyway, Gus is still working on Andrew. Let 'em stew."

Early in '72 Gus reported that no more could be gained by sweating Andrew, and the dance began in earnest. First the Foreign Office agreed to "exploratory talks," with the proviso that nobody tipped the Press in either country.

"One thing's for certain," C told the Minister. "None of this must become public property, and, if we do reach an agreement, the first specific has got to be a five-year blanket of silence."

The Minister nodded, and the talks went ahead. In early August, agreement in principle was reached. In the last week of that month, the whole thing was signed and sealed. The exchange would go ahead, under a five-year cloak of silence, on September 10. The Soviets would have made the exchange straightaway, but the Foreign Office, on advice from C, needed time to assemble their forces, to refit the secure guest suite at Warminster, and make decisions on exactly who should know the facts, and who should be kept in ignorance. They required a good fortnight, and were ready only twenty-four hours before the exchange.

TWENTY-THREE

1

Naldo Railton knew nothing of his impending exchange until it happened. On the contrary, his impression was that they were removing him from the hospital to stand trial in Moscow.

It began with a slow weaning off the sedation, around the middle of July. They had done this from time to time before, so he thought nothing of it. But now they went on, cutting down the sedation and making certain he did not go to pieces with withdrawal. Then they got him out of bed and allowed him to dress and sit in a chair. They had only done this for a few hours at a time before; now the hours turned into whole days. He was appalled at the way clothes hung on him, as though they had been bought from a mail order firm who had sent garments two sizes larger than ordered.

They kept the door locked and bolted on the outside, and after a few weeks he found he was able to walk quite well. On the morning of September 5—at least they told him that was the date—two young KGB officers came, with the doctor, and asked him if he was fit enough to travel. The pair of men were correct, neither polite nor authoritarian. They made it clear that they would abide by his decision, and doctor's advice, as to whether he was really well enough to endure what they said would be "Quite a long journey."

Naldo asked where they were taking him, and for what reason. Both men shook their heads and said these things were, as yet, operational matters. Their jobs, they intimated, would be at risk if they told him. In any case they were only taking him on the first leg of the trip. It all depended on his health.

The doctor examined him and said in his opinion he was fit. Even though, by this time, Naldo was convinced the show trial was about to start, and had probably been triggered by some political event, he could not shirk it. "I'll go with you," he said, and they were off within the hour.

They took him by car to a small airstrip, and it was only during this short ride that Naldo was able to confirm that he had been kept near Sochi. That night he was in a safe house in Moscow. They had landed after dark, and he could see little, for the rear compartment of the car had been blacked out with a special glass, but he knew it was Moscow, for the city, like many in the world, has its specific smell: a vague sourness in the air; just as Paris smells of Gauloise cigarettes, coffee, and garlic; and New York has a particular scent which, combined with the echoing noise of traffic, makes it easy to identify. Oddly, Naldo thought, London had become bland. He could recall days when they might have put him down blindfolded and he would recognize the capital city of his native country by its particular scent—soot, and something undefinable, but London's own. Since it had, rightly, become a smokeless zone, the odor of London had disappeared.

In the safe house, his two young guardians were replaced by half a dozen new men who offered him a change of clothes. "They will fit you better," the most senior officer told him, but Naldo refused. By now he was not so sure of the trial, and had become confused and tired. Part of his mind told him they were going to kill him when the moment was ripe. But, for the time being, another doctor came and checked him out. He was given vitamins and food, then told to rest. He wondered if he was paranoid, for he felt certain the food had been drugged. Within an hour of eating, he could hardly stand up: requiring only a bed and sleep.

When he woke it was day again, though he had no idea what day. They had removed the ill-fitting clothes so he was forced to dress in gray cords, a rollneck sweater, and a matching cord jacket. The labels, he noticed, had been removed, but he would put money on them having come from Marks & Spencer.

That evening the man he knew only as Jacob arrived, dressed as ever in civilian clothes. Was he ready for the final lap of the journey? Jacob asked. That depended on where they were going. Once more, Naldo became preoccupied with death. If they could shoot down Arnie, Spatukin, and Kati in the open, then he would be easy meat.

"We're going to Berlin." Jacob smiled.

"That the end of the line for me?"

Jacob shook his head. "Just the beginning, I think."

They made the journey by night and he saw the lights of Berlin below them, with the obscene snake of brilliance that was the Wall, blazing with its high-security illumination. The plainclothed KGB men formed a human wall around Naldo to get him off the airplane and into the waiting car, which drove at high speed to yet another safe house. He ate and slept again. In the morning, Jacob returned and said as they would be in the house for a couple of days, he would like to talk over certain things.

The questions were oddly standard—bearing in mind that he was a member of the British Secret Service. Had he been treated well? Had any of his views regarding the Soviet Union changed since he had lived there? What were his views on the United States? The CIA? What were his views on KGB?—"After all, you were treated as one of our own for a time." Jacob's eyes went stony, as if to say, "You know more than most people."

Naldo was still confused. He did not know why the questions were being asked. He had no idea whether this was still some kind of final statement, for they were quite capable of killing him and dumping his body in the West. It had been done before. It had been done to one of his own people. He answered the questions in the most ambivalent way he could, but Jacob merely pressed him for more detailed answers. In all, this interrogation went on until the night of September 9, though Naldo had no idea of time or date, for they kept the windows of his room covered with frames of thick black material. It reminded Naldo of wartime England and the blackout frames that went up at dusk throughout those long years of fighting.

At last (it was in reality around seven P.M. on September 9) Jacob said enough was enough. "We have a small banquet prepared in your honor."

"The condemned man ate a hearty breakfast," Naldo said somberly.

Jacob made a gesture with his hands, as though throwing away all responsibility. "You consider being returned to your own people as being condemned?"

"My own . . . ?" Later Naldo was to say he really did not believe it.

"Dawn tomorrow. In less than twelve hours. We're exchanging you for your cousin, Andrew."

They took him, in tight security and secrecy, to the eastern side of the Heerstrasse Checkpoint. Naldo sat in a car parked in the shadows and waited, thinking that, in all the spy fiction he had read the exchanges took place at Checkpoint Charlie. That was often true; he had, himself, brought in people via Charlie.

He could see the harsh sodium lighting around both sides of the checkpoint, and a distant glow as dawn approached to kill the street-lights of the West. As the sky turned to a pearl-like morning, an airplane, in the far distance, climbed away. Probably from Tempelhof.

Jacob walked back to the car and opened the door. "Come," he said, beckoning. "They are ready. Your cousin is with them, and we have all the people we need." They walked slowly towards the huts and the double sets of booms. As they neared the first boom, so a figure emerged from one of the checkpoint huts. He was tall, and wearing Western clothes, a dark overcoat with a rose in his buttonhole. His face seemed to have been lit by a lone spotlight: a touch theatrical.

"Who's that?" Naldo nodded in the direction of the lone man.

"Nobody in particular." Jacob did not even look at the figure. "He's a man we use sometimes. His name's Philip. But now there's something I wish you to do for me."

They had reached the first frontier boom, white with red rings, hinged poles placed one above the other and joined by a crisscross of heavy metal strips. From the far distance of his memory, Naldo thought of nursery teas and sugar tongs that reached out, in that same pattern of joined silver Xs. The place could easily have been a railway crossing. As the dawn began to take hold on the sky, Naldo shivered. They had not bothered with an overcoat. One of the soldiers came out of the small blockhouse from which the booms were operated. "Comrade Colonel General, they're ready. All is in order," he said in German.

"Colonel General?" Naldo raised an eyebrow.

"Give *Schnitzer* my good wishes," Jacob said. Naldo looked at him harder, as though seeing his face for the first time. He knew *Schnitzer* had been Big Herbie's crypto—*Blunderer*—when he had worked on both sides of the Wall. "Tell him I look forward to seeing him again soon. It will happen. Tell him Jacob Vascovsky says it will happen."

The first set of booms was raised and, some fifty yards away, a similar set came up on the other side, rising and juddering as they almost reached at right angles to the road. Naldo could just make out the group of figures under the lights.

"Go," said the soldier in the box. The second set rose.

Vascovsky tapped Naldo lightly on the shoulder. "Goodbye, until the next time, Comrade Railton." He laughed, then thrust something into Naldo's hand: an envelope; a stiff envelope. "Go now."

Naldo turned away and started to walk. He saw the other figure moving towards him and, slowly, he recognized him clearly as Andrew. His cousin had lost weight, but his shoulders were stooped and he walked stolidly, like a farm boy following the plow. Perhaps that was what he had been doing all these years, following the plow that was his conscience, his ideal, his life. The plow that was Communism.

As they passed, Andrew did not raise his head or make eye contact. Naldo saw there was no point in even opening his mouth, so he looked away. Seconds later he saw Max, the Warminster heavy, with three of his sidekicks closing in towards him.

"Stay in the center of our circle, Mr. Railton, sir." Max did his usual trick of speaking without moving his lips. "Keep close. They've taken out people before this, right here at the exchange. Good to have you back, sir."

There were three cars. He glimpsed Curry Shepherd standing by the lead car, and Herbie beckoning him to hurry.

"Nald. Oh, good you come back, Naldo. In get quick." And the bearlike arm went around his shoulders, almost pushing him into the car next to Gus Keene, who was smiling. Minutes later, they were off, traveling fast, one car in front and another behind, Naldo sitting between Herbie and Gus.

"You okay, Nald?" from Herbie.

"I will be. Bewildered. Bit confused. Just left a fellow who sent you a message."

"Oh?" Herbie leaned forward and the car seemed to creak.

Naldo told him about Jacob Vascovsky and the message to *Schnitzer.* He felt Herbie's muscles tense, the whole of the big man seemed to go rigid next to him. An age passed before he spoke, and then it was poetry of some kind—

> *"I am not going to the green clover!*
> *The garden of weapons*
> *Full of halberds*
> *Is where I am posted."*

"Come again, Herb?" Gus spoke at last.

"Ach, is only poem. Poem set to music by Gustav Mahler, Gus. Mahler is my saint, my conscience, and my hiding place. I ever tell you that, Gus?"

"Several times, Herbie. Let me have a word with Naldo. Got to tell him the order of march and all that." Then he reached out and grasped Naldo's hand. "Good to have you back. I fear I'm going to be a pain in your arse for a few weeks." He went on to say they were going straight to the RAF facility. There was an aircraft ready. "Fly us into Northolt," he said, and that brought back a whole wasp's nest of memories. It was in an ugly little house in Northolt that he had plotted with the then C; with Arnie and Caspar as well. Ages ago. Yesterday. Time did a loop then rolled off the top.

Gus talked on. They would go straight from Northolt to Warminster where Barbara was waiting. "She's longing to see you. What you got there? Parting gift?" Gus' hand stole the stiff envelope out of Naldo's grip. "Pretty pix by the look of them. Mind if I hang on to the pictures, Naldo? For the time being, eh? See if they're of any interest."

"I know what they are." Naldo turned his eyes onto Gus and nodded. "I know, and I don't want to look. I saw one of the set a few years ago, and I think they showed me one of the people involved before shoving me across their cursed border. Keep 'em, Gus. There might even be some of me, with a lady who's long dead as well."

"Okay. I'll have them somewhere safe." Keene went on to specifics. How they would live in the Warminster bunker for a while, and how he, and others, would, to use his language, "take a steady trip through your time abroad. Barbara can stay with you if you want it. You both have to talk about that . . . "

"We'll want it." Naldo snapped out. "I want to see the kids as well . . ."

"All grown up, Nald." Herbie chipped in. "Young Arthur's in the Foreign Office; Emma working in the publishing business. She is in purr—that right?" He looked at Gus.

"PR," said Gus. "Public Relations, looks after authors and the Press, goes with them when they're trying to sell their bloody books. PR, Herb."

Naldo smiled. "I have a few favors to ask of you, Gus. Important favors."

"So they'll wait until we get to Warminster, right, Naldo?"

It wasn't going to be all that simple, Naldo thought. Gus would be resistant; could not be hurried. But he had to be hurried, because Caspar's memory was slipping away with each minute and Naldo wanted to get his hands on the diaries that would blow their crazy notions to hell and gone.

They hung about at the RAF facility, and Naldo had the feeling that, perhaps, they were buggering about with time—making him wait; putting him off balance. Then he realized there was no way they would fly him back in daylight.

There was a P4 doctor waiting, and he gave Naldo a more thorough going-over than the Russians. He also asked very pertinent questions. "Do you know what they've had you on for the last few months?"— this after he had taken a urine test. Naldo did not know, but said it was some kind of sedative. The doctor's eyebrows rose, and he said that a new and strict regimen was needed. "You've been kept short of exercise, I think."

"I've been in bloody bed," Naldo told him.

They ate. Then ate again, and, at last, when it was almost dusk, they took off. He could not believe it when he saw London from the air, and a real evening paper left lying in the flight room where they waited for the car.

Three hours later they turned into the wide drive, through the security gates at Warminster. They drove to the far end of the compound and helped him out. "Down the stairs, and through the doors facing you," Gus said. "We'll give you an hour to get organized."

Barbara was waiting, standing in front of an imitation fireplace, for they had tried to give the guest suite a welcoming look.

"Naldo?" It was almost a question. He merely nodded. He recalled his father telling him of the time, at the end of the First World War, when, as a prisoner in some German *Schloss*, they had brought his cousin in and told them they were to be taken home. He had thought his cousin dead. James always said, "Only when I saw her did I know what that Biblical phrase meant—'they fell on each other's necks and wept.' "

Now, Naldo knew, and the pair of them just clung on to one another, sobbing, touching each other's wet faces, tracing their fingers over noses, chins, ears, like blind people making sure they would never forget how they looked.

"Love me a bit?" Barbara said, trying to smile through the hail that was her tears as she used their old familiar code.

"Big bit." It sounded false, childish, and sentimental, but, as Herbie would have said—"Who is doing the counting, Nald?"

"Marry me?" She did the asking, and did not take it for granted.

"Of course. As soon as they can get a priest."

"No. Christmas Eve. At Redhill. Start at our beginning."

He nodded, sight still blurred. Then Gus came down, with Herbie like a big bear out of control, knocking things over and riddling the conversation with trivia until Gus had to banish him.

"We'll start in the morning," Gus told them. "You don't have to be around, Barbara. In fact best if you're not. Come back each evening. Why not bring the children down tomorrow night?"

Before things got under way, on the following day, one of the Legal & General people came down with a sheaf of forms for Naldo's signature. "Annulment of your Russian marriage," he said.

"But she's dead. In Russia I'm a widower." Naldo frowned.

"Best to be on the safe side." The lawyer smiled a legal smile, and Naldo signed. A long time was to pass before the whole truth filtered through to him.

2

It was the old team, Gus said. Himself, his wife, Carole, and Martin Brook, the one they called the Fat Boy. "We've been on all this for eight years, Naldo," he said. "Just, for God's sake, tell us the truth and we'll get it finished with." He added that there would be others who had to be present.

"Damage control?" Naldo asked.

"Not really. They've already presumed that you told them all that mattered." Gus gave him an encouraging smile. "No, people like myself and the medics. We'll want some idea of how they do it. But let's get all the routine over with. You ready?"

Naldo settled himself and lighted the first cigarette he had smoked in years. "Shoot."

"Why, Naldo? Why, in heaven's name, did you go?"

"Revenge. Vengeance. The usual common or garden reasons."

"Vengeance for what?"

"For putting a great, splendid old man in the dirt."

"Caspar?"

"Who else, Gus?"

"How?"

"How what?"

"How could you wreak revenge for Caspar's misfortunes?"

"I did it. I killed the man who shat on the Yanks, on the country, and on Caspar."

"Who?"

"Oh, come on, Gus. You must have been comparing notes with the dear Cousins at Langley. Oleg Penkovsky, of course."

C had warned them. "He'll tell you he went to get Penkovsky, who's been dead these nine years. You might even think about believing him. I've had sight of some corroboration, but you're getting nothing from me until you've talked to Naldo. Let him spill the lot to you."

Now, in the air-conditioned room below the ground that was part of Warminster's guest suite, Gus said, "Naldo, Oleg Penkovsky was tried and shot in the spring of 1963. He's dead."

"He is now." Naldo smiled. It was the smile of a man who knew the truth.

"You're telling me that you went into the Soviet Union, with Arnie Farthing, to kill a man who's already dead?"

"Sit back, Gus, and let me tell you a tale." He smiled again and quoted Shakespeare, remembering that Arnold had quoted the same passage at him, in the Berlin green house, though Arnie had taken liberties—

> "For God's sake, let us sit upon the ground,
> And tell sad stories of the death of kings—
> How some have been deposed; some slain in war;
> Some haunted by the ghosts they have deposed;
> Some poisoned by their wives; some sleeping killed;
> All murdered . . . "

Then Naldo Railton talked. They sent for coffee and sandwiches, and he talked on. He was still talking when it was time to end the day's session. He told of Caspar's funeral; of the meeting in Berlin; of everything that happened, leaving out only Caspar's diaries and the document the old man had called *Bogeyman,* for that contained the trap; the way to whoever it was who had really sold the Service and Country for less than thirty pieces of silver. By the time they left, and his children had come happily into the room, Naldo had got as far as the night he went out, stood face to face with Penkovsky, and killed him, only to find his three companions dead when he walked from the dacha.

"It can't be true, but I believe him," Carole said in Gus' office in the main house.

"Me too," from Martin, who had lost weight in the last year but was still known to them as the Fat Boy.

"It *can* be true, and I have to find out." Gus picked up the telephone and put through a call directly to the shop. He caught C as he was leaving the office.

"I have to go now," Gus told them. "Should be back late tonight." He shot a severe look at Martin Brook. "I leave you to look after my wife while I'm gone, and, if you cuckold me, I'll know."

Carole threw a hefty pillow at him.

"It's the death of Arnold I don't follow," Brook said as they had a drink before dinner. "We know he's still around, yet Naldo believes he saw him dead. There's no doubt there."

"It's the one thing that concerns me." Carole fished a piece of lemon from her gin and tonic. "If he swears to Arnold being shot to pieces, could they have taken him for a ride about Penkovsky?"

"Let's see what the Guv'nor brings back from the great white chief. Either Naldo's off his chump or it's true . . ."

"Or Naldo's lying in his teeth, and *we* never believed Caspar's diary and the Credit findings, so he's either mad or honest."

Gus returned at three in the morning. Carole muttered in her sleep and then half woke. "Is he mad or true?" she mumbled, and Gus knew exactly what she meant. "He's true. Now go to sleep. Tomorrow all will be there, laid in front of you with only one very vital piece missing."

"Good. You haven't got a vital piece missing, have you, my darling?"

"Not when I last looked." But she was off into her dreams and did not hear him.

3

Naldo was in fine form when they gathered on the next day. His children had grown from adolescence to adulthood, and he was amazed at their strength of character. He knew he must have looked as though he could not believe them as they told him of their lives in the present, but he was proud.

They took the news of the remarriage almost as a foregone conclusion, neither Arthur nor Emma even asked what their father had been up to, and he did not have to make a speech about keeping his return a secret, for they already knew, like the rest of the family.

Arthur and Emma had stayed the night, in the nearby garrison town, and Barbara left early to go back to London with them. She would do some shopping and be back by the time the day's work was done.

"Right, Naldo," Gus began. "We want you to go over the murder of Oleg Penkovsky, and the deaths of Arnie, Spatukin, and Kati again. Everything. All the tiny details. Don't spare our stomachs."

It took a long while, for Gus interrupted a great number of times, asking him to repeat the actual moment of Penkovsky's death again and again—"He spoke to you? You're certain of that? Now, Naldo, tell us again. Tell us exactly what happened when the bullets hit. Make us live it with you."

They then passed to the three deaths outside the dacha. Again, Gus almost morbid about detail. "You saw bullets hit?"

"Yes. I saw Arnold jerked off his feet."

"You saw blood, but—think, Naldo—did you actually see the kind of thing you witnessed in the dacha? Did you see flesh being ripped apart?"

"Not exactly, no."

"Ah."

Then, just before Barbara returned, Gus told him that Arnold Farthing was still alive and in Russia. He did not believe it, so Gus took out a folder of photographs. They were of Arnie and also Spatukin. All were taken with some date visible—on a newspaper, a big digital clock on a Russian railway station.

Naldo went white, then became angry.

"It's okay, Naldo. You killed Penkovsky. That's for certain. We believe you. What is difficult is the game Arnie's been playing. We have evidence that he's still operating on behalf of the United States. He *used* you as—they say—collateral."

The anger died. "If that's all, it's okay by me. I've done that much for Caspar. What more can I do? I have things that should be brought in front of the so-called Credit Committee, and I'd like to do it now."

"Then you'll have to be patient, Nald. Our instructions are to complete a full investigation. You have KGB operational stuff that could be like hen's teeth."

"Later. Please." Naldo was almost pleading. "Look, Gus. I've never done anything to discredit this Service. Others have, and I want at least one of them brought down. I also want to finish the job I began—to clear Caspar's name, okay?"

"See what I can do." From the tone of Gus Keene's voice, there was little he could do as yet. "You should make application to C now, this minute, to appear before the Credit Committee as soon as possible."

"Let's get on with it, then."

On the following day, Keene's fears were confirmed. Naldo was refused permission to appear before the Committee until the interrogation unit were satisfied their work was complete.

Yet, unknown to Naldo, C had instructed Keene to get the bulk of the interrogation over with speed. At the same time he called in Willis Maitland-Wood, telling him to stand by to resurrect his beloved committee.

"Naldo going to do a whitewash?" BMW all but sneered.

"I think," C told him, "Naldo might just give you the real truth."

Keene and his team worked solidly for the next three weeks. Specialists came in to ask their own pertinent questions; doctors spent four days discussing the effects of Naldo's KGB interrogation under drugs; Covert and Counterintelligence people arrived at all hours and fired friendly questions, then left, happy with their answers.

Each night, Barbara was there, and, together, they planned their future. Naldo constantly spoke of "going private." In plain talk, retiring.

One morning towards the end of October, Gus came down and said they were finished. "Now you can set the date for your evidence before the committee," he told Naldo. "When?"

"Will you drive me to Slough today, Gus?" Naldo asked.

"If I must."

"If you do, I'll start giving them evidence at nine tomorrow morning."

"You're on."

That night, having gone to collect the papers, under the name of Bernard Carpenter, Naldo sat down and went through the material he had last seen in the Hôtel Victoria Jungfrau at Interlaken. Gus allowed him full use of the big photocopier, and he took three hours running off complete copies of both diaries and the covering letter. *Bogeyman*, the document which spelled out the hidden entrapment which Caspar had embedded, was not copied. On the following morning he left with all of it except the *Bogeyman* papers. Those, he considered, would be used to do the biggest, and most unpleasant burn of his career.

As he drove to London, with Gus at the wheel and Max as a personal protector, Naldo was very quiet. Gus put it down to nerves. After all, the man had waited a long time for this moment. Now it was here, he would feel apprehensive. Who would not?

In reality, Naldo was thinking about childhood. He had a long memory, and could recall those early days when he lived with his mother and sister, in the Kensington house to which he hoped to return. Those were days without his father, for it was during the First World War, when James was holed up, under arrest, and in fear of being shot as a spy in Germany.

He remembered the day his mother had opened the bedroom door singing and telling them that Daddy was coming home. It was much later that he learned she had said it on instinct, yet all her instincts were accurate. His mother was uncanny, and her rapport with his father, James, had always been extraordinary.

He could see, quite clearly, whole excerpts from his life, running like film clips—outtakes—in his head. First days at school; holidays between the wars, when they went all over Europe together. On the first day of the summer holiday, as he recalled it, James would pick him up from school and say, "Tomorrow we're off, Naldo." He always took his entire quota of leave during the summer holidays—that was, apart from one week, saved for the riotous Redhill Christmases.

They went without any known plan. The train to Dover, and then the boat to Calais and a train to Paris. From there they searched out places all over Europe. His father could speak enough of every tongue to get them by. There were plots and plans as they moved south, and then into Italy and Switzerland. Naldo recalled it all during that drive to London.

The pensions and hotels, the little restaurants where such a fuss was made of them. The Swiss lakes and swimming as the ferries chugged to and fro; Italy—he remembered Milan, and being shown the cathedral, with the mummified body of St. Charles Borromeo in the crypt; Rome, and having pictures taken with a box Brownie on the Spanish Steps; Berlin, when they sat at cafés along the Kurfürstendamm and sipped coffee; mountain country, near the Soviet border; his first ever glass of champagne in Paris.

Lights, glitter, strange voices, odd smells, coffee, foreign cigarettes; the newspapers, and everywhere they went there were friends. Men and women who would suddenly appear, as if out of nowhere, and embrace his father, and gravely shake his mother's hand. He always thought, as a growing boy that, somehow, this was the wrong way round. And, later, he realized these people were probably more than just old friends. They were his father's agents. Later still, he saw some of their photographs in old files in the shop's registry.

With a touch of sadness he remembered them meeting with Uncle Caspar, he thought it was on the Channel coast, Dieppe, or Calais. They had all gone to a café to eat eggs and chips, and an itinerant clown came in dressed as Charlie Chaplin.

Caspar and his father had got a little drunk. He could hear Cas now. "We have heard the chimes at midnight. Oh, what days we've seen," quoting and misquoting Shakespeare and punching his father's arm. "What days we've seen."

When they reached the shop, Naldo could have wept for the loving wonderful memories. All gone. Like the golden lads and lasses. All turned to dust.

"They're waiting for you, Nald." Gus brought him out of the reverie.

"Right." Naldo took a deep breath. "Okay, Gus, let's put this calumny to rest once and for all."

TWENTY-FOUR

1

They looked at him as though he had come from another planet which, he thought, was, in a way, true. Their eyes were hard, like colored pebbles, and their faces blank, like a jury about to show no mercy.

Nobody could doubt the hostility that came from the re-formed Credit Committee. They were quite prepared to reject the fact that black was black and white was white. Big Herb would have called them "flat-earthers."

Willis Maitland-Wood glared from the head of the long table; Tubby Fincher tilted his skull-like head, his eyes failing to meet those of Naldo. The charming, well-groomed David Barnard smoothed a hand over his silky hair; Indigo Belper fiddled with his watch chain; Desmond Elms, of the Soviet Desk, tried to outstare Naldo: his eyes said he had heard and seen it all before, and he would not be fooled; of them all, Arden Elder, Gus Keene's second in command from Warminster, appeared to be interested; while the usually pert and pretty Beryl Williamson's mouth was set, and there were patches of color high on her cheekbones.

Naldo, with Gus Keene's assistance, had carried in the large parcels of papers and set them on a table just inside the door. Now he stood, facing down the table so that he looked towards the chairman, BMW.

"This is going to be short, and, for me, very sweet." There was no malice in his voice. "Might I ask, sir, if this is the whole of the Credit Committee, responsible for passing internal judgment on my uncle, Sir Caspar Railton?"

"Yes. Of course, yes." BMW's voice was as steely as his eyes.

"I have brought further documents, authenticated by a solicitor of high reputation, Mr. Leo Morris. I do not blame you for coming to the conclusion you did, with the evidence at your disposal . . . "

362

Indigo Belper made a "ptcha" kind of noise, as though he was already dismissing what Naldo had said.

"However," pause counting three. "However, you did *not* have all the documents available. That was, I know, Sir Caspar's intention. He wished to set a small trap. Before anyone can deal with this device—which must eventually be defused—I ask you to examine what I am now going to place before you. C has already seen the originals. Each of you will get copies, apart from Mr. Maitland-Wood, who will also get the originals.

"Caspar Railton's denunciation, by this committee, is understandable. You had copies of one diary, covering those years during the nineteen-thirties when Sir Caspar was living out of the discipline of the Service. I fear the diary you read is a fake . . . "

"Absolute nonsense . . . !" Belper began.

Naldo continued to speak, using the actor's trick of dropping his voice, hands by his sides, using no gestures, never once stooping to histrionics which could later return and haunt him. "A fake," he repeated. "For Caspar *did* see everyone he claims to have seen in that diary; his movements *were* the movements he made. Meetings; journeys; conversations. They all took place. But he kept two diaries. One a fake, intended to mislead and, possibly, condemn him. The other, the true diary, his own reality, will show that all the events so neatly itemized in Diary One, the fake, take on a new, and significant meaning in the true diary—Diary Two."

He went on to suggest that they should subject the originals to stringent forensic tests; to get every piece of expert advice on paper-dating and machines used for typing. "You're going to need it," he told them, hinting that they would almost certainly find the true, and original, diary was written while the events were happening in the 1930s, and typed from notes made in the field.

"My Uncle Caspar had a sense of humor." He did not smile or allow his manner to show frivolity. "He was also possessed with a great sense of honor to the Service, together with an almost overpowering love of country and the monarchy. He grew up with these attributes, which, as we all know to our cost, are not much in vogue, here in Britain, these days."

He went on to explain that the sense of humor was displayed in the diary they had already examined: the fake diary; the diary that was written in the early 1960s, almost thirty years after the events; written when Caspar knew his time was running out.

"I trust you're going to discover that Caspar's devotion to his country went as far as attempting to penetrate the Soviet intelligence services. By the time the 1939–'45 conflict broke out, he had already obtained the blueprint for what was then Stalin's plan for all Europe." He paused again, as his eyes roamed the room, and, in the back of his head, he thought of the real treason. Lowering his voice again, he continued, "In more subtle ways, that is probably still the Soviet plan. I leave you to judge."

Then Naldo put the boot in. "There are people still close to the Service, still living, who helped pour water on Caspar's private secret work. Certainly the truth, bought by my uncle and paid for with his reputation, was never believed. So, his little joke was to leave spurious evidence. He can smile happily now, because I am revealing his practical joke." Naldo smiled at them, each in turn, as though inviting them to share the jest of dead Caspar.

"I hope that, when you have reached your final conclusions, based on the true facts, I shall be informed. I shall also be out of the Service by then. I am now going to hand out the documents, then leave you in peace while I tender my own resignation to C."

He passed down the table, placing a photostated bundle in front of each member of the committee. Every pile of papers contained both diaries and the first covering letter in which Caspar had given his detailed instructions, and the résumé of what he had done. As he went, Naldo thought of The Wind in the Willows, and the moment where the Rat makes piles of accoutrements, in readiness for the attack on the Wild Wooders in Toad Hall. 'Here's-a-belt-for-the-Rat, here's-a-belt-for-the-Toad, here's-a-belt-for-the-Badger, here's-a-belt-for-the-Mole!'' BMW was classed as the Rat; but who was the Mole?

At last, he placed the copies in front of Maitland-Wood, and added to them the original true diaries. In silence he walked to the door. The air somehow felt cleaner on the other side.

2

C reminded Naldo Railton of the deal that had been done with the Soviets. No releases to the Press; no public affirmation of any kind regarding the exchange of Andrew for a matter of five years. "I feel it should probably be longer," he said. "However, that will depend on the Soviets—whether they wish to make capital out of it or not."

He was also clear about what he called the "limitations of your release from the Secret Intelligence Service." Gus Keene had to give him a clean bill of health; and, once gone, Naldo would remain under the disciplines which are normal to the intelligence and security services: namely, that he should never disclose anything he had seen, learned about or taken part in while a member of the Service.

"You can take all that as read, sir. There is one request—for old time's sake; not for anything devious."

"Well?" The CSS had met with too many requests termed not to be devious. His mind hovered on the poisoned chalice of suspicion.

"A stroll down memory lane, sir."

"Registry?"

Naldo nodded. "Just a gentle tour down all my days. Mine, my Uncle Caspar's, my father's even."

C coughed. "Take you one thousand and one nights."

"Week, sir. Ten days tops."

C gave a jerk of his head. "No notes. Search on going in and coming out. No current files. Nothing running now. Nothing Cosmic. All right for you?"

"Generous, sir. Thank you."

With these provisos agreed, the Chief asked, "What shall you do, Donald?" He hated the diminutive used by everybody, including himself.

"There's some family money. My pension'll be forfeit, I know. But, between us, Barbara and I should have plenty. I shall probably leave this septic island and live in the United States."

C did not approve of the Shakespearean misquote, and glared Naldo out of his office. Gus drove him back to Warminster, said he would make arrangements to see him, maybe once or twice a week, "To finish the debrief." Apart from that, as long as they kept their heads down, there was no reason why they should not return to the house off Kensington Gore.

"Before we get back to what you charmingly call the debrief, Gus . . . ?"

"Yes?" Gus did not snap back, but some sense told Naldo there were suspicions lurking around in the Inquisitor's mind.

"Just a couple of things. Family matters. Real family matters. My family."

"Mmmm?" Again the sound was edged with caution.

"You ever break my revolting little cousin, Alexander?"

Keene sighed, and admitted failure. "His prints were all over that house," he said. "But he gave no explanation. Swore he hadn't been near." Then, after a long pause, "You know they're taking him back?"

"Jesus, what's it coming to, Gus? He's about as reliable as a whore in a monastery."

"The positive vetting cleared him."

"You cleared him?"

"I pointed out that no satisfactory answers had been given regarding the Eccleston Square house."

"And what did the vetting committee say to that?"

"Irrelevant. It was a Railton property; he had every right to go in, and to remain silent about it. I pointed out the devious nature of the deed. They went on saying it was a reasonable risk. Your cousin's very good at his job. They need men like him."

"In spite of *his* brother's treason? Not to mention the findings of the Credit Committee."

"No, probably because of it. Their argument is that Andrew's folly more or less cleared up everything else."

"They didn't take the view that my family's history is eaten through with maggots? One rotten apple? That kind of stuff?"

"Didn't even touch on it. Anyway, it's not your business now, Naldo. In a week or two you'll have no need-to-know. You'll be out."

There was a long pause, during which Gus negotiated a pair of narrow S-bends. They were returning by the scenic route, and England was looking at its best. Naldo loved the autumn, the trees turning to the gold and browns of the year's death. Smoke drifted from fields and gardens. A time of melancholy, and a time of hope. In autumn, Naldo thought, the death of the year was signaled by great beauty, hinting at rebirth.

"Mrs. Ross?" he queried.

"What about the unpleasant Mrs. Ross?"

Was Gus suddenly on his guard again?

"I've met Mrs. Ross in another life, haven't I, Gus?"

"I wouldn't know. Have you?"

"I think so. I met her several times in my youth. When she was Alice Pritchard. I was a growing boy, Gus. Parents often think children don't know their special secrets. I don't think my mother ever knew about Alice Pritchard, but she was young and pretty. Much younger than my father. She worked in the shop then, didn't she?"

"Yes."

"It was hinted at during the trial."

"Could've made nasty headlines."

"But it didn't."

So, a deal was struck, Naldo thought. Back across the years he saw himself watching his father fondle Alice Pritchard's hand for a second. He was being taken to the theater in the school holidays, and was to meet the Old Man—as he always called him—outside one of the bland government buildings which housed some department of the secret trade. James had told him to wait outside for him, and he saw the looks, the fondling of the hand, and a final, loving caress, as his father touched her shoulder.

"Best my mother never finds out." Naldo seemed to be giving Gus a warning.

That night, while Naldo was dining with Barbara, Gus gathered his special cabal around him: Carole, his wife, and Martin Brook. "He's resigning, but still into a personal vendetta," Gus told them. "It's family business; but it's our kind of *family* as well. We know there's at least one more high-powered source. I think it might well be that Naldo'll lead us there. I don't want round-the-clock watchers on him, because he'd spot them at two miles. In this we have to be discreet, so let him take us there very gently." Carole was instructed to follow up on what Gus was certain would be a paper chase through Registry. "Just see what files he pulls and how he cross-indexes them. Use someone he doesn't know. Plonk your own mole into Registry, doing research for some classified pamphlet, eh?"

"A doddle." Carole nodded. "I've got just the girl to take care of that."

For the time being Naldo and Barbara remained in the guest suite at Warminster with Naldo slipping away for a couple of days at a time to the Registry, where he collected names and cross-indexes, shuffled through red-flagged files and old cases. He read for ten hours at a stretch sometimes, flipping from file to file and back again. As agreed, he made no notes while doing the work. But, in the evening, back at Warminster he copied things into a little cheap notebook, for he always returned with his head stuffed full of solid fact—names, cities, old operations. But mainly names that came rising from very old files. And so he prepared for his final days within the world of secrets, which also harbored more obvious facts, together with a disillusionment that seemed so heavy that he thought his bones might break with the weariness of it.

They left the confines of Warminster at the end of October, and, on the night of their return, went to dine with his parents, James and Margaret Mary, at the pleasant town house in King Street, a family property that had once belonged to old Caspar's own father. There were no other guests, but the elderly couple had learned to manage by themselves in spite of encroaching age. Margaret Mary had prepared a quite lavish dinner, and Naldo expressed surprise at the smoked salmon mousse, rack of lamb, and the almost sickly, but delicious, pudding that had been a childhood favorite—a lime jelly studded with banana slices and filled with double cream, whipped with bananas.

"What else have I to do, my dear? Anyway, we seem to entertain more than ever these days." His mother's smile removed any signs of her years. To Naldo her face was that of the woman who had so cared for him as a child. Again, his mind went back to the days of his youth and childhood. He saw her at the piano, playing with immense style and effortlessness, so that, in the present, the sounds became jumbled in his head, a whole montage of Brahms, Chopin, Liszt, and other fashionable composers, clashed with popular songs of the day: "Keep the Home Fires Burning"; "If You Were the Only Girl in the World"; and a hundred more that he and his now religious sister had frolicked to as tiny children.

"I can tell you that growing old's not the greatest thing about life." His mother was still speaking. "But you have to make the best of it. We have and we do."

"Well, neither of you look or behave like elderly people, that's for sure," Barbara said. She meant it, for James could be taken for a man in his late sixties instead of early eighties: still a fine, handsome man, alert and amusing in conversation. When they arrived he had told them of his first flight in Concorde, during the spring. He spoke with the excitement of a young man. Margaret Mary had been with him, of course, but James' passion had always been aircraft. After all, he had met Dick Railton-Farthing as a young man and persuaded him into letting him fly an early Maurice Farman airplane, a day which had ended in near disaster, but also in future pleasure. It was Dick who had taught the young James to fly, and James' passion had prophesied what would eventually happen, for he had informed the very first Chief of Service that future intelligence operations would rely on flying machines. In his life, James Railton had witnessed the whole panorama, from the wood and string planes before the 1914–'18 war, to the satellites that were now starting to lift intelligence from the air. He went on for a good while about the Concorde flight before turning to his wife and saying lamely, "You enjoyed it as well, dear, didn't you?"

She gave a twinkling smile, and said he knew very well that she loathed flying, just as much as he adored it.

"So what was Russia really like, Nald?" his father asked over the dinner table.

"Sour, boring, paranoid, but I wouldn't have missed it for anything."

"You're an odd one. I'd have given my right arm to have avoided my own incarceration during the first war."

Naldo smiled. "But you didn't get a chance to do something quite special."

"Oh? Tell us. What . . . ?" But Naldo shut him off with a wink and a quick shake of the head. It did not stop James from returning to the question when the ladies went into the drawing room.

"Russia, now we're alone?" James looked clear-eyed at his son. "Someone told me you actually worked in Dzerzhinsky Square. True?"

"Who told you that?"

James gave a sly smile. "They all come and see me, old son." The charm, ever present, twinkled in his eyes like beacons. "I might have retired, but I keep abreast of things."

"Sorry, Pa. No deal. I don't talk about it and I won't talk about it."

"But it's family."

"That's why I won't talk, Pa. You *know* why I'll keep quiet. It's in the contract."

"My contract as well." His father lit a cigar and passed the brandy across the table.

"A good, sound contract." Naldo poured himself a drink.

"What's this I hear about that damned Credit Committee opening their bloody investigation again?"

"I wouldn't know. All I'll tell you is that I think Caspar's going to be cleared."

"That all came out of the job I passed on to you, didn't it?" James was in a pressing mood. "Everything stemmed from that."

"I did as you were instructed, Pa. It was a job left for you. I did it. It's over now. You surely never believed all that rubbish about Caspar?"

"Not for a moment. But I was out of the picture."

"And out of the frame," his son wanted to say. In one of those revelations that seemed of late to flash without warning through his mind, he saw the whole scene of their conversation in the Reform Club, when James had first talked of Caspar's wishes, so long ago now. He also saw behind the words and actions of that evening, and wondered what would have happened had James carried out Caspar's wishes. Another thought trailed through his head, ragged as barbed wire. He saw the salutation at the beginning of that letter, and realized how someone had already tampered with it. Would the forensic boys detect *that,* he wondered?

Naldo looked his father full in the face, then allowed his eyes to focus on the wall behind him. Directly over James' left shoulder was a painting of Berlin between the wars. The Unter den Linden in spring with the blossom making the trees look as though they were shimmering in the warmth of the afternoon sun. "Remember when we were last there together?" He nodded towards the picture.

"Around thirty-eight, or was it thirty-seven?" James shifted in his chair to look back at the painting. "I picked that up for a song at the end of the war."

"It was 1936 to be exact." Naldo relaxed, poured brandy for himself and waited, expecting a flood of memories to come from his father.

"Changed, hasn't it?" was all the old man said.

"I guess it has, but I don't really know. That's in the East now. I haven't been in the Unter den Linden since soon after the war, when we were chasing about over there. I've often seen it from the other side of the Brandenburg Gate, but never walked down it. Have you, Pa?"

His father seemed lost in thought, and replied as though he had not heard the last question, his fingers curling around the bowl of the brandy glass. "Thirty-six, yes. Yes, you're right."

"On our last night there together, you met a guy you always saw in Berlin. Hans Schnaffel. Remember Hans?" Naldo seemed to be humoring him.

"Hans, yes. Yes, I remember him. Young. About your age—a little older—at the time."

"You saw him every time we went to Berlin."

"Good times, those." James drew on his cigar. "Naldo, you remember that time when we got into terrible trouble with your mother, in Poitiers?"

"I remember we always stopped in Poitiers, on our journeys back to Paris. We used to eat in the same little restaurant. We stopped only for dinner, before catching the next train to Paris, and a fellow called . . . ? Oh, what was his name . . . ?"

"No, I'm talking about the bust-up we had with your mother, Naldo. On the train we would always plan our menu, what we would eat at the St. Hilaire . . ."

That was it, Naldo thought. He could even name the little restaurant. Could he not name the man?

". . . We had eaten a very large lunch, on the train as I recall it. But the two of us said we wanted to start with that magnificent soup they served there, thick and full of vegetables. We always ate the pork chops. Chops the size of plates . . ."

"Whenever we were there," Naldo interjected, "every time we broke for dinner there, a fellow came in, was it Jean something?"

"Jean Brissault." James supplied it as though throwing the name away. "I don't think Jean came in *every* time we stopped there. It's your memory, Naldo. From childhood we always remember long hot summers and cold snowbound winters. The Christmases of our child-hood are always white. The memory is selective. But, this time, do you recall, your mother put a veto on the soup." He began to laugh. "She said we'd never finish the pork chops if we had the soup. We stuck to our guns, and had the soup, and your mother was right. We smug-gled most of the chops out in our handkerchiefs. Oh, my, but your mother was cross."

Naldo had a vague memory of the incident. What he had plainly fixed in his mind was the man called Jean Brissault. "I wonder what-ever happened to Jean?" He seemed to muse aloud.

"Long gone, I should imagine. Now *he* was much older than you, almost my age. He'll be in his box by now, Naldo."

"And Lena Legarto, in Milan?"

"Who?"

"Lena. Pretty, dark girl. Now she *was* about my age, because I fancied her something rotten as a teenager. But she only had eyes for you, Pa. Every time we went to Milan we used to bump into her in that huge arcade near the Duomo. I used to think that she sought you out. Lena Legarto."

James shook his head. "No. Your memory's better than mine, Naldo. But you would remember a pretty girl from years back. Come, let's ask your mother."

They went through into the small room they insisted on calling the drawing room. It was filled with James' memories: framed photographs of him as a young man, standing in front of fragile flying machines with Dick; one of him soon after the war with Mansfield-Cumming, the first CSS. "Look at old C," he would say. "Old fraud that he was. After he lost his leg in that car accident they put it about that he had cut the trapped leg away with a penknife to get to his dying son. Not so, but it added to the mystique, the legend. Old Caspar told me the story first, and I believed it for a long time."

There were other things, a framed coded cable from the second war;

medals that really should not have been on display, for they were awarded in secret. The Americans called them jockstrap medals. A letter from Churchill. A photograph of the famous Yalta conference showing Churchill, Stalin, and Roosevelt. On the sidelines, James stood with other men in civilian clothes, his face partly obscured by shadow, as though he was deliberately trying to hide his features.

"Your son has a prodigious memory, my dear." James threw a crisp clean smile in the direction of his wife. "Says we always ran into some chit of a girl when we passed through Milan. Name of . . . What did you say, Naldo?"

"Lena." He sounded bored now. "Lena Legarto. You always stopped to talk with her, Pa. I used to walk on with Ma, feeling very jealous."

Margaret Mary shook her head slowly, brow creased. "I can't recall it, or the girl. We didn't go to Milan that often, did we?" It was as though she was closing the topic of conversation.

They discussed trivia for an hour or so, James constantly pretending to be in the sulks with Naldo because his son would not talk about Russia.

Back home, Naldo asked how Barbara had felt about them. "Amazing," she replied. "You'd never think they were in their eighties. So bloody agile, physically and mentally. I feel decrepit next to them."

During the first week in November, visiting Gus at Warminster, Naldo heard the Credit Committee had reversed their decision. Caspar was completely exonerated. The one thing Naldo could never forgive was the fact that no official statement was made, and there was no hint of apology. He asked Gus to get the original documents back for him. "They are family papers, after all, and valuable," he told the Grand Inquisitor.

A week later, the papers arrived at the Kensington Gore house by special messenger. Naldo took the first page from the letter of instructions and carried it out to Maida Vale, to a stooped old man called Hammerstein. His friends called him Oscar, though he admitted no kinship to the librettist. Closer friends knew him as "Handy." Handy Hammerstein had spent various segments of his life in jail, but people like Naldo accepted him for what he was: one of the world's greatest forgers.

"Naldo, come in, come in, why I not seen you so long? Come." The old forger was thinner than Tubby Fincher, and his stoop, caused by long hours of extraordinary penmanship, often in bad light, made him look like a walking question mark. His home was small but neat and clean. "Clean as a nun's knickers," the old man would say with a dry laugh. His granddaughter lived with him, looked after the house, cooked and slaved for him. She had lost her husband in warfare somewhere in the Middle East, and had taken a vow of chastity, determined to tend her grandfather to the grave.

Naldo was always very formal with "Handy," who, in his time, had done excellent pieces of work for the Service, between his letters from Napoleon to Josephine, and many other ladies; scribbled notes from Lord Nelson; and beautifully penned memos from Disraeli. This work had earned him a fortune at Sotheby's and Christie's.

The grandchild, a woman in her middle thirties, brought them tea and sweet biscuits, moving silently and clucking over an imagined speck of dust on the mantel.

"Naldo, is good to see you. What you want, eh? A certificate for some painting or what?" He gave his dry laugh again, winked, and laid a finger alongside his nose. Hammerstein had built his own legend with gestures and mannerisms, rather as Big Herbie had built his in malapropisms and a general immolation of the English language.

Naldo opened his briefcase and drew out the single sheet of typewritten paper, covered in clear plastic. He handed it to the forger whose expertise he would back against a dozen forensic document specialists any day. "Handy, I want to know if any of that first line could have been added at a later date. It looks okay to me, but there *is* room, and I need to know."

Hammerstein took the paper to his table, set in the bay of a window, and pulled an angled, lighted magnifying glass over it. A few seconds later he gave a little cry, which could be taken as "Eureka," or a howl of anguish. "You need the truth on this, Naldo. Truth given without prejudice?"

"Nothing matters but the truth, Handy."

"Is mine." The old man turned. "Is my work. I do this, Naldo. You set me up, huh?"

"No, it's okay. I'll pay you a fee. All I need to know is who asked you to do it."

"Cost you, Naldo."

"So it costs me. Who?"

Hammerstein told him, and Naldo should not have been surprised; but, like a man waiting over a long time to hear of a death, he was shocked. However well-prepared you are, death always comes as a huge blow to the heart.

"Nobody make trouble, Nald, eh?"

"Don't give it another thought." He had come with a large amount of cash on him. Naldo had never in his life paid Handy by check. In his eyes that was good tradecraft. When he got home he sat down alone and wept.

3

On the first Thursday of December, Naldo woke feeling deeply depressed. Barbara, once more attuned to his moods, asked if he was unwell.

"Depressed for some stupid reason." Naldo's brow creased. There were many reasons for him to feel depression, but not as leaden and heavy as this. "Don't know why." He kissed her, like a child wanting affection from a mother.

"You really don't know why?" Barbara cradled him in her arms. "Look at the date, my darling," and it came to him—it was the anniversary of Caspar's death. Eight years ago the old man had gone out like a light, and his nephew still mourned him.

"You loved Caspar more than any of us," Barbara said in an almost matter-of-fact way.

"I know. I'm sorry. It's inexplicable."

"It's very understandable. The children know, and so do I. You've nothing to apologize for. Men sometimes have relationships with other men that are more binding than with wives, children—anybody. I mean straight relationships, of course. There was nothing more binding and close than your attachment to Caspar. You loved him, Nald. I sometimes think you loved him more than Phoebe did, which is saying a great deal."

Naldo planned to drive them both to Redhill that day. "Drop in unexpectedly. It's the kind of thing Sara and Dick would like," he said.

But, as they made preparations, the telephone rang. It was Willis Maitland-Wood and he sounded on top of the world. "The Chief's compliments," he said. "Would you step over to his office?"

"Don't you mean could I step over?" They had long since removed the scrambling devices, and BMW or C had no true jurisdiction over his life, but he knew instinctively this was important.

"It's in your interest, Naldo. Soon as you can make it. They'll give you a special pass."

They were all gathered together in C's office: BMW, Tubby Fincher, and, of all people, cousin Alexander, who looked more like a jockey than ever. Like many tall men, Naldo did not take to other members of his sex who were short of stature: particularly one of his own family, for the males were normally very long boned.

Sitting close to C's desk was a distinguished-looking man whose appearance screamed the word lawyer. He wore the old-fashioned uniform of the profession: striped trousers and a black jacket. His face was round but very smooth, as though he shaved twice daily, and his silver hair was swept back, thick and well-groomed. He gazed at Naldo through thick spectacles set into gold wire frames, and he rose as they were introduced by C.

"Donald Railton: Mr. Leo Morris, your late Uncle Caspar's solicitor."

The handshake was, Naldo noted, very firm.

C spoke again as Morris lowered himself back into his chair. "You're not going to like this, I fear. Mr. Morris should give you the facts first."

Leo Morris' voice was calm, controlled, and gentle. "As you know," he began, "I acted for your late uncle, who was, to say the least, slightly eccentric in his habits."

Naldo nodded, and waited for the blow he knew would come as Morris continued. "On the day after Sir Caspar's death, I received a letter from him. It had, I think, been posted on the very day he died, so my receiving it the day after his death was a minor miracle." The smile was pleasant, as though he knew the small joke was minute. "There was a letter inside a long manila envelope, marked for myself, personal and private, and another letter, which you will see in a moment."

Naldo felt that BMW was smiling as though in victory. "Sir Caspar instructed me to keep the enclosed letter safe, and under seal, until the eighth anniversary of his death." Morris looked straight at Naldo. He was telling the same story twice. "On that anniversary, he instructed me to bring the sealed letter and place it personally into the hands of the CSS, who would almost certainly understand its contents. I understand your father should also be present, but the CSS tells me he has a slight chill and cannot leave his house. The CSS, I gather, has already passed on the contents of this letter to him." He made a little bowing movement towards C, as though he was a judge.

The Chief of Service handed two pieces of heavy paper to Naldo. Both sheets were letter size, around five inches by eight, and the top page bore the printed address of Eccleston Square. The letter was typed.

Dear C,

Forgive me for not addressing you by name, but I shall have been eight years gone by the time you read this, and you might well not be the C I knew at the time of my death.

Nevertheless, you will, I am certain, be familiar with my case, for my cousin, James Railton, will almost certainly have been through flood and fire on my behalf. After all, I instructed him to do certain things. For all I know, he might even, if he is alive, be in jail, for I set some very small traps which could just have pointed to him being a Soviet penetration agent. Whether he had the shrewdness to follow my devious plotting, I shall never know. If he did, then it is possible nothing at all has come out. If he did not, then others might well have picked up what he missed. I know we harbour such idiots in the trade. If anyone has been foolish enough to fall for innuendo then this is to clear James' name. There was no reason for me to point fingers elsewhere, for James has always been a good and loyal friend and cousin. But one has to do something to cover tracks, and I am aware, at the moment I write this, that I am under some form of investigation.

I trust that, by now, my diaries will have been discovered, together with my letter to James, and the papers I coded BOGEYMAN. This letter is to give the posthumous lie to my truth, if you follow me.

What I mean by this is that the Diary written as the Diary of Truth, is, in fact, the Diary of Lies, and vice versa. Since Tuesday August 5th 1939 I have, sporadically, and later consistently, worked for various intelligence departments of the Soviet Union. During wartime I provided them with military information denied to them by our own military. In peace I gave them information of various kinds. What I gave them is KGB operational knowledge, and I shall not detail it here.

I worked without interconsciousness with any other deep penetration agents. I was not known to them, and they did not have the benefit of knowing me. Also, on one occasion, I was instructed to betray an NKVD source within my own family.

Here the page break took the letter to a matching sheet with no printed address. Unconsciously, Naldo recognized the paper from countless letters and notes he had received from his uncle.

There are no regrets, the letter continued. **I have long believed that when the time is right, one should grasp it. I did just that, and if God exists he will allow me to look down and smile on you now. Farewell, a long farewell, and the rest of that Shakespearean tag.**

Sincerely,
Caspar Railton

Naldo read the letter twice, his mind numb. Of one thing he was certain. The signature was genuine. He needed no graphologist, or even his most reliable Handy Hammerstein, to tell him that. He looked around the room and quietly said that this was impossible. "If you believe this, then you'll believe anything. If I have to spend my whole life disproving this idiocy, then I'll do it." His voice was filled with wormwood and gall.

It was the lawyer, Leo Morris, who came to his side. "I do assure you, this came from Caspar, and you can see it is his signature. There can be no doubt."

"I admit to the signature. As for the content, it is lunatic. So there is *my* doubt." Naldo's voice went out of control. "And while I doubt, I shall . . ." he trailed off. Indeed, what could he do? Nothing. What he had been about to say would have sounded cheap and melodramatic. Forget it, he thought. Forget the whole bloody business. Just let the whole of his rotten family rest in peace.

By the time he reached the street, he knew there was no way in which he could leave things as they were. With great reluctance, Naldo had gathered a whole case against his own father, James. He had been ready to commit a kind of mental patricide. Now, he had to see it through to the end. If he was wrong, then so be it.

TWENTY-FIVE

1

Naldo arrived back in the Kensington house like a whirlwind. Barbara took in the shocked, gray look of his face, and the bleak fury in his eyes. He kissed her, then made signals from their other life in Moscow—touching his ear, circling the air with a finger, pointing at the telephone and light fixtures. She could almost smell the stale cabbage, the sour odor of that ghastly flat opposite Factory No. 2. She even shivered with cold, though the winter had yet to set in.

"Was it important, darling?" She fed him for the tapes, if there were tapes.

"Caspar," he said. "Caspar left a letter . . ." He went on, into the facts that were true but could not be true, and she knew her own expression was one of disbelief, the look of someone who has just been struck by bullet, blackjack, stroke, or some other sudden, near fatal, disaster. She heard herself speaking, but the words had little meaning—"Oh, Nald, no! How? Why? I don't believe it."

As she said it, so Naldo was writing fast, on the telephone pad. *Meet you in the Gardens. Ten minutes.* Aloud he said he wanted to rest; to think; to lie down. Then silence as he slipped out of the front door.

Ten minutes later they were both in Kensington Gardens, walking arm in arm past the Peter Pan statue, and the smattering of Norland Nannies, with their charges, the rich tots. Every year there were fewer of them. The uniforms had started to disappear, yet these were scenes that allowed the left-wing socialists to still claim a great class division in Britain, Naldo thought. Them and us had really gone, the old aristocracy was fading like a slow dissolve in a movie. The Trade Unions had won their battles, yet they still fought them, and fomented hatred on picket line and factory floor. They did not understand the rewards for responsibility, any more than they understood the other side of wealth. All they wanted was what they called a fair distribution of money, with no thought of hours spent toiling, or

378

weekends lost to hard work, management who had to labor hours the union leaders would never tolerate. The sight of a Rolls-Royce, and even a Norland Nannie, made them see red and sing the Internationale.

But, as Barbara and Naldo walked, they spoke of other things— Naldo of the course of action they must take to dig for the truth. Play spy on the spies, he said. Go out into the streets and create their own network. Bring the buggers to book.

In an hour they had a prototype ready to fly. The next morning they started the test flights, with Naldo going off to Maida Vale to see his expert, Handy Hammerstein, and Barbara into the West End, to an estate agent who dealt with short leases on small furnished properties. She gave her name as Mrs. Brenda Roberts, and they took her out to three small apartments. She chose one in New Cavendish Street, in a block with an entrance next to a shop that sold model kits and model railway accessories. The charges were extortionate, but she said she would bring her husband tomorrow. In the meantime here was the deposit, in cash. On the way to the agent she had withdrawn four thousand pounds from a savings account. She would bring the remainder, with Mr. Daniel Roberts, the next day. They would move in, she thought, around Christmas, or just after. Yes, she was ready to sign the lease. They would both do it in the morning.

On her way back to Kensington, Barbara took the long way, stopping off at Paddington Railway Station to take her own photograph in one of the little automatic booths that had sprung up in recent years. The photographs on show outside the booth looked like "Wanted" posters. When she next saw Naldo, Barbara could claim she was ninety-nine percent certain there was nobody on her back. Naldo had spelled it out for her. Always assume people are listening. It was the old rule. Take care, even if you're speaking from a public telephone box. Now, more than ever, they had to assume that, for a while at least, the shop would keep their private telephone bugged. Also they should use caution when moving about. They—this particular "they" being BMW and his cronies, plus all those on the old Credit Committee—would make certain that Barbara and Naldo did nothing to throw even a small wrench in the works. The late Sir Caspar Railton was trapped, dead to rights, condemned by his own mouth from the grave.

They were always short-staffed, though, so movement was probably fairly safe, as long as he took the usual precautions.

While Barbara was off fixing their private safe-flat, Naldo talked to Handy Hammerstein. His instructions were precise, and Handy took his personal threats very much to heart. Naldo quite simply said he would kill the old man with his bare hands if any of this was passed back. Hammerstein believed him. If he talked, then his granddaughter would sit *shiva* for him within a week of his talking.

On his way to Maida Vale, Naldo had also had his photograph taken, and called in at a small branch of Barclays Bank where he kept what he liked to call his "running money." He cleaned out the account in cash, closed it, and left with ten grand in his briefcase.

At home, they pooled information by writing everything down, just as they had done in Moscow, carrying on conversations laced with venom aimed towards his former employers, who still had a stake in him, for the long debriefing continued.

On this very same day, Naldo wrote a note to Herbie Kruger, which, on the surface, seemed bland enough, but contained, first, the New Cavendish flat address and a code word that would bring the large German running.

This was posted, in the normal box, up near the Kensington Gardens entrance, together with one of Barbara's photographs, sealed in a plain envelope and addressed to a postbox number which Hammerstein cleared every day. Some of the old man's clientele were a trifle on the naughty side, and the old boy kept certain parts of his work exceptionally quiet. At his age he did not wish to make a return trip to the Scrubs or Pentonville.

On the following morning, Naldo watched Barbara's back—and kept an eye on his own—when they went down to the estate agent's office. There they paid a full three months' rent in advance, had their excellent references checked, and signed the contract. It didn't matter when they moved in, the lease began from the current date, and the telephone was activated.

In the afternoon, Naldo met Gus Keene in the shop's safe house on the corner of South Audley and Mount streets. The irony of being debriefed at that location had escaped neither Keene nor Naldo, for this had been the very site to which Naldo had taken the retired Sir Caspar to meet Penkovsky, on the first night of *Alex*'s own debriefing.

Gus had carried out the whole business on a very friendly basis. They had long since accepted the bulk of Naldo's testimony, including the fact that he had shot Penkovsky at Sochi. Today they went on digging back over the years, for Gus had started at the present and slowly worked backwards. They had reached Naldo's early days with the SIS, after he had taken up his appointment following the transfer made from the Royal Air Force. Naldo had fought in the Battle of Britain, ending up with what was commonly called "the twitch." It had been a bad war for him by the end of 1940, and the transfer was made without rancor or innuendo on either side.

At the end of this particular session, Naldo said he had a favor to ask.

"Ask away." Gus lit his pipe and drew in with a bubbling noise.

"We want to take a short holiday," Naldo supplied. "Around Christmas. In a couple of weeks, in fact."

"So?"

"So we'd like our passports back, Gus."

Keene thought for a while. "Shouldn't be a problem. As long as you're on the level, Naldo. This has nothing to do with the late Sir Caspar's letter, I hope?"

"That's something we all have to live with, Gus. It's unbelievable, but we have to accept it. That's all there is."

"Mmmm." Gus, if the truth had been known, had reservations about Caspar's letter, but the facts could not be disputed. The graphologists had been at work. It was Caspar's typewriter, his paper, and, definitely, his signature. There was no sidestepping Sir Caspar's confession from the grave. "I give you a ring tomorrow?" Gus asked. "Have to clear it with the Chief. BMW would say no just for the hell of it, so I'd rather go over his head. Christmas, you say?"

"As soon as possible."

"What about the great tradition? The Redhill Christmas party?"

"I want to put a lot of miles between myself and the rest of my family, this year. Isn't that what you'd do in my situation?"

Gus nodded, understanding.

As they were leaving, Naldo said he would be popping in and out of the Eccleston Square house during the next week or so. Purely family stuff. "I have to talk with my father, and Dick, sometime. We don't intend to hang around in this country for longer than is necessary, so the place'll either have to go to young Arthur or one of the other Railton children. I want to make sure the obnoxious Alexander doesn't get hold of it."

"Understood." Gus gave a wink and a conspiratorial smile which said, "I'm with you there."

The truth was at odds with the information Naldo had given to Gus. The only other person who knew the facts was Barbara. During their first walk in Kensington Gardens, Naldo had gone through his theory: a thesis that had materialized, as though from the blue, on his way back from the shop to Kensington, after the meeting with the respectable Leo Morris, who was as Caesar's wife.

The mind, under pressure, and subjected to a shock as great as Caspar's call from the dead, had produced a sudden, ready-made, solution. It was as though Naldo's brain had been poked with a sharp knife. Until then, the jigsaw had been only partly completed: the deceit of the Penkovsky affair, which in turn had cast the first doubts on Caspar, had been taken care of. Naldo felt happy only when he thought of the shots fired in Sochi. How could there be remorse at righting both a personal and international wrong?

The rest, though painful, was all in place. Only a couple of pieces of the puzzle remained unanswered. Andrew's arrest had been another shock, unaccounted for at the time. Yet now, with the knife of Caspar's letter plunged into his head, the entire picture, with all its duplicities, intrigues, and betrayals, lay in front of him, an unclouded landscape in his mind.

As he went through each step, striding through the nebula of nannies, and the kite-flying children in Kensington Gardens, Barbara had asked, "Would there have been time?"

"Just." Naldo still wore the grim look of a man hearing of sudden death. "There would just have been time, all I need are the backup facts—doctor's evidence; a sign that he was not where he should have been on that day. The funny thing was that I didn't really take in the poor old thing's words while I waited for Alexander and Andrew to arrive. Only came back this morning, as I left the shop. The brain is an oddity. But there's just time for it to have been done that way. No problem, if he had a following wind and some luck. The rest is obvious, and proven."

In the present, with Gus, just as they were leaving, Naldo asked if they had ever got anything out of Caspar's widow. "Anything of value, I mean?"

"Spit and a cough." Gus shrugged. "Poor old thing was too far gone for anything lucid. You saw her, Nald. She simply got worse as time went on."

"And then she died."

Gus repeated the words, in agreement, "And then she died."

That night, at dusk, with Barbara watching his back, Naldo returned to Eccleston Square and let himself in. Even though Maitland-Wood's bully boys had turned the place over, it had been put back together with care. Now he prayed that Caspar's sons did not know their father as well as he, the nephew.

The first search bore no fruit. Nothing in the bathroom cabinet and medicine chest, so he tried the bedside table in his uncle's room. It was arranged with the same neatness Caspar had used all his life. A small tape machine stood on top, next to the alarm clock and telephone. A pair of headphones neatly fitted into a corner of the drawer. Tapes lay in two piles of three in the opposite corner: Mozart, Bach's *"Goldberg" Variations,* and Vivaldi clashed with *West Side Story.* All there if the old boy could not sleep. A pad and silver ballpoint pen, then, there it was, a porcelain pillbox with Hatchards, that most famous of book-shops, transferred in color on the lid.

Naldo removed the lid, taking a cheap tin pillbox from his own pocket. The two tablets he had hoped to find lay in the palm of his hand for a second before he tipped them into his pillbox, then replaced lids and closed the drawer.

He went downstairs, for one piece of evidence was of no use without the other. In the room they called The Hide he opened the large roll-topped desk and went straight to the secret drawer. Caspar had showed him all the workings, years ago. "Even your pa doesn't know this, Naldo," he had said. "Old Giles, my grandpapa, used it all his life."

You had to remove the first two small drawers to the right of the upright paper slots, which still held some of the stationery Naldo had seen, in C's office. The dead letter had been typed neatly on this kind of paper. Next, the bottom matching drawer on the far left. They all came right out with no pushing or pulling. Then, down to the underside of the desk itself. He pushed in on the tiny catch and there was a click as the central section moved. Naldo lifted it away, and there, as he had hoped, were pages of notes and letters, all in Caspar's hand and in green ink. There were crossings out, and scrib-bled marginal notes, and that was only to be expected. Caspar never committed himself to a full letter, typed personally, until he was satisfied with a draft. And it was his old practice to keep all drafts for three months.

He had kept to the routine right up to the end. What Naldo required was at the top of the pile, on plain white A4 paper. He sat in front of the desk, the paper in gloved hands, as he deciphered his uncle's writing. Then he shed tears. Weeping was often a release of tension, and Naldo had never been afraid to weep, especially now when tension had to be wrung out.

"Not a tickle," Barbara told him when they met back in Kensington Gore. The next day they both did a temporary move to the rented three-room apartment in New Cavendish Street. The passports had been picked up, by messenger from Hammerstein; C had released their own passports, and they had booked their short break. Naldo had even given Gus all details. It was out of season in Corfu, true, but the weather usually remained mild.

They were all set. Barbara dialed Herbie's number at ten that night, from New Cavendish Street, and simply said one word—"Karl."

"Groucho," Herbie grunted back. An hour later he was at the door, a bottle of wine in one hand and a bunch of flowers in the other. "Is housewarming." He grinned.

2

On the night that Naldo made his raid on the Eccleston Square house, other things were taking place on the fifth floor of the shop, in C's own office.

Mark Bertram-Prince, tall, tough and expert at reading accounts upside down, had dropped in from Washington for the day. He was to leave that night and his report mainly concerned the pressures that were building up around the American Agency.

Things had started to happen during the Presidential election campaign. They were only now coming to a head. Rumor had piled itself on rumor, particularly after the strange break-in at the Democratic National Committee headquarters in the smart, cool gray Watergate building on the night of June 17th, almost six months previously. Nixon had won the election in November, and next month, January 1973, he would be sworn in for his second term as President of the United States.

But rumors traveled, and word had reached the fifth floor in London that the Agency was already battening down hatches, covering trails, and reorganizing. C wanted to know exactly what was what, from the horse's mouth. Bertram-Prince was gathering up his belongings, ready to head out to Heathrow for the evening Washington flight, when he dropped a cloud, no bigger than a man's hand, into the clear air of C's office.

"Arnie Farthing," he said. *"Heartbreak,"* he said.

"Yes?" C did not even look up, which was a bad sign.

"I gather things have gone very quiet."

"How quiet?"

"Deafeningly."

"And?"

"And people're looking very unhappy."

"Fill me in." C leaned back in his chair.

"First, I caught a whiff during late summer, which is the silly season anyway, apart from this Watergate thing which had started to develop. God knows where that's finally going to land . . ."

"The whiff?"

"Uncomfortable. If I read it correctly, the standard of intelligence they were getting back dropped alarmingly."

"You know how these things go." C was patting him along the road.

"Usually, yes. Good stuff, followed by a bucketful of chicken crap, then, bingo, sixty-five gold ingots in a row. My feeling is that the chicken crap became normal. Now I don't think there's even a dribble. Heads are on the line. People are worried."

"Where did you get this?"

"Here and there. Then, last week, a chance remark—overheard, of course."

"Of course." C gave a solemn nod. "The chance remark?"

"Gave me the impression that Arnie's disappeared, whether into the cellars of Lubyanka or Lefortovo; or the high table out at the main complex, I cannot tell. But some of the CA people're looking gloomy as hell."

"Thanks for the tip." C was on the verge of saying, "We have problems of our own," but stopped himself in time. All he knew was that Naldo and Barbara Railton were booked to go off to Corfu for a couple of weeks over Christmas, and bells had started to ring in his head. He did not have the manpower to follow them. He could only trust that they were not up to anything devious.

3

"So, what game we playing, Naldo?" The three of them were seated in the small apartment's largest room. They had drunk Big Herbie's bottle and broached another of their own.

"Not a game, Herb." Naldo poured what looked like arterial blood into Barbara's glass. "No games now. A private operation. Run from here, by me."

"You're out, Naldo. You gone private."

"When did that ever stop anyone?"

"Is games when you go private."

"You call clearing Caspar for good, and putting the record straight, mere games?"

"You reckon you can do that, Nald?"

"More'n that. I can do it, and I want to do it with the highest possible cooperation. You going to help, or am I going to have to get myself some casual labor?"

"You serious?"

"Never more so."

"You *really* believe that can be done?"

"With your help. In or out now."

"Count in. Me!" Herbie banged his breast with a clenched palm.

They drank to it, and Naldo began to rattle off instructions. "It shouldn't take more than four, maybe five, days as the crow flies."

"Is Christmas. Give me an extra day for the holidays."

"Six maximum. The end of the Christmas break is essential, Herb. It's our safest way back in. Got me?"

Herbie said he was receiving loud and clear.

"As soon as you've put it together, I want you to send this cable. We'll call you around three, maybe four, days after the cable reaches us. Don't fret if it's longer. We're dealing with the Greek postal service here. Sometimes they take longer, okay?"

"I just wait. No worries."

"And you're not to go to Redhill if they ask you. Get some nice jolly young woman to spend Christmas with you; make the red cabbage stuff you like, cook her a turkey, but stay indoors."

"All the way." Herbie's large head did its Buddha nod.

The next morning, Naldo and Barbara took a hire car to Gatwick and joined the charter flight to Corfu, under their own paper: Mr & Mrs Donald Railton.

They had not booked themselves into anywhere near the main town. In 1972 the large hotels and the crowds had yet to mushroom, but the signs that it would happen were everywhere. They took a cab to a small hotel, perched above a bay in Paliokastritsa. There were only half a dozen other guests, the food was terrible, but the weather stayed mild, and there was a splendid taverna a short walk down through the hotel gardens and quarter of a mile down the road.

Below, and along the coast, they could see from their balcony the beginnings of the blight that would eventually ruin this isle of ginger beer, cricket, and eccentrics. Two beehive hotels were growing from piles of rubble. By the summer, they supposed, the place would be swarming with men in Dr. Scholl sandals, and girls in bikinis, straight from the fleshpots of Wiggan, Scunthorpe, and Ruislip. Nothing wrong with the people, but, like deforestation, a place of calm beauty would be transformed into a kind of Golden Mile with sun. After that, the American tourists would find it. Nothing wrong with that either, but it would bring inflated prices, ripoff tours, and fake souvenirs.

But, for now, the couple basked in pleasant loafing. They would walk, lie in what was called the sun lounge, and each evening totter down the hill and along the road, lined with huge dusty trees. The landscape looked very Victorian to Naldo, but he could not tell why.

They, naturally, struck up a good relationship with the people who ran the taverna, and the two waiters, Spiros and Dimitri. They would eat well, drink quite a lot of ouzo, and, inevitably, learn to dance, as Alan Bates and Anthony Quinn had danced in *Zorba.*

On Christmas Day they went through the routine of giving each other little gifts—a cloth shoulder bag, with Greek designs on it for Barbara, and a set of worry beads for Naldo. They bought small gifts for the boys at the taverna as well, so, though the place was officially closed for the day, they were allowed to eat there—lobsters, freshly caught, salads and sweet cakes.

On 27th December the cable arrived, with much clucking and head shaking. Naldo had, rightly, presumed it would be read, and the contents passed on to the hotel management, who were not bothered about their eating out.

It was bad news, for the English. The staff passed it around, and it reached the taverna before they arrived for their evening meal, when they were greeted with the reverence shown only to those on the brink of a death watch.

The cable had read—DEEPLY REGRET WORST FEARS CONFIRMED REGARDING UNCLE STOP NOT EXPECTED TO LIVE FOR MORE THAN A FEW DAYS STOP SUGGEST YOU GET HOME WITH ALL HASTE.

There was much telephoning, and they departed on the following morning, taking an Olympic flight to Athens, where they were booked onto a British European Airways flight to Gatwick. Strangely, the nice Railton couple, waved off from the hotel by the staff, arrived in Athens, but, once there, they canceled the flight to Gatwick.

On the next morning they reappeared as Mr & Mrs Roberts, on an Air France to Paris, Orly. From there, a last-minute decision put them onto Aer Lingus to Dublin, where they spent a merry evening at the Shelbourne, hopping into London, Heathrow, on the last flight of the day.

Nobody even bothered to ask for passports; what was more, nobody even noticed. Five had a watch out, but they used the small staff available to check on the ex-Athens flights. "The soft route always works," Naldo smiled as they directed the taxi to New Cavendish Street.

But as they disembarked, he thought he saw a familiar silhouette, framed in the back of another passing cab. It was caught in their taxi's headlights for a fraction of a second, no more, but Naldo took one stride away, into the darkness of the building. It remained in his mind, and, during the following couple of days, he moved with extra caution.

Barbara dialed Herbie five minutes after they checked the flat, taking the telephone apart, examining walls, lamps, the undersides of tables and chairs. "Doing the rounds," as Naldo called it. It was far from being a hundred percent foolproof, but better than nothing.

Herbie arrived at one in the morning, and Naldo immediately asked if he had been followed.

"I play it safe all ways, Nald." Herbie was not happy, he seemed to have lost use of the facial muscles which allowed him to smile. "Three taxis and a bus. Nobody here."

Naldo asked them to turn out the lights, and he pulled back the curtain a fraction. The street seemed deserted, though he saw that a car, a blue Rover 3.4, had parked directly opposite. It had not been there when they arrived, and it appeared to be unoccupied.

"He's coming?" Naldo asked when the lights went on again.

"About half an hour. You want details before he gets in?"

"If you would, Herb."

"Okay. Subject one. No postmortem. Heart attack. Saw his doctor the night before so no need, the duck says . . ."

"Quack, Herb," from Barbara.

"No need, the quack says, okay."

"Okay."

"Subject two. They have some fancy name, but basically they're stuff called digoxin. Fifty milligrams is fatal dose. Subject three. Yes, a silver pillbox among the effects. Seen it myself. Still at the shop. Empty. Okay?"

Naldo did not speak.

"Subject four. Yes, you completely right, Nald. Didn't show that morning. Got in around two forty-five. Fourteen forty-five as the twenty-four-hours has it. All there, I got everything in writing. I even ask the duck—the quack—to sign statement, official." He pulled out a sheaf of notes from the small briefcase, which looked even smaller when carried by Herbie.

Barbara asked if that was it.

"The whole thing. Tied up almost with pink string and sealing wax." Naldo pursed his lips. "All we've got to do now is prove it."

The entryfone buzzed, and Barbara called out "Yes?" into the little telephone speaker by the door.

"Hunter," said the disembodied voice.

"Come home, then, sir." She pressed the button to open the ground-floor electronic lock.

Naldo was beside the window. As the front doorbell rang, he saw the Rover drive away, and noted that a small white van had parked up the street.

"Well, Naldo, this had better be good because I've kept quiet, and not told a living soul," C said from the threshold. He looked tired and much older. Naldo put it down to the time of day. "If you want a laugh, I know the few people watching for you haven't got a scent." He was shrugging out of his topcoat. "Damned cold out there. There's been a heavy frost, and, maybe, snow before long."

"Nobody on your back, sir?"

"Only my own man. You know him. The best. Max."

Naldo poured a large brandy and set it before the CSS. "You're probably going to need that, sir."

"Let us say, I'd better need it, Naldo. It's the last . . ." The telephone began to ring with that strident urgency that only comes late at night or in the early hours.

"Who the hell?" Naldo said calmly. He picked up the instrument and said nothing. "For you, Chief. Max," handing it to C. How did the old devil get the number? he thought to himself.

"Can't be . . . Right . . . Yes, if he comes round for a third look . . . I'll flash three times . . . Okay." C put down the telephone. "Max says he thinks someone's doing a round the houses. Taxi. It's passed twice since he's been watching."

Naldo felt his heart give a jump. He wondered if it was the same cab he had seen before. "You ready, sir?"

"Depends what you've got."

Naldo gave a sigh: long, a great expelling of his breath, as though his lungs needed emptying before he started. "It's not easy for me, sir. I have a prima facie case against my father for being a Soviet long-term penetration; an explanation for Sir Caspar's letter reaching Mr. Morris when it did; evidence that the letter's a forgery; possible means of handling; and the probable involvement of yet another of my family. The entire business appears to be a family business. Betrayal's our second name. I'm sorry."

"How solid's your evidence, Naldo?" The Chief spoke as though trying to soothe a sick child. Barbara and Herbie saw how ill and lonely Naldo looked, from the bleakness deep in his eyes, to the slight shaking of his fingers.

"Only up to a point, sir. I think we'll need watchers to catch them, and my father's an old man. I don't know how discovery's going to affect him. I . . .''

"Just lay out the facts. Tell us how it lies, Naldo."

Naldo Railton placed the sheaf of papers from Herbie on the table, and a further document next to it. Then, softly, with occasional breaks in his voice, he began to talk.

Thousand-and-One-Nights time, Big Herbie Kruger thought.

4

In the King Street house, James Railton sat alone, gazing into the fire. For some strange reason he had begun to feel older in the last few weeks, as though another winter had brought his body and mind into that chill last season of his life. Even Margaret Mary had noticed the change, and seemed to be constantly asking him if he was all right.

He told her "Yes," but they both knew he was lying, as he had lied for so long now. Even in retirement he lied, and schemed, doubled to and fro, hid in the mental shadows.

God, it had been so long, he thought, catching the pictures of faces in the fire. So long since he had thought of honor, family, God, and country. He supposed it was the country and his own values—or the old family values—that had started the slide.

It was the first war, the Great War as they had called it, that had been the turning point. James really had believed that God, honor, country, and family had meant something then. When it was over, he knew a new order would replace the old; that Great Britain would be a land fit for heroes. Yet the heroes remained unsung, for the most part. Some begged in the streets—EX-SERVICEMAN: WIFE & CHILDREN TO SUPPORT; selling matches or bootlaces from cardboard trays, or playing an instrument, lonely in the gutter; marching from North to South for fair wages, while others prospered, if they had the right contacts, the correct look, the proper school. Nothing altered. Nothing was ventured and nothing gained. Each year they paid lip service to the glorious dead, while the unemployment figures rose and love of country became tarnished.

James remembered now how he had woken one morning to see clearly that he was ashamed of his background, sick to death with his family and their strength of rank and privilege.

It must have shown, for suddenly—in The Travellers Club of all places—the approach was made. Already Hitler was on the rise, the scent of war hung in the air. If Hitler and his Fascist Nazi Party were to be defeated there was only one way: one way to be certain, this time, that at the end Britain would blossom into a new Jerusalem. After all, Communism was only a form of political Christianity, and in that way lay hope.

He recalled the tall, languid man, talking quietly, and for hours on end. The government's way of appeasement was of no value. Fascism could only be put down through a political ideology fully opposed to the evil that Germany had embraced.

Slowly he had seen the full light. What Britain needed was the ruthless discipline of Stalin's Marxism; the weeding of politicians and military leaders; the clean sweep of class; the organization of the people, and the equality it would bring. In the end, he had totally embraced the only way.

Certainly there was danger, but James had always thrived on that: the code word telephone calls, the drops, and the meetings. Within a year the old arcane rituals were replaced by new ones. In the giant chess game he had changed sides and it was as easy as crossing the road.

James Railton did not think of himself as a traitor. It was his country that had betrayed him. The old country had become a nonentity. The Empire was in twilight time and the saviors had approached him just as his disillusioned view of country, family, God, and honor was at its lowest ebb. And he was not alone. Even younger members of his own family had followed him when he cast the fly. Moscow Center used guile, handled them in a way his own old Service could never have handled them. They cosseted the three of them and kept them safe. Not even the archmole Blunt, who had led so many others, knew of their existence.

Because of them, and others of like mind, it would come: the dream; just as it had come to Russia. He had no regrets, just hatred for the past. At his age, the future mattered little, except that he had done his best to point the way. One day his secret efforts, his personal contribution to the Soviet future, would be recognized. For now it was as though his country was a private luxury motor car about to be crushed between two lorries. James was sure it was not an original thought. He had read it somewhere. At least he had done something positive with his life, not like so many of the dissatisfied poor and rich kids of today who sought shelter in the dropout subculture of drugs and pop groups.

He let the fire warm him, and delved back into his memories, wondering how long men and women would have to fight in secret for true freedom and equality.

TWENTY-SIX

1

"Weep if it'll help, Naldo." C was ever a man's man, but, once Naldo had finished, his sense of comprehension and compassion showed clear. Herbie had taken out a handkerchief and blown his nose loudly, muttering something about "Foolish. Blubbings. Foolish. Unmanly, the blubbings." Barbara, who knew it all anyway, did nothing to stop the tears trickling silently down her cheeks.

Later, one of them thought C had wiped the corner of an eye. "It's not every day that a man is forced to betray an elderly father whom he's always loved," C said. "Nor outline a possible corruption which has eaten the heart of his family." He paused, going over to the window, motioning them to turn off the lights, then drawing back the curtains. It was day. A milk truck went up the street, and the sound of heels on the pavement below merged with the early morning traffic.

"I guess you loved your uncle more than most," C said, not even looking at Naldo as he walked back to the table. "As for the evidence. Well, it makes sense. As you said at the beginning, we need them redhanded, and that means a surveillance team. There's the question of forgery in Caspar's papers. You know *who,* but *when's* the question." It was always the problem with counterintelligence. There was no case unless you caught the target guilty, in the act, or got a clean confession.

As though he had not heard his Chief's last words, Naldo said, "It needs one that can be trusted." His voice was gritty, his throat dry. He spoke of the surveillance team.

"Quite." C understood, and went towards the window. Then, as though caught by a sudden memory, he turned back into the room. Barbara had gone off into the kitchen to make tea and raise the level of the central heating. There was frost on the windows. Naldo remem-

392

bered childhood and his father pointing out the incredible kaleidoscopic and beautiful patterns formed within the droplets of frost.

"We can deal with telephones and spikes. No problem." C seemed
to be speaking to himself. "I can have the telephones wired in a matter
of an hour. The spikes can probably be put in later today. They
changed King Street much in the last few years?"

He called it King Street, but, in reality, James Railton's house stood
in King Street St. James's, at the bottom of the wide street off Piccadilly
called St. James's, because of the palace with its colorful guard which
stood at the far end. King Street branched off to the left. Offices, some
exclusive shops, a few very good houses—some now dissected into
flats—towards the point where the street filtered into St. James's
Square.

"Hardly at all," Naldo answered.

"We get a team in?"

"I should think Special Branch can arrange it, sir. Directly opposite
the house they've refurbished the building. What was once four
houses is now a damned ugly office block. The SB should be able to
put on some pressure."

"You want to be in on it, Naldo?"

"It'd be best." He answered slowly, laboriously even, as though the
long relating of facts through the early hours had left him without
words.

C nodded. "I'll be back to you. Must get a move on. This line's clear,
I presume?" pointing at the telephone.

"Should be, sir."

"I'll send a man around." C was shrugging himself into his coat.
"Suggest Barbara lets him in and then both of you stay out of sight.
I must go . . ."

"No tea, sir?" Barbara came through with a tray.

"Like to, but this is probably more important than any of you think.
I might return and brief you here. Otherwise I'll call." He stopped,
strangely hesitant for a man used to making very fast decisions.
Then—"It's possible Gus'll be over sometime. I might want you to go
over everything with him, Naldo. Sorry to put you through the ordeal,
but it's necessary." He moved his body, from the trunk, his feet
staying in the same position: it was how they were taught to change
an aiming point with a pistol. C looked at Kruger. "Herb, you got
anything vital on today?"

"It'll keep, actually." Herbie sounded very precise.

"Right. Would you stay and babysit these two?"

"Best nannie in the business, Chief." Pause, as though counting beats like an actor. "Like to be at the kill, please."

C nodded agreement. Then—"Now, I'd be obliged if someone would flash these lights three times, I don't want to incur Max's wrath. It can be awful."

"Yes, I've seen it," Naldo said, flashing the lights, on-off, on-off, on-off.

They filled the day somehow. Herbie lumbered out to get cigarettes, and returned to tell them there was heavy surveillance on the block. "The Chief's got bodies from every way which . . ."

"*Which* way, Herb," Naldo and Barbara spoke in unison.

"They have this place completely covered. I think Max really did see something last night, maybe."

Naldo was smoking more than ever. Lighting cigarette from cigarette. They tried to behave normally, but all knew the horror that would come, if not that night, the next, or the following week. At one point Naldo said, "They might have talked recently. At Redhill. We need something to flush them."

"Ja. Ja, I think, maybe, the Chief knows that, Nald." Herbie spoke as one who had a whole plan of battle laid out in front of him; the pieces set in place. The big German was always surprising them. He did so now, seeing the look on Naldo's face. "I tell you, Nald. I tell you what the Chinaman Sun Tzu said. He said, 'Your surviving spy must be of keen intellect, though in outward appearance, a fool.' This brings great comfort to me."

Later, in the middle of the afternoon, Naldo suddenly quoted Shakespeare for no apparent reason—

> "*How sometimes nature will betray its folly,*
> *Its tenderness, and make itself a pastime*
> *To harder bosoms! Looking on the lines*
> *Of my boy's face, methoughts I did recoil*
> *Twenty-three years, and saw myself unbreeched.*"

Then he laughed and asked the air, "I wonder if my old father will curse the day, and remember himself unbreeched when I was conceived?"

At around five in the afternoon, C turned up with Gus. Max stood outside the door and handed his Chief a small tape recorder, similar to the one Naldo had seen beside Caspar's bed. Gus looked like a gentleman farmer, in rough tweeds, pipe clamped between his teeth.

"I want you to talk it all through with Gus." C laid a hand on his shoulder. "I think it will be tonight, Naldo. The telephone was done this morning, I've got young Curry Shepherd in place with a team. Curry's in charge and I'm not going to be present when it happens. He'll give you plenty of warning."

"How is it going to be tonight?" Naldo sounded oddly indifferent.

Gus found a wall socket and plugged in the tape machine. "Two conversations," he said, and pressed the "play" button.

They heard the ringing tone, then James answering in the guarded way of their trade. Not giving the number: simply saying, "Yes?"

It was C himself on the tape. "James. You recognize my voice?"

"Of course." Calm.

"A tiny problem. I wonder if you'd do me the favor of coming in sometime tomorrow."

A long pause. Then—"Er . . . When?"

"Just suit yourself. We need your wisdom."

"For what?"

"I don't know if it's around the family yet, but Caspar's provided us with a letter from the grave. You heard about that? From Naldo, perhaps?"

"Naldo seems to have disappeared, but I did hear a whisper, yes."

"Need to talk with you about it, James. Caspar's letter isn't kosher, you see. Just a friendly chat."

James' voice, which until then had been clear, almost young, now sank beneath his years, and the stress with which he must have lived. "Yes, of course. Of course I'll come in. You say to suit myself: would noon be convenient?"

"Noon it is. Look forward to seeing you, James."

C had hung up abruptly.

"There must have been a little panic, and some thought." It was Gus speaking. "The next call was an hour later. To Alex himself. At work. At GCHQ, where he's reinstalled, but under restraint regarding confidential documents."

"Alex Railton's office," the secretary said.

"Is Alex around?" James appeared to have got his wind back. His voice had regained its strength.

"Who's calling."

"Tell him it's his Uncle James."

"James?" Alex guarded, knowing for certain the tapes would be picking it up.

"Alex, sorry to bother you, but we've got a small family crisis. Can you get to town tonight?"

"Tonight?"

"I think it would be a mistake to leave it any later. You know our bloody relatives panic."

"Ten. I can't make it until about ten, and I'll need feeding."

"Good. See you tonight then, Alex."

The click as the "stop" button was pressed sounded like a gunshot. Gus spoke. "Ten could mean eight, nine, or eleven. It won't be ten on the dot. You caught the key words, Naldo?"

Naldo nodded. "Crisis. Panic. Feeding."

"That's it. I think we should all be ready by eight. Though there's a team at Cheltenham, so we'll get some idea, once he's left."

C left them, saying he would be by the telephone. Barbara brought tea, and Gus set up the tape machine with a recording device. "Just tell it as it lies," he said.

Naldo sighed. "Once is never enough is it, Gus?"

"Hardly. Take it gently."

"Well," Naldo began, "It starts, I suppose, by Caspar's grave." He told the story of the voice in his head saying "Now it begins." "It took me a long time to realize that it was my father who said it, aloud. It's difficult to accept that, down the years, one's family has lied and betrayed, almost on a regular basis. You know everyone, up to Andrew?"

Gus said he did, reeling off the names.

"So it took me a long time to come to terms with Caspar's sons, and *my* father. It's understandable, I think."

This time Gus just nodded. Naldo rambled a little. He told of the meeting with Arnie, the dossiers Arnie had seen, and his own feeling of hatred for Penkovsky, whom he saw as a double-dyed villain. "I could forgive him, his international duplicity, because that saved the world from disaster, which was what the Soviets wanted anyway. I could never forgive him for the stuff he fed everyone about Caspar. I can't forgive Blunt, period. Blunt just rubbed it in."

"Blunt's the number one in my book: ran the entire Cambridge lot. First one recruited and last one unmasked. Might even have helped the Ks run your dad. Now, just give us the time scale, Naldo. The nuts and bolts. How the setting up was achieved."

First, Naldo said, he was set up by his own father. "He knew exactly what Caspar had, and who he'd be pointing at. How, I don't know, but it would be after Caspar gave him a spare set of keys to Eccleston Square. There is a space, though. A couple of weeks before my dear father passed the buck to me, old Caspar and Phoeb spent five days with Sara and Dick. I should imagine that was when James went in and took a good look through the documents. Also, I think he had, for years, relied on his relationship with his cousin. He pretty well knew that Caspar, as honorable as he was, would never turn him in. It's even just possible that Caspar refused to believe anyone else was involved."

"It would be easy for a man like Cas to go into a psychological block. To refuse belief that his sons had been turned."

Naldo nodded. "And James continued to rely on family . . ."

Gus said that Caspar probably considered James to be too old to do more damage.

"It would be in character for Cas, yes. But James was still seeing so many people. Little dinner parties, meetings with Maitland-Wood, Tubby, a lot of the active gang. They talked, just as old mates talked to Blunt. Both Blunt and James simply passed on the chat. James did it through Alex, I suspect. Anyway, when he looked at Caspar's plan—the two diaries, the document called *Bogeyman:* everything—he knew that whoever went through it was bound, in the end, to see that Caspar was fingering him. It's quite plain, Gus. Caspar all but gives the name. James played *Croesus* to Caspar's *Dionysus.*"

"And so blocked all the intelligence Caspar had risked his life for in the 1930s. I even followed that myself."

"There was no way my father could hide it. For all he knew, there were other copies of the real diary, and *Bogeyman*, around. He had only one course, and that was to rely on family loyalty. The original covering letter, a copy of which I'll bet Mr. Morris has somewhere in his office, was doctored."

"You're certain of this?"

Naldo told of how he had gone to old Handy Hammerstein with the first page of the original covering letter, "The one that asked James to remove the diaries and all else from the Eccleston Square house." And how Handy admitted to the forgery. "I was always puzzled by it, especially when I realized Caspar was fingering James in those documents, setting the trap. I suppose the old boy was appealing to James' better nature. He was certainly saying, 'James old love, I know what you did. I know who you worked for. Do the decent thing.' "

"The forgery," Gus egged him on.

"There was plenty of room for it. The original letter began:

My Dear James,
This is a brief résumé of the contents of my private box . . . etc. Then, even at the start, in the letter, he began to spell out to James exactly what he was doing. Now, when I got the letter, it began:

My Dear James, or Naldo who'll doubtless be reading this if his father's not available."

He told of the evidence gleaned from the frightened Hammerstein. "He admitted to me that James had brought him *that* page, and that he inserted the bit about me. So, once my father had passed the buck, in the Reform Club that night, the letter was already doctored. Even then I was being set up on the grounds that a son like me would never betray a father like James."

"Flaps and seals?" Gus asked. He was inquiring if James had the ability to remove the letter from its envelope and return it with no signs of tampering.

"No problem for my father. I've seen him do it a hundred times. In fact he taught me all the ways: from steam and carbon tet to tweezers and bamboo."

"And you're sure there was time?"

Naldo gave a mirthless laugh. "Gus, *we* know there was time, for Christ's sake. We both know he's guilty."

"Maybe, but we might have to make the evidence stick. I'm playing defense counsel. You've given us one end of the documents. What about the other? What about the letter from the grave?"

Naldo went through it all, just as he had done for C. This was the hardest part, but he spoke steadily, showing no emotion until towards the end.

He had known his Uncle Caspar probably a shade too well. He knew the man's hiding places, and his obsessions. "He always made drafts of important letters, and always kept them for three months at the least. I knew where the bodies were buried."

Naldo described how his first suspicion came. "The covering note to Leo Morris—the one that gave the eight-year instruction—was unsigned. Nobody bothered about that. Morris wouldn't because Caspar sometimes didn't sign memos. Often he left them blank or, as a personal joke, signed them *C,* in green ink. This one was so important that, knowing the man as I did, Caspar *would* have signed it. But he didn't, so I looked at his letter of confession very carefully. The signature was undoubtedly his. You didn't have to be a graphologist to tell that. But there were two sheets—you've seen it?"

Gus gave him a quick nod, not looking up from the notes he was taking. The tape recorder rolled on, but, as many have noticed, Gus Keene was always a thorough man.

"It's that last page." Naldo was starting to speak quietly. "Cas was under stress, visited his doctor the day before his death. We now know what the doctor told him, and what decision he took."

"How?" Gus asked, even though C had given him the answer.

"Because I knew where Cas kept all the drafts of his letters. At the point of death he wouldn't change the habits of a lifetime. That was dear old Caspar's way. Neat. Efficient. Obsessive even. He always felt that, being minus one arm and one leg, he had to make up for it in other ways. When he worked for the first C, for instance . . .''

Gus held up a hand to halt the conversation, knowing that unconsciously Naldo was playing for time, delaying the worst moment.

Naldo said he was sorry. Told how he had gone to Eccleston Square and found the draft of Caspar's letter. "When you type it, the second page comes out just as it does in the so-called letter from the grave. It reads—

There are no regrets. I have long believed that when the time is right, one should grasp it. I did just that, and if God exists he will allow me to look down and smile on you now. Farewell, a long farewell, and the rest of that Shakespearean tag.

Sincerely

"Then Caspar's signature. But it's the first page that's altogether different. Here's the draft." He pushed the pages of neat writing towards Gus. Even the corrections on the page were neat.

"Read it to me," Gus said evenly.

"Must I?"

"It's best. You've done it once for C. I need it for the tapes. With luck you'll never have to read it again."

Big Herbie's lips moved. He was counting down the silence in German.

"Caspar committed suicide, you know that, Gus?"

Once more the nod.

"He carefully polished a suicide note, meant only for C's eyes."

"Read it from the draft."

Naldo's voice cracked only once—

My Dear C,

Forgive me. You will already have heard of my death when you read this later today. I ask you to comfort old Phoeb for me, and not let anyone else into a last secret. Alas, there is another little secret which will have to be

unveiled, but, for the moment, let us stay with my death.

I went to the quack yesterday afternoon. The pain has been getting worse, and I cannot bear to go on any longer. It has been with me, as you know, for years. Now, my mutilated body cannot cope. The quack tells me it could happen any time. In fact, I know as I write this, I could feel the pain and leave in the twinkling of an eye. Therefore I have chosen to make my own terms. I am on some stuff for my heart and, yesterday, the doc pointedly told me that I must on no account take more than the required dose. So, I am lunching with three men who we both knew of as Paul, John and George—you might as well call me Ringo, eh?

I shall take well over the prescribed dose with my coffee, and the rest will be silence. Thank God I'm not afraid to die.

The other secret. It will come out for I have left instructions for James. If he does not do the right thing, then you must go for him. I am sorry. I have betrayed you. You should have been told years ago. I should have gone to your predecessor in the early forties. I could not betray my beloved cousin, even though I know he is a Soviet penetration, and probably has been since the 1930s. There is evidence. He is retired, and so surely can do little more harm. Forgive me for not feeling his collar when I first knew. I still have no idea why, though I think I know how. It could not be money, so he must be a believer. Please, please, forgive me.

There are no regrets. I have long believed that when the time is right, one should grasp it. I did just that, and if God exists he will allow me to look down and smile on you now. Farewell, a long farewell, and the rest of that Shakespearean tag.

Sincerely,
Caspar Railton

"That's it." Naldo lit a cigarette, his fingers shaking.

"So how did a suicide note to C become a letter from the dead, Naldo?"

"It's a puzzle, but then my whole bloody family's devious. You live so long in the damned labyrinth of secrets that you cannot escape. Everything my family has ever done has been devious: illusions; blind corners that are not there; mirage effects; nothing straight or plain; everything web upon web of complexities. The Service makes you like that, Gus. This whole bloody country makes you like that, and, when we all become a sort of United States of Europe, it'll be more devious than ever."

"Tell me, Naldo. I need it for the tape." Gus spoke sharply. "Anyway, time's running out."

Naldo said okay, right, he would tell Gus what he figured out. First, he checked on the letter. "Sat down and typed it at his machine and saw how the second page came out. All that had to be done was write the first page and send the thing off. There must have been a temptation to post it to C himself, but I think my father jibbed at that."

"So what's your theory?"

"I thought it out logically. Couldn't get it straight, then realized it had been sitting in front of me from the very day of Caspar's death. I thought Phoebe was rambling when she said things like 'Is Alex coming back?' which she *did* say. She also said, 'Has James been told?' and 'I think Alex phoned James.' You bet Alex phoned James. I don't know why, but Alex drove to London on the day Caspar died. Maybe he'll tell us—or you, Gus, when you sweat the little bastard. But he came down, and, somehow, he went into The Hide, Caspar's study. There, I guess, was the letter, all prominent and addressed to C, Private and Confidential. If you were Alex, and working in close harmony with James, what would you do? Open it, which is what I guess Alex did, and, when he read it, I guess he panicked. Phoebe knew he had spoken to James. He told her so, and I suppose James stayed very cool and dictated a new letter which would fit on page one, leaving page two original and with Caspar's signature.

"It must have been very inviting. 'Put it in the post, Alex. Pop it in and we'll be home and dry.' But my dear old father knew his trade. 'Best not use it now,' he would have said. 'Better later.' I'd even put money on him first thinking of giving it ten years—I know he doesn't expect to live long. He talked about it before Cas died. So, in the end, I would think he compromised and dictated a memo over the telephone. Alex would do the rest. It would be easy. Destroy the evidence. Probably took the original envelope, together with page one, with him and burned it back in Cheltenham. He'd post it on his way out, and then risk ad libbing if his visit was mentioned. Bet he drove like the wind, Gus. Little shit. If I . . . .''

"Go through the timings for me, Naldo." Gus hammered at him, knowing now how Naldo, wound like a spring, could launch himself into tributaries of hate and venom.

"Timings? Yes, Alex's timings. We don't know, probably we'll never know—unless you beat it out of him, Gus—why he chose *that* particular day to come up to town. We do know he must have arrived after eleven, because Caspar left Eccleston Square for The Travellers, and death, at about that time. He got there between eleven-thirty and eleven forty-five, according to the barman. He and his old friends drank quite a lot before going into lunch, at just after one. So Alex drives in, sometime after eleven. If it had been any earlier, Caspar wouldn't have left until Alexander was out of the way. I'm pretty certain of that."

"So Alex hung around Eccleston Square for how long?"

"Till about one-thirty, I'd guess. That would've given him time, plenty of time, to have found the letter to C, gone through his panic with James, and done the rewriting. Caspar died at the end of lunch, around three-ten. C and I were at the house just after three-thirty, and I spoke to Alex, in Cheltenham, at three forty-five. We know he wasn't in during the morning. We don't know *why* he came up to town at all."

Gus gave a curt nod. "But we do know it couldn't have been for anything sinister?"

"We know he couldn't have had any hint of Caspar's plans. Unless Cas rang him and said something to alert him, but I doubt it."

"Coincidence then. Funny thing, coincidence. Was it coincidence that brought Alexander back, later?"

"When he left his fingerprints all over the place? I doubt it. He never did come clean on that, did he, Gus?"

"Denied it again and again. But he *was* there?"

"No doubt. He tripped all my little traps, and I thought it was BMW's boys."

"Why? I mean why did Alex go back?"

"Maybe to check I'd taken everything. That would've been on James' orders. Or he might well have wanted to be sure he'd left nothing incriminating behind. By the time he returned nobody had mentioned his visit on the day of Caspar's death. Who knows . . ."

The telephone rang.

Outside, it was growing dark, and freezing hard. Naldo thought of the green house in Berlin. Looking out of the window to see the snow falling, while Arnie Farthing gave him due warning that Caspar's name was on the shit list, and the rest of his family would follow pretty soon.

"He's on his way," Gus Keene said. "We've got about an hour and a half. They're bringing a car for you and Herb in one hour."

Naldo turned his head, and Barbara bent to kiss him, lovingly. "I'm so bloody proud of you," she whispered.

"Proud?" he said. "Proud because I've done my uncle's dirty work for him? The sooner we all get out of this fucking country; out of Europe; away from the lies; then the better it will be for me."

"Oh, Naldo . . ."

"No! I belong to a family who, down its secret generations, has committed every capital sin in the book, and, while I would never work for the Sovs, I believe a lot of them were right not to work for England. We live in a little, tight, bright island, where everything has to be done in bloody triplicate. You been into a public lavatory lately? It's like being in a prison. Nobody cares; really cares anymore—the Labour Party rabble or the Conservative shits. *They just don't care.* We ceased to be a great nation years ago, yet we still pretend. Rule Bloody Britannia; Britons never never shall be slaves; wider still and wider. We have to forget our one-time greatness before we can begin to atone."

"Naldo." Gus laid a hand on his shoulder, having come around the table during the outburst. "Naldo, you're angry. It's natural. You feel injustice." He turned his head to Barbara. "Coffee, I think." Then, to Naldo, "Just a little way to go now, Nald."

Big Herbie Kruger sat, hunched in a chair, his huge shoulders shaking, hands over his face to hide the tears. Herb had loved them all: Caspar, James. Arnie Farthing, Naldo.

"What else you fucking want to know, Gus, so that you can flay my old dad? Isn't it enough that I've done what my saintly—and I mean saintly—uncle couldn't do? You want me to provide iron for the branding, leather for the whips? What?"

"Just when you first suspected."

A long silence draped the room. It seemed to Naldo that he was speaking from a distance. "I don't know. Maybe I've known since he played soldiers with me. Maybe since he sat up with me all night when I was ill. Maybe since he read me to sleep with *Treasure Island.* I don't know. I know I suspected him, but, Oh Christ . . ." The tears came now, and he shook. Even Gus had turned white, his hands locked together, fingers laced.

"Oh, dear sweet Jesus," Naldo sobbed. "I knew from childhood that it wasn't right. Then I put it down to his job. Gus, you should have known him really well. You couldn't love him like Caspar, but I can never forget—picnics, outings, learning to shoot and fish, learning to drive, listening to him and Ma play the piano. Hearing him quote Shakespeare. He was better at that than anyone in the family."

Then he seemed to pull himself together, and reeled off a series of facts. "C let me into the Registry. I asked for it. Asked to take a stroll through the past. I wanted to take a stroll through James' past, and I found it all." He had picked three names—three from many locked in childhood and adolescent memory. "There was this guy called Jean Brissault. We used to meet him, almost regularly, in Poitiers on holiday; and another when we were in Berlin, Hans Schnaffel. And a girl used to bump into us, every time we visited Milan. Lena. Lena Legarto. The old man said he could hardly remember any of them. He'd forgotten the Italian girl completely, he said."

Naldo had toiled in Registry, followed trails and cross-references. "It was all there. Brissault was caught by the French in the fifties. Tried and shot—they don't fuck about in France. Long-term. Soviet, of course. They even found a tiny lead with James at the end. I think someone from your lot spent an afternoon with him, Gus. But he walked away. The German was the same. They never caught dear old Hans, and he ended up happy as a lark in Moscow."

"And Lena?"

"The Italian bitch. Still at it. They know. She's worked in Rome since the war. An old lady now, but she goes into the office three times a week. They drew her sting, even though she made PR to the head of bloody Puccini-singing Counterespionage. All they did was shuffle her sideways and cut off the material. If she hears about this, it'll be the last act of *Tosca*, won't it."

"That's all in the files, is it?"

"Oh, and more. Bring Alice Ross, née Pritchard, to book, Gus. Five years isn't enough, even at her age. James dallied with her, and lord knows what else went on. There, I've broken my staff and drowned my book."

They drank coffee, and Naldo went off to clean up. The car arrived at seven, and they wondered if the last act would play true to form. They should have been so lucky.

2

They had placed four heavies downstairs, in the building opposite James' house in King Street. The walkie-talkies crackled as Big Herbie led Naldo up the stairs and into the eyrie. A room with no lights on, only the glow from some communications equipment and the receivers which picked up every word from the privacy of James Railton's home.

Curry Shepherd was at the window with another man and a pair of binoculars on one tripod, and a camera with a lens that would reach to Trafalgar Square on a good day on another.

"Nobody on your backs, was there?" Curry sounded anxious, as though he was worried about the whole thing.

"We were clean as scrubbed cats," Herbie said, using this strange image as though it was a normal English simile.

"Why?" Naldo asked, a shade briskly.

"Don't know really." The usually languid Curry Shepherd was far from languid tonight. "Don't know, but things haven't got the right smell. It's like having another team that's not under your control."

Naldo remembered the taxi of the previous night, and wondered. Later he did not regret remaining silent, but, for years after, he saw the silhouette in the taxi when he dreamed.

Everyone was silent, and very still.

They heard Margaret Mary constantly asking questions inside the house across the road. "Why tonight, darling? It's damned cold and they've forecast snow."

"Because Alex is coming all the way from Cheltenham, and he wants a private talk." James sounded almost too relaxed. "I'll take him to the club. He likes that. Likes a good dinner at the club."

"They're going to do a runner," Curry said. Then he turned to Naldo. "C suggests that you go first. Ring the bell and get your ma to open up. The boys'll pile in after that. All be over before you can say Klaus Fuchs. Okay by you, Nald?"

"It'll save nastiness."

"Oh, I doubt that. Maybe Herb should go with you."

"I definitely go with him, actually, Curry. I carry. Know what I mean."

"Oh, right. Good."

A radio crackled. "Red Robin entering St. James's Square," a disembodied voice said.

"Red Robin?" Naldo muttered in disbelief.

"Okay, here we go," Curry said. "Want to nip downstairs and join the others?"

"Wait till he gets here and parks." Naldo sounded as though he had the authority to give the order.

"If you say so, old dear," from Curry.

From the window, they watched as Alexander Percival Railton's Mercedes took a parking space in front of James' house. Special Branch had made sure the local law kept it clear.

They saw the small figure get out, glance up the street, down, then up again. He did not lock the Merc, but went straight up the steps and rang the bell.

"Now?" Curry asked.

"Leave it a minute." Naldo knew it was right to wait, though he could not have given a logical explanation if someone had asked him.

"Nald, it should be now," from Herbie.

"In a second!" angry, almost shouted. "Damn it, Herb, it's my old dad."

"It's a fucking Soviet agent," someone said from the communications gear.

"Christ!" from Curry as the taxi came hurtling down the street, to stop next to the Merc. "Now, for God's sake. Now, Naldo!"

Naldo just had time to see the tall figure leap from the cab and run for the steps. "Yes," he said quietly, already at the run towards the door. "This way we get the lot."

James' front door was closed and the cab had gone when they reached the street. Naldo felt the ice on the pavement but made it in fifteen seconds to the front door, where he leaned against the buzzer, Herbie at his shoulder, and the other hoods in the street behind him.

"Naldo? What . . . ?" his mother asked, shocked, surprised, as she opened the door, but Herbie's long arm shot out, pushing her back and pinning her against the wall.

"Where, Ma? Where are . . . ?" Naldo got out before the shot. Two shots, quick, one after the other, from what they called the drawing room. He lunged for the door, but it was Big Herbie who was in first.

"Drop it, Arn or I'll take you out now." Herbie's English was commanding.

James stood, white and shaking, by the mantelpiece, his eyes wide, looking across the room where the bloodstains on the wall pointed to Alexander Railton's body crumpled and smashed by the 9mm bullets from Arnold Farthing's automatic.

"Shit!" said Arnie, pausing for a second, before dropping the gun, which was turned towards James.

As he did so, the tall figure of Paul Schillig seemed to appear, like the Demon King from an unseen star-trap, behind Naldo. He pushed his way through and strode, furious, across the room. "You good-for-nothing, lowdown jerk, Farthing. You bastard." Schillig hit him twice, once with the palm and once with the back of his hand, then spun him around.

"I've spoken with C," Schillig said, looking not the least bit ruffled. "This one's ours, and I hope he doesn't even make it to Washington."

"I hoped the bastard was mine." Naldo's shoulders drooped. "I hoped it since I saw him last night. How long did it take Washington to work out which side of the street *he* was working? And how did he know we were . . . ?"

"Never mind. That's not your department, Railton." Schillig had Arnie in an armlock and had begun to push him out of the room.

"Why did you let me kill Penkovsky?" Naldo asked, incredibly quietly as they passed him.

"Because it was your right, and he was getting greedy. You got your Alex, and I got mine. Pity I lost your father."

"Afraid they'd blow the lot?"

"Of course. Your old man's got everything to spill." Then they were gone, and the hoods were all over the place: pronouncing Alex Farthing dead while a Special Branch officer read James his rights.

"Why, Pa? Why?" Naldo looked his father straight in the face.

"Because, for me, it was the only way. I'd rather go down with them than with the other kind of corruption. No ideology is perfect, but theirs has an equality about it. It is the end of privilege."

"You're still *that* naive. God help you." Naldo's eyes were brimming again.

"Shouldn't you kiss me or something, Naldo? Isn't that what Judas did?" James' had regained strength, his eyes blazing towards his son.

"Ah, but that was Christ." Naldo shook with rage. "That was blessèd Mary's son . . ." Before he could stop himself he continued the Shakespearian quote, most of it under his breath as Herbie helped him from the house, down the steps into the waiting car—

"This land of much dear souls, this dear dear land,
Dear for her reputation through the world
Is now leased out—I die pronouncing it—
Like to a tenement or pelting farm.
England, bound in with the triumphant sea,
Whose rocky shore beats back the envious siege
Of watery Neptune, is now bound in with shame,
With inky blots and rotten parchment bonds.

> *That England that was wont to conquer others*
> *Hath made a shameful conquest of itself."*

And all the time, in his head, Big Herbie Kruger could only hear the sudden crash and thump of the double timpani strokes at the start of the third movement of Mahler's Second.

When they got back to the Kensington house, where Barbara said she would meet them, they saw something was wrong from the moment she opened the door.

"Nald." She touched him as though he was a bomb unfused and likely to explode. "Bad news, I'm afraid."

He gave a dry laugh. "What could be bad after the night we've had?" Then he saw the fresh tears on her cheek. "What?"

"Dick." She made a hopeless gesture, arms rising and falling. "Dick Railton-Farthing died suddenly this afternoon at Redhill."

"Thank God for that. He was James' idol. It would have killed him anyway. They're all dying off. Amen to that."

Herbie helped him inside and closed the door, as though to shut out the world forever.

3

Almost everyone turned up for Dick's funeral. James was not there, of course, but Naldo and Barbara flanked Margaret Mary. Even Anne and Andrew's children were present. Anne erect, brave-faced and dry-eyed. Stalks and one of the nurses wheeled Sara, who remained bold until the interment, when she broke, and Stalks quickly hurried her back into the house.

When they left, Naldo took a quick glance over his shoulder. He knew it was not likely he would ever return to Redhill. He did not care anymore. Sara was still Sara, and he would adore her for the rest of his life. Odd that the only truly unscathed Railtons had been Railtons by marriage.

They did not attend Alex's funeral. Later, Naldo heard that Gus had been present, and he knew the coroner's court had found "Death by misadventure." Quite a lot of things were left unsaid and, for a change, the Press were either muzzled or kept their peace.

There was still the debriefing with Gus to occupy his time, while they made plans to leave London, and indeed England, forever.

"Arnie?" he asked of Gus, towards the end of their long series of talks.

"What about Arnie?"

"How did he know? How was he so certain we had James and Alexander in our sights? And how did he manage to get in and sniff us out?"

"Nobody's talking about Arnie." Gus drew on his pipe. "They flew him out within an hour of what the Press called the 'incident.' I heard he was being held in a safe house in Washington."

"Any theories?" Naldo asked.

"Private theories, yes. I'll tell you all I know. Grosvenor Square put out an alert three days ago. Arnie was out of Russia and on the rampage. No explanation apart from the fact that he was out and had joined the bears. They got a sniff of him in Amsterdam, and a tiny whiff in Folkstone. After that, nothing, except that he was about to break all the rules. Clever boy, that Arnie. Well, *you* know that, Nald. You've worked with him. Arnie could hide in an empty street at high noon. I knew he was around when C brought me to New Cavendish Street that night. By which time Paul Schillig had been given the nod. I don't suppose C wanted Arnie on his plate as well."

"But how did he know?"

"You're as wise as I am, Nald. You tell me."

"Try this on for size." Naldo dug into his logic. "From the little I heard, James and Alex were going to do a Burgess and Maclean. Disappear into the night, then turn up in Moscow. We didn't give them much time, but it's possible someone already tipped James that we were closing in. Make sense?"

"It's how I see it. Quite like the old days." Gus sucked at his pipe. "I believe there is one more unaccounted for. It might even be you, Naldo, but I don't think so . . ."

"You'd better bloody well not."

"I believe that your poor old father had already asked to get out. Arnie, being an acceptable choice, was possibly sent over to take them—one way or the other. When he arrived, you were just warming up. That could have pushed him, particularly if someone else was, and is, telling tales out of school."

After a long silence Gus said, "In our trade there are always things you never really untangle. I don't think we'll ever untangle Arnie and his part in things—except that he doubled: that's not in dispute."

On his last visit to the shop, Naldo bumped into Paul Schillig hurrying out. "Paul!" He thrust out a hand.

"No, Naldo." Schillig beamed as he spoke. "No, I can't tell you, and I never will. As far as you're concerned, Arnold Farthing died the last time you saw him, okay?"

"I wasn't going to ask," Naldo lied. In the far reaches of his mind, he heard unrecognized voices quoting the Railtons' beloved Shakespeare—"Our watchword was 'Hem boys! Come, let's to dinner; come let's to dinner. Jesus, the days that we have seen! Come, come.' "

EPILOGUE

1989

In 1989, eight years after Sara Railton died, aged ninety-six and fighting to the end, at Redhill Manor, an horrific disaster was averted in the British Crown Colony of Hong Kong. Hong Kong was now usually spoken of simply as the Territories, out of respect for the People's Republic of China, who, in 1997, would reclaim the Fragrant Harbour, Hong Kong Island itself, together with Kowloon and the 588 square kilometers of mainland.

Special celebrations were planned, to coincide with the June 1989 Dragon Boat Festival, when the Governor would entertain Royalty and distinguished members of the Government of the People's Republic of China. Many of these functions were planned in the years leading up to the takeover by China. All were symbolic, acts of goodwill between the British and the Chinese.

On the first day there was to be a grand parade and inspection, in which members of the British Royal Family and the Chinese politicians would take part. Three bands from a trio of great British regiments were to provide the music, while an Honour Guard was flown in from the Royal Scots Greys.

On the evening before this event, a secret operation, involving MI5, the SIS, and the Special Air Service uncovered a bomb plot by the Provisional Irish Republican Army.

Six members of the Provos were shot dead before they were able to explode a huge car bomb. The bomb was remote-controlled, and the Provos had planned this "spectacular"—as they called such horrors—to show they were capable of taking death to any part of the globe where British forces were still stationed. The deaths of many innocent people, plus the Royals and Chinese politicians, would merely have been a side effect.

There followed the usual cries of outrage from both sides. The SAS was accused of brutal murder by those who claimed these elite troops were simply British assassins; while others pointed to the policy of murder and war waged by a minority in the North of Ireland.

Distanced from these events, Naldo and Barbara watched the television coverage and listened to the BBC World Service from their pleasant small estate in Virginia.

Following the horrors of his last days with the SIS, Naldo had remained adamant about leaving the United Kingdom. Barbara, who shared his anxiety about the future of Europe, was only too happy to follow her husband. So, in 1975, the couple packed their bags, shipped their furniture, and set off to make a new life in the United States.

James Railton's betrayal, together with the unmasking of Arnie Farthing, had broken Naldo's will. What he needed now was to put a lot of distance between him and his old roots. Down the years, his family had posed, lied, and betrayed. He wanted no more of that, and this sense of disillusion had spread deeply into his views of life and country. The England he saw around him in the mid-1970s had altered out of recognition. No more, he repeated many times, was this the country of his birth, the country he had fought for, and been betrayed for. His England had passed away, and something new and unrecognizable had risen in its place. England was betrayed, and, in return, had betrayed its citizens.

He was aware that by residing in the United States he was in many ways avoiding issues, but he could live with that. Here, in the U.S.A., as an alien, he did not have a vote. He paid his taxes, but was not forced by conscience to cast his lot for British politicians who, in his heart, disgusted him. The coziness of the old socialism had turned into a rabble, with cardboard leaders, ready to be burned down by the firebrands of the far left; the present government practiced an outward show of Victorian paternalism, together with values that had little meaning in the modern world—and often no meaning at all for the civil servants who acted on its behalf. The middle ground Naldo saw as a scattering of foxholes, peopled by men and women who dreamed impossible dreams, and had not one clear, original, or feasible political thought between them.

So now the couple lived a simple life. Naldo began to write and, for a number of years, had been engaged in a long history of the Western intelligence and security services, taking care not to break the Official Secrets Act, as some had in recent times. Indeed, he would have cheerfully gone and strangled Mr. Peter Wright, who had so blatantly broken his binding agreement of service with MI5, making the government of the day look stupid in the process.

Naldo's theory about the government's continued legal attempts to ban Wright's book, *Spycatcher*, was that they feared innocent men and women would *actually believe* Wright's garbage, while anyone who knew the truth of these things could spot the multitude of holes, and manufactured "truths," which were simply an old man's unbridled vengeance, coupled with an unnatural swallowing of Soviet disinformation.

It was a quiet, warm Friday night when the telephone rang. Barbara and Naldo had been sitting on their sun deck, looking out towards the Blue Ridge Mountains and trying to summon up energy to bathe and change for a dinner party with friends.

Naldo answered, immediately recognizing his son's, Arthur's, voice.

"How does a bloke, and his wife-to-be, get to your neck of the woods, Pa?" Arthur asked.

"Where in hell are you?"

"Dulles International." You could hear the smile in his voice.

"It'll only take you an hour from Dulles. There's a flight every two hours." Naldo did not try to cloak his excitement. "Look, why don't you get the first one available? I'll check it out from this end. We'll be at the airport. What a wonderful surprise."

Their hosts for the evening understood the sudden change of plan, but it was not until they were in the car, heading towards the local airport, that they took in the full magnitude of what Arthur had said.

"You're sure?" Barbara's eyes opened wide. "You're sure he said 'wife-to-be'? Arthur's going to be married?"

"That's what he said. Wonder why he's here? With the girl as well."

"She'll never be good enough for him." Barbara laughed. In fun, she echoed exactly what her own mother had said when she had broken the news of *her* engagement to Naldo, all those years ago.

Both of them had long accepted that Arthur was a member of the Secret Intelligence Service, having been recruited while working for the Foreign Office. But what Arthur was doing this far afield made them curious. They both hoped, with some fervor, that their son would be the last Railton to dabble in secret affairs.

Arthur was fit and well, brimming with energy: taller than his father, and dressed casually in jeans and a leather jacket. Privately, Naldo thought the boy resembled any other SIS hood. The girl, whose name was Elizabeth McGregor, had a fresh, clean, scrubbed look about her, with fair fluffy hair, freckles, and a mischievous sense of fun.

Naldo and Barbara were delighted. Only Naldo felt a twitch of concern, for Liz, as she liked to be called, had traces of an Irish brogue

413

in her voice: not the soft accent of the South, but the slightly more harsh vowel sounds of the North.

They heard all the news; were careful not to ask questions which might embarrass Arthur; laughed, joked, heaped congratulations on the couple, and drew Liz closely to them, making her feel part of the family from the start.

Barbara, the soul of tact, took Arthur aside and asked if they wanted two guest rooms or only one.

He smiled his charming smile—looking just like his father had once appeared to Barbara—and told her that two rooms were needed. "We're both a shade old-fashioned about these things," he said. "It's not like it used to be in your day, Ma," ducking a feigned left hook.

So it was that, later in the evening, Naldo found himself alone, on the deck, but behind the wire grille to keep the insects out, having a nightcap with his son.

"When's the wedding, then? And where will it be?"

Arthur looked up at his father from beneath lowered lids. "In about a year," he said softly. "Don't worry, it's going to happen, but we need a year. I'm probably being posted to Washington, and I—well, *we* really—wondered if Liz could stay with you for a while. She needs somewhere safe and unlikely."

Naldo felt his instincts sit bolt upright. "Where've you flown in from, Art?" It was his interrogating voice.

"Hong Kong, actually."

"Ah."

"Don't get it wrong, Pa. I've known Liz for eighteen months now."

"And you've worked with her, haven't you?"

"I'd only admit it to you."

"You were in the recent thing? The Hong Kong thing? And she was involved?"

His son nodded. "Yes. She *has* to go to earth, Pa. You have to look after her for me. I love her. I want to marry her."

"And you ran her, didn't you?"

"In a way. She's a very brave girl. She was our mole inside the Provos. She blew the Hong Kong thing for us."

Silently, Naldo sipped his drink. Yes, he would let her stay, but he was aware of the dangers, and the care that he would have to take. He also knew he should turn his son down and send both of them packing.

Then he thought of his own father, who had died in an open prison during 1984, without giving any convincing explanation for his treachery or even when he had started to work for the Soviets. His

414

clearest answer was that he had been motivated by conviction alone. He had even said that it was to save his own country.

Naldo's mother, the once lovely Margaret Mary, had come out to live with them, depressed and only a fragment of her former self. She followed her husband within a year.

"Of course," Naldo now said to his son. "Of course she can stay. But your Service must know I'm not going to make a habit of it. Also, I want your boss, whoever he is, to pay a call: take me through the minefield so to speak."

"Nobody alters in this business, do they, Pa? Even after all this time your tradecraft is second nature. Nobody changes."

"Some do. Some alter out of all recognition, Arthur."

Shakespeare went through his head, and a night bird called from the woods at the far edge of his property.

And trust no agent: for beauty is a witch
Against whose charms faith melteth into blood.

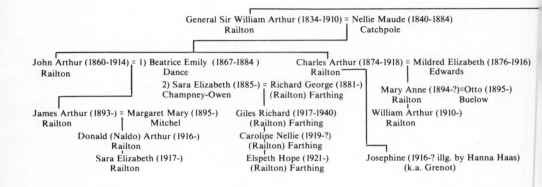

General Sir William Arthur (1834-1910) = Nellie Maude (1840-1884)
Railton   Catchpole

John Arthur (1860-1914) = 1) Beatrice Emily (1867-1884)   Charles Arthur (1874-1918) = Mildred Elizabeth (1876-1916)
Railton   Dance   Railton   Edwards

                                    2) Sara Elizabeth (1885-) = Richard George (1881-)   Mary Anne (1894-?)=Otto (1895-)
                                       Champney-Owen   (Railton) Farthing   Railton   Buelow

James Arthur (1893-) = Margaret Mary (1895-)   Giles Richard (1917-1940)   William Arthur (1910-)
Railton   Mitchel   (Railton) Farthing   Railton

        Donald (Naldo) Arthur (1916-)   Caroline Nellie (1919-?)
                Railton   (Railton) Farthing
        Sara Elizabeth (1917-)   Elspeth Hope (1921-)   Josephine (1916-? illg. by Hanna Haas)
                Railton   (Railton) Farthing   (k.a. Grenot)

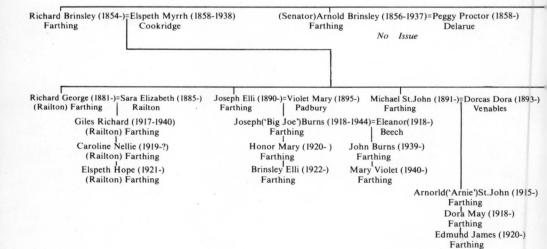

Richard Brinsley (1854-)=Elspeth Myrrh (1858-1938)   (Senator)Arnold Brinsley (1856-1937)=Peggy Proctor (1858-)
Farthing   Cookridge   Farthing   Delarue
                                                                                    No   Issue

Richard George (1881-)=Sara Elizabeth (1885-)   Joseph Elli (1890-)=Violet Mary (1895-)   Michael St.John (1891-)=Dorcas Dora (1893-)
(Railton) Farthing   │   Railton   Farthing   │   Padbury   Farthing   Venables
        Giles Richard (1917-1940)   Joseph('Big Joe')Burns (1918-1944)=Eleanor(1918-)
        (Railton) Farthing   Farthing   Beech
        Caroline Nellie (1919-?)   Honor Mary (1920-)   John Burns (1939-)
        (Railton) Farthing   Farthing   Farthing
        Elspeth Hope (1921-)   Brinsley Elli (1922-)   Mary Violet (1940-)
        (Railton) Farthing   Farthing   Farthing

                                                                            Arnorld('Arnie')St.John (1915-)
                                                                                    Farthing
                                                                            Dora May (1918-)
                                                                                    Farthing
                                                                            Edmund James (1920-)
                                                                                    Farthing